Raven Baker

# MASTERS OF THE MACABRE

# Masters

# of the

# Macabre

AN ANTHOLOGY OF MYSTERY,
HORROR AND DETECTION ∂∾ EDITED
BY SEON MANLEY AND GOGO LEWIS
∂∾ DOUBLEDAY & COMPANY, INC.
GARDEN CITY, NEW YORK

Library of Congress Cataloging in Publication Data
Manley, Seon, comp.
Masters of the macabre.
SUMMARY: An anthology of horror and suspense tales arranged chronologically from
early Gothic writing characterized by Mary Shelley to detective stories of today by Ellery
Queen and Dorothy Sayers.
1. Horror tales. 2. Detective and mystery stories.
[1. Horror stories. 2. Mystery and detective stories]
I. Lewis, Gogo, joint comp. II. Title.
PZ5.M3Mas [Fic]

ISBN 0-385-00883-X Trade
0-385-03270-6 Prebound
Library of Congress Catalog Card Number 69–11002
Copyright © 1975 by Seon Manley and Gogo Lewis
All Rights Reserved
Printed in the United States of America

We are grateful to the authors, agents, and publishers who have given us permission to
reprint the following selections:

"The House of the Dead Hand" (copyright 1904 The Atlantic Monthly) by Edith
Wharton is reprinted by permission of Charles Scribner's Sons from *The Collected Short
Stories of Edith Wharton.*

"The Adventure of the Creeping Man" by Sir Arthur Conan Doyle from *The Casebook
of Sherlock Homes,* John Murray (publishers) Ltd. and Baskerville Investments Ltd. Permission to reprint also granted by the author's American agents, Joan and Robert Franklin.

"A Revolver in the Corner Cupboard" from *The Lost Childhood and Other Essays* by
Graham Greene. Copyright 1951 by Graham Greene. Reprinted by permission of The
Viking Press, Inc. Permission to reprint also granted by Laurence Pollinger Limited.

"The Dark Brotherhood" by H. P. Lovecraft & August Derleth. Copyright © 1966 by
August Derleth. Reprinted by permission of the authors' Estates and agents for their
Estates, Scott Meredith Literary Agency, Inc., 580 Fifth Avenue, New York, New York,
10036.

"Abraham Lincoln's Clue" by Ellery Queen. Copyright © 1965, 1968 by Ellery Queen.
Reprinted by permission of the author and the author's agents, Scott Meredith Literary
Agency, Inc., 580 Fifth Avenue, New York, New York, 10036.

"Absolutely Elsewhere" by Dorothy L. Sayers. Reprinted by permission of the author's
agent, A. Watkins, Inc. from LORD PETER: *A Collection of all the Lord Peter Wimsey
Stories,* copyright © 1972 by Harper & Row Publishers, Inc.

Our thanks also to Susan Belcher, the staff of the Bellport Memorial Library, Bellport,
New York; the staff of the Patchogue Library, Patchogue, New York; the staff of the
Greenwich Library, Greenwich, Connecticut; our husbands, Robert R. Manley and Wil-
liam W. Lewis; and our daughters Sara Lewis, Carol Lewis, and Shivaun Manley.

# CONTENTS

THIS BOOK IS FOR
MILDRED AND RICHARD PERSINGER

# INTRODUCTION

JUST FIFTY years ago, the great master of the supernatural, H. P. Lovecraft, decreed that "the appeal of the macabre tale is generally narrow because it demands from the reader a certain degree of imagination and a capacity for detachment from everyday life."

Times have certainly changed. Interest in the macabre, the tale of horror, suspense, detection is at an all-time high. Perhaps we are in a period of a rebirth of the imagination; perhaps we are in a period in which we are not detached from life, but one in which the technological life of today has detached itself from us—in any case weird and wonderful stories are enjoying a true renascence.

Here are many phases of the macabre in the hands of superb masters of the genre; men and women who have explored—and expressed—the dark heritage of literature and the human mind from the days of Mary Shelley to our own contemporary Ellery Queen.

SEON MANLEY
GOGO LEWIS

# Great Writers of the Gothic Landscape: Mary Shelley, Bram Stoker, and Edith Wharton (The Gothic Movement Through the Centuries)

# THE MORTAL IMMORTAL

## BY MARY SHELLEY

THE ANCESTRY of all contemporary supernatural tales is grounded in the gothic romantic tale. The gothic story used the terrible malignant forces of the natural world as a projection of the dark, confused passions of man. When the gothic story came to its full flowering in the eighteenth century, it was a natural product of its age. It was an age that truly believed in the supernatural; the telling of ghost stories and folk tales of horror were daily events. Leisure hung heavy in the hands of the eighteenth century and so did the books, great three-decker novels of gloomy castles, secret rooms, rotting tapestries.

Mary Shelley was a true daughter of that age. Among her novels, inspired by many gothic elements, was the famous *Frankenstein* and an extraordinary book entitled *The Last Man*. The latter which tells a story about the end of mankind, compelled the writer Muriel Spark to say, "She created an entirely new genre, compounded of a domestic romance, a gothic extravaganza and the sociological novel."

Mary Shelley also wrote a number of remarkable short stories. *The Mortal Immortal* is based on a theme often used in gothic literature. Indeed, the theme was used by her father before her, William Godwin, in his own fable of immortality entitled *St. Leon*, in which the leading character drinks an elixir of life and wanders deathlessly throughout the world.

Mary Shelley's story of immortality, first published in 1834, shows not only that she was inspired by her father's book, but contributed her own talent and insight in the tale of a man who might live forever. ॐ

July 16, 1833—This is a memorable anniversary for me; on it I complete my three hundred and twenty-third year!

The Wandering Jew?—certainly not. More than eighteen centuries have passed over his head. In comparison with him, I am a very young Immortal.

Am I, then, immortal? This is a question which I have asked myself, by day and night, for now three hundred and three years, and yet cannot answer it. I detected a gray hair amidst my brown locks this very day—that surely signifies decay. Yet it may have remained concealed there for three hundred years—for some persons have become entirely white-headed before twenty years of age.

I will tell my story, and my reader shall judge for me. I will tell my story, and so contrive to pass some few hours of a long eternity, become so wearisome to me. For ever! Can it be? to live for ever! I have heard of enchantments, in which the victims were plunged into a deep sleep, to wake after a hundred years, as fresh as ever: I have heard of the Seven Sleepers—thus to be immortal would not be so burdensome: but, oh! the weight of never-ending time—the tedious passage of the still-succeeding hours! How happy was the fabled Nourjahad!—but to my task.

All the world has heard of Cornelius Agrippa. His memory is as immortal as his arts have made me. All the world had also heard of his scholar, who, unawares, raised the foul fiend during his master's absence, and was destroyed by him. The report, true or false, of this accident was attended with many inconveniences to the renowned philosopher. All his scholars at once deserted him—his servants disappeared. He had no one near him to put coals on his ever-burning fires while he slept, or to attend to the changeful colors of his medicines while he studied. Experiment after experiment failed, because one pair of hands was insufficient to complete them: the dark spirits laughed at him for not being able to retain a single mortal in his service.

I was then very young—very poor—and very much in love. I had been for about a year the pupil of Cornelius, though I was absent when this accident took place. On my return my friends implored me not to return to the alchemist's abode. I trembled as I listened to the dire tale they told; I required no second warning; and when Cornelius came and offered me a purse of gold if I would remain under his roof, I felt as if Satan himself tempted me. My teeth chattered—my hair stood on end: —I ran off as fast as my trembling knees would permit.

My failing steps were directed whither for two years they had every evening been attracted,—a gently bubbling spring of pure living waters, beside which lingered a dark-haired girl, whose beaming eyes were fixed on the path I was accustomed each night to tread. I cannot remember the hour when I did not love Bertha; we had been neighbors and playmates from infancy—her parents, like mine, were of humble life, yet respectable—our attachment had been a source of pleasure to them. In an evil hour a malignant fever carried off both her father and mother, and Bertha became an orphan. She would have found a home beneath my paternal roof, but unfortunately, the old lady of the near castle, rich, childless, and solitary, declared her intention to adopt her. Henceforth Bertha was clad in silk—inhabited a marble palace—and was looked on as being highly favored by fortune. But in her new situation among her new associates, Bertha remained true to the friend of her humbler days; she often visited the cottage of my father, and when forbidden to go thither, she would stray toward the neighboring wood, and meet me beside its shady fountain.

She often declared that she owed no duty to her new protectress equal in sanctity to that which bound us. Yet still I was too poor to marry, and she grew weary of being tormented on my account. She had a haughty but an impatient spirit, and grew angry at the obstacles that prevented our union. We met now after an absence, and she had been sorely beset while I was away; she complained bitterly, and almost reproached me for being poor. I replied hastily,—

"I am honest, if I am poor—were I not, I might soon become rich!"

This explanation produced a thousand questions. I feared to shock her by owning the truth, but she drew it from me: and then, casting a look of disdain on me: she said

"You pretend to love, and you fear to face the Devil for my sake!"

I protested that I had only dreaded to offend her;—while she dwelt on the magnitude of the reward that I should receive. Thus encouraged —shamed by her—led on by love and hope, laughing at my late fears, with quick steps and a light heart I returned to accept the offers of the alchemist, and was instantly installed in my office.

A year passed away. I became possessed of no insignificant sum of money. Custom had banished my fears. In spite of the most painful vigilance, I had never detected the trace of a cloven foot; nor was the studious silence of our abode ever disturbed by demoniac howls. I still continued my stolen interviews with Bertha, and hope dawned on me— hope—but not perfect joy; for Bertha fancied that love and securities were enemies, and her pleasure was to divide them in my bosom. Though true of heart, she was somewhat of a coquette in manner; and I was jealous as a Turk. She slighted me in a thousand ways, yet would never acknowledge herself to be in the wrong. She would drive me mad with anger, and then force me to beg her pardon. Sometimes she fancied that I was not sufficiently submissive, and then she had some story of a rival, favored by her protectress. She was surrounded by silk-clad youths—the rich and gay—What chance had the sad-robed scholar of Cornelius compared with these?

On one occasion the philosopher made such large demands upon my time that I was unable to meet her as I was wont. He was engaged in some mighty work, and I was forced to remain, day and night, feeding his furnaces and watching his chemical preparations. Bertha waited for me in vain at the fountain. Her haughty spirit fired at this neglect; and when at last I stole out during the few short minutes allotted to me for slumber, and hoped to be consoled by her, she received me with disdain, dismissed me in scorn, and vowed that any man should possess her hand rather than he who could not be in two places at once for her sake. She would be revenged!—And truly she was. In my dingy retreat I heard that she had been hunting, attended by Albert Hoffer. Albert Hoffer was favored by her protectress, and the three passed in cavalcade before my smoky window. Methought that they mentioned my name —it was followed by a laugh of derision, as her dark eyes glanced contemptuously toward my abode.

Jealousy, with all its venom and all its misery, entered my breast. Now I shed a torrent of tears, to think that I should never call her mine; and, anon, I imprecated a thousand curses on her inconstancy. Yet still I must stir the fires of the alchemist, still attend on the changes of his unintelligible medicines.

Cornelius had watched for three days and nights, nor closed his eyes. The progress of his alembics was slower than he expected: in spite of his anxiety, sleep weighed upon his eyelids. Again and again he threw off drowsiness with more than human energy; again and again it stole away his senses. He eyes his crucibles wistfully. "Not ready yet," he murmured; "will another night pass before the work is accomplished? Winzy, you are vigilant—you are faithful—you have slept, my boy— you slept last night. Look at that glass vessel. The liquid it contains is of a soft rose color: the moment it begins to change its hue, awaken me —till then I may close my eyes. First, it will turn white, and then emit golden flashes: but wait not till then; when the rose-color fades, rouse me." I scarcely heard the last words muttered as they were in sleep. Even then he did not quite yield to nature. "Winzy, my boy," he said, "do not touch the vessel—do not put it to your lips; it's a philter —a philter to cure love; you would not cease to love your Bertha—beware to drink!"

And he slept. His venerable head sunk on his breast, and I scarce heard his regular breathing. For a few minutes I watched the vessel— the rosy hue of the liquid remained unchanged. Then my thoughts wandered—they visited the fountain, and dwelt on a thousand charming scenes never to be renewed—never! Serpents and adders were in my heart as the word "Never!" half formed itself on my lips. False girl!— false and cruel! Never more would she smile on me as that evening she smiled on Albert. Worthless, detested woman! I would not remain unrevenged—she should see Albert expire at her feet—she should die beneath my vengeance. She had smiled in disdain and triumph—she knew my wretchedness and her power. Yet what power had she?—the power of exciting my hate—my utter scorn—my—oh, all but indifference. Could I attain that—could I regard her with careless eyes, transferring my rejected love to one fairer and more true, that were indeed a victory!

A bright flash darted before my eyes. I had forgotten the medicine of the adept; I gazed on it with wonder: flashes of admirable beauty, more bright than those which the diamond emits when the sun's rays are on it, glanced from the surface of the liquid; an odor the most fragrant and grateful stole over my sense; the vessel seemed one globe of living radiance, lovely to the eye, and most inviting to the taste. The first thought, instinctively inspired by the grosser sense, was, I will—I must drink. I raised the vessel to my lips. "It will cure me of love—of torture!" Already I had quaffed half of the most delicious liquor ever tasted by the palate of man, when the philosopher stirred. I started—I dropped the glass—the fluid flamed and glanced along the floor, while I felt Cornelius's grip at my throat, as he shrieked aloud, "Wretch! you have destroyed the labor of my life!"

The philosopher was totally unaware that I had drunk any portion of his drug. His idea was, and I gave a tacit assent to it, that I raised the vessel from curiosity, and that, frighted at its brightness, and the flashes of intense light it gave forth, I had let it fall. I never undeceived him. The fire of the medicine was quenched—the fragrance died away —he grew calm, as a philosopher should under the heaviest trials, and dismissed me to rest.

I will not attempt to describe the sleep of glory and bliss which bathed my soul in paradise during the remaining hours of that memorable night. Words would be faint and shallow types of my enjoyment, or of the gladness that possessed my bosom when I woke. I trod air—my thoughts were in heaven. Earth appeared heaven, and my inheritance upon it was to be one trance of delight. "This it is to be cured of love," I thought; "I will see Bertha this day, and she will find her lover cold and regardless; too happy to be disdainful, yet how utterly indifferent to her!"

The hours danced away. The philosopher secure that he had once succeeded, and believing that he might again, began to concoct the same medicine once more. He was shut up with his books and drugs, and I had a holiday. I dressed myself with care; I looked in an old but polished shield, which served me for a mirror; methought my good looks had wonderfully improved. I hurried beyond the precincts of the town, joy in my soul, the beauty of heaven and earth around me. I turned my steps toward the castle—I could look on its lofty turrets with lightness of heart, for I was cured of love. My Bertha saw me afar off, as I came up the avenue. I know not what sudden impulse animated her bosom, but at the sight she sprung with a light fawn-like bound down the marble steps, and was hastening toward me. But I had been perceived by another person. The old high-born hag, who called herself her protectress, and was her tyrant, had seen me also; she hobbled, panting, up the terrace; a page, as ugly as herself, held up her train, and fanned her as she hurried along, and stopped my fair girl with a "How, now, my bold mistress? whither so fast? Back to your cage—hawks are abroad!"

Bertha clasped her hands—her eyes were still bent on my approaching figure. I saw the contest. How I abhorred the old crone who checked the kind impulses of my Bertha's softening heart. Hitherto, respect for her rank had caused me to avoid the lady of the castle; now I disdained such trivial considerations. I was cured of love and lifted above all human fears; I hastened forward, and soon reached the terrace. How lovely Bertha looked! her eyes flashing fire, her cheeks glowing with impatience and anger, she was a thousand times more graceful and charming than ever—I no longer loved—Oh! no, I adored—worshipped—idolized her!

She had that morning been persecuted, with more than usual vehemence, to consent to an immediate marriage with my rival. She was reproached with the encouragement that she had shown him—she was threatened with being turned out of doors with disgrace and shame. Her proud spirit rose in arms at the threat; but when she remembered the scorn that she had heaped upon me, and how, perhaps, she had thus lost one whom she now regarded as her only friend, she wept with remorse and rage. At that moment I appeared, "O, Winzy!" she exclaimed, "take me to your mother's cot; swiftly let me leave the detested luxuries and wretchedness of this noble dwelling—take me to poverty and happiness."

I clasped her in my arms with transport. The old lady was speechless with fury, and broke forth into invective only when we were far on our road to my natal cottage. My mother received the fair fugitive, escaped from a gilt cage to nature and liberty, with tenderness and joy; my father, who loved her, welcomed her heartily; it was a day of rejoicing, which did not need the addition of the celestial potion of the alchemist to steep me in delight.

Soon after this eventful day I became the husband of Bertha. I ceased to be the scholar of Cornelius, but I continued his friend. I always felt grateful to him for having, unawares, procured me that delicious draft of a divine elixir, which instead of curing me of love (sad cure! solitary and joyless remedy for evils which seem blessings to the memory), had inspired me with courage and resolution thus winning for me an inestimable treasure in my Bertha.

I often called to mind that period of trance-like inebriation with wonder. The drink of Cornelius had not fulfilled the task for which he affirmed that it had been prepared, but its effects were more potent and blissful than words can express. They had faded by degrees, yet they lingered long—and painted life in hues of splendor. Bertha often wondered at my lightness of heart and unaccustomed gaiety; for, before, I had been rather serious, or even sad, in my disposition. She loved me the better for my cheerful temper, and our days were winged by joy.

Five years afterward I was suddenly summoned to the bedside of the dying Cornelius. He had sent for me in haste, conjuring my instant presence. I found him stretched on his pallet, enfeebled even to death; all of life that yet remained animated his piercing eyes, and they were fixed on a glass vessel, full of a roseate liquid.

"Behold," he said, in a broken and inward voice, "the vanity of human wishes! a second time my hopes are about to be crowned, a second time they are destroyed. Look at that liquor—you remember five years ago I had prepared the same, with the same success;—then, as now, my thirsting lips expected to taste the immortal elixir—you dashed it from me! and at present it is too late."

He spoke with difficulty, and fell back on his pillow. I could not help saying—

"How, revered master, can a cure for love restore you to life?"

A faint smile gleamed across his face as I listened earnestly to his scarcely intelligible answer.

"A cure for love and for all things—the Elixir of Immortality. Ah! if now I might drink, I should live for ever!"

As he spoke, a golden flash gleamed from the fluid; a well remem-

bered fragrance stole over the air; he raised himself, all weak as he was —strength seemed miraculously to re-enter his frame—he stretched forth his hand—a loud explosion startled me—a ray of fire shot up from the elixir, and the glass vessel which contained it was shivered to atoms! I turned my eyes toward the philosopher; he had fallen back— his eyes were glassy—his features rigid—he was dead!

But I lived, and was to live for ever! So said the unfortunate alchemist, and for a few days I believed his words. I remembered the glorious drunkenness that had followed my stolen draft. I reflected on the change I had felt in my frame—in my soul. The bounding elasticity of the one—the buoyant lightness of the other. I surveyed myself in a mirror, and could perceive no change in my features during the space of five years which had elapsed. I remembered the radiant hues and grateful scent of that delicious beverage—worthy the gift it was capable of bestowing—I was, then, *Immortal!*

A few days after I laughed at my credulity. The old proverb, that "a prophet is least regarded in his own country," was true with respect to me and my defunct master. I loved him as a man—I respected him as a sage—but I derided the notion that he could command the powers of darkness, and laughed at the superstitious fears with which he was regarded by the vulgar. He was a wise philosopher, but had no acquaintance with any spirits but those clad in flesh and blood. His science was simply human; and human science, I persuaded myself, could never conquer nature's laws so far as to imprison the soul for ever within its carnal habitation. Cornelius had brewed a soul-refreshing drink—more inebriating than wine—sweeter and more fragrant than any fruit: it possessed probably strong medicinal powers, imparting gladness to the heart and vigor to the limbs; but its effects would wear out; already were they diminished in my frame. I was a lucky fellow to have quaffed health and joyous spirits, and perhaps long life, at my master's hands; but my good fortune ended there: longevity was far different from immortality.

I continued to entertain this belief for many years. Sometimes a thought stole across me—Was the alchemist indeed deceived? But my habitual credence was, that I should meet the fate of all the children of Adam at my appointed time—a little late, but still at a natural age. Yet it was certain that I retained a wonderfully youthful look. I was laughed at for my vanity in consulting the mirror so often, but I consulted it in vain—my brow was untrenched—my cheeks—my eyes—my whole person continued as untarnished as in my twentieth year.

I was troubled. I looked at the faded beauty of Bertha—I seemed more like her son. By degrees our neighbors began to make similar observations, and I found at last that I went by the name of the scholar bewitched. Bertha herself grew uneasy. She became jealous and peevish, and at length she began to question me. We had no children; we were all in all to each other; and though, as she grew older, her vivacious spirit became a little allied to ill-temper, and her beauty sadly diminished. I cherished her in my heart as the mistress I had idolized, the wife I had sought and won with such perfect love.

At last our situation became intolerable: Bertha was fifty—I twenty years of age. I had in very shame, in some measure adopted the habits of a more advanced age; I no longer mingled in the dance among the young and gay, but my heart bounded along with them while I restrained my feet; and a sorry figure I cut among the Nestors of our village. But before the time I mention things were altered—we were universally shunned; we were—at least, I was—reported to have kept up an iniquitous acquaintance with some of my former master's supposed friends. Poor Bertha was pitied, but deserted. I was regarded with horror and detestation.

What was to be done? we sat by our winter fire—poverty had made itself felt, for none would buy the produce of my farm; and often I had been forced to journey twenty miles, to some place where I was not known, to dispose of our property. It was true we had saved something for an evil day—that day was come.

We sat by our lone fireside—the old-hearted youth and his antiquated wife. Again Bertha insisted on knowing the truth; she recapitulated all she had ever heard said about me, and added her own observations. She conjured me to cast off the spell; she described how much more comely gray hairs were than my chestnut locks; she descanted on the reverence and respect due to age—how preferable to the slight regard paid to mere children: could I imagine that the despicable gifts of youth and good looks outweighed disgrace, hatred, and scorn? Nay, in the end I should be burned as a dealer in the black art, while she, to whom I had not deigned to communicate any portion of my good fortune, might be stoned as my accomplice. At length she insinuated that I must share my secret with her, and bestow on her like benefits to those I myself enjoyed, or she would denounce me—and then she burst into tears.

Thus beset, methought it was the best way to tell the truth. I revealed it as tenderly as I could, and spoke only of a *very long life*, not of immortality—which representation, indeed, coincided best with my own ideas. When I ended, I rose and said,

"And now, my Bertha, will you denounce the lover of your youth?—You will not, I know. But it is too hard, my poor wife, that you should suffer from my ill-luck and the accursed arts of Cornelius. I will leave you—you have wealth enough, and friends will return in my absence. I will go; young as I seem, and strong as I am, I can work and gain my bread among strangers, unsuspected and unknown. I loved you in youth; God is my witness that I would not desert you in age, but that your safety and happiness require it."

I took my cap and moved toward the door; in a moment Bertha's arms were around my neck, and her lips were pressed to mine. "No, my husband, my Winzy," she said, "you shall not go alone—take me with you; we will remove from this place, and, as you say, among strangers we shall be unsuspected and safe. I am not so very old as quite to shame you, my Winzy; and I dare say the charm will soon wear off, and, with the blessing of God, you will become more elderly-looking, as is fitting; you shall not leave me."

I returned the good soul's embrace heartily. "I will not, my Bertha, but for your sake, I had not thought of such a thing. I will be your true, faithful husband while you are spared to me, and do my duty by you to the last."

The next day we prepared secretly for our emigration. We were obliged to make great pecuniary sacrifices—it could not be helped. We realized a sum sufficient, at least, to maintain us while Bertha lived; and without saying adieu to anyone, quitted our native country to take refuge in a remote part of western France.

It was a cruel thing to transport poor Bertha from her native village, and the friends of her youth, to a new country, new language, new customs. The strange secret of my destiny rendered this removal immaterial to me; but I compassionated her deeply, and was glad to perceive that she found compensation for her misfortunes in a variety of little ridiculous circumstances. Away from all tell-tale chroniclers, she sought to decrease the apparent disparity of our ages by a thousand feminine arts—rouge, youthful dress, and assumed juvenility of manner. I could not be angry—Did not I myself wear a mask? Why quarrel with hers, because it was less successful? I grieved deeply when I remembered that this was my Bertha, whom I had loved so fondly, and won with such transport—the dark-eyed, dark-haired girl, with smiles of enchanting archness and a step like a fawn—this mincing, simpering, jealous old woman. I should have revered her gray locks and withered cheeks; but thus?—It was my work, I knew; but I did not the less deplore this type of human weakness.

Her jealousy never slept. Her chief occupation was to discover that, in spite of outward appearances, I was myself growing old. I verily believed that the poor soul loved me truly in her heart, but never had woman so tormenting a mode of displaying fondness. She would discern wrinkles in my face and decrepitude in my walk, while I bounded along in youthful vigor, the youngest looking of twenty youths. I never dared address another woman: on one occasion, fancying that the bellé of the village regarded me with favoring eyes, she brought me a gray wig. Her constant discourse among her acquaintances was, that though I looked so young, there was ruin at work within my frame; and she affirmed that the worst symptom about me was my apparent health. My youth was a disease, she said, and I ought at all times to prepare for a sudden and awful death, at least to awake some morning white-headed, and bowed down with all the marks of advanced years. I let her talk— I often joined in her conjectures. Her warnings chimed in with my never-ceasing speculations concerning my state, and I took an earnest, though painful, interest in listening to all that her quick wit and excited imagination could say on the subject.

Why dwell on these minute circumstances? We lived on for many long years. Bertha became bedridden and paralytic; I nursed her as a mother might a child. She grew peevish, and still harped upon one string—of how long I should survive her. It has ever been a source of consolation to me, that I performed my duty scrupulously toward her. She had been mine in youth, she was mine in age, and at last, when I heaped the sod over her corpse, I wept to feel that I had lost all that really bound me to humanity.

Since then how many have been my cares and woes, how few and empty my enjoyments! I pause here in my history—I will pursue it no further. A sailor without rudder or compass, tossed on a stormy sea—a traveler lost on a widespread heath, without landmark or stone to guide him—such have I been: more lost, more hopeless than either. A nearing ship, a gleam from some far cot, may save them; but I have no beacon except the hope of death.

Death! mysterious, ill-visaged friend of weak humanity! Why alone of all mortals have you cast me from your sheltering fold? O, for the peace of the grave! the deep silence of the iron-bound tomb! that thought would cease to work in my brain, and my heart beat no more with emotions varied only by new forms of sadness!

Am I immortal? I return to my first question. In the first place, is it not more probable that the beverage of the alchemist was fraught rather with longevity than eternal life? Such is my hope. And then be it remembered, that I only drank *half* of the potion prepared by him. Was not the whole necessary to complete the charm? To have drained half the Elixir of Immortality is but to be half immortal—for Forever is thus truncated and null.

But again, who shall number the years of the half of eternity? I often try to imagine by what rule the infinite may be divided. Sometimes I fancy age advancing upon me. One gray hair I have found. Fool! do I lament? Yes, the fear of age and death often creeps coldly into my heart; and the more I live, the more I dread death, even while I abhor life. Such an enigma is man—born to perish—when he wars, as I do, against the established laws of his nature.

But for this anomaly of feeling surely I might die: the medicine of the alchemist would not be proof against fire—sword—and the strangling waters. I have gazed upon the blue depths of many a placid lake, and the tumultuous rushing of many a mighty river, and have said, Peace inhabits those waters; yet I have turned my steps away, to live yet another day. I have asked myself, whether suicide would be a crime in one to whom thus only the portals of the other world could be open. I have done all, except presenting myself as a soldier or duelist, an object of destruction to my—no, *not* my fellow-mortals, and therefore I have shrunk away. They are not my fellows. The inextinguishable power of life in my frame, and their ephemeral existence, places us wide as the poles asunder. I could not raise a hand against the meanest or the most powerful among them.

Thus I have lived on for many a year—alone and weary of myself—desirous of death, yet never dying—a mortal immortal. Neither ambition nor avarice can enter my mind, and the ardent love that gnaws at my heart, never to be returned—never to find an equal on which to expend itself—lives there only to torment me.

This very day I conceived a design by which I may end all—without self-slaughter, without making another man a Cain—an expedition, which mortal frame can never survive, even endued with the youth and strength that inhabits mine. Thus I shall put my immortality to the test, and rest forever—or return, the wonder and benefactor of the human species.

Before I go, a miserable vanity has caused me to pen these pages. I would not die, and leave no name behind. Three centuries have passed since I quaffed the fatal beverage; another year shall not elapse before, encountering gigantic dangers—warring with the powers of frost in their home—beset by famine, toil, and tempest—I yield this body, too tenacious a cage for a soul which thirsts for freedom to the destructive elements of air and water—or, if I survive, my name shall be recorded as one of the most famous among the sons of men; and, my task achieved, I shall adopt more resolute means, and, by scattering and annihilating the atoms that compose my frame set at liberty the life imprisoned within, and so cruelly prevented from soaring from this dim earth to a sphere more congenial to its immortal essence.

# THE SQUAW

## BY BRAM STOKER

BRAM STOKER, the author of the most obsessive book in literature, *Dracula*, was often confined to bed in ill health. During those early years his mother regaled and terrified him with Irish fairy and horror stories. She had seen the terrible cholera epidemic in Sliggo in 1832, and her stories of the pestilence inspired Stoker to use later a background of vampire pestilence in *Dracula*.

After his college years, Bram, as he was known throughout his life (his name was Abraham), inundated himself in the theatrical world. Once, seeing the great Henry Irving in the Dublin theater, he described his reactions to the part Irving was playing in a description worthy of *Dracula*, "The awful horror . . . the blood of avenging spite . . . eyes as inflexible as fate, eloquent hands slowly moving, outspread, fanlike." Although Stoker said he became hysterical that night at the theater, he was so impressed by Irving that he became the actor's private secretary for twenty-seven years. But he had two other lasting passions, the study of vampirism and the gothic novel.

Determined to write a vampire story of his own, he sought out the friendship of a Hungarian scholar, Professor Arminium Vambrey, who gave him background material about the cruel, bloodthirsty prince of Transylvania, Dracula, a nickname, meaning son of the devil. In many languages the words devil and vampire are synonymous. Stoker was never in Transylvania, but when *Dracula* was first published, he was congratulated for knowing the country firsthand. He also knew his vampires; his Count Dracula lived his vampire life for centuries, and his horror life continues forever on the screen of television.

"The Squaw" was intended by Stoker to be published as part of *Dracula*. The publishers eliminated it for reason of space in the early editions, but his wife saw that this remarkable tale was published after his death. &

NURNBERG at the time was not so much exploited as it has been since then. Irving had not been playing *Faust*, and the very name of the old town was hardly known to the great bulk of the traveling public. My wife and I being in the second week of our honeymoon, naturally wanted someone else to join our party, so that when the cheery stranger, Elias P. Hutcheson, hailing from Isthmian City, Bleeding Gulch, Maple Tree County, Neb., turned up at the station at Frankfort, and casually remarked that he was going on to see the most all-fired old Methuselah of a town in Yurrup, and that he guessed that so much traveling alone was enough to send an intelligent, active citizen into the melancholy ward of a daft house, we took the pretty broad hint and suggested that we should join forces. We found, on comparing notes afterward, that we had intended to speak with some diffidence or hesitation so as not to appear too eager, such not being a good compliment to the success of our married life; but the effect was entirely marred by our both beginning to speak at the same instant—stopping simultaneously and then going on together again. Anyhow, no matter how, it was done; and Elias P. Hutcheson became one of our party. Straightway Amelia and I found the pleasant benefit; instead of quarreling, as we had been doing, we found that the restraining influence of a third party was such that we now took every opportunity of spooning in odd corners. Amelia declares that ever since she has, as the result of that experience, advised all her friends to take a friend on the honeymoon. Well, we "did" Nurnberg together, and much enjoyed the racy remarks of our Transatlantic friend, who, from his quaint speech and his wonderful stock of adventures, might have stepped out of a novel. We kept for the last object of interest in the city to be visited the Burg, and on the day appointed for the visit strolled around the outer wall of the city by the eastern side.

The Burg is seated on a rock dominating the town, and an immensely deep fosse guards it on the northern side. Nurnberg has been happy in that it was never sacked; had it been it would certainly not be so spick and span perfect as it is at present. The ditch has not been used for centuries, and now its base is spread with tea-gardens and orchards, of which some of the trees are of quite respectable growth. As we wandered around the wall, dawdling in the hot July sunshine, we often paused to admire the views spread before us, and in especial the great plain covered with towns and villages and bounded with a blue line of hills, like a landscape of Claude Lorraine. From this we always turned with new delight to the city itself, with its myriad of quaint old gables and acre-wide red roofs dotted with dormer windows, tier upon tier. A little to our right rose the towers of the Burg, and nearer still, standing grim, the Torture Tower, which was, and is, perhaps, the most interesting place in the city. For centuries the tradition of the Iron Virgin of Nurnberg has been handed down as an instance of the horrors of cruelty of which man is capable; we had long looked forward to seeing it; and here at last was its home.

In one of our pauses we leaned over the wall of the moat and looked down. The garden seemed quite fifty or sixty feet below us, and the sun pouring into it with an intense, moveless heat like that of an oven. Beyond rose the gray, grim wall seemingly of endless height, and losing itself right and left in the angles of bastion and counterscarp. Trees and bushes crowned the wall, and above again towered the lofty houses on whose massive beauty Time has only set the hand of approval. The sun was hot and we were lazy; time was our own, and we lingered, leaning on the wall. Just below us was a pretty sight—a great black cat lying stretched in the sun, while around her gamboled prettily a tiny black kitten. The mother would wave her tail for the kitten to play with, or would raise her feet and push away the little one as an encouragement to further play. They were just at the foot of the wall, and Elias P. Hutcheson, in order to help the play, stopped and took from the walk a moderate sized pebble.

"See!" he said, "I will drop it near the kitten, and they will both wonder where it came from."

"Oh, be careful," said my wife; "you might hit the dear little thing!"

"Not me, ma'am," said Elias P. "Why, I'm as tender as a Maine cherry-tree. Lor, bless ye, I wouldn't hurt the poor pooty little critter more'n I'd scalp a baby. An' you may bet your variegated socks on that! See, I'll drop it fur away on the outside so's not to go near her!" Thus saying, he leaned over and held his arm out at full length and dropped the stone. It may be that there is some attractive force which draws lesser matters to greater; or more probably that the wall was not plumb but sloped to its base—we not noticing the inclination from above; but the stone fell with a sickening thud that came up to us through the hot air, right on the kitten's head, and shattered out its little brains then and there. The black cat cast a swift upward glance, and we saw her eyes like green fire fixed an instant on Elias P. Hutcheson; and then her attention was given to the kitten, which lay still with just a quiver of her tiny limbs, while a thin red stream trickled from a gaping wound. With a muffled cry, such as a human being might give, she bent over the kitten, licking its wound and moaning. Suddenly she seemed to realize that it was dead, and again threw her eyes up at us. I shall never forget the sight, for she looked the perfect incarnation of hate. Her green eyes blazed with lurid fire, and the white, sharp teeth seemed to almost shine through the blood which dabbled her mouth and whiskers. She gnashed her teeth, and her claws stood out stark and at full length on every paw. Then she made a wild rush up the wall as if to reach us, but when the momentum ended fell back, and further added to her horrible appearance for she fell on the kitten, and rose with her back fur smeared with its brains and blood. Amelia turned quite faint, and I had to lift her back from the wall. There was a seat close by in shade of a spreading plane-tree, and here I placed her while she composed herself. Then I went back to Hutcheson, who stood without moving, looking down on the angry cat below.

As I joined him, he said:

"Wall, I guess that air the savagest beast I ever see—'cept once when an Apache squaw had an edge on a half-breed what they nicknamed 'Splinters' 'cos of the way he fired up her papoose which he stole on a raid just to show that he appreciated the way they had given his mother the fire torture. She got that kinder look so set on her face that it just seemed to grow there. She followed Splinters more'n three year till at last the braves got him and handed him over to her. They did say that no man, white or Injun, had ever been so long a-dying under the tortures of the Apaches. The only time I ever see her smile was when I wiped her out. I kem on the camp just in time to see Splinters pass in his checks, and he wasn't sorry to go either. He was a hard citizen, and though I never could shake with him after that papoose business—for it was bitter bad—I see he had got paid out in full. Durn me, but I took a piece of his hide from one of his skinnin posts an' had it made into a pocket-book. It's here now!" and he slapped the breast pocket of his coat.

While he was speaking the cat was continuing her frantic efforts to get up the wall. She would take a run back and then charge up, sometimes reaching an incredible height. She did not seem to mind the heavy fall which she got each time but started with renewed vigor; and at every tumble her appearance became more horrible. Hutcheson was a kind-hearted man—my wife and I had both noticed little acts of kindness to animals as well as to persons—and he seemed concerned at the state of fury to which the cat had wrought herself.

"Wall now!" he said, "I du declare that that poor critter seems quite desperate. There! there! poor thing, it was all an accident—though that won't bring back your little one to you. Say! I wouldn't have had such a thing happen for a thousand! Just shows what a clumsy fool of a man can do when he tries to play! Seems I'm too darned slipperhanded to even play with a cat. Say Colonel!"—it was a pleasant way he had to bestow titles freely—"I hope your wife don't hold no grudge against me on account of this unpleasantness? Why, I wouldn't have had it occur on no account."

He came over to Amelia and apologized profusely, and she with her usual kindness of heart hastened to assure him that she quite understood that it was an accident. Then we all went again to the wall and looked over.

The cat missing Hutcheson's face had drawn back across the moat, and was sitting on her haunches as though ready to spring. Indeed, the

very instant she saw him she did spring, and with a blind unreasoning
fury, which would have been grotesque, only that it was so frightfully
real. She did not try to run up the wall, but simply launched herself at
him as though hate and fury could lend her wings to pass straight
through the great distance between them. Amelia, womanlike, got quite
concerned, and said to Elias P. in a warning voice:

"Oh! you must be very careful. That animal would try to kill you if
she were here; her eyes look like positive murder."

He laughed out jovially. "Excuse me, ma'am," he said, "but I can't
help laughin'. Fancy a man that has fought grizzlies an' Injuns bein'
careful of bein' murdered by a cat!"

When the cat heard him laugh, her whole demeanor seemed to
change. She no longer tried to jump or run up the wall, but went quietly
over, and sitting again beside the dead kitten began to lick and fondle it
as though it were alive.

"See!" said I, "the effect of a really strong man. Even that animal in
the midst of her fury recognizes the voice of a master, and bows to
him!"

"Like a squaw!" was the only comment of Elias P. Hutcheson, as we
moved on our way around the city fosse. Every now and then we looked
over the wall and each time saw the cat following us. At first she had
kept going back to the dead kitten, and then as the distance grew
greater took it in her mouth and so followed. After a while, however, she
abandoned this, for we saw her following all alone; she had evidently
hidden the body somewhere. Amelia's alarm grew at the cat's persist-
ence, and more than once she repeated her warning; but the American
always laughed with amusement, till finally, seeing that she was beginning to be worried, he said:

"I say, ma'am, you needn't be skeered over the cat. I go heeled, I du!"
Here he slapped his pistol pocket at the back of his lumbar region.
"Why sooner'n have you worried, I'll shoot the critter, right here, an'
risk the police interferin' with a citizen of the United States for carryin'
arms contrairy to reg'lations!" As he spoke he looked over the wall, but
the cat, on seeing him, retreated, with a growl, into a bed of tall flowers,
and was hidden. He went on: "Blest if that ar critter ain't got more
sense of what's good for her than most Christians. I guess we've seen the

last of her! You bet, she'll go back now to that busted kitten and have a private funeral of it, all to herself!"

Amelia did not like to say more, lest he might, in mistaken kindness to her, fulfill his threat of shooting the cat: and so we went on and crossed the little wooden bridge leading to the gateway whence ran the steep paved roadway between the Burg and the pentagonal Torture Tower. As we crossed the bridge we saw the cat again down below us. When she saw us her fury seemed to return, and she made frantic efforts to get up the steep wall. Hutcheson laughed as he looked down at her, and said:

"Good-bye, old girl. Sorry I in-jured your feelin's, but you'll get over it in time! So long!" And then we passed through the long, dim archway and came to the gate of the Burg.

When we came out again after our survey of this most beautiful old place which not even the well-intended efforts of the Gothic restorers of forty years ago have been able to spoil—though their restoration was then glaring white—we seemed to have quite forgotten the unpleasant episode of the morning. The old lime tree with its great trunk gnarled with the passing of nearly nine centuries, the deep well cut through the heart of the rock by those captives of old, and the lovely view from the city wall whence we heard, spread over almost a full quarter of an hour, the multitudinous chimes of the city, had all helped to wipe out from our minds the incident of the slain kitten.

We were the only visitors who had entered the Torture Tower that morning—so at least said the old custodian—and as we had the place all to ourselves were able to make a minute and more satisfactory survey than would have otherwise been possible. The custodian, looking to us as the sole source of his gains for the day, was willing to meet our wishes in any way. The Torture Tower is truly a grim place, even now when many thousands of visitors have sent a stream of life, and the joy that follows life, into the place; but at the time I mention it wore its grimmest and most gruesome aspect. The dust of ages seemed to have settled on it, and the darkness and the horror of its memories seem to have become sentient in a way that would have satisfied the Pantheistic souls of Philo or Spinoza. The lower chamber where we entered was seemingly, in its normal state, filled with incarnate darkness; even the hot sunlight streaming in through the door seemed to be lost in the vast thickness of the walls, and only showed the masonry rough as when the builder's scaffolding had come down, but coated with dust and marked here and there with patches of dark stain which, if walls could speak, could have given their own dread memories of fear and pain. We were glad to pass up the dusty wooden staircase, the custodian leaving the outer door open to light us somewhat on our way; for to our eyes the one long-wick'd, evil-smelling candle stuck in a sconce on the wall gave an inadequate light. When we came up through the open trap in the corner of the chamber overhead, Amelia held on to me so tightly that I could actually feel her heart beat. I must say for my own part that I was not surprised at her fear, for this room was even more gruesome than that below. Here there was certainly more light, but only just sufficient to realize the horrible surroundings of the place. The builders of the tower had evidently intended that only they who should gain the top should have any of the joys of light and prospect. There, as we had noticed from below, were ranges of windows, albeit of medieval small-ness, but elsewhere in the tower were only a very few narrow slits such as were habitual in places of medieval defense. A few of these only lit the chamber, and these so high up in the wall that from no part could the sky be seen through the thickness of the walls. In racks, and leaning in disorder against the walls, were a number of headsmen's swords, great double-handed weapons with broad blade and keen edge. Hard by were several blocks whereon the necks of the victims had lain, with here and there deep notches where the steel had bitten through the guard of flesh and shored into the wood. Around the chamber, placed in all sorts of ir-regular ways, were many implements of torture which made one's heart ache to see—chairs full of spikes which gave instant and excruciating pain; chairs and couches with dull knobs whose torture was seemingly less, but which, though slower, were equally efficacious; racks, belts, boots, gloves, collars, all made for compressing at will; steel baskets in which the head could be slowly crushed into a pulp if necessary; watch-men's hooks with long handle and knife that cut at resistance—this a specialty of the old Nurnberg police system; and many, many other de-vices for man's injury to man. Amelia grew quite pale with the horror of the things, but fortunately did not faint, for being a little overcome she sat down on a torture chair, but jumped up again with a shriek, all tendency to faint gone. We both pretended that it was the injury done to her dress by the dust of the chair, and the rusty spikes which had up-set her, and Mr. Hutcheson acquiesced in accepting the explanation with a kind-hearted laugh.

But the central object in the whole of this chamber of horrors was the engine known as the Iron Virgin, which stood near the center of the room. It was a rudely-shaped figure of a woman, something of the bell order, or, to make a closer comparison, of the figure of Mrs. Noah, in the children's Ark, but without that slimness of waist and perfect *rondeur* of hip which marks the aesthetic type of the Noah family. One would hardly have recognized it as intended for a human figure at all had not the founder shaped on the forehead a rude semblance of a woman's face. This machine was coated with rust without, and covered with dust; a rope was fastened to a ring in the front of the figure, about where the waist should have been, and was drawn through a pulley, fastened on the wooden pillar which sustained the flooring above. The custodian pulling this rope showed that a section of the front was hinged like a door at one side; we then saw that the engine was of considerable thick-ness, leaving just room enough inside for a man to be placed. The door was of equal thickness and of great weight, for it took the custodian all his strength, aided though he was by the contrivance of the pulley, to open it. This weight was partly due to the fact that the door was of manifest purpose hung so as to throw its weight downward, so that it might shut of its own accord when the strain was released. The inside was honeycombed with rust—nay more, the rust alone that comes through time would hardly have eaten so deep into the iron walls; the rust of the cruel stains was deep indeed! It was only, however, when we came to look at the inside of the door that the diabolical intention was manifest to the full. Here were several long spikes, square and massive, broad at the base and sharp at the points, placed in such a position that when the door should close the upper ones would pierce the eyes of the victim, and the lower ones his heart and vitals. The sight was too much for poor Amelia, and this time she fainted dead off, and I had to carry her down the stairs, and place her on a bench outside till she recovered. That she felt it to the quick was afterward shown by the fact that my eldest son bears to this day a rude birthmark on his breast, which has, by family consent, been accepted as representing the Nurnberg Virgin.

When we got back to the chamber we found Hutcheson still opposite the Iron Virgin; he had been evidently philosophizing, and now gave us the benefit of his thought in the shape of a sort of exordium.

"Wall, I guess I've been learnin' somethin' here while madam has been gettin' over her faint. 'Pears to me that we're a long way behind the times on our side of the big drink. We uster think out on the plains that the Injun could give us points in tryin' to make a man oncomfortable; but I guess your old medieval law-and-order party could raise him every time. Splinters was pretty good in his bluff on the squaw, but this here young miss held a straight flush all high on him. The points of them spikes air sharp enough still, though even the edges air eaten out by what uster be on them. It'd be a good thing for our Indian section to get some specimens of this here play-toy to send round to the Reservations jest to knock the stuffin' out of the bucks, and the squaws too, by showing them as how old civilization lays over them at their best. Guess but I'll get in that box a minute jest to see how it feels!"

"Oh no! no!" said Amelia. "It is too terrible!"

"Guess, ma'am, nothin's too terrible to the explorin' mind. I've been in some queer places in my time. Spent a night inside a dead horse while a prairie fire swept over me in Montana Territory—an' another time slept inside a dead buffler when the Comanches was on the war path an' I didn't keer to leave my kyard on them. I've been two days in a caved-in tunnel in the Billy Broncho gold mine in New Mexico, an' was one of the four shut up for three parts of a day in the caisson what slid over on her side when we was settin' the foundations of the Buffalo Bridge. I've not funked an odd experience yet, an' I don't propose to begin now!"

We saw that he was set on the experiment, so I said: "Well, hurry up, old man, and get through it quick?"

"All right, General," said he, "but I calculate we ain't quite ready yet. The gentlemen, my predecessors, what stood in that thar canister, didn't volunteer for the office—not much! And I guess there was some ornamental tyin' up before the big stroke was made. I want to go into this thing fair and square, so I must get fixed up proper first. I dare say this old galoot can rise some string and tie me up accordin' to sample?"

This was said interrogatively to the old custodian, but the latter, who understood the drift of his speech, though perhaps not appreciating to the full the niceties of dialect and imagery, shook his head. His protest was, however, only formal and made to be overcome. The American thrust a gold piece into his hand, saying, "Take it, pard! it's your pot; and don't be skeer'd. This ain't no necktie party that you're asked to assist in!" He produced some thin frayed rope and proceeded to bind our companion, with sufficient strictness for the purpose. When the upper part of his body was bound, Hutcheson said:

"Hold on a moment, Judge. Guess I'm too heavy for you to tote into the canister. You jest let me walk in, and then you can wash up re-gardin' my legs!"

While speaking he had backed himself into the opening which was just enough to hold him. It was a close fit and no mistake. Amelia looked on with fear in her eyes, but she evidently did not like to say anything. Then the custodian completed his task by tying the American's feet together so that he was now absolutely helpless and fixed in his voluntary prison. He seemed to really enjoy it, and the incipient smile which was habitual to his face blossomed into actuality as he said:

"Guess this here Eve was made out of the rib of a dwarf! There ain't much room for a full-grown citizen of the United States to hustle. We uster make our coffins more roomier in Idaho territory. Now, Judge, you just begin to let this door down, slow, on to me. I want to feel the same pleasure as the other jays had when those spikes began to move toward their eyes!"

"Oh no! no! no!" broke in Amelia hysterically. "It is too terrible! I can't bear to see it!—I can't! I can't."

But the American was obdurate. "Say, Colonel," said he, "why not take Madame for a little promenade? I wouldn't hurt her feelin's for the world; but now that I am here, havin' kem eight thousand miles, wouldn't it be too hard to give up the very experience I've been pinin' and pantin' fur? A man can't get to feel like canned goods every time! Me and the Judge here'll fix up this thing in no time, an' then you'll come back, an' we'll all laugh together!"

Once more the resolution that is born of curiosity triumphed, and Amelia stayed holding tight to my arm and shivering while the custodian began to slacken slowly inch by inch the rope that held back the iron door. Hutcheson's face was positively radiant as his eyes followed the first movement of the spikes.

"Wall!" he said. "I guess I've not had enjoyment like this since I left Noo York. Bar a scrap with a French sailor at Wapping—an' that warn't much of a picnic neither—I've not had a show fur real pleasure in this dod-rotted Continent, where there ain't no b'ars nor no Injuns, an' where nary man goes heeled. Slow there, Judge! Don't you rush this business! I want a show for my money this game—I du!"

The custodian must have had in him some of the blood of his predecessors in that ghastly tower, for he worked the engine with a deliberate and excruciating slowness which after five minutes, in which the outer edge of the door had not moved half as many inches, began to overcome Amelia. I saw her lips whiten, and felt her hold upon my arm relax. I looked around an instant for a place whereon to lay her, and when I looked at her again found that her eye had become fixed on the side of the Virgin. Following its direction I saw the black cat crouching out of sight. Her green eyes shone like danger lamps in the gloom of the place, and their color was heightened by the blood which still smeared her coat and reddened her mouth. I cried out:

"The cat! look out for the cat!" for even then she sprang out before the engine. At this moment she looked like a triumphant demon. Her eyes blazed with ferocity, her hair bristled out till she seemed twice her normal size, and her tail lashed about as does a tiger's when the quarry is before it. Elias P. Hutcheson when he saw her was amused, and his eyes positively sparkled with fun as he said:

"Darned if the squaw hain't got on all her war paint! Jest give her a glove off if she comes any of her tricks on me, for I'm so fixed everlastingly by the boss, that durn my skin if I can keep my eyes from her if she wants them! Easy there, Judge! Don't you slack that ar rope or I'm euchered!"

At this moment Amelia completed her faint, and I had to clutch hold of her around the waist or she would have fallen to the floor. While attending to her I saw the black cat crouching for a spring, and jumped up to turn the creature out.

But at that instant, with a sort of hellish scream, she hurled herself, not as we expected at Hutcheson, but straight at the face of the custodian. Her claws seemed to be tearing wildly as one sees in the Chinese drawings of the dragon rampant, and as I looked I saw one of them light on the poor man's eye, and actually tear through it and down his cheek, leaving a wide band of red where the blood seemed to spurt from every vein.

With a yell of sheer terror which came quicker than even his sense of pain, the man leaped back, dropping as he did so the rope which held back the iron door. I jumped for it, but was too late, for the cord ran like lightning through the pulley-block, and the heavy mass fell forward from its own weight.

As the door closed I caught a glimpse of our poor companion's face. He seemed frozen with terror. His eyes stared with a horrible anguish as if dazed, and no sound came from his lips.

And then the spikes did their work. Happily the end was quick, for when I wrenched open the door they had pierced so deep that they had locked in the bones of the skull through which they had crushed, and actually tore him—it—out of his iron prison till, bound as he was, he fell at full length with a sickly thud upon the floor, the face turning upward as he fell.

I rushed to my wife, lifted her up and carried her out, for I feared for her very reason if she should wake from her faint to such a scene. I laid her on the bench outside and ran back. Leaning against the wooden column was the custodian moaning in pain while he held his reddening handkerchief to his eyes. And sitting on the head of the poor American was the cat, purring loudly as she licked the blood which trickled through the gashed sockets of his eyes.

I think no one will call me cruel because I seized one of the old executioner's swords and shore her in two as she sat.

# THE HOUSE OF
# THE DEAD HAND

## BY EDITH WHARTON

EDITH WHARTON, the grand dame of American letters in the earlier twentieth century, used many elements of the gothic story as well as a contemporary straightforwardness of her own. She credited her ability with the supernatural story to the fact that she was, if not, a ghost feeler, at least a ghost seer, "a person whose extrasensory tentacles are so well developed that they use their sense of sight to submit to the brain presences which otherwise could only make themselves vaguely felt."

After meeting Osbert Sitwell one day, she wrote: "He informed us the other day that ghosts went out when electricity came in, but surely this is to misapprehend the nature of the ghostly. What drives ghosts away is not the aspidistra or the electric cooker; I can more easily imagine them haunting a mean, modern house in a dull, modern street than the battlemented castle with the boring stage properties. What the ghost really needs is not the echoing passages and hidden doors behind the tapestry, but only continuity and silence. It obviously prefers the silent hours when the wireless has ceased to jazz. These hours, pathetically called small, are growing smaller. And even if so few diviners as keep their wands, the ghost may after all succumb first to the impossibility of finding standing room in a roaring and discontinuous universe."

In *The House of the Dead Hand,* using a most gothic background, she tells an extraordinary tale that shows that she was not only a ghost seer, but a ghost teller of remarkable talent.  ⅊

I

"ABOVE ALL," the letter ended, "don't leave Siena without seeing Doctor Lombard's Leonardo. Lombard is a queer old Englishman, a mystic or a madman (if the two are not synonymous), and a devout student of the Italian Renaissance. He has lived for years in Italy, exploring its remotest corners, and has lately picked up an undoubted Leonardo, which came to light in a farmhouse near Bergamo. It is believed to be one of the missing pictures mentioned by Vasari, and is at any rate, according to the most competent authorities, a genuine and almost untouched example of the best period.

"Lombard is a queer stick, and jealous of showing his treasures; but we struck up a friendship when I was working on the Sodomas in Siena three years ago, and if you will give him the enclosed line you may get a peep at the Leonardo. Probably not more than a peep, though, for I hear he refuses to have it reproduced. I want badly to use it in my monograph on the Windsor drawings, so please see what you can do for me, and if you can't persuade him to let you take a photograph or make a sketch, at least jot down a detailed description of the picture and get from him all the facts you can. I hear that the French and Italian governments have offered him a large advance on his purchase, but that he refuses to sell at any price, though he certainly can't afford such luxuries; in fact, I don't see where he got enough money to buy the picture. He lives in the Via Papa Giulio."

Wyant sat at the table d'hôte of his hotel, re-reading his friend's letter over a late luncheon. He had been five days in Siena without having found time to call on Doctor Lombard; not from any indifference to the opportunity presented, but because it was his first visit to the strange red city and he was still under the spell of its more conspicuous wonders—the brick palaces flinging out their wrought-iron torch-holders with a gesture of arrogant suzerainty; the great council chamber emblazoned with civic allegories; the pageant of Pope Julius on the Library walls; the Sodomas smiling balefully through the dusk of moldering chapels—and it was only when his first hunger was appeased that he remembered that one course in the banquet was still untasted.

He put the letter in his pocket and turned to leave the room, with a nod to its only other occupant, an olive-skinned young man with lustrous eyes and a low collar, who sat on the other side of the table perusing the *Fanfulla di Domenica*. This gentleman, his daily vis-à-vis, returned the nod with a Latin eloquence of gesture, and Wyant passed on to the ante-chamber, where he paused to light a cigarette. He was just restoring the case to his pocket when he heard a hurried step behind him, and the lustrous-eyed young man advanced through the glass doors of the dining-room.

"Pardon me, sir," he said in measured English, and with an intonation of exquisite politeness; "you have let this letter fall."

Wyant, recognizing his friend's note of introduction to Doctor Lombard, took it with a word of thanks, and was about to turn away when he perceived that the eyes of his fellow diner remained fixed on him with a gaze of melancholy interrogation.

"Again pardon me," the young man at length ventured, "but are you by chance the friend of the illustrious Doctor Lombard?"

"No," returned Wyant, with the instinctive Anglo-Saxon distrust of foreign advances. Then, fearing to appear rude, he said with a guarded politeness: "Perhaps, by the way, you can tell me the number of his house. I see it is not given here."

The young man brightened perceptibly. "The number of the house is thirteen; but any one can indicate it to you—it is well known in Siena. It is called," he continued after a moment, "the House of the Dead Hand."

Wyant stared. "What a queer name!" he said.

"The name comes from an antique hand of marble which for many hundred years has been above the door."

Wyant was turning away with a gesture of thanks, when the other added: "If you would have the kindness to ring twice."

"To ring twice?"

"At the doctor's." The young man smiled. "It is the custom."

It was a dazzling March afternoon, with a shower of sun from the mid-blue, and a marshaling of slaty clouds behind the umber-colored hills. For nearly an hour Wyant loitered on the Lizza, watching the shadows race across the naked landscape and the thunder blacken in the west; then he decided to set out for the House of the Dead Hand. The map in his guidebook showed him that the Via Papa Giulio was one of the streets which radiate from the Piazza, and thither he bent his course, pausing at every other step to fill his eye with some fresh image of weather-beaten beauty. The clouds had rolled upward, obscuring the sunshine and hanging like a funereal baldachin above the projecting cornices of Doctor Lombard's street, and Wyant walked for some distance in the shade of the beetling palace fronts before his eye fell on a doorway surmounted by a sallow marble hand. He stood for a moment staring up at the strange emblem. The hand was a woman's—a dead drooping hand, which hung there convulsed and helpless, as though it had been thrust forth in denunciation of some evil mystery within the house, and had sunk struggling into death.

A girl who was drawing water from the well in the court said that the English doctor lived on the first floor, and Wyant, passing through a glazed door, mounted the damp degrees of a vaulted stairway with a plaster Aesculapius moldering in a niche on the landing. Facing the Aesculapius was another door, and as Wyant put his hand on the bell-rope he remembered his unknown friend's injunction, and rang twice.

His ring was answered by a peasant woman with a low forehead and small close-set eyes, who, after a prolonged scrutiny of himself, his card, and his letter of introduction, left him standing in a high, cold ante-chamber floored with brick. He heard her wooden pattens click down an interminable corridor, and after some delay she returned and told him to follow her.

They passed through a long saloon, bare as the ante-chamber, but loftily vaulted, and frescoed with a seventeenth-century Triumph of Scipio or Alexander—martial figures following Wyant with the filmed melancholy gaze of shades in limbo. At the end of this apartment he was admitted to a smaller room, with the same atmosphere of mortal cold, but showing more obvious signs of occupancy. The walls were covered with tapestry which had faded to the gray-brown tints of decaying vegetation, so that the young man felt as though he were entering a sunless autumn wood. Against these hangings stood a few tall cabinets on heavy gilt feet, and at a table in the window three persons were seated: an elderly lady who was warming her hands over a brazier, a girl bent above a strip of needle-work, and an old man.

As the latter advanced toward Wyant, the young man was conscious of staring with unseemly intentness at his small round-backed figure, dressed with shabby disorder and surmounted by a wonderful head, lean, vulpine, eagle-beaked as that of some art-loving despot of the Renaissance: a head combining the venerable hair and large prominent eyes of the humanist with the greedy profile of the adventurer. Wyant, in musing on the Italian portrait-medals of the fifteenth century, had often fancied that only in that period of fierce individualism could types so paradoxical have been produced; yet the subtle craftsmen who committed them to the bronze had never drawn a face more strangely stamped with contradictory passions than that of Doctor Lombard.

"I am glad to see you," he said to Wyant, extending a hand which seemed a mere framework held together by knotted veins. "We lead a quiet life here and receive few visitors, but any friend of Professor Clyde's is welcome." Then, with a gesture which included the two women, he added dryly: "My wife and daughter often talk of Professor Clyde."

"Oh yes—he used to make me such nice toast; they don't understand toast in Italy," said Mrs. Lombard in a high plaintive voice.

It would have been difficult, from Doctor Lombard's manner and appearance, to guess his nationality; but his wife was so inconsciently and ineradicably English that even the silhouette of her cap seemed a protest against Continental laxities. She was a stout fair woman, with pale cheeks netted with red lines. A brooch with a miniature portrait sustained a bogwood watch-chain upon her bosom, and at her elbow lay a heap of knitting and an old copy of *The Queen*.

The young girl, who had remained standing, was a slim replica of her mother, with an apple-cheeked face and opaque blue eyes. Her small head was prodigally laden with braids of dull fair hair, and she might have had a kind of transient prettiness but for the sullen droop of her round mouth. It was hard to say whether her expression implied ill-temper or apathy; but Wyant was struck by the contrast between the fierce vitality of the doctor's age and the inanimateness of his daughter's youth.

Seating himself in the chair which his host advanced, the young man tried to open the conversation by addressing to Mrs. Lombard some random remark on the beauties of Siena. The lady murmured a resigned assent, and Doctor Lombard interposed with a smile: "My dear sir, my wife considers Siena a most salubrious spot, and is favorably impressed by the cheapness of the marketing; but she deplores the total absence of muffins and cannel coal, and cannot resign herself to the Italian method of dusting furniture."

"But they don't, you know—they don't dust it!" Mrs. Lombard protested, without showing any resentment of her husband's manner.

"Precisely—they don't dust it. Since we have lived in Siena we have not once seen the cobwebs removed from the battlements of the Mangia. Can you conceive of such housekeeping? My wife has never yet dared to write it home to her aunts at Bonchurch."

Mrs. Lombard accepted in silence this remarkable statement of her views, and her husband, with a malicious smile at Wyant's embarrassment, planted himself suddenly before the young man.

"And now," said he, "do you want to see my Leonardo?"

"Do I?" cried Wyant, on his feet in a flash.

The doctor chuckled. "Ah," he said, with a kind of crooning deliberation, "that's the way they all behave—that's what they all come for." He turned to his daughter with another variation of mockery in his smile. "Don't fancy it's for your *beaux yeux*, my dear; or for the mature charms of Mrs. Lombard," he added, glaring suddenly at his wife, who had taken up her knitting and was softly murmuring over the number of her stitches.

Neither lady appeared to notice his pleasantries, and he continued, addressing himself to Wyant: "They all come—they all come; but many are called and few are chosen." His voice sank to solemnity. "While I live," he said, "no unworthy eye shall desecrate that picture. But I will not do my friend Clyde the injustice to suppose that he would send an unworthy representative. He tells me he wishes a description of the picture for his book; and you shall describe it to him—if you can."

Wyant hesitated, not knowing whether it was a propitious moment to put in his appeal for a photograph.

"Well, sir," he said, "you know Clyde wants me to take away all I can of it."

Doctor Lombard eyed him sardonically. "You're welcome to take away all you can carry," he replied; adding, as he turned to his daughter: "That is, if he has your permission, Sybilla."

The girl rose without a word, and laying aside her work, took a key from a secret drawer in one of the cabinets, while the doctor continued in the same note of grim jocularity: "For you must know that the picture is not mine—it is my daughter's."

He followed with evident amusement the surprised glance which Wyant turned on the young girl's impassive figure.

"Sybilla," he pursued, "is a votary of the arts; she has inherited her fond father's passion for the unattainable. Luckily, however, she also recently inherited a tidy legacy from her grandmother; and having seen the Leonardo, on which its discoverer had placed a price far beyond my reach, she took a step which deserves to go down to history: she invested her whole inheritance in the purchase of the picture, thus enabling me to spend my closing years in communion with one of the world's masterpieces. My dear sir, could Antigone do more?"

The object of this strange eulogy had meanwhile drawn aside one of the tapestry hangings, and fitted her key into a concealed door.

"Come," said Doctor Lombard, "let us go before the light fails us."

Wyant glanced at Mrs. Lombard, who continued to knit impassively.

"No, no," said his host, "my wife will not come with us. You might not suspect it from her conversation, but my wife has no feeling for art —Italian art, that is; for no one is fonder of our early Victorian school."

"Frith's *Railway Station*, you know," said Mrs. Lombard, smiling. "I like an animated picture."

Miss Lombard, who had unlocked the door, held back the tapestry to let her father and Wyant pass out; then she followed them down a narrow stone passage with another door at its end. This door was iron-barred, and Wyant noticed that it had a complicated patent lock. The girl fitted another key into the lock, and Doctor Lombard led the way into a small room. The dark paneling of this apartment was irradiated by streams of yellow light slanting through the disbanded thunder clouds and in the central brightness hung a picture concealed by a curtain of faded velvet.

"A little too bright, Sybilla," said Doctor Lombard. His face had grown solemn, and his mouth twitched nervously as his daughter drew a linen drapery across the upper part of the window.

"That will do—that will do." He turned impressively to Wyant. "Do you see the pomegranate bud in this rug? Place yourself there—keep your left foot on it, please. And now, Sybilla, draw the cord."

Miss Lombard advanced and placed her hand on a cord hidden behind the velvet curtain.

"Ah," said the doctor, "one moment: I should like you, while looking at the picture, to have in mind a few lines of verse. Sybilla—"

Without the slightest change of countenance, and with a promptness which proved her to be prepared for the request, Miss Lombard began to recite, in a full round voice like her mother's, St. Bernard's invocation to the Virgin, in the thirty-third canto of the *Paradise*.

"Thank you, my dear," said her father, drawing a deep breath as she ended. "That unapproachable combination of vowel sounds prepares one better than anything I know for the contemplation of the picture."

As he spoke the folds of velvet slowly parted, and the Leonardo appeared in its frame of tarnished gold.

From the nature of Miss Lombard's recitation Wyant had expected a sacred subject, and his surprise was therefore great as the composition was gradually revealed by the widening division of the curtain.

In the background a steel-colored river wound through a pale calcareous landscape; while to the left, on a lonely peak, a crucified Christ hung livid against indigo clouds. The central figure of the foreground, however, was that of a woman seated in an antique chair of marble with bas-reliefs of dancing maenads. Her feet rested on a meadow sprinkled with minute wild-flowers, and her attitude of smiling majesty recalled that of Dosso Dossi's Circe. She wore a red robe, flowing in closely fluted lines from under a fancifully embroidered cloak. Above her high forehead the crinkled golden hair flowed sideways beneath a veil; one hand drooped on the arm of her chair; the other held up an inverted human skull, into which a young Dionysus, smooth, brown and sidelong as the

St. John of the Louvre, poured a stream of wine from a high-poised flagon. At the lady's feet lay the symbols of art and luxury: a flute and a roll of music, a platter heaped with grapes and roses, the torso of a Greek statuette, and a bowl overflowing with coins and jewels; behind her, on the chalky hilltop, hung the crucified Christ. A scroll in a corner of the foreground bore the legend: *Lux Mundi.*

Wyant, emerging from the first plunge of wonder, turned inquiringly toward his companions. Neither had moved. Miss Lombard stood with her hand on the cord, her lids lowered, her mouth drooping; the doctor, his strange Thoth-like profile turned toward his guest, was still lost in rapt contemplation of his treasure.

Wyant addressed the young girl.

"You are fortunate," he said, "to be the possessor of anything so perfect."

"It is considered very beautiful," she said coldly.

"Beautiful—*beautiful!*" the doctor burst out. "Ah, the poor, worn out, overworked word! There are no adjectives in the language fresh enough to describe such pristine brilliancy: all their brightness has been worn off by misuse. Think of the things that have been called beautiful, and then look at *that!*"

"It is worthy of a new vocabulary," Wyant agreed.

"Yes," Doctor Lombard continued, "my daughter is indeed fortunate. She has chosen what Catholics call the higher life—the counsel of perfection. What other private person enjoys the same opportunity of understanding the master? Who else lives under the same roof with an untouched masterpiece of Leonardo's? Think of the happiness of being always under the influence of such a creation; of living *into* it; of partaking of it in daily and hourly communion! The room is a chapel; the sight of that picture is a sacrament. What an atmosphere for a young life to unfold itself in! My daughter is singularly blessed. Sybilla, point out some of the details to Mr. Wyant: I see that he will appreciate them."

The girl turned her dense blue eyes toward Wyant; then, glancing away from him, she pointed to the canvas.

"Notice the modeling of the left hand," she began in a monotonous voice; "it recalls the hand of the Mona Lisa. The hand of the naked genius will remind you of that of the St. John of the Louvre, but it is more purely pagan and is turned a little less to the right. The embroidery on the cloak is symbolic: you will see that the roots of this plant have burst through the vase. This recalls the famous definition of Hamlet's character in *Wilhelm Meister*. Here are the mystic rose, the flame, and the serpent, emblem of eternity. Some of the other symbols we have not yet been able to decipher."

Wyant watched her curiously: she seemed to be reciting a lesson.

"And the picture itself?" he said. "How do you explain that? *Lux Mundi*—what a curious device to connect with such a subject! What can it mean?"

Miss Lombard dropped her eyes: the answer was evidently not included in her lesson.

"What, indeed?" the doctor interposed. "What does life mean? As one may define it in a hundred different ways, so one may find a hundred different meanings in this picture. Its symbolism is as many-faceted as a well-cut diamond. Who, for instance, is that divine lady? Is it she who is the true *Lux Mundi*—the light reflected from jewels and young eyes, from polished marble and clear waters and statues of bronze? Or is that the Light of the World, extinguished on yonder stormy hill, and is this lady the Pride of Life, feasting blindly on the wine of iniquity, with her back turned to the light which has shone for her in vain? Something of both these meanings may be traced in the picture; but to me it symbolizes rather the central truth of existence: that all that is raised in incorruption is sown in corruption; art, beauty, love, religion; that all our wine is drunk out of skulls, and poured for us by the mysterious genius of a remote and cruel past."

The doctor's face blazed: his bent figure seemed to straighten itself and become taller.

"Ah," he cried, growing more dithyrambic, "how lightly you ask what it means! How confidently you expect an answer! Yet here am I who have given my life to the study of the Renaissance; who have violated its tomb, laid open its dead body, and traced the course of every muscle, bone and artery; who have sucked its very soul from the pages of poets and humanists; who have wept and believed with Joachim of Flora, smiled and doubted with Aeneas Sylvius Piccolomini; who have patiently followed to its source the least inspiration of the masters, and groped in neolithic caverns and Babylonian ruins for the first unfolding tendrils of the arabesques of Mantegna and Crivelli; and I tell you that I stand abashed and ignorant before the mystery of this picture. It means nothing—it means all things. It may represent the period which saw its creation; it may represent all ages past and to come. There are volumes of meaning in the tiniest emblem on the lady's cloak; the blossoms of its border are rooted in the deepest soil of myth and tradition. Don't ask what it means, young man, but bow your head in thankfulness for having seen it!"

Miss Lombard laid her hand on his arm.

"Don't excite yourself, father," she said in the detached tone of a professional nurse.

He answered with a despairing gesture. "Ah, it's easy for you to talk. You have years and years to spend with it; I am an old man, and every moment counts!"

"It's bad for you," she repeated with gentle obstinacy.

The doctor's sacred fury had in fact burnt itself out. He dropped into a seat with dull eyes and slackening lips, and his daughter drew the curtain across the picture.

Wyant turned away reluctantly. He felt that his opportunity was slipping from him, yet he dared not refer to Clyde's wish for a photograph. He now understood the meaning of the laugh with which Doctor Lombard had given him leave to carry away all the details he could remember. The picture was so dazzling, so unexpected, so crossed with elusive and contradictory suggestions, that the most alert observer, when placed suddenly before it, must lose his coördinating faculty in a sense of confused wonder. Yet how valuable to Clyde the record of such a work would be! In some ways it seemed to be the summing up of the master's thought, the key to his enigmatic philosophy.

The doctor had risen and was walking slowly toward the door. His daughter unlocked it, and Wyant followed them back in silence to the room in which they had left Mrs. Lombard. That lady was no longer there, and he could think of no excuse for lingering.

He thanked the doctor, and turned to Miss Lombard, who stood in the middle of the room as though awaiting further orders.

"It is very good of you," he said, "to allow one even a glimpse of such a treasure."

She looked at him with her odd directness. "You will come again?" she said quickly; and turning to her father she added: "You know what Professor Clyde asked. This gentleman cannot give him any account of the picture without seeing it again."

Doctor Lombard glanced at her vaguely; he was still like a person in a trance.

"Eh?" he said, rousing himself with an effort.

"I said, father, that Mr. Wyant must see the picture again if he is to tell Professor Clyde about it," Miss Lombard repeated with extraordinary precision of tone.

Wyant was silent. He had the puzzled sense that his wishes were being divined and gratified for reasons with which he was in no way connected.

"Well, well," the doctor muttered, "I don't say no—I don't say no. I know what Clyde wants—I don't refuse to help him." He turned to Wyant. "You may come again—you may make notes," he added with a sudden effort. "Jot down what occurs to you. I'm willing to concede that."

Wyant again caught the girl's eye, but its emphatic message perplexed him.

"You're very good," he said tentatively, "but the fact is the picture is so mysterious—so full of complicated detail—that I'm afraid no notes I could make would serve Clyde's purpose as well as—as a photograph, say. If you would allow me—"

Miss Lombard's brow darkened, and her father raised his head furiously.

"A photograph? A photograph, did you say? Good God, man, not ten people have been allowed to set foot in that room! A *photograph?*"

Wyant saw his mistake, but saw also that he had gone too far to retreat.

"I know, sir, from what Clyde has told me, that you object to having any reproduction of the picture published; but he hoped you might let me take a photograph for his personal use—not to be reproduced in his book, but simply to give him something to work by. I should take the photograph myself, and the negative would of course be yours. If you wished it, only one impression would be struck off, and that one Clyde could return to you when he had done with it."

Doctor Lombard interrupted him with a snarl. "When he had done with it? Just so: I thank thee for that word! When it had been rephotographed, drawn, traced, autotyped, passed about from hand to hand, defiled by every ignorant eye in England, vulgarized by the blundering praise of every art-scribbler in Europe! Pah! I'd as soon give you the picture itself: why don't you ask for that?"

"Well, sir," said Wyant calmly, "if you will trust me with it, I'll engage to take it safely to England and back, and to let no eye but Clyde's see it while it is out of your keeping."

The doctor received this remarkable proposal in silence; then he burst into a laugh.

"Upon my soul!" he said with sardonic good humor.

It was Miss Lombard's turn to look perplexedly at Wyant. His last words and her father's unexpected reply had evidently carried her beyond her depth.

"Well, sir, am I to take the picture?" Wyant smilingly pursued.

"No, young man; nor a photograph of it. Nor a sketch, either; mind that,—nothing that can be reproduced. Sybilla," he cried with sudden passion, "swear to me that the picture shall never be reproduced! No photograph, no sketch—now or afterward. Do you hear me?"

"Yes, father," said the girl quietly.

"The vandals," he muttered, "the desecrators of beauty; if I thought it would ever get into their hands I'd burn it first, by God!" He turned to Wyant, speaking more quietly. "I said you might come back—I never retract what I say. But you must give me your word that no one but Clyde shall see the notes you make."

Wyant was growing warm.

"If you won't trust me with a photograph I wonder you trust me not to show my notes!" he exclaimed.

The doctor looked at him with a malicious smile.

"Humph!" he said; "would they be of much use to anybody?"

Wyant saw that he was losing ground and controlled his impatience.

"To Clyde, I hope, at any rate," he answered, holding out his hand.

The doctor shook it without a trace of resentment, and Wyant added: "When shall I come, sir?"

"To-morrow—to-morrow morning," cried Miss Lombard, speaking suddenly.

She looked fixedly at her father, and he shrugged his shoulders.

"The picture is hers," he said to Wyant.

In the ante-chamber the young man was met by the woman who had admitted him. She handed him his hat and stick, and turned to unbar the door. As the bolt slipped back he felt a touch on his arm.

"You have a letter?" she said in a low tone.

"A letter?" He stared. "What letter?"

She shrugged her shoulders, and drew back to let him pass.

## II

As WYANT emerged from the house he paused once more to glance up at its scarred brick façade. The marble hand drooped tragically above the entrance: in the waning light it seemed to have relaxed into the passiveness of despair, and Wyant stood musing on its hidden meaning. But the Dead Hand was not the only mysterious thing about Doctor Lombard's house. What were the relations between Miss Lombard and her father? Above all, between Miss Lombard and her picture? She did not look like a person capable of a disinterested passion for the arts; and there had been moments when it struck Wyant that she hated the picture.

The sky at the end of the street was flooded with turbulent yellow light, and the young man turned his steps toward the church of San Domenico, in the hope of catching the lingering brightness of Sodoma's St. Catherine.

The great bare aisles were almost dark when he entered, and he had to grope his way to the chapel steps. Under the momentary evocation of the sunset, the saint's figure emerged pale and swooning from the dusk, and the warm light gave a sensual tinge to her ecstasy. The flesh seemed to glow and heave, the eyelids to tremble; Wyant stood fascinated by the accidental collaboration of light and color.

Suddenly he noticed that something white had fluttered to the ground at his feet. He stooped and picked up a small thin sheet of notepaper, folded and sealed like an old-fashioned letter, and bearing the superscription:—

*To the Count Ottaviano Celsi.*

Wyant stared at this mysterious document. Where had it come from? He was distinctly conscious of having seen it fall through the air, close to his feet. He glanced up at the dark ceiling of the chapel; then he turned and looked about the church. There was only one figure in it, that of a man who knelt near the high altar.

Suddenly Wyant recalled the question of Doctor Lombard's maid-servant. Was this the letter she had asked for? Had he been unconsciously carrying it about with him all the afternoon? Who was Count Ottaviano Celsi, and how came Wyant to have been chosen to act as the nobleman's ambulant letter-box?

Wyant laid his hat and stick on the chapel steps and began to explore his pockets, in the irrational hope of finding there some clue to the mystery; but they held nothing which he had not himself put there, and he was reduced to wondering how the letter, supposing some unknown hand to have bestowed it on him, had happened to fall out while he stood motionless before the picture.

At this point he was disturbed by a step on the floor of the aisle, and turning, he saw his lustrous-eyed neighbor of the table d'hôte.

The young man bowed and waved an apologetic hand.

"I do not intrude?" he inquired suavely.

Without waiting for a reply, he mounted the steps of the chapel, glancing about him with the affable air of an afternoon caller.

"I see," he remarked with a smile, "that you know the hour at which our saint should be visited."

Wyant agreed that the hour was indeed felicitous.

The stranger stood beamingly before the picture.

"What grace! What poetry!" he murmured, apostrophizing the St. Catherine, but letting his glance slip rapidly about the chapel as he spoke.

Wyant, detecting the maneuver, murmured a brief assent.

"But it is cold here—mortally cold; you do not find it so?" The intruder put on his hat. "It is permitted at this hour—when the church is

empty. And you, my dear sir—do you not feel the dampness? You are
an artist, are you not? And to artists it is permitted to cover the head
when they are engaged in the study of the paintings."

He darted suddenly toward the steps and bent over Wyant's hat.

"Permit me—cover yourself!" he said a moment later, holding out the
hat with an ingratiating gesture.

A light flashed on Wyant.

"Perhaps," he said, looking straight at the young man, "you will
tell me your name. My own is Wyant."

The stranger, surprised, but not disconcerted, drew forth a coroneted
card, which he offered with a low bow. On the card was engraved:—
*Il Conte Ottaviano Celsi.*

"I am much obliged to you," said Wyant; "and I may as well tell you
that the letter which you apparently expected to find in the lining of
my hat is not there, but in my pocket."

He drew it out and handed it to its owner, who had grown very pale.

"And now," Wyant continued, "you will perhaps be good enough to
tell me what all this means."

There was no mistaking the effect produced on Count Ottaviano
by this request. His lips moved, but he achieved only an ineffectual
smile.

"I suppose you know," Wyant went on, his anger rising at the sight
of the other's discomfiture, "that you have taken an unwarrantable
liberty. I don't yet understand what part I have been made to play, but
it's evident that you have made use of me to serve some purpose of
your own, and I propose to know the reason why."

Count Ottaviano advanced with an imploring gesture.

"Sir," he pleaded, "you permit me to speak?"

"I expect you to," cried Wyant. "But not here," he added, hearing
the clank of the verger's keys. "It is growing dark, and we shall be turned
out in a few minutes."

He walked across the church, and Count Ottaviano followed him
out into the deserted square.

"Now," said Wyant, pausing on the steps.

The Count, who had regained some measure of self-possession, began
to speak in a high key, with an accompaniment of conciliatory gesture.

"My dear sir—my dear Mr. Wyant—you find me in an abominable position—that, as a man of honor, I immediately confess. I have taken advantage of you—yes! I have counted on your amiability, your chivalry —too far, perhaps? I confess it! But what could I do? It was to oblige a lady"—he laid a hand on his heart—"a lady whom I would die to serve!" He went on with increasing volubility, his deliberate English swept away by a torrent of Italian, through which Wyant, with some difficulty, struggled to a comprehension of the case.

Coung Ottaviano, according to his own statement, had come to Siena some months previously, on business connected with his mother's property; the paternal estate being near Orvieto, of which ancient city his father was syndic. Soon after his arrival in Siena the young Count had met the incomparable daughter of Doctor Lombard, and falling deeply in love with her, had prevailed on his parents to ask her hand in marriage. Doctor Lombard had not opposed his suit, but when the question of settlements arose it became known that Miss Lombard, who was possessed of a small property in her own right, had a short time before invested the whole amount in the purchase of the Bergamo Leonardo. Thereupon Count Ottaviano's parents had politely suggested that she should sell the picture and thus recover her independence; and this proposal being met by a curt refusal from Doctor Lombard, they had withdrawn their consent to their son's marriage. The young lady's attitude had hitherto been one of passive submission; she was horribly afraid of her father, and would never venture openly to oppose him, but she had made known to Ottaviano her intention of not giving him up, of waiting patiently till events should take a more favorable turn. She seemed hardly aware, the Count said with a sigh, that the means of escape lay in her own hands; that she was of age, and had a right to sell the picture, and to marry without asking her father's consent. Meanwhile her suitor spared no pains to keep himself before her, to remind her that he, too, was waiting and would never give her up.

Doctor Lombard, who suspected the young man of trying to persuade Sybilla to sell the picture, had forbidden the lovers to meet or to correspond; they were thus driven to clandestine communication, and had several times, the Count ingenuously avowed, made use of the doctor's visitors as a means of exchanging letters.

"And you told the visitors to ring twice?" Wyant interposed.

The young man extended his hands in a deprecating gesture. Could Mr. Wyant blame him? He was young, he was ardent, he was enamored! The young lady had done him the supreme honor of avowing her attachment, of pledging her unalterable fidelity; should he suffer his devotion to be outdone? But his purpose in writing to her, he admitted, was not merely to reiterate his fidelity; he was trying by every means in his power to induce her to sell the picture. He had organized a plan of action; every detail was complete; if she would but have the courage to carry out his instructions he would answer for the result. His idea was that she should secretly retire to a convent of which his aunt was the Mother Superior, and from that stronghold should transact the sale of the Leonardo. He had a purchaser ready, who was willing to pay a large sum; a sum, Count Ottaviano whispered, considerably in excess of the young lady's original inheritance; once the picture sold, it could, if necessary, be removed by force from Doctor Lombard's house, and his daughter, being safely in the convent, would be spared the painful scenes incidental to the removal. Finally, if Doctor Lombard were vindictive enough to refuse his consent to her marriage, she had only to make a *sommation respectueuse,* and at the end of the prescribed delay no power on earth could prevent her becoming the wife of Count Ottaviano.

Wyant's anger had fallen at the recital of this simple romance. It was absurd to be angry with a young man who confided his secrets to the first stranger he met in the streets, and placed his hand on his heart whenever he mentioned the name of his betrothed. The easiest way out of the business was to take it as a joke. Wyant had played the wall to this new Pyramus and Thisbe, and was philosophic enough to laugh at the part he had unwittingly performed.

He held out his hand with a smile to Count Ottaviano.

"I won't deprive you any longer," he said, "of the pleasure of reading your letter."

"Oh, sir, a thousand thanks! And when you return to the casa Lombard, you will take a message from me—the letter she expected this afternoon?"

"The letter she expected?" Wyant paused. "No, thank you. I thought you understood that where I come from we don't do that kind of thing—knowingly."

"But, sir, to serve a young lady!"

"I'm sorry for the young lady, if what you tell me is true"—the Count's expressive hands resented the doubt—"but remember that if I am under obligations to any one in this matter, it is to her father, who has admitted me to his house and has allowed me to see his picture."

"*His* picture? Hers!"

"Well, the house is his, at all events."

"Unhappily—since to her it is a dungeon!"

"Why doesn't she leave it, then?" exclaimed Wyant impatiently.

The Count clasped his hands. "Ah, how you say that—with what force, with what virility! If you would but say it to *her* in that tone—you, her countryman! She has no one to advise her; the mother is an idiot; the father is terrible; she is in his power; it is my belief that he would kill her if she resisted him. Mr. Wyant, I tremble for her life while she remains in that house!"

"Oh, come," said Wyant lightly, "they seem to understand each other well enough. But in any case, you must see that I can't interfere—at least you would if you were an Englishman," he added with an escape of contempt.

III

WYANT'S AFFILIATIONS in Siena being restricted to an acquaintance with his landlady, he was forced to apply to her for the verification of Count Ottaviano's story.

The young nobleman had, it appeared, given a perfectly correct account of his situation. His father, Count Celsi-Mongirone, was a man of distinguished family and some wealth. He was syndic of Orvieto, and lived either in that town or on his neighboring estate of Mongirone. His wife owned a large property near Siena, and Count Ottaviano, who was the second son, came there from time to time to look into its management. The eldest son was in the army, the youngest in the Church; and an aunt of Count Ottaviano's was Mother Superior of the Visitandine convent in Siena. At one time it had been said that Count Ottaviano, who was a most amiable and accomplished young man, was to marry the daughter of the strange Englishman, Doctor Lombard, but difficulties having arisen as to the adjustment of the young lady's dower, Count Celsi-Mongirone had very properly broken off the match. It was sad for the young man, however, who was said to be deeply in love, and to find frequent excuses for coming to Siena to inspect his mother's estate.

Viewed in the light of Count Ottaviano's personality the story had a tinge of opera bouffe; but the next morning, as Wyant mounted the stairs of the House of the Dead Hand, the situation insensibly assumed another aspect. It was impossible to take Doctor Lombard lightly; and there was a suggestion of fatality in the appearance of his gaunt dwelling. Who could tell amid what tragic records of domestic tyranny and fluttering broken purposes the little drama of Miss Lombard's fate was being played out? Might not the accumulated influences of such a house modify the lives within it in a manner unguessed by the inmates of a suburban villa with sanitary plumbing and a telephone?

One person, at least, remained unperturbed by such fanciful problems; and that was Mrs. Lombard, who, at Wyant's entrance, raised a placidly wrinkled brow from her knitting. The morning was mild, and her chair had been wheeled into a bar of sunshine near the window, so that she made a cheerful spot of prose in the poetic gloom of her surroundings.

"What a nice morning!" she said; "it must be delightful weather at Bonchurch."

Her dull blue glance wandered across the narrow street with its threatening house fronts, and fluttered back baffled, like a bird with clipped wings. It was evident, poor lady, that she had never seen beyond the opposite houses.

Wyant was not sorry to find her alone. Seeing that she was surprised at his reappearance he said at once: "I have come back to study Miss Lombard's picture."

"Oh, the picture—" Mrs. Lombard's face expressed a gentle disappointment, which might have been boredom in a person of acuter sensibilities. "It's an original Leonardo, you know," she said mechanically.

"And Miss Lombard is very proud of it, I suppose? She seems to have inherited her father's love for art."

Mrs. Lombard counted her stitches, and he went on: "It's unusual in so young a girl. Such tastes generally develop later."

Mrs. Lombard looked up eagerly. "That's what I say! I was quite different at her age, you know. I liked dancing, and doing a pretty bit of fancy-work. Not that I couldn't sketch, too; I had a master down from London. My aunts have some of my crayons hung up in their drawing-room now—I did a view of Kenilworth which was thought pleasing. But I liked a picnic, too, or a pretty walk through the woods with young people of my own age. I say it's more natural, Mr. Wyant; one may have a feeling for art, and do crayons that are worth framing, and yet not give up everything else. I was taught that there were other things."

Wyant, half-ashamed of provoking these innocent confidences, could not resist another question. "And Miss Lombard cares for nothing else?"

Her mother looked troubled.

"Sybilla is so clever—she says I don't understand. You know how self-confident young people are! My husband never said that of me, now—he knows I had an excellent education. My aunts were very particular; I was brought up to have opinions, and my husband has always respected them. He says himself that he wouldn't for the world miss hearing my opinion on any subject; you may have noticed that he often refers to my tastes. He has always respected my preference for living in England; he likes to hear me give my reasons for it. He is so much interested in my ideas that he often says he knows just what I am going to say before I speak. But Sybilla does not care for what I think—"

At this point Doctor Lombard entered. He glanced sharply at Wyant. "The servant is a fool; she didn't tell me you were here." His eye turned to his wife. "Well, my dear, what have you been telling Mr. Wyant? About the aunts at Bonchurch, I'll be bound!"

Mrs. Lombard looked triumphantly at Wyant, and her husband rubbed his hooked fingers, with a smile.

"Mrs. Lombard's aunts are very superior women. They subscribe to the circulating library, and borrow *Good Words* and the *Monthly Packet* from the curate's wife across the way. They have the rector to tea twice a year, and keep a page boy, and are visited by two baronets' wives. They devoted themselves to the education of their orphan niece, and I think I may say without boasting that Mrs. Lombard's conversation shows marked traces of the advantages she enjoyed."

Mrs. Lombard colored with pleasure.

"I was telling Mr. Wyant that my aunts were very particular."

"Quite so, my dear; and did you mention that they never sleep in anything but linen, and that Miss Sophia puts away the furs and blankets every spring with her own hands? Both those facts are interesting to the student of human nature." Doctor Lombard glanced at his watch. "But we are missing an incomparable moment; the light is perfect at this hour."

Wyant rose, and the doctor led him through the tapestried door and down the passageway.

The light was, in fact, perfect, and the picture shone with an inner radiancy, as though a lamp burned behind the soft screen of the lady's flesh. Every detail of the foreground detached itself with jewel-like precision. Wyant noticed a dozen accessories which had escaped him on the previous day.

He drew out his note-book, and the doctor, who had dropped his sardonic grin for a look of devout contemplation, pushed a chair forward, and seated himself on a carved settle against the wall.

"Now, then," he said, "tell Clyde what you can; but the letter killeth."

He sank down, his hands hanging on the arm of the settle like the claws of a dead bird, his eyes fixed on Wyant's note-book with the obvious intention of detecting any attempt at a surreptitious sketch.

Wyant, nettled at this surveillance, and disturbed by the speculations which Doctor Lombard's strange household excited, sat motionless for a few minutes, staring first at the picture and then at the blank pages of the note-book. The thought that Doctor Lombard was enjoying his discomfiture at length roused him, and he began to write.

He was interrupted by a knock on the iron door. Doctor Lombard rose to unlock it, and his daughter entered.

She bowed hurriedly to Wyant, without looking at him.

"Father, had you forgotten that the man from Monte Amiato was to come back this morning with an answer about the bas-relief? He is here now; he says he can't wait."

"The devil!" cried her father impatiently. "Didn't you tell him—"

"Yes; but he says he can't come back. If you want to see him you must come now."

"Then you think there's a chance?—"

She nodded.

He turned and looked at Wyant, who was writing assiduously.

"You will stay here, Sybilla; I shall be back in a moment."

He hurried out, locking the door behind him.

Wyant had looked up, wondering if Miss Lombard would show any surprise at being locked in with him; but it was his turn to be surprised, for hardly had they heard the key withdrawn when she moved close to him, her small face pale and tumultuous.

"I arranged it—I must speak to you," she gasped. "He'll be back in five minutes."

Her courage seemed to fail, and she looked at him helplessly.

Wyant had a sense of stepping among explosives. He glanced about him at the dusky vaulted room, at the haunting smile of the strange picture overhead, and at the pink-and-white girl whispering of conspiracies in a voice meant to exchange platitudes with a curate.

"How can I help you?" he said with a rush of compassion.

"Oh, if you would! I never have a chance to speak to any one; it's so difficult—he watches me—he'll be back immediately."

"Try to tell me what I can do."

"I don't dare; I feel as if he were behind me." She turned away, fixing her eyes on the picture. A sound startled her. "There he comes, and I haven't spoken! It was my only chance; but it bewilders me so to be hurried."

"I don't hear any one," said Wyant, listening. "Try to tell me."

"How can I make you understand? It would take so long to explain." She drew a deep breath, and then with a plunge—"Will you come here again this afternoon—at about five?" she whispered.

"Come here again?"

"Yes—you can ask to see the picture,—make some excuse. He will come with you, of course; I will open the door for you—and—and lock you both in"—she gasped.

"Lock us in?"

"You see? You understand? It's the only way for me to leave the house—if I am ever to do it"—She drew another difficult breath.

"The key will be returned—by a safe person—in half an hour—perhaps sooner—"

She trembled so much that she was obliged to lean against the settle for support.

Wyant looked at her steadily; he was very sorry for her.

"I can't, Miss Lombard," he said at length.

"You can't?"

"I'm sorry; I must seem cruel; but consider—"

He was stopped by the futility of the word: as well ask a hunted rabbit to pause in its dash for a hole!

Wyant took her hand; it was cold and nerveless.

"I will serve you in any way I can; but you must see that this way is impossible. Can't I talk to you again? Perhaps—"

"Oh," she cried, starting up, "there he comes!"

Doctor Lombard's step sounded in the passage.

Wyant held her fast. "Tell me one thing: he won't let you sell the picture?"

"No—hush!"

"Make no pledges for the future, then; promise me that."

"The future?"

"In case he should die: your father is an old man. You haven't promised?"

She shook her head.

"Don't, then; remember that."

She made no answer, and the key turned in the lock.

As he passed out of the house, its scowling cornice and façade of ravaged brick looked down on him with the startlingness of a strange face, seen momentarily in a crowd, and impressing itself on the brain as part of an inevitable future. Above the doorway, the marble hand reached out like the cry of an imprisoned anguish.

Wyant turned away impatiently.

"Rubbish!" he said to himself. "*She* isn't walled in; she can get out if she wants to."

## IV

WYANT HAD any number of plans for coming to Miss Lombard's aid: he was elaborating the twentieth when, on the same afternoon, he stepped into the express train for Florence. By the time the train reached Certaldo he was convinced that, in thus hastening his departure, he had followed the only reasonable course; at Empoli, he began to reflect that the priest and the Levite had probably justified themselves in much the same manner.

A month later, after his return to England, he was unexpectedly relieved from these alternatives of extenuation and approval. A paragraph in the morning paper announced the sudden death of Doctor Lombard, the distinguished English dilettante who had long resided in Siena. Wyant's justification was complete. Our blindest impulses become evidence of perspicacity when they fall in with the course of events.

Wyant could now comfortably speculate on the particular complications from which his foresight had probably saved him. The climax was unexpectedly dramatic. Miss Lombard, on the brink of a step which, whatever its issue, would have burdened her with retrospective compunction, had been set free before her suitor's ardor could have had time to cool, and was now doubtless planning a life of domestic felicity on the proceeds of the Leonardo. One thing, however, struck Wyant as odd—he saw no mention of the sale of the picture. He had scanned the papers for an immediate announcement of its transfer to one of the great museums; but presently concluding that Miss Lombard, out of filial piety, had wished to avoid an appearance of unseemly haste in the disposal of her treasure, he dismissed the matter from his mind. Other affairs happened to engage him; the months slipped by, and gradually the lady and the picture dwelt less vividly in his mind.

It was not till five or six years later, when chance took him again to Siena, that the recollection started from some inner fold of memory. He found himself, as it happened, at the head of Doctor Lombard's street, and glancing down that grim thoroughfare, caught an oblique glimpse of the doctor's house front, with the Dead Hand projecting above its threshold.

The sight revived his interest, and that evening, over an admirable *frittata*, he questioned his landlady about Miss Lombard's marriage.

"The daughter of the English doctor? But she has never married, signore."

"Never married? What, then, became of Count Ottaviano?"

"For a long time he waited; but last year he married a noble lady of the Maremma."

"But what happened—why was the marriage broken?"

"The landlady enacted a pantomime of baffled interrogation.

"And Miss Lombard still lives in her father's house?"

"Yes, signore; she is still there."

"And the Leonardo—"

"The Leonardo, also, is still there."

The next day, as Wyant entered the House of the Dead Hand, he remembered Count Ottaviano's injunction to ring twice, and smiled mournfully to think that so much subtlety had been vain. But what could have prevented the marriage? If Doctor Lombard's death had been long delayed, time might have acted as a dissolvent, or the young lady's resolve have failed; but it seemed impossible that the white heat of ardor in which Wyant had left the lovers should have cooled in a few short weeks.

As he ascended the vaulted stairway the atmosphere of the place seemed a reply to his conjectures. The same numbing air fell on him, like an emanation from some persistent willpower, a something fierce and imminent which might reduce to impotence every impulse within its range. Wyant could almost fancy a hand on his shoulder, guiding him upward with the ironical intent of confronting him with the evidence of its work.

A strange servant opened the door, and he was presently introduced to the tapestried room, where, from their usual seats in the window, Mrs. Lombard and her daughter advanced to welcome him with faint ejaculations of surprise.

Both had grown oddly old, but in a dry, smooth way, as fruits might shrivel on a shelf instead of ripening on the tree. Mrs. Lombard was still knitting, and pausing now and then to warm her swollen hands above the brazier; and Miss Lombard, in rising, had laid aside a strip of needle-work which might have been the same on which Wyant had first seen her engaged.

Their visitor inquired discreetly how they had fared in the interval, and learned that they had thought of returning to England, but had somehow never done so.

"I am sorry not to see my aunts again," Mrs. Lombard said resignedly; "but Sybilla thinks it best that we should not go this year."

"Next year, perhaps," murmured Miss Lombard, in a voice which seemed to suggest that they had a great waste of time to fill.

She had returned to her seat, and sat bending over her work. Her hair enveloped her head in the same thick braids, but the rose color of her cheeks had turned to blotches of dull red, like some pigment which has darkened in drying.

"And Professor Clyde—is he well?" Mrs. Lombard asked affably; continuing, as her daughter raised a startled eye: "Surely, Sybilla, Mr. Wyant was the gentleman who was sent by Professor Clyde to see the Leonardo?"

Miss Lombard was silent, but Wyant hastened to assure the elder lady of his friend's well-being.

"Ah—perhaps, then, he will come back some day to Siena," she said, sighing. Wyant declared that it was more than likely; and there ensued a pause, which he presently broke by saying to Miss Lombard: "And you still have the picture?"

She raised her eyes and looked at him. "Should you like to see it?" she asked.

On his assenting, she rose, and extracting the same key from the same secret drawer, unlocked the door beneath the tapestry. They walked down the passage in silence, and she stood aside with a grave gesture, making Wyant pass before her into the room. Then she crossed over and drew the curtain back from the picture.

The light of the early afternoon poured full on it: its surface appeared to ripple and heave with a fluid splendor. The colors had lost none of their warmth, the outlines none of their pure precision; it seemed to Wyant like some magical flower which had burst suddenly from the mold of darkness and oblivion.

He turned to Miss Lombard with a movement of comprehension.

"Ah, I understand—you couldn't part with it, after all!" he cried.

"No—I couldn't part with it," she answered.

"It's too beautiful,—too beautiful,"—he assented.

"Too beautiful?" She turned on him with a curious stare. "I have never thought it beautiful, you know."

He gave back the stare. "You have never—"

She shook her head. "It's not that. I hate it; I've always hated it. But he wouldn't let me—he will never let me now."

Wyant was startled by her use of the present tense. Her look surprised him, too: there was a strange fixity of resentment in her innocuous eye. Was it possible that she was laboring under some delusion? Or did the pronoun not refer to her father?

"You mean that Doctor Lombard did not wish you to part with the picture?"

"No—he prevented me; he will always prevent me."

There was another pause. "You promised him, then, before his death—"

"No; I promised nothing. He died too suddenly to make me." Her voice sank to a whisper. "I was free—perfectly free—or I thought I was till I tried."

"Till you tried?"

"To disobey him—to sell the picture. Then I found it was impossible. I tried again and again; but he was always in the room with me."

She glanced over her shoulder as though she had heard a step; and to Wyant, too, for a moment, the room seemed full of a third presence.

"And you can't"—he faltered, unconsciously dropping his voice to the pitch of hers.

She shook her head, gazing at him mystically. "I can't lock him out; I can never lock him out now. I told you I should never have another chance."

Wyant felt the chill of her words like a cold breath in his hair.

"Oh"—he groaned; but she cut him off with a grave gesture.

"It is too late," she said; "but you ought to have helped me that day."

*August 1904*

# PIONEERS OF THE DETECTIVE STORY: WILKIE COLLINS, CHARLES DICKENS, SIR ARTHUR CONAN DOYLE, AND L. T. MEADE & ROBERT EUSTACE

## (THE BIRTH AND DEVELOPMENT OF THE DETECTIVE STORY)

# THE POLICEMAN
# AND THE COOK

## BY WILKIE COLLINS

WILKIE COLLINS, the author of *The Woman in White*, published in 1850, is generally acknowledged to be the innovator of the full-length detective story. *The Woman in White* is one of the most popular books ever written. It was also critically applauded. Thackeray stayed up all night to finish it, Edward Fitzgerald said it was far beyond anything Jane Austen ever wrote, and reread it four times. Prince Albert and Queen Victoria were enchanted by it, and the great Prime Minister Gladstone canceled engagements so that nothing could interrupt the reading of "that great book."

Eighteen years later Collins wrote *The Moonstone*, the first detective police novel in English. The character of Sergeant Cuff in *The Moonstone* is the ancestor of all modern police detectives in contemporary novels.

Wilkie Collins was also a very successful short story writer. He was one of the most important contributors to *Household Words*, a periodical edited by his friend and associate Charles Dickens.

"The Policeman and the Cook" never before anthologized in this country, or elsewhere, is one of the earliest "police procedure" tales in the history of detective fiction. 🐦


WHEN I was a young man of five-and-twenty, I became a member of the London police force. After nearly two years' ordinary experience of the responsible and ill-paid duties of that vocation, I found myself employed on my first serious and terrible case of official inquiry—relating to nothing less than the crime of Murder.

The circumstances were these:

I was then attached to a station in the northern district of London—which I beg permission not to mention more particularly. On a certain Monday in the week, I took my turn of night duty. Up to four in the morning, nothing occurred at the station-house out of the ordinary way. It was then springtime, and, between the gas and the fire, the room became rather hot. I went to the door to get a breath of fresh air—much to the surprise of our Inspector on duty, who was constitutionally a chilly man. There was a fine rain falling; and a nasty damp in the air sent me back to the fireside. I don't suppose I had sat down for more than a minute when the swinging-door was violently pushed open. A frantic woman ran in with a scream, and said: "Is this the station-house?"

Our Inspector (otherwise an excellent officer) had, by some perversity of nature, a hot temper in his chilly constitution. "Why, bless the woman, can't you *see* it is?" he says. "What's the matter now?"

"Murder's the matter!" she burst out. "For God's sake, come back with me. It's at Mrs. Crosscapel's lodging-house, number 14 Lehigh Street. A young woman has murdered her husband in the night! With a knife, sir. She says she thinks she did it in her sleep."

I confess I was startled by this; and the third man on duty (a sergeant) seemed to feel it too. She was a nice-looking young woman, even in her terrified condition, just out of bed, with her clothes huddled on anyhow. I was partial in those days to a tall figure—and she was, as they say, my style. I put a chair for her; and the sergeant poked the fire. As for the Inspector, nothing ever upset *him*. He questioned her as coolly as if it had been a case of petty larceny.

"Have you seen the murdered man?" he asked.

"No, sir."

"Or the wife?"

"No, sir. I didn't dare go into the room; I only heard about it!"

"Oh? And who are you? One of the lodgers?"

"No, sir. I'm the cook."

"Isn't there a master in the house?"

"Yes, sir. He's frightened out of his wits. And the housemaid's gone for the doctor. It all falls on the poor servants, of course. Oh, why did I ever set foot in that horrible house?"

The poor soul burst out crying, and shivered from head to foot. The Inspector made a note of her statement, and then asked her to read it, and sign it with her name. The object of this proceeding was to get her to come near enough to give him the opportunity of smelling her breath. "When people make extraordinary statements," he afterward said to me, "it sometimes saves trouble to satisfy yourself that they are not drunk. I've known them to be mad—but not often. You will generally find *that* in their eyes."

She roused herself and signed her name—"Priscilla Thurlby." The Inspector's own test proved her to be sober; and her eyes—a nice light blue color, mild and pleasant, no doubt, when they were not staring with fear, and red with crying—satisfied him (as I supposed) that she was not mad. He turned the case over to me, in the first instance. I saw that he didn't believe in it, even yet.

"Go back with her to the house," he says. "This may be a stupid hoax, or a quarrel exaggerated. See to it yourself, and hear what the doctor says. If it *is* serious, send word back here directly, and let nobody enter the place or leave it till we come. Stop! You know the form if any statement is volunteered?"

"Yes, sir. I am to caution the persons that whatever they say will be taken down, and may be used against them."

"Quite right. You'll be an Inspector yourself one of these days. Now, miss!" With that he dismissed her, under my care.

Lehigh Street was not very far off—about twenty minutes' walk from the station. I confess I thought the Inspector had been rather hard on Priscilla. She was herself naturally angry with him. "What does he mean," she says, "by talking of a hoax? I wish he was as frightened as I am. This is the first time I have been out at service, sir— and I did think I had found a respectable place."

I said very little to her—feeling, if the truth must be told, rather anxious about the duty committed to me. On reaching the house the door was opened from within, before I could knock. A gentleman stepped out, who proved to be the doctor. He stopped the moment he saw me.

"You must be careful, policeman," he says. "I found the man lying on his back, in bed, dead—with the knife that had killed him left sticking in the wound."

Hearing this, I felt the necessity of sending at once to the station. Where could I find a trustworthy messenger? I took the liberty of asking the doctor if he would repeat to the police what he had already said to me. The station was not much out of his way home. He kindly granted my request.

The landlady (Mrs. Crosscapel) joined us while we were talking. She was still a young woman; not easily frightened, as far as I could see, even by a murder in the house. Her husband was in the passage behind her. He looked old enough to be her father; and he so trembled with terror that some people might have taken him for the guilty person. I removed the key from the street door, after locking it; and I said to the landlady: "Nobody must leave the house, or enter the house, till the Inspector comes. I must examine the premises to see if anyone has broken in."

"There is the key of the area gate," she said, in answer to me. "It's always kept locked. Come downstairs and see for yourself." Priscilla went with us. Her mistress set her to work to light the kitchen fire. "Some of us," says Mrs. Crosscapel, "may be the better for a cup of tea." I remarked that she took things easy, under the circumstances. She answered that the landlady of a London lodging-house could not afford to lose her wits, no matter what might happen.

I found the gate locked, and the shutters of the kitchen window fastened. The back kitchen and back door were secured in the same way. No person was concealed anywhere. Returning upstairs, I examined the front parlor window. There, again, the barred shutters answered for the security of that room. A cracked voice spoke through the door of the back parlor. "The policeman can come in," it said, "if he will promise not to look at me." I turned to the landlady for information. "It's my parlor lodger, Miss Mybus," she said, "a most respectable lady." Going into the room, I saw something rolled up perpendicularly in the bed curtains. Miss Mybus had made herself modestly invisible in that way. Having now satisfied my mind about the security of the lower part of the house, and having the keys safe in my pocket, I was ready to go upstairs.

On our way to the upper regions I asked if there had been any visitors on the previous day. There had been only two visitors, friends of the lodgers—and Mrs. Crosscapel herself had let them both out. My next inquiry related to the lodgers themselves. On the ground floor there was Miss Mybus. On the first floor (occupying both rooms) Mr. Barfield, an old bachelor, employed in a merchant's office. On the second floor, in the front room, Mr. John Zebedee, the murdered man, and his wife. In the back room, Mr. Deluc; described as a cigar agent, and supposed to be a Creole gentleman from Martinique. In the front garret, Mr. and Mrs. Crosscapel. In the back garret, the cook and the housemaid. These were the inhabitants, regularly accounted for. I asked about the servants. "Both excellent characters," says the landlady, "or they would not be in my service."

We reached the second floor, and found the housemaid on the watch outside the door of the front room. Not as nice a woman, personally, as the cook, and sadly frightened of course. Her mistress had posted her, to give the alarm in the case of an outbreak on the part of Mrs. Zebedee, kept locked up in the room. My arrival relieved the housemaid of further responsibility. She ran downstairs to her fellow-servant in the kitchen.

I asked Mrs. Crosscapel how and when the alarm of the murder had been given.

"Soon after three this morning," says she, "I was woke by the screams of Mrs. Zebedee. I found her out here on the landing, and Mr. Deluc, in great alarm, trying to quiet her. Sleeping in the next room, he had only to open his door, when her screams woke him. 'My dear John's murdered! I am the miserable wretch—I did it in my sleep!' She repeated those frantic words over and over again, until she dropped in a swoon. Mr. Deluc and I carried her back into the bedroom. We both thought the poor creature had been driven distracted by some dreadful dream. But when we got to the bedside—don't ask me what we saw; the doctor has told you about it already. I was once a nurse in a hospital, and accustomed, as such, to horrid sights. It turned me cold and giddy, notwithstanding. As for Mr. Deluc, I thought *he* would have had a fainting fit next."

Hearing this, I inquired if Mrs. Zebedee had said or done any strange things since she had been Mrs. Crosscapel's lodger.

"You think she's mad?" says the landlady. "And anybody would be of your mind, when a woman accuses herself of murdering her husband in her sleep. All I can say is that, up to this morning, a more quiet, sensible, well-behaved little person than Mrs. Zebedee I never met with. Only just married, mind, and as fond of her unfortunate husband as a woman could be. I should have called them a pattern couple, in their own line of life."

There was no more to be said on the landing. We unlocked the door and went into the room.

## II

HE LAY in bed on his back as the doctor had described him. On the left side of his nightgown, just over his heart, the blood on the linen told its terrible tale. As well as one could judge, looking unwillingly at a dead face, he must have been a handsome young man in his lifetime. It was a sight to sadden anybody—but I think the most painful sensation was when my eyes fell next on his miserable wife.

She was down on the floor, crouched up in a corner—a dark little woman, smartly dressed in gay colors. Her black hair and her big brown eyes made the horrid paleness of her face look even more deadly white than perhaps it really was. She stared straight at us without appearing to see us. We spoke to her, and she never answered a word. She might have been dead—like her husband—except that she perpetually picked at her fingers, and shuddered every now and then as if she was cold. I went to her and tried to lift her up. She shrank back with a cry that wellnigh frightened me—not because it was loud, but because it was more like the cry of some animal than of a human being. However quietly she might have behaved in the landlady's previous experience of her, she was beside herself now. I might have been moved by a natural pity for her, or I might have been completely upset in my mind—I only know this, I could not persuade myself that she was guilty. I even said to Mrs. Crosscapel, "I don't believe she did it."

While I spoke there was a knock at the door. I went downstairs at once, and admitted (to my great relief) the Inspector, accompanied by one of our men.

He waited downstairs to hear my report, and he approved of what I had done. "It looks as if the murder has been committed by somebody in the house." Saying this, he left the man below, and went up with me to the second floor.

Before he had been a minute in the room, he discovered an object which had escaped my observation.

It was the knife that had done the deed.

The doctor had found it left in the body—had withdrawn it to probe the wound—and had laid it on the bedside table. It was one of those useful knives which contain a saw, a corkscrew, and other like implements. The big blade fastened back, when open, with a spring. Except where the blood was on it, it was as bright as when it had been purchased. A small metal plate was fastened to the horn handle, containing an inscription, only partly engraved, which ran thus: "*To John Zebedee, from—*" there it stopped, strangely enough.

Who or what had interrupted the engraver's work? It was impossible even to guess. Nevertheless, the Inspector was encouraged.

"This ought to help us," he said—and then he gave an attentive ear (looking all the while at the poor creature in the corner) to what Mrs. Crosscapel had to tell him.

The landlady having done, he said he must now see the lodger who slept in the next bed-chamber.

Mr. Deluc made his appearance, standing at the door of the room, and turning away his head with horror from the sight inside.

He was wrapped in a splendid blue dressing-gown, with a golden girdle and trimmings. His scanty brownish hair curled (whether artificially or not, I am unable to say) in little ringlets. His complexion was yellow; his greenish-brown eyes were of the sort called "goggle"—they looked as if they might drop out of his face, if you held a spoon under them. His mustache and goat's beard were beautifully oiled; and, to complete his equipment, he had a long black cigar in his mouth.

"It isn't insensibility to this terrible tragedy," he explained. "My nerves have been shattered, Mr. Policeman, and I can only repair the mischief in this way. Be pleased to excuse and feel for me."

The Inspector questioned this witness sharply and closely. He was not a man to be misled by appearances; but I could see that he was far from liking, or even trusting, Mr. Deluc. Nothing came of the examination, except what Mrs. Crosscapel had in substance already mentioned to me. Mr. Deluc returned to his room.

"How long has he been lodging with you?" the Inspector asked, as soon as his back was turned.

"Nearly a year," the landlady answered.

"Did he give you a reference?"

"As good a reference as I could wish for." Thereupon, she mentioned the names of a well-known firm of cigar merchants in the city. The Inspector noted the information in his pocketbook.

I would rather not relate in detail what happened next: it is too distressing to be dwelt on. Let me only say that the poor demented woman was taken away in a cab to the station-house. The Inspector possessed himself of the knife, and of a book found on the floor, called "The World of Sleep." The portmanteau containing the luggage was locked —and then the door of the room was secured, the keys in both cases being left in my charge. My instructions were to remain in the house, and allow nobody to leave it, until I heard again shortly from the Inspector.

### III

THE CORONER'S inquest was adjourned; and the examination before the magistrate ended in a remand—Mrs. Zebedee being in no condition to understand the proceedings in either case. The surgeon reported her to be completely prostrated by a terrible nervous shock. When he was asked if he considered her to have been a sane woman before the murder took place, he refused to answer positively at that time.

A week passed. The murdered man was buried; his old father attending the funeral. I occasionally saw Mrs. Crosscapel and the two servants, for the purpose of getting such further information as was thought desirable. Both the cook and the housemaid had given their month's notice to quit; declining, in the interest of their characters, to remain in a house which had been the scene of a murder. Mr. Deluc's nerves led also to his removal; his rest was now disturbed by frightful dreams. He paid the necessary forfeit-money, and left without notice. The first-floor lodger, Mr. Barfield, kept his rooms, but obtained leave of absence from his employers, and took refuge with some friends in the country. Miss Mybus alone remained in the parlors. "When I am comfortable," the old lady said, "nothing moves me, at my age. A murder up two pairs of stairs is nearly the same thing as a murder in the next house. Distance, you see, makes all the difference."

It mattered little to the police what the lodgers did. We had men in plain clothes watching the house night and day. Everybody who went away was privately followed; and the police in the district to which they retired were warned to keep an eye on them, after that. As long as we failed to put Mrs. Zebedee's extraordinary statement to any sort of test—to say nothing of having proved unsuccessful, thus far, in tracing the knife to its purchaser—we were bound to let no person living under Mr. Crosscapel's roof, on the night of the murder, slip through our fingers.

### IV

IN A fortnight more, Mrs. Zebedee had sufficiently recovered to make the necessary statement—after the preliminary caution addressed to persons in such cases. The surgeon had no hesitation, now, in reporting her to be a sane woman.

Her station in life had been domestic service. She had lived for four years in her last place as lady's-maid, with a family residing in Dorsetshire. The one objection to her had been the occasional infirmity of sleep-walking, which made it necessary that one of the other female servants should sleep in the same room, with the door locked and the key under her pillow. In all other respects the lady's-maid was described by her mistress as "a perfect treasure."

In the last six months of her service, a young man named John Zebedee entered the house (with a written character) as a footman. He soon fell in love with the nice little lady's-maid, and she heartily returned the feeling. They might have waited for years before they were in a pecuniary position to marry, but for the death of Zebedee's uncle, who left him a little fortune of two thousand pounds. They were now, for persons in their station, rich enough to please themselves; and they were married from the house in which they served together, the little daughters of the family showing their affection for Mrs. Zebedee by acting as her bridesmaids.

The young husband was a careful man. He decided to employ his small capital to the best advantage, by sheep-farming in Australia. His wife made no objection; she was ready to go wherever John went.

Accordingly they spent their short honeymoon in London, so as to see for themselves the vessel in which their passage was to be taken. They went to Mrs. Crosscapel's lodging-house because Zebedee's uncle had always stayed there when in London. Ten days were to pass before the day of embarkation arrived. This gave the young couple a welcome holiday, and a prospect of amusing themselves to their heart's content among the sights and shows of the great city.

On their first evening in London they went to the theater. They were both accustomed to the fresh air of the country, and they felt half stifled by the heat and the gas. However, they were so pleased with an amusement which was new to them that they went to another theater on the next evening. On this second occasion, John Zebedee found the heat unendurable. They left the theater, and got back to their lodgings toward ten o'clock.

Let the rest be told in the words used by Mrs. Zebedee herself. She said:

"We sat talking for a little while in our room, and John's headache got worse and worse. I persuaded him to go to bed, and I put out the candle (the fire giving sufficient light to undress by), so that he might the sooner fall asleep. But he was too restless to sleep. He asked me to read him something. Books always made him drowsy at the best of times.

"I had not myself begun to undress. So I lit the candle again, and I opened the only book I had. John had noticed it at the railway bookstall by the name of 'The World of Sleep.' He used to joke with me about my being a sleepwalker; and he said, 'Here's something that's sure to interest you'—and he made me a present of the book.

"Before I had read to him for more than half an hour he was fast asleep. Not feeling that way inclined, I went on reading to myself.

"The book did indeed interest me. There was one terrible story which took a hold on my mind—the story of a man who stabbed his own wife in a sleep-walking dream. I thought of putting down my book after that, and then changed my mind again and went on. The next chapters were not so interesting; they were full of learned accounts of why we fall asleep, and what our brains do in that state, and such like. It ended in my falling asleep, too, in my armchair by the fireside.

"I don't know what o'clock it was when I went to sleep. I don't know how long I slept, or whether I dreamed or not. The candle and the fire had both burned out, and it was pitch dark when I woke. I can't even say why I woke—unless it was the coldness of the room.

"There was a spare candle on the chimneypiece. I found the matchbox, and got a light. Then for the first time, I turned round toward the bed; and I saw—"

She had seen the dead body of her husband, murdered while she was unconsciously at his side—and she fainted, poor creature, at the bare remembrance of it.

The proceedings were adjourned. She received every possible care and attention; the chaplain looking after her welfare as well as the surgeon.

I have said nothing of the evidence of the landlady and servants. It was taken as a mere formality. What little they knew proved nothing against Mrs. Zebedee. The police made no discoveries that supported her first frantic accusation of herself. Her master and mistress, where she had been last in service, spoke of her in the highest terms. We were at a complete deadlock.

It had been thought best not to surprise Mr. Deluc, as yet, by citing him as a witness. The action of the law was, however, hurried in this case by a private communication received from the chaplain.

After twice seeing, and speaking with, Mrs. Zebedee, the reverend gentleman was persuaded that she had no more to do than himself with the murder of her husband. He did not consider that he was justified in repeating a confidential communication—he would only recommend that Mr. Deluc should be summoned to appear at the next examination. This advice was followed.

The police had no evidence against Mrs. Zebedee when the inquiry was resumed. To assist the ends of justice she was now put into the witness-box. The discovery of her murdered husband, when she woke in the small hours of the morning, was passed over as rapidly as possible. Only three questions of importance were put to her.

First, the knife was produced. Had she ever seen it in her husband's possession? Never. Did she know anything about it? Nothing whatever.

Secondly: Did she, or did her husband, lock the bedroom door when they returned from the theater? No. Did she afterward lock the door herself? No.

Thirdly: Had she any sort of reason to give for supposing that she had murdered her husband in a sleep-walking dream? No reason, except that she was beside herself at the time, and the book put the thought into her head.

After this the other witnesses were sent out of court. The motive for the chaplain's communication now appeared. Mrs. Zebedee was asked if anything unpleasant had occurred between Mr. Deluc and herself.

Yes. He had caught her alone on the stairs at the lodging-house; had presumed to make love to her; and had carried the insult still further by attempting to kiss her. She had slapped his face, and had declared that her husband should know of it, if his misconduct was repeated. He was in a furious rage at having his face slapped; and he said to her: "Madam, you may live to regret this."

After consultation, and at the request of our Inspector, it was decided to keep Mr. Deluc in ignorance of Mrs. Zebedee's statement for the present. When the witnesses were recalled, he gave the same evidence which he had already given to the Inspector—and he was then asked if he knew anything of the knife. He looked at it without any guilty signs in his face, and swore that he had never seen it until that moment. The resumed inquiry ended, and still nothing had been discovered.

But we kept an eye on Mr. Deluc. Our next effort was to try if we could associate him with the purchase of the knife.

Here again (there really did seem to be a sort of fatality in this case) we reached no useful result. It was easy enough to find out the wholesale cutlers, who had manufactured the knife at Sheffield, by the mark on the blade. But they made tens of thousands of such knives, and disposed of them to retail dealers all over Great Britain—to say nothing of foreign parts. As to finding out the person who had engraved the imperfect inscription (without knowing where, or by whom, the knife had been purchased) we might as well have looked for the proverbial needle in the bundle of hay. Our last resource was to have the knife photographed, with the inscribed side uppermost, and to send copies to every police-station in the kingdom.

At the same time we reckoned up Mr. Deluc—I mean that we made investigations into his past life—on the chance that he and the murdered man might have known each other, and might have had a quarrel, or a rivalry about a woman, on some former occasion. No such discovery rewarded us.

We found Deluc to have led a dissipated life, and to have mixed with very bad company. But he had kept out of reach of the law. A man may be a profligate vagabond; may insult a lady; may say threatening things to her, in the first stinging sensation of having his face slapped—but it doesn't follow from these blots on his character that he has murdered her husband in the dead of the night.

Once more, then, when we were called upon to report ourselves, we had no evidence to produce. The photographs failed to discover the owner of the knife, and to explain its interrupted inscription. Poor Mrs. Zebedee was allowed to go back to her friends, on entering into her own recognizance to appear again if called upon. Articles in the newspapers began to inquire how many more murderers would succeed in baffling the police. The authorities at the Treasury offered a reward of a hundred pounds for the necessary information. And the weeks passed, and nobody claimed the reward.

Our Inspector was not a man to be easily beaten. More inquiries and examinations followed. It is needless to say anything about them. We were defeated—and there, so far as the police and the public were concerned, was an end of it.

The assassination of the poor young husband soon passed out of notice, like other undiscovered murders. One obscure person only was foolish enough, in his leisure hours, to persist in trying to solve the problem of Who Killed Zebedee? He felt that he might rise to the highest position in the police force if he succeeded where his elders and betters had failed—and he held to his own little ambition, though everybody laughed at him. In plain English, I was the man.

## V

WITHOUT MEANING it, I have told my story ungratefully.

There were two persons who saw nothing ridiculous in my resolution to continue the investigation, single-handed. One of them was Miss Mybus; and the other was the cook, Priscilla Thurlby.

Mentioning the lady first, Miss Mybus was indignant at the resigned manner in which the police accepted their defeat. She was a little bright-eyed wiry woman; and she spoke her mind freely.

"This comes home to me," she said. "Just look back for a year or two. I can call to mind two cases of persons found murdered in London—and the assassins have never been traced. I am a person, too; and I ask myself if my turn is not coming next. You're a nice-looking fellow—and I like your pluck and perseverance. Come here as often as you think right; and say you are my visitor, if they make any difficulty about letting you in. One thing more! I have nothing particular to do, and I am no fool. Here, in the parlors, I see everybody who comes into the house or goes out of the house. Leave me your address—I may get some information for you yet."

With the best intentions, Miss Mybus found no opportunity of helping me. Of the two, Priscilla Thurlby seemed more likely to be of use.

In the first place, she was sharp and active, and (not having succeeded in getting another situation as yet) was mistress of her own movements.

In the second place, she was a woman I could trust. Before she left home to try domestic service in London, the parson of her native parish gave her a written testimonial, of which I append a copy. Thus it ran:

> I gladly recommend Priscilla Thurlby for any respectable employment which she may be competent to undertake. Her father and mother are infirm old people, who have lately suffered a diminution of their income; and they have a younger

daughter to maintain. Rather than be a burden on her parents, Priscilla goes to London to find domestic employment, and to devote her earnings to the assistance of her father and mother. This circumstance speaks for itself. I have known the family many years; and I only regret that I have no vacant place in my own household which I can offer to this good girl.

(*Signed*)

HENRY DERRINGTON, *Rector of Roth.*

After reading those words, I could safely ask Priscilla to help me in re-opening the mysterious murder case to some good purpose.

My notion was that the proceedings of the persons in Mrs. Cross-capel's house had not been closely enough inquired into yet. By way of continuing the investigation, I asked Priscilla if she could tell me anything which associated the housemaid with Mr. Deluc. She was unwilling to answer. "I may be casting suspicion on an innocent person," she said. "Besides, I was for so short a time the housemaid's fellow-servant—"

"You slept in the same room with her," I remarked; "and you had opportunities of observing her conduct toward the lodgers. If they had asked you, at the examination, what I now ask, you would have answered as an honest woman."

To this argument she yielded. I heard from her certain particulars, which threw a new light on Mr. Deluc, and on the case generally. On that information I acted. It was slow work, owing to the claims on me of my regular duties; but with Priscilla's help, I steadily advanced toward the end I had in view.

Besides this, I owed another obligation to Mrs. Crosscapel's nice-looking cook. The confession must be made sooner or later—and I may as well make it now. I first knew what love was, thanks to Priscilla. I had delicious kisses, thanks to Priscilla. And, when I asked if she would marry me, she didn't say No. She looked, I must own, a little sadly, and she said: "How can two such poor people as we are ever hope to marry?" To this I answered: "It won't be long before I lay my hand on the clue which my Inspector has failed to find. I shall be in a position to marry you, my dear, when that time comes."

At our next meeting we spoke of her parents. I was now her promised husband. Judging by what I had heard of the proceedings of other people in my position, it seemed to be only right that I should be made known to her father and mother. She entirely agreed with me; and she wrote home that day to tell them to expect us at the end of the week.

I took my turn of night-duty, and so gained my liberty for the greater part of the next day. I dressed myself in plain clothes, and we took our tickets on the railway for Yateland, being the nearest station to the village in which Priscilla's parents lived.

## VI

THE TRAIN stopped, as usual, at the big town of Waterbank. Supporting herself by her needle, while she was still unprovided with a situation, Priscilla had been at work late in the night—she was tired and thirsty. I left the carriage to get her some soda-water. The stupid girl in the refreshment room failed to pull the cork out of the bottle, and refused to let me help her. She took a corkscrew, and used it crookedly. I lost all patience, and snatched the bottle out of her hand. Just as I drew the cork, the bell rang on the platform. I only waited to pour the soda-water into a glass—but the train was moving as I left the refreshment room. The porters stopped me when I tried to jump on to the step of the carriage. I was left behind.

As soon as I had recovered my temper, I looked at the time-table. We had reached Waterbank at five minutes past one. By good luck, the next train was due at forty-four minutes past one, and arrived at Yateland (the next station) ten minutes afterward. I could only hope that Priscilla would look at the time-table too, and wait for me. If I had attempted to walk the distance between the two places, I should have lost time instead of saving it. The interval before me was not very long; I occupied it in looking over the town.

Speaking with all due respect to the inhabitants, Waterbank (to other people) is a dull place. I went up one street and down another—and stopped to look at a shop which struck me; not from anything in itself, but because it was the only shop in the street with the shutters closed.

A bill was posted on the shutters, announcing that the place was to let. The outgoing tradesman's name and business, announced in the customary painted letters, ran thus: *James Wycomb, Cutler, etc.*

For the first time, it occurred to me that we had forgotten an obstacle in our way, when we distributed our photographs of the knife. We had none of us remembered that a certain proportion of cutlers might be placed, by circumstances, out of our reach—either by retiring from business or by becoming bankrupt. I always carried a copy of the photograph about me; and I thought to myself, "Here is the ghost of a chance of tracing the knife to Mr. Deluc!"

The shop door was opened, after I had twice rung the bell, by an old man, very dirty and very deaf. He said: "You had better go upstairs, and speak to Mr. Scorrier—top of the house."

I put my lips to the old fellow's ear-trumpet, and asked who Mr. Scorrier was.

"Brother-in-law to Mr. Wycomb. Mr. Wycomb's dead. If you want to buy the business apply to Mr. Scorrier."

Receiving that reply, I went upstairs, and found Mr. Scorrier engaged in engraving a brass door-plate. He was a middle-aged man, with a cadaverous face and dim eyes. After the necessary apologies, I produced my photograph.

"May I ask, sir, if you know anything of the inscription on that knife?" I said.

He took his magnifying glass to look at it.

"This is curious," he remarked quietly. "I remember the queer name —Zebedee. Yes, sir; I did the engraving, as far as it goes. I wonder what prevented me from finishing it?"

The name of Zebedee, and the unfinished inscription on the knife, had appeared in every English newspaper. He took the matter so coolly that I was doubtful how to interpret his answer. Was it possible that he had not seen the account of the murder? Or was he an accomplice with prodigious powers of self-control?

"Excuse me," I said, "do you read the newspapers?"

"Never! My eyesight is failing me. I abstain from reading, in the interests of my occupation."

"Have you not heard the name of Zebedee mentioned—particularly by people who do read the newspapers?"

"Very likely; but I didn't attend to it. When the day's work is done, I take my walk. Then I have my supper, my drop of grog, and my pipe. Then I go to bed. A dull existence you think, I daresay! I had a miserable life, sir, when I was young. A bare subsistence, and a little rest, before the last perfect rest in the grave—that is all I want. The world has gone by me long ago. So much the better."

The poor man spoke honestly. I was ashamed of having doubted him. I returned to the subject of the knife.

"Do you know where it was purchased, and by whom?" I asked.

"My memory is not so good as it was," he said; "but I have got something by me that helps it."

He took from a cupboard a dirty old scrapbook. Strips of paper, with writing on them, were pasted on the pages, as well as I could see. He turned to an index, or table of contents, and opened a page. Something like a flash of life showed itself on his dismal face.

"Ha! now I remember," he said. "The knife was bought of my late brother-in-law, in the shop downstairs. It all comes back to me, sir. A person in a state of frenzy burst into this very room, and snatched the knife away from me, when I was only half way through the inscription!"

I felt that I was now close on discovery. "May I see what it is that has assisted your memory?" I asked.

"Oh yes. You must know, sir, I live by engraving inscriptions and addresses, and I paste in this book the manuscript instructions which I receive, with marks of my own on the margin. For one thing, they serve as a reference to new customers. And for another thing, they do certainly help my memory."

He turned the book toward me, and pointed to a slip of paper which occupied the lower half of a page.

I read the complete inscription, intended for the knife that killed Zebedee, and written as follows:

"To John Zebedee. From Priscilla Thurlby."

## VII

I DECLARE that it is impossible for me to describe what I felt when Priscilla's name confronted me like a written confession of guilt. How long it was before I recovered myself in some degree, I cannot say. The only thing I can clearly call to mind is, that I frightened the poor engraver.

My first desire was to get possession of the manuscript inscription. I told him I was a policeman, and summoned him to assist me in the discovery of a crime. I even offered him money. He drew back from my hand. "You shall have it for nothing," he said, "if you will only go away and never come here again." He tried to cut it out of the page—but his trembling hands were helpless. I cut it out myself, and attempted to thank him. He wouldn't hear me. "Go away!" he said, "I don't like the look of you."

It may be here objected that I ought not to have felt so sure as I did of the woman's guilt, until I had got more evidence against her. The knife might have been stolen from her, supposing she was the person who had snatched it out of the engraver's hands, and might have been afterward used by the thief to commit the murder. All very true. But I never had a moment's doubt in my own mind, from the time when I read the damnable line in the engraver's book.

I went back to the railway without any plan in my head. The train by which I had proposed to follow her had left Waterbank. The next train that arrived was for London. I took my place in it—still without any plan in my head.

At Charing Cross a friend met me. He said, "You're looking miserably ill. Come and have a drink."

I went with him. The liquor was what I really wanted; it strung me up, and cleared my head. He went his way, and I went mine. In a little while more, I determined what I would do.

In the first place, I decided to resign my situation in the police, from a motive which will presently appear. In the second place, I took a bed at a public-house. She would no doubt return to London, and she would go to my lodgings to find out why I had broken my appointment. To bring to justice the one woman whom I had dearly loved was too cruel a duty for a poor creature like me. I preferred leaving the police force. On the other hand, if she and I met before time had helped me to control myself, I had a horrid fear that I might turn murderer next, and kill her then and there. The wretch had not only all but misled me into marrying her, but also into charging the innocent housemaid with being concerned in the murder.

The same night I hit on a way of clearing up such doubts as still harassed my mind. I wrote to the rector of Roth, informing him that I was engaged to marry her, and asking if he would tell me (in consideration of my position) what her former relations might have been with the person named John Zebedee.

By return of post I got this reply:

SIR—Under the circumstances, I think I am bound to tell you confidentially what the friends and well-wishers of Priscilla have kept secret, for her sake.

Zebedee was in service in this neighborhood. I am sorry to say it, of a man who has come to such a miserable end—but his behavior to Priscilla proves him to have been a vicious and heartless wretch. They were engaged—and, I add with indignation, he tried to seduce her under a promise of marriage. Her virtue resisted him, and he pretended to be ashamed of himself. The banns were published in my church. On the next day Zebedee disappeared, and cruelly deserted her. He was a capable servant; and I believe he got another place. I leave you to imagine what the poor girl suffered under the outrage inflicted on her. Going to London, with my recommendation, she answered the first advertisement that she saw, and was unfortunate enough to begin her career in domestic service in the very lodging-house to which (as I gather from the newspaper report of the murder) the man Zebedee took the person whom he married, after deserting Priscilla. Be assured that you are about to unite yourself to an excellent girl, and accept my best wishes for your happiness.

It was plain from this that neither the rector nor the parents and friends knew anything of the purchase of the knife. The one miserable man who knew the truth was the man who had asked her to be his wife.

I owed it to myself—at least so it seemed to me—not to let it be supposed that I, too, had meanly deserted her. Dreadful as the prospect was, I felt that I must see her once more, and for the last time.

She was at work when I went into her room. As I opened the door she started to her feet. Her cheeks reddened, and her eyes flashed with anger. I stepped forward—and she saw my face. My face silenced her.

I spoke in the fewest words I could find.

"I have been to the cutler's shop at Waterbank," I said. "There is the unfinished inscription on the knife, complete in your handwriting. I could hang you by a word. God forgive me—I can't say the word."

Her bright complexion turned to a dreadful clay-color. Her eyes were fixed and staring, like the eyes of a person in a fit. She stood before me, still and silent. Without saying more, I dropped the inscription into the fire. Without saying more, I left her.

I never saw her again.

## VIII

But I heard from her a few days later. The letter has long since been burned. I wish I could have forgotten it as well. It sticks to my memory. If I die with my senses about me, Priscilla's letter will be my last recollection on earth.

In substance it repeated what the rector had already told me. Further, it informed me that she had bought the knife as a keepsake for Zebedee, in place of a similar knife which he had lost. On the Saturday, she made the purchase, and left it to be engraved. On the Sunday, the banns were put up. On the Monday, she was deserted; and she snatched the knife from the table while the engraver was at work.

She only knew that Zebedee had added a new sting to the insult inflicted on her when he arrived at the lodgings with his wife. Her duties as cook kept her in the kitchen—and Zebedee never discovered that she was in the house. I still remember the last lines of her confession: "The devil entered into me when I tried their door, on my way up to bed, and found it unlocked, and listened a while, and peeped in. I saw them by the dying light of the candle—one asleep on the bed, the other asleep by the fireside. I had the knife in my hand, and the thought came to me to do it, so that they might hang *her* for the murder. I couldn't take the knife out again, when I had done it. Mind this! I did really like you—I didn't say Yes, because you could hardly hang your own wife, if you found out who killed Zebedee."

Since the past time I have never heard again of Priscilla Thurlby; I don't know whether she is living or dead. Many people may think I deserve to be hanged myself for not having given her up to the gallows. They may, perhaps, be disappointed when they see this confession, and hear that I have died decently in my bed. I don't blame them. I am a penitent sinner. I wish all merciful Christians good-by forever.

# THE SOFA

## BY CHARLES DICKENS

CHARLES DICKENS is the great master of Victorian sensationalism. He was a genius who knew what the public wanted. All his work was directed to a new social class, a reading public which emerged in the first half of the nineteenth century. "I write for the public," he said, "and the public cares less for a dead lion than for a living ass." The public was ecstatic about his work.

Dickens was not only a great writer, but a great editor as well, and the magazines that he supervised constantly demanded new stories and articles. The magazines of the Victorian period were like the television of today—a giant maw, endlessly demanding more and more material—and more and more sensation.

The emergence of effective police departments and the omnipresent presence of crime during the mid-Victorian period made police stories unusually popular. This almost unknown Dickens story, "The Sofa," was directed to the hungry reading audience that was interested in the new hero of the time, the policeman.

So began the birth of the detective police story, which G. K. Chesterton described so magnificently: "When the detective in a police romance stands alone, and somewhat fatuously fearless amid the knives and fists of a thief's kitchen, it does certainly serve to make us remember that it is the agent of social justice who is the original and poetic figure, while the burglars and footpads are merely placid old cosmic conservatives, happy in the immemorial respectability of apes and wolves. The romance of the police force is thus the whole romance of man. It is based on the fact that morality is the most dark and daring of conspiracies. It reminds us that the whole noiseless and unnoticeable police management by which we are ruled and protected is only a successful knight-errantry." ૨ઌ

"WHAT YOUNG men will do, sometimes, to ruin themselves, and break their friends' hearts," said Sergeant Dornton, "it's surprising! I had a case at St. Blank's Hospital which was of this sort. A bad case, indeed, with a bad end!

"The Secretary, and the House-Surgeon, and the Treasurer, of Saint Blank's Hospital, came to Scotland Yard to give information of numerous robberies having been committed on the students. The students could leave nothing in the pockets of their great-coats while the great-coats were hanging at the hospital, but it was almost certain to be stolen. Property of various descriptions was constantly being lost; and the gentlemen were naturally uneasy about it, and anxious, for the credit of the institution, that the thief or thieves should be discovered. The case was entrusted to me, and I went to the hospital.

" 'Now, gentlemen,' said I, after we had talked it over; 'I understand this property is usually lost from one room.'

"Yes, they said. It was.

" 'I should wish, if you please,' said I, 'to see the room.'

"It was a good sized bare room down-stairs, with a few tables and forms in it, and a row of pegs all around for hats and coats.

" 'Next, gentlemen,' said I, 'do you suspect anybody?'

"Yes, they said. They did suspect somebody. They were sorry to say, they suspected one of the porters.

" 'I should like,' said I, 'to have that man pointed out to me, and to have a little time to look at him.'

"He was pointed out, and I looked at him, and then I went back to the hospital, and said, 'Now, gentlemen, it's not the porter. He's, unfortunately for himself, a little too fond of drink, but he's nothing worse. My suspicion is, that these robberies are committed by one of the students; and if you'll put me a sofa into that room where the pegs are—as there's no closet—I think I shall be able to detect the thief. I wish the sofa, if you please, to be covered with chintz, or something of that sort, so that I may lie on my chest, underneath it, without being seen.'

"The sofa was provided, and next day at eleven o'clock, before any of the students came, I went there with those gentlemen, to get under it. It turned out to be one of those old-fashioned sofas with a cross-beam at the bottom, that would have broken my back in no time if I could ever have got below it. We had quite a job to break all this away in time; however, I fell to work, and they fell to work, and we broke it out, and made a clear place for me. I got under the sofa, lay down on my chest, took out my knife, and made a convenient hole in the chintz to look through. It was then settled between me and the gentlemen that when the students were all up in the wards, one of the gentlemen should come in, and hang up a great-coat on one of the pegs. And that great-coat should have, in one of the pockets, a pocket-book containing marked money.

"After I had been there some time, the students began to drop into the room, by ones, and twos, and threes, and to talk about all sorts of things, little thinking there was anyone under the sofa—and then to go up-stairs. At last there came in one who remained until he was alone in the room by himself. A tallish, good-looking young man of one or two and twenty, with a light whisker. He went to a particular hat-peg, took off a good hat that was hanging there, tried it on, hung his own hat in its place, and hung that on another peg, nearly opposite to me. I then felt quite certain that he was the thief, and would come back by-and-by.

"When they were all up-stairs, the gentleman came in with the great-coat. I showed him where to hang it, so that I might have a good view of it; and he went away; and I lay under the sofa on my chest, for a couple of hours or so, waiting.

"At last the same young man came down. He walked across the room, whistling—stopped and listened—took another walk and whistled—stopped again, and whistled—then began to go regularly round the pegs, feeling in pockets of all the coats. When he came to THE great-coat, and felt the pocket-book, he was so eager and so hurried that he broke the strap in tearing it open. As he began to put the money in his pocket, I crawled out from under the sofa, and his eyes met mine.

"My face, as you may perceive, is brown now, but it was pale at that time, my health not being good; and looked as long as a horse's. Besides which there was a great draught of air from the door, underneath the sofa, and I had tied a handkerchief round my head; so what I looked like, altogether, I don't know. He turned blue—literally blue—when he saw me crawling out, and I couldn't feel surprised at it.

" 'I am an officer of the Detective Police,' said I, 'and have been lying here since you first came this morning. I regret, for the sake of yourself and your friends, that you should have done what you have; but this case is complete. You have the pocket-book in your hand and the money about you; and I must take you into custody!'

"It was impossible to make out any case in his behalf, and on his trial he pleaded guilty. How or when he got the means I don't know; but while he was awaiting his sentence, he poisoned himself in Newgate."

We inquired of this officer, on the conclusion of the foregoing anecdote, whether the time appeared long, or short, when he lay in that constrained position under the sofa?

"Why, you see, sir," he replied, "if he hadn't come in, the first time, and I had not been quite sure he was the thief, and would return, the time would have seemed long. But, as it was, I being dead certain of my man, the time seemed pretty short."

# THE ADVENTURE OF THE CREEPING MAN

## BY SIR ARTHUR CONAN DOYLE

IT WAS the great master Arthur Conan Doyle who brought detective fiction to its finest maturity. Edgar Allan Poe was of course the true father of short detective fiction. His stories are still so popular and so easily available, they are not reprinted in this present book; however, many of the great stories about Sherlock Holmes are relatively unknown to the general reader. "The Adventure of the Creeping Man" is one such story.

The great Sherlock Holmes sprang almost full grown from the brain of a young English doctor in his mid-twenties. As a doctor, Arthur Conan Doyle was unsuccessful. However, in 1886 the idea of creating a great literary character made the name Arthur Conan Doyle known throughout the world. The character was, of course, the Great Detective Sherlock Holmes. Actually, Sherlock Holmes was based on a great surgeon, Dr. Joseph Bell, whom Doyle knew, but Doyle also was Sherlock Holmes himself. More than once Doyle showed his unusual skills of deduction in real-life murder cases.

Doyle was a superb storyteller. All of his tales are as exciting today as when they were written. Many of his rivals of the time tried their hand at such stories, but they have long since been forgotten. Only Doyle can make us feel the peculiar horror of the moors, the fog and mist of the London street, and exquisite fineness of pure deduction summed up so beautifully in few words "by a man's finger-nails, by his coat-sleeve, by his boots, by his trouser knees, by the callosities of his forefinger and thumb, by his expression, by his shirt-cuffs—by each of these things a man's calling is plainly revealed." ⟨⟩

MR. SHERLOCK HOLMES was always of opinion that I should publish the singular facts connected with Professor Presbury, if only to dispel once for all the ugly rumors which some twenty years ago agitated the university and were echoed in the learned societies of London. There were, however, certain obstacles in the way, and the true history of this curious case remained entombed in the tin box which contains so many records of my friend's adventures. Now we have at last obtained permission to ventilate the facts which formed one of the very last cases handled by Holmes before his retirement from practice. Even now a certain reticence and discretion have to be observed in laying the matter before the public.

It was one Sunday evening early in September of the year 1903 that I received one of Holmes's laconic messages:

Come at once if convenient—if inconvenient come all the same.

S.H.

The relations between us in those latter days were peculiar. He was a man of habits, narrow and concentrated habits, and I had become one of them. As an institution I was like the violin, the shag tobacco, the old black pipe, the index books, and others perhaps less excusable. When it was a case of active work and a comrade was needed upon whose nerve he could place some reliance, my role was obvious. But apart from this I had uses. I was a whetstone for his mind. I stimulated him. He liked to think aloud in my presence. His remarks could hardly be said to be made to me—many of them would have been as appropriately addressed to his bedstead—but none the less, having formed the habit, it had become in some way helpful that I should register and interject. If I irritated him by a certain methodical slowness in my mentality, that irritation served only to make his own flame-like intuitions and impressions flash up the more vividly and swiftly. Such was my humble role in our alliance.

When I arrived at Baker Street I found him huddled up in his arm-chair with updrawn knees, his pipe in his mouth and his brow furrowed with thought. It was clear that he was in the throes of some vexatious problem. With a wave of his hand he indicated my old armchair, but otherwise for half an hour he gave no sign that he was aware of my presence. Then with a start he seemed to come from his reverie, and with his usual whimsical smile he greeted me back to what had once been my home.

"You will excuse a certain abstraction of mind, my dear Watson," said he. "Some curious facts have been submitted to me within the last twenty-four hours, and they in turn have given rise to some speculations of a more general character. I have serious thoughts of writing a small monograph upon the uses of dogs in the work of the detective."

"But surely, Holmes, this has been explored," said I. "Bloodhounds—sleuthhounds——"

"No, no, Watson, that side of the matter is, of course, obvious. But there is another which is far more subtle. You may recollect that in the case which you, in your sensational way, coupled with the Copper Beeches, I was able, by watching the mind of the child, to form a de-duction as to the criminal habits of the very smug and respectable fa-ther."

"Yes, I remember it well."

"My line of thoughts about dogs is analogous. A dog reflects the family life. Whoever saw a frisky dog in a gloomy family, or a sad dog in a happy one? Snarling people have snarling dogs, dangerous people have dangerous ones. And their passing moods may reflect the passing moods of others."

I shook my head. "Surely, Holmes, this is a little far-fetched," said I.

He had refilled his pipe and resumed his seat, taking no notice of my comment.

"The practical application of what I have said is very close to the problem which I am investigating. It is a tangled skein, you understand, and I am looking for a loose end. One possible loose end lies in the question: Why does Professor Presbury's wolfhound, Roy, endeavor to bite him?"

I sank back in my chair in some disappointment. Was it for so trivial a question as this that I had been summoned from my work? Holmes glanced across at me.

"The same old Watson!" said he. "You never learn that the gravest issues may depend upon the smallest things. But is it not on the face of it strange that a staid, elderly philosopher—you've heard of Presbury, of course, the famous Camford physiologist?—that such a man, whose friend has been his devoted wolfhound, should now have been twice attacked by his own dog? What do you make of it?"

"The dog is ill."

"Well, that has to be considered. But he attacks no one else, nor does he apparently molest his master, save on very special occasions. Curious, Watson—very curious. But young Mr. Bennett is before his time if that is his ring. I had hoped to have a longer chat with you before he came."

There was a quick step on the stairs, a sharp tap at the door, and a moment later the new client presented himself. He was a tall, handsome youth about thirty, well dressed and elegant, but with something in his bearing which suggested the shyness of the student rather than the self-possession of the man of the world. He shook hands with Holmes, and then looked with some surprise at me.

"This matter is very delicate, Mr. Holmes," he said. "Consider the relation in which I stand to Professor Presbury both privately and publicly. I really can hardly justify myself if I speak before any third person."

"Have no fear, Mr. Bennett. Dr. Watson is the very soul of discretion, and I can assure you that this is a matter in which I am very likely to need an assistant."

"As you like, Mr. Holmes. You will, I am sure, understand my having some reserves in the matter."

"You will appreciate it, Watson, when I tell you that this gentleman, Mr. Trevor Bennett, is professional assistant to the great scientist, lives under his roof, and is engaged to his only daughter. Certainly we must agree that the professor has every claim upon his loyalty and devotion. But it may best be shown by taking the necessary steps to clear up this strange mystery."

"I hope so, Mr. Holmes. That is my one object. Does Dr. Watson know the situation?"

"I have not had time to explain it."

"Then perhaps I had better go over the ground again before explaining some fresh developments."

"I will do so myself," said Holmes, "in order to show that I have the events in their due order. The professor, Watson, is a man of European reputation. His life has been academic. There has never been a breath of scandal. He is a widower with one daughter, Edith. He is, I gather, a man of very virile and positive, one might almost say combative, character. So the matter stood until a very few months ago.

"Then the current of his life was broken. He is sixty-one years of age, but he became engaged to the daughter of Professor Morphy, his colleague in the chair of comparative anatomy. It was not, as I understand, the reasoned courting of an elderly man but rather the passionate frenzy of youth, for no one could have shown himself a more devoted lover. The lady, Alice Morphy, was a very perfect girl both in mind and body, so that there was every excuse for the professor's infatuation. None the less, it did not meet with full approval in his own family."

"We thought it rather excessive," said our visitor.

"Exactly. Excessive and a little violent and unnatural. Professor Presbury was rich, however, and there was no objection upon the part of the father. The daughter, however, had other views, and there were already several candidates for her hand, who, if they were less eligible from a worldly point of view, were at least more of an age. The girl seemed to like the professor in spite of his eccentricities. It was only age which stood in the way.

"About this time a little mystery suddenly clouded the normal routine of the professor's life. He did what he had never done before. He left home and gave no indication where he was going. He was away a fortnight and returned looking rather travel-worn. He made no allusion to where he had been, although he was usually the frankest of men. It chanced, however, that our client here, Mr. Bennett, received a letter from a fellow-student in Prague, who said that he was glad to have seen Professor Presbury there, although he had not been able to talk to him. Only in this way did his own household learn where he had been.

"Now comes the point. From that time onward a curious change came over the professor. He became furtive and sly. Those around him had always the feeling that he was not the man that they had known, but that he was under some shadow which had darkened his higher qualities. His intellect was not affected. His lectures were as brilliant as ever. But always there was something new, something sinister and unexpected. His daughter, who was devoted to him, tried again and again to resume the old relations and to penetrate this mask which her father seemed to have put on. You, sir, as I understand, did the same—but all was in vain. And now, Mr. Bennett, tell in your own words the incident of the letters."

"You must understand, Dr. Watson, that the professor had no secrets from me. If I were his son or his younger brother I could not have more completely enjoyed his confidence. As his secretary I handled every paper which came to him, and I opened and subdivided his letters. Shortly after his return all this was changed. He told me that certain letters might come to him from London which would be marked by a cross under the stamp. These were to be set aside for his own eyes only. I may say that several of these did pass through my hands, that they had the E.C. mark, and were in an illiterate handwriting. If he answered them at all the answers did not pass through my hands nor into the letter-basket in which our correspondence was collected."

"And the box," said Holmes.

"Ah, yes, the box. The professor brought back a little wooden box from his travels. It was the one thing which suggested a Continental tour, for it was one of those quaint carved things which one associates with Germany. This he placed in his instrument cupboard. One day, in looking for a canula, I took up the box. To my surprise he was very angry, and reproved me in words which were quite savage for my curiosity. It was the first time such a thing had happened, and I was deeply hurt. I endeavored to explain that it was a mere accident that I had touched the box, but all the evening I was conscious that he looked at me harshly and that the incident was rankling in his mind." Mr. Bennett drew a little diary book from his pocket. "That was on July 2d," said he.

"You are certainly an admirable witness," said Holmes. "I may need some of these dates which you have noted."

"I learned method among other things from my great teacher. From the time that I observed abnormality in his behavior I felt that it was my duty to study his case. Thus I have it here that it was on that very day, July 2d, that Roy attacked the professor as he came from his study into the hall. Again, on July 11th, there was a scene of the same sort, and then I have a note of yet another upon July 20th. After that we had to banish Roy to the stables. He was a dear, affectionate animal—but I fear I weary you."

Mr. Bennett spoke in a tone of reproach, for it was very clear that Holmes was not listening. His face was rigid and his eyes gazed abstract-edly at the ceiling. With an effort he recovered himself.

"Singular! Most singular!" he murmured. "These details were new to me, Mr. Bennett. I think we have now fairly gone over the old ground, have we not? But you spoke of some fresh developments."

The pleasant, open face of our visitor clouded over, shadowed by some grim remembrance. "What I speak of occurred the night before last," said he. "I was lying awake about two in the morning, when I was aware of a dull muffled sound coming from the passage. I opened my door and peeped out. I should explain that the professor sleeps at the end of the passage——"

"The date being——?" asked Holmes.

Our visitor was clearly annoyed at so irrelevant an interruption.

"I have said, sir, that it was the night before last—that is, September 4th."

Holmes nodded and smiled.

"Pray continue," said he.

"He sleeps at the end of the passage and would have to pass my door in order to reach the staircase. It was a really terrifying experience, Mr. Holmes. I think that I am as strong-nerved as my neighbors, but I was shaken by what I saw. The passage was dark save that one window half-way along it threw a patch of light. I could see that something was com-ing along the passage, something dark and crouching. Then suddenly it emerged into the light, and I saw that it was he. He was crawling, Mr. Holmes—crawling! He was not quite on his hands and knees. I should rather say on his hands and feet, with his face sunk between his hands. Yet he seemed to move with ease. I was so paralyzed by the sight that it was not until he had reached my door that I was able to step forward and ask if I could assist him. His answer was extraordinary. He sprang up, spat out some atrocious word at me, and hurried on past me, and down the staircase. I waited about for an hour, but he did not come back. It must have been daylight before he regained his room."

"Well, Watson, what make you of that?" asked Holmes with the air of the pathologist who presents a rare specimen.

"Lumbago, possibly. I have known a severe attack make a man walk in just such a way, and nothing would be more trying to the temper."

"Good, Watson! You always keep us flat-footed on the ground. But we can hardly accept lumbago, since he was able to stand erect in a moment."

"He was never better in health," said Bennett. "In fact, he is stronger than I have known him for years. But there are the facts, Mr. Holmes. It is not a case in which we can consult the police, and yet we are utterly at our wit's end as to what to do, and we feel in some strange way that we are drifting towards disaster. Edith—Miss Presbury—feels as I do, that we cannot wait passively any longer."

"It is certainly a very curious and suggestive case. What do you think, Watson?"

"Speaking as a medical man," said I, "it appears to be a case for an alienist. The old gentleman's cerebral processes were disturbed by the love affair. He made a journey abroad in the hope of breaking himself of the passion. His letters and the box may be connected with some other private transaction—a loan, perhaps, or share certificates, which are in the box."

"And the wolfhound no doubt disapproved of the financial bargain. No, no, Watson, there is more in it than this. Now, I can only suggest——"

What Sherlock Holmes was about to suggest will never be known, for at this moment the door opened and a young lady was shown into the room. As she appeared Mr. Bennett sprang up with a cry and ran forward with his hands out to meet those which she had herself outstretched.

"Edith, dear! Nothing the matter, I hope?"

"I felt I must follow you. Oh, Jack, I have been so dreadfully frightened! It is awful to be there alone."

"Mr. Holmes, this is the young lady I spoke of. This is my fiancée."

"We were gradually coming to that conclusion, were we not, Watson?" Holmes answered with a smile. "I take it, Miss Presbury, that there is some fresh development in the case, and that you thought we should know?"

Our new visitor, a bright, handsome girl of a conventional English type, smiled back at Holmes as she seated herself beside Mr. Bennett.

"When I found Mr. Bennett had left his hotel I thought I should probably find him here. Of course, he had told me that he would consult you. But, oh, Mr. Holmes, can you do nothing for my poor father?"

"I have hopes, Miss Presbury, but the case is still obscure. Perhaps what you have to say may throw some fresh light upon it."

"It was last night, Mr. Holmes. He had been very strange all day. I am sure that there are times when he has no recollection of what he does. He lives as in a strange dream. Yesterday was such a day. It was not my father with whom I lived. His outward shell was there, but it was not really he."

"Tell me what happened."

"I was awakened in the night by the dog barking most furiously. Poor Roy, he is chained now near the stable. I may say that I always sleep with my door locked; for, as Jack—as Mr. Bennett—will tell you, we all have a feeling of impending danger. My room is on the second floor. It happened that the blind was up in my window, and there was bright moonlight outside. As I lay with my eyes fixed upon the square of light, listening to the frenzied barkings of the dog, I was amazed to see my father's face looking in at me. Mr. Holmes, I nearly died of surprise and horror. There it was pressed against the window-pane, and one hand seemed to be raised as if to push up the window. If that window had opened, I think I should have gone mad. It was no delusion, Mr. Holmes. Don't deceive yourself by thinking so. I dare say it was twenty seconds or so that I lay paralyzed and watched the face. Then it vanished, but I could not—I could not spring out of bed and look out after it. I lay cold and shivering till morning. At breakfast he was sharp and fierce in manner, and made no allusion to the adventure of the night. Neither did I, but I gave an excuse for coming to town—and here I am."

Holmes looked thoroughly surprised at Miss Presbury's narrative.

"My dear young lady, you say that your room is on the second floor. Is there a long ladder in the garden?"

"No, Mr. Holmes, that is the amazing part of it. There is no possible way of reaching the window—and yet he was there."

"The date being September 15th," said Holmes. "That certainly complicates matters."

It was the young lady's turn to look surprised. "This is the second time that you have alluded to the date, Mr. Holmes," said Bennett. "Is it possible that it has any bearing upon the case?"

"It is possible—very possible—and yet I have not my full material at present."

"Possibly you are thinking of the connection between insanity and phases of the moon?"

"No, I assure you. It was quite a different line of thought. Possibly you can leave your notebook with me, and I will check the dates. Now I think, Watson, that our line of action is perfectly clear. This young lady has informed us—and I have the greatest confidence in her intuition —that her father remembers little or nothing which occurs upon certain dates. We will therefore call upon him as if he had given us an appointment upon such a date. He will put it down to his own lack of memory. Thus we will open our campaign by having a good close view of him."

"That is excellent," said Mr. Bennett. "I warn you, however, that the professor is irascible and violent at times."

Holmes smiled. "There are reasons why we should come at once— very cogent reasons if my theories hold good. To-morrow, Mr. Bennett, will certainly see us in Camford. There is, if I remember right, an inn called the Chequers where the port used to be above mediocrity and the linen was above reproach. I think, Watson, that our lot for the next few days might lie in less pleasant places."

Monday morning found us on our way to the famous university town —an easy effort on the part of Holmes, who had no roots to pull up, but one which involved frantic planning and hurrying on my part, as my practice was by this time not inconsiderable. Holmes made no allusion to the case until after we had deposited our suitcases at the ancient hostel of which he had spoken.

"I think, Watson, that we can catch the professor just before lunch. He lectures at eleven and should have an interval at home."

"What possible excuse have we for calling?"

Holmes glanced at his notebook.

"There was a period of excitement upon August 26th. We will assume that he is a little hazy as to what he does at such times. If we insist that we are there by appointment I think he will hardly venture to contradict us. Have you the effrontery necessary to put it through?"

"We can but try."

"Excellent, Watson! Compound of the Busy Bee and Excelsior. We can but try—the motto of the firm. A friendly native will surely guide us."

Such a one on the back of a smart hansom swept us past a row of ancient colleges and, finally turning into a tree-lined drive, pulled up at the door of a charming house, girt round with lawns and covered with purple wistaria. Professor Presbury was certainly surrounded with every sign not only of comfort but of luxury. Even as we pulled up, a grizzled head appeared at the front window, and we were aware of a pair of keen eyes from under shaggy brows which surveyed us through large horn glasses. A moment later we were actually in his sanctum, and the mysterious scientist, whose vagaries had brought us from London, was standing before us. There was certainly no sign of eccentricity either in his manner or appearance, for he was a portly, large-featured man, grave, tall, and frock-coated, with the dignity of bearing which a lecturer needs. His eyes were his most remarkable feature, keen, observant, and clever to the verge of cunning.

He looked at our cards. "Pray sit down, gentlemen. What can I do for you?"

Mr. Holmes smiled amiably.

"It was the question which I was about to put to you, Professor."

"To me, sir!"

"Possibly there is some mistake. I heard through a second person that Professor Presbury of Camford had need of my services."

"Oh, indeed!" It seemed to me that there was a malicious sparkle in the intense gray eyes. "You heard that, did you? May I ask the name of your informant?"

"I am sorry, Professor, but the matter was rather confidential. If I have made a mistake there is no harm done. I can only express my regret."

"Not at all. I should wish to go further into this matter. It interests me. Have you any scrap of writing, any letter or telegram, to bear out your assertion?"

"No, I have not."

"I presume that you do not go so far as to assert that I summoned you?"

"I would rather answer no questions," said Holmes.

"No, I dare say not," said the professor with asperity. "However, that particular one can be answered very easily without your aid."

He walked across the room to the bell. Our London friend, Mr. Bennett, answered the call.

"Come in, Mr. Bennett. These two gentlemen have come from London under the impression that they have been summoned. You handle all my correspondence. Have you a note of anything going to a person named Holmes?"

"No, sir," Bennett answered with a flush.

"That is conclusive," said the professor, glaring angrily at my companion. "Now, sir"—he leaned forward with his two hands upon the table—"it seems to me that your position is a very questionable one."

Holmes shrugged his shoulders.

"I can only repeat that I am sorry that we have made a needless intrusion."

"Hardly enough, Mr. Holmes!" the old man cried in a high screaming voice, with extraordinary malignancy upon his face. He got between us and the door as he spoke, and he shook his two hands at us with furious passion. "You can hardly get out of it so easily as that." His face was convulsed, and he grinned and gibbered at us in his senseless rage. I am convinced that we should have had to fight our way out of the room if Mr. Bennett had not intervened.

"My dear Professor," he cried, "consider your position! Consider the scandal at the university! Mr. Holmes is a well-known man. You cannot possibly treat him with such discourtesy."

Sulkily our host—if I may call him so—cleared the path to the door.

We were glad to find ourselves outside the house and in the quiet of the tree-lined drive. Holmes seemed greatly amused by the episode.

"Our learned friend's nerves are somewhat out of order," said he. "Perhaps our intrusion was a little crude, and yet we have gained that personal contact which I desired. But, dear me, Watson, he is surely at our heels. The villain still pursues us."

There were the sounds of running feet behind, but it was, to my relief, not the formidable professor but his assistant who appeared round the curve of the drive. He came panting up to us.

"I am so sorry, Mr. Holmes. I wished to apologize."

"My dear sir, there is no need. It is all in the way of professional experience."

"I have never seen him in a more dangerous mood. But he grows more sinister. You can understand now why his daughter and I are alarmed. And yet his mind is perfectly clear."

"Too clear!" said Holmes. "That was my miscalculation. It is evident that his memory is much more reliable than I had thought. By the way, can we, before we go, see the window of Miss Presbury's room?"

Mr. Bennett pushed his way through some shrubs, and we had a view of the side of the house.

"It is there. The second on the left."

"Dear me, it seems hardly accessible. And yet you will observe that there is a creeper below and a water-pipe above which give some foothold."

"I could not climb it myself," said Mr. Bennett.

"Very likely. It would certainly be a dangerous exploit for any normal man."

"There was one other thing I wish to tell you, Mr. Holmes. I have the address of the man in London to whom the professor writes. He seems to have written this morning, and I got it from his blotting-paper. It is an ignoble position for a trusted secretary, but what else can I do?"

Holmes glanced at the paper and put it into his pocket.

"Dorak—a curious name. Slavonic, I imagine. Well, it is an important link in the chain. We return to London this afternoon, Mr. Bennett. I see no good purpose to be served by our remaining. We cannot arrest the professor because he has done no crime, nor can we place him under constraint, for he cannot be proved to be mad. No action is as yet possible."

"Then what on earth are we to do?"

"A little patience, Mr. Bennett. Things will soon develop. Unless I am mistaken, next Tuesday may mark a crisis. Certainly we shall be in Camford on that day. Meanwhile, the general position is undeniably unpleasant, and if Miss Presbury can prolong her visit——"

"That is easy."

"Then let her stay till we can assure her that all danger is past. Meanwhile, let him have his way and do not cross him. So long as he is in a good humor all is well."

"There he is!" said Bennett in a startled whisper. Looking between the branches we saw the tall, erect figure emerge from the hall door and look around him. He stood leaning forward, his hands swinging straight before him, his head turning from side to side. The secretary with a last wave slipped off among the trees, and we saw him presently rejoin his employer, the two entering the house together in what seemed to be animated and even excited conversation.

"I expect the old gentleman has been putting two and two together," said Holmes as we walked hotelward. "He struck me as having a particularly clear and logical brain from the little I saw of him. Explosive, no doubt, but then from his point of view he has something to explode about if detectives are put on his track and he suspects his own household of doing it. I rather fancy that friend Bennett is in for an uncomfortable time."

Holmes stopped at a post-office and sent off a telegram on our way. The answer reached us in the evening, and he tossed it across to me.

> Have visited the Commercial Road and seen Dorak. Suave person, Bohemian, elderly. Keeps large general store.
>
> MERCER.

"Mercer is since your time," said Holmes. "He is my general utility man who looks up routine business. It was important to know something of the man with whom our professor was so secretly corresponding. His nationality connects up with the Prague visit."

"Thank goodness that something connects with something," said I.

"At present we seem to be faced by a long series of inexplicable incidents with no bearing upon each other. For example, what possible connection can there be between an angry wolfhound and a visit to Bohemia, or either of them with a man crawling down a passage at night? As to your dates, that is the biggest mystification of all."

Holmes smiled and rubbed his hands. We were, I may say, seated in the old sitting-room of the ancient hotel, with a bottle of the famous vintage of which Holmes had spoken on the table between us.

"Well, now, let us take the dates first," said he, his finger-tips together and his manner as if he were addressing a class. "This excellent young man's diary shows that there was trouble upon July 2d, and from then onward it seems to have been at nine-day intervals, with, so far as I remember, only one exception. Thus the last outbreak upon Friday was on September 3d, which also falls into the series, as did August 26th, which preceded it. The thing is beyond coincidence."

I was forced to agree.

"Let us, then, form the provisional theory that every nine days the professor takes some strong drug which has a passing but highly poisonous effect. His naturally violent nature is intensified by it. He learned to take this drug while he was in Prague, and is now supplied with it by a Bohemian intermediary in London. This all hangs together, Watson!"

"But the dog, the face at the window, the creeping man in the passage?"

"Well, well, we have made a beginning. I should not expect any fresh developments until next Tuesday. In the meantime we can only keep in touch with friend Bennett and enjoy the amenities of this charming town."

In the morning Mr. Bennett slipped round to bring us the latest report. As Holmes had imagined, times had not been easy with him. Without exactly accusing him of being responsible for our presence, the professor had been very rough and rude in his speech, and evidently felt some strong grievance. This morning he was quite himself again, however, and had delivered his usual brilliant lecture to a crowded class. "Apart from his queer fits," said Bennett, "he has actually more energy and vitality than I can ever remember, nor was his brain ever clearer. But it's not he—it's never the man whom we have known."

"I don't think you have anything to fear now for a week at least," Holmes answered. "I am a busy man, and Dr. Watson has his patients to attend to. Let us agree that we meet here at this hour next Tuesday, and I shall be surprised if before we leave you again we are not able to explain, even if we cannot perhaps put an end to, your troubles. Meanwhile, keep us posted in what occurs."

I saw nothing of my friend for the next few days, but on the following Monday evening I had a short note asking me to meet him next day at the train. From what he told me as we traveled up to Camford all was well, the peace of the professor's house had been unruffled, and his own conduct perfectly normal. This also was the report which was given us by Mr. Bennett himself when he called upon us that evening at our old quarters in the Chequers. "He heard from his London correspondent to-day. There was a letter and there was a small packet, each with the cross under the stamp which warned me not to touch them. There has been nothing else."

"That may prove quite enough," said Holmes grimly. "Now, Mr. Bennett, we shall, I think, come to some conclusion to-night. If my deductions are correct we should have an opportunity of bringing matters to a head. In order to do so it is necessary to hold the professor under observation. I would suggest, therefore, that you remain awake and on the lookout. Should you hear him pass your door, do not interrupt him, but follow him as discreetly as you can. Dr. Watson and I will not be far off. By the way, where is the key of that little box of which you spoke?"

"Upon his watch-chain."

"I fancy our researches must lie in that direction. At the worst the lock should not be very formidable. Have you any other able-bodied man on the premises?"

"There is the coachman, Macphail."

"Where does he sleep?"

"Over the stables."

"We might possibly want him. Well, we can do no more until we see how things develop. Good-bye—but I expect that we shall see you before morning."

It was nearly midnight before we took our station among some bushes immediately opposite the hall door of the professor. It was a fine night, but chilly, and we were glad of our warm overcoats. There was a breeze, and clouds were scudding across the sky, obscuring from time to time the half-moon. It would have been a dismal vigil were it not for the expectation and excitement which carried us along, and the assurance of my comrade that we had probably reached the end of the strange sequence of events which had engaged our attention.

"If the cycle of nine days holds good then we shall have the professor at his worst to-night," said Holmes. "The fact that these strange symptoms began after his visit to Prague, that he is in secret correspondence with a Bohemian dealer in London, who presumably represents someone in Prague, and that he received a packet from him this very day, all point in one direction. What he takes and why he takes it are still beyond our ken, but that it emanates in some way from Prague is clear enough. He takes it under definite directions which regulate this ninth-day system, which was the first point which attracted my attention. But his symptoms are most remarkable. Did you observe his knuckles?"

I had to confess that I did not.

"Thick and horny in a way which is quite new in my experience. Always look at the hands first, Watson. Then cuffs, trouser-knees, and boots. Very curious knuckles which can only be explained by the mode of progression observed by——" Holmes paused and suddenly clapped his hand to his forehead. "Oh, Watson, Watson, what a fool I have been! It seems incredible, and yet it must be true. All points in one direction. How could I miss seeing the connection of ideas? Those knuckles—how could I have passed those knuckles? And the dog! And the ivy! It's surely time that I disappeared into that little farm of my dreams. Look out, Watson! Here he is! We shall have the chance of seeing for ourselves."

The hall door had slowly opened, and against the lamplit background we saw the tall figure of Professor Presbury. He was clad in his dressing-gown. As he stood outlined in the doorway he was erect but leaning forward with dangling arms, as when we saw him last.

Now he stepped forward into the drive, and an extraordinary change came over him. He sank down into a crouching position and moved along upon his hands and feet, skipping every now and then as if he

were overflowing with energy and vitality. He moved along the face of
the house and then around the corner. As he disappeared Bennett
slipped through the hall door and softly followed him.

"Come, Watson, come!" cried Holmes, and we stole as softly as we
could through the bushes until we had gained a spot whence we could
see the other side of the house, which was bathed in the light of the
half-moon. The professor was clearly visible crouching at the foot of the
ivy-covered wall. As we watched him he suddenly began with incredible
agility to ascend it. From branch to branch he sprang, sure of foot and
firm of grasp, climbing apparently in mere joy at his own powers, with
no definite object in view. With his dressing-gown flapping on each side
of him, he looked like some huge bat glued against the side of his own
house, a great square dark patch upon the moonlit wall. Presently he
tired of this amusement, and, dropping from branch to branch, he
squatted down into the old attitude and moved toward the stables,
creeping along in the same strange way as before. The wolfhound was
out now, barking furiously, and more excited than ever when it actually
caught sight of its master. It was straining on its chain and quivering
with eagerness and rage. The professor squatted down very deliberately
just out of reach of the hound and began to provoke it in every possible
way. He took handfuls of pebbles from the drive and threw them in the
dog's face, prodded him with a stick which he had picked up, flicked his
hands about only a few inches from the gaping mouth, and endeavored
in every way to increase the animal's fury, which was already beyond all
control. In all our adventures I do not know that I have ever seen a
more strange sight than this impassive and still dignified figure crouching frog-like upon the ground and goading to a wilder exhibition of
passion the maddened hound, which ramped and raged in front of him,
by all manner of ingenious and calculated cruelty.

And then in a moment it happened! It was not the chain that broke,
but it was the collar that slipped, for it had been made for a thick-
necked Newfoundland. We heard the rattle of falling metal, and the
next instant dog and man were rolling on the ground together, the one
roaring in rage, the other screaming in a strange shrill falsetto of terror.
It was a very narrow thing for the professor's life. The savage creature
had him fairly by the throat, its fangs had bitten deep, and he was

senseless before we could reach them and drag the two apart. It might have been a dangerous task for us, but Bennett's voice and presence brought the great wolfhound instantly to reason. The uproar had brought the sleepy and astonished coachman from his room above the stables. "I'm not surprised," said he, shaking his head. "I've seen him at it before. I knew the dog would get him sooner or later."

The hound was secured, and together we carried the professor up to his room, where Bennett, who had a medical degree, helped me to dress his torn throat. The sharp teeth had passed dangerously near the carotid artery, and the hemorrhage was serious. In half an hour the danger was past, I had given the patient an injection of morphia, and he had sunk into deep sleep. Then, and only then, were we able to look at each other and to take stock of the situation.

"I think a first-class surgeon should see him," said I.

"For God's sake, no!" cried Bennett. "At present the scandal is confined to our own household. It is safe with us. If it gets beyond these walls it will never stop. Consider his position at the university, his European reputation, the feelings of his daughter."

"Quite so," said Holmes. "I think it may be quite possible to keep the matter to ourselves, and also to prevent its recurrence now that we have a free hand. The key from the watch-chain, Mr. Bennett. Macphail will guard the patient and let us know if there is any change. Let us see what we can find in the professor's mysterious box."

There was not much, but there was enough—an empty phial, another nearly full, a hypodermic syringe, several letters in a crabbed, foreign hand. The marks on the envelopes showed that they were those which had disturbed the routine of the secretary, and each was dated from the Commercial Road and signed "A. Dorak." They were mere invoices to say that a fresh bottle was being sent to Professor Presbury, or receipt to acknowledge money. There was one other envelope, however, in a more educated hand and bearing the Austrian stamp with the postmark of Prague. "Here we have our material!" cried Holmes as he tore out the enclosure.

HONORED COLLEAGUE [*it ran*]:

Since your esteemed visit I have thought much of your case, and though in your circumstances there are some special reasons for the treatment, I would none the less enjoin caution, as my results have shown that it is not without danger of a kind.

It is possible that the serum of anthropoid would have been better. I have, as I explained to you, used black-faced langur because a specimen was accessible. Langur is, of course, a crawler and climber, while anthropoid walks erect and is in all ways nearer.

I beg you to take every possible precaution that there be no premature revelation of the process. I have one other client in England, and Dorak is my agent for both.

Weekly reports will oblige.

Yours with high esteem,<br>H. LOWENSTEIN.

Lowenstein! The name brought back to me the memory of some snippet from a newspaper which spoke of an obscure scientist who was striving in some unknown way for the secret of rejuvenescence and the elixir of life. Lowenstein of Prague! Lowenstein with the wondrous strength-giving serum, tabooed by the profession because he refused to reveal its source. In a few words I said what I remembered. Bennett had taken a manual of zoology from the shelves. "'Langur,'" he read, "'the great black-faced monkey of the Himalayan slopes, biggest and most human of climbing monkeys.' Many details are added. Well, thanks to you, Mr. Holmes, it is very clear that we have traced the evil to its source."

"The real source," said Holmes, "lies, of course, in that untimely love affair which gave our impetuous professor the idea that he could only gain his wish by turning himself into a younger man. When one tries to rise above Nature one is liable to fall below it. The highest type of man may revert to the animal if he leaves the straight road of destiny." He sat musing for a little with the phial in his hand, looking at the clear liquid within. "When I have written to this man and told him that I hold him criminally responsible for the poisons which he circulates, we will have no more trouble. But it may recur. Others may find a better way. There is danger there—a very real danger to humanity. Consider, Watson, that the material, the sensual, the worldly would all prolong their worthless lives. The spiritual would not avoid the call to something higher. It would be the survival of the least fit. What sort of cesspool may not our poor world become?" Suddenly the dreamer disappeared, and Holmes, the man of action, sprang from his chair. "I think there is nothing more to be said, Mr. Bennett. The various incidents will now fit themselves easily into the general scheme. The dog, of course, was aware of the change far more quickly than you. His smell would insure that. It was the monkey, not the professor, whom Roy attacked, just as it was the monkey who teased Roy. Climbing was a joy to the creature, and it was a mere chance, I take it, that the pastime brought him to the young lady's window. There is an early train to town, Watson, but I think we shall just have time for a cup of tea at the Chequers before we catch it."

# WHERE THE AIR
# QUIVERED

## BY L. T. MEADE & ROBERT EUSTACE

SHERLOCK HOLMES catapulted the short detective story into fame. During the late nineteenth century and the early twentieth century, torrents of short stories of murder and mystery flooded all the periodicals.

It was a period well described by one of the great women practitioners of the detective story, Dorothy Sayers: "In the century the vast, unexplored limits of the world began to shrink at an amazing and unprecedented rate. The electric telegraph circled the globe; railways brought remote villages into touch with civilization; photographs made known to the stay-at-homes the marvels of foreign landscapes, customs and animals; science reduced seeming miracles to mechanical marvels; popular education and improved policing made town and country safer for the common man than they had ever been. In place of the adventurer and the knight errant, popular imagination hailed the doctor, the scientist, and the policeman as saviors and protectors. But if one could no longer hunt the manticora, one could still hunt the murderer; if the armed escort had grown less necessary, yet one still needed the analyst to frustrate the wiles of the poisoner; from this point of view, the detective steps into his right place as the protector of the weak—the latest of the popular heroes, the true successor of Roland and Lancelot."

L. T. Meade was one of the products of this fascinating period. She turned her skill to the investigation of one of the great developments in the age, science, and was one of the pioneers in the medical mystery story. She often worked in collaboration with Robert Eustace, who was a doctor and often supplied thematic material. Everything was grist to their literary mill, murder by gas, by X rays, by acid, stories of hypnotism, catalepsy, somnambulism, insanity, and always murder most foul.  ॐ

WHEN MY daughter Vivien became engaged to Archie Forbes I naturally took a great interest in the circumstance. Vivien was my only child, and her mother had died at her birth. She was a handsome, bright, sensible girl, worthy to be the wife of any good fellow, and with as much pluck and common sense as I have ever seen in anyone.

Archie was a landed proprietor on a small scale, and had not a debt in the world; his past was a clean record, and his future was as bright as health, intelligence, and a fair amount of money could make it. He was devotedly attached to Vivien, and I gave my hearty consent to the engagement.

I am a doctor by profession, and thoroughly enjoy the life. In the ordinary course of things the physician comes into close contact with the stranger and rarer forms of human nature, and being myself a lover of all that is out of the common, this outlook weighed with me in my choice. After many years of hard work I secured an enormous practice, and when I settled down as a specialist in Harley Street I was already a wealthy man.

On a certain warm evening in June I sat smoking at the open window of my dining-room when Vivien entered.

She held a telegram in her hand.

"This has just come," she cried, in some excitement; "it is from Archie. He has returned, and will be here this evening."

She sat down as she spoke on the edge of the table, and put her slim hand affectionately on my shoulder.

"You won't be sorry to see him, Vi, will you?" was my answer.

"Sorry!" she cried. "I cannot tell you how thankful I am! You never supposed I was nervous, did you, father; but the fact is, I hated Archie going away with Jack Fletcher. Oh, I know that Jack is a right good fellow, but he is terribly wild and daring. Lately I have had most uncomfortable dreams about both of them. Yes, it is a relief to get this telegram. Archie promises to call about ten o'clock; how nice it will be to see him again!"

Her bright eyes sparkled as she spoke, and into them stole that radiant look which girls wear when they speak of the man they love best on earth.

"Ah! Vivien," I answered, "there are two sides to every question. Archie will be taking you away, and what shall I do?"

"You will have another home to go to," she replied; but her face suddenly became graver.

"I wonder what their adventures have been," she said, a moment later.

"They will tell you themselves before another hour is out," I answered. I glanced, as I spoke, at a small clock on the mantel-piece. Vivien gave a quick sigh and stood up. She was in full evening dress, of some soft, white texture, and wore a bunch of yellow roses at her belt.

"Aunt Mary wishes me to go with her to Lady Farrell's reception," she said; "but I will be back, if possible, within the hour."

"Well, go, my dear, and enjoy yourself," I answered, standing up and kissing her. "If Archie should arrive before you are back, I will get him to wait."

She slowly left the room. I lay back in my chair and thought over my girl's prospects. The moments flew quickly. Shortly after ten o'clock I heard the hall-door bell ring, and the next instant Archie burst into the room.

"Here you are, old fellow, and you are welcome," I said, grasping him by the hand.

He came to me hurriedly; his dress was in considerable disorder, and his face wore a wild and terribly disturbed expression. To my hearty grip of the hand he scarcely responded.

"Is anything wrong?" I said, giving him a quick glance.

"I am in awful trouble," was the reply. "Is Vivien in?"

"No, she is out with her aunt, but she got your telegram, and will be back almost immediately."

"I cannot see her; not just yet. Do you mind if I lock the door?"

"What is wrong, my dear fellow?"

"Oh, I am in terrible trouble," he repeated. He strode across the room as he spoke, turned the key in the lock, and then sank into the nearest chair.

"I want your advice and help badly, Dr. Kennedy," he continued.

"But, my dear boy, what is the matter? What has happened?"

He raised his sunburned face and looked at me gravely.

"Poor Jack is dead," he said then, in a broken sort of voice.

"Jack Fletcher!" I cried, springing to my feet.

"Yes, he died an hour ago, quite suddenly, at the Savoy Hotel, in his room. We got into London all right at six o'clock, and drove off to the Savoy at once. I never saw Jack in better spirits. We went to our rooms and had a wash and sat down to dinner at half-past seven. At half-past eight he went to his room for something. He did not come back, and after a time I followed him. I found his door locked and called to him, but he made no reply. In great alarm I went for help, and we had the door burst open. Jack was lying on the floor. Everything was done, of course. A doctor happened to be in the house, who applied all the usual restoratives, but it was too late; he was quite dead. My God, it is awful! I don't seem able to think. You must think for me, and come to the Savoy at once to see to things. What can have caused his death? You will come round, won't you?"

"Yes, I'll come," I replied. "I'll just scribble a note to Vivien first. It is fearfully sad. Death must have been caused by heart failure, of course."

I scribbled a few words on a card, laid it on the table to be given to my daughter, and then went into the hall. A few moments later Archie and I were on our way in a hansom to the Savoy.

"Of course, there will be an inquest," he said, "and you will be present, won't you, Dr. Kennedy? The death must have been due to natural causes."

"Why, of course," I answered, looking round at him in some surprise. "What do you mean?"

"Oh nothing, nothing," he said, "only it seems so strange. He was in the best of health and spirits."

"All the same, there may have been lesion of the heart," I answered; "but we shall soon know. You say you found the door of his room locked?"

"Yes, fast, and the key was within; the window was open, though."

"What had that to do with it?"

"Nothing." Archie hung his head. Painful as the occasion was, his gloom and depression seemed greater than the circumstances warranted.

We soon reached the hotel. I saw poor Fletcher's body. Until a post-mortem was made it was impossible to tell the cause of death, so I superintended all the details of the removal, sent off a wire and letter to the poor fellow's mother in Lancashire, and then rejoined Archie in his private sitting-room. I found him pacing up and down the room, a wild gleam in his eye, a restlessness about his manner which I had never observed before. Once more I thought that Jack Fletcher's death could scarcely account for the disordered state of his whole appearance.

"You must pull yourself together, my boy," I said. "Men have died suddenly before now. Of course it is fearfully sad, but you have got Vivien to think of."

"I don't want to see her to-night," he said eagerly.

"Why so?" I asked.

"She must be acquainted with the fact of Jack's death; it will upset her, and I—the fact is, I am completely done up; I don't know myself, doctor."

"Nor do I know you, Archie, in your present state. You must pull yourself together; and I tell you what, the very best thing you can do is to come away with me, and let us put you up for the night. Vivien will naturally expect to see you, whatever has happened, and the sooner you unburden your mind to her the better."

"My nerves are shaken to bits," he replied. "I have the strangest feeling about this whole matter. There is a cloud over me. The fact is, I don't believe Vivien and I will ever be married."

"Oh, nonsense, my dear fellow; come and have a talk with my sensible, matter-of-fact girl, and you will feel a new man. I am not going to leave you here, so come at once."

I got him to do so, but evidently with extreme unwillingness.

When we got home Vivien was waiting for us. She came into the hall. One glance into her face caused Archie to change color. He went up to her, kissed her, took her hand, and then dropped it again.

"Something very sad has happened, Vivien," I remarked, "and Archie wants to tell you. Take him into your private room, my love, and have a good talk."

"Come, Archie, this way," said the girl. She led him down one of the corridors, opened the door of her own sitting-room, and closed it behind them.

"This is a queer affair," I could not help murmuring to myself. "Strange and disastrous as Jack Fletcher's death is, I am more disturbed about Archie. What can be the matter with him?"

The next day, with the consent of the coroner, I assisted at the autopsy. I need not go into details, but merely state at once that, after two hours' careful and most minute investigation, the cause of Jack Fletcher's death still remained an absolute mystery. Every organ was sound, there was no wound anywhere, and not a trace of poison was discovered. Dr. Benjamin Curtis, the skilled pathologist and analyst, was present, and the last sentence of his exhaustive report I append herewith:—

"There is absolutely nothing to account for the cause of death; and the only remaining alternative is that it was probably due to some very severe nervous shock of central origin, the nature of which is wholly obscure."

I flung the report down in annoyance, and went to meet Archie, who was waiting for me outside the coroner's court. I told him what Dr. Curtis had said. To my astonishment his face turned ashy white, and he almost reeled as he walked.

"Then it is as I thought," he said.

"What do you think?" I said. "Forbes, you are keeping something from us; you have something on your mind. What is wrong?"

"Nothing, nothing," he said, hurriedly. "I hoped the coroner would find a cause for death. Dr. Curtis's report has upset me."

I asked a few more questions, and felt now absolutely convinced that Forbes was concealing something. Whatever it was, he was determined to keep it to himself. I went home considerably troubled.

A week after poor Jack's funeral, Vivien came into my consulting-room. Archie had only been to the house once, and on that occasion he could not be got to say a word with regard to their approaching marriage.

"Now, father," said my girl, closing the door, and coming up and planting herself in front of me, "there is something wrong, and you have got to find out what it is."

I looked full into her eyes; they were brighter than usual, and had a suspicion of tears about them.

"Archie is terribly changed," she said; "you must have noticed it."

"I have," I answered, in a low tone.

"I know he was very much attached to Jack," continued Vivien, "but this is no ordinary grief. There is something terrible weighing on his mind. If I did not know that he was a thoroughly brave fellow, I should say that he was oppressed by a fearful sense of overmastering fear. It cannot be that. What, then, can it be?"

I made no answer. She continued to stand upright before me, and to keep her eyes fixed on my face.

"What can it be?" she repeated. "I puzzle myself over the whole thing day and night. I don't believe he is tired of me."

"Assuredly that is not the case," was my quick response.

"But all the same, he is completely changed," she continued. "Before he went on this cruise, he was devoted to me—each moment in my presence was paradise to him—now it may be likened to purgatory. He is restless until he gets away from me. When he is with me he is unhappy and *distrait*. In short, there is something terribly wrong, and you must help me to find out what it is."

"Ask him yourself, my dear. I have seen just what you have seen, but cannot get him to say a word."

"I am glad you agree with me," she said, the gloom of her brow lightening for a moment. "I will write to him at once and ask him to come here."

She had scarcely said the words before the door was opened and Forbes himself came in.

"Ah, that's right, Archie," I cried, in a tone of relief. "Come over here, dear fellow, and sit down. The fact is, Vivien is thoroughly unhappy. She sees that there is something wrong with you, and is discontented with the present state of matters. You have something on your mind, and you ought to tell us what it is."

Forbes raised two lack-luster eyes and fixed them on the girl's face. The tears which were close to her gray eyes now brimmed over.

"Archie," she said, going to him and laying her hand on his shoulder, "I want to ask you a plain question. Would you like our engagement to be broken off?"

"I was coming here to propose it, Vivien," was his strange reply.

She turned very white, and fell back as if someone had dealt her a blow.

"Good God!" she said. "It is then as I feared; there is something terribly wrong."

"It is not that I do not love you as much as ever," continued the poor fellow; "but I have no right to bind you to me. I scarcely dare to tell you what has happened. I am unworthy of you, Vivien, and besides, I am doomed. It is only a matter of time."

He flung himself into the nearest chair, and covered his face with two hands which trembled from nervous terror.

I nodded to Vivien.

"You had better leave him with me for a few moments," I said.

"No, I will not," she answered, desperately. "I have a right to know the truth, and I am determined to get at it. What is wrong, Archie? You are not tired of me? You still love me, don't you?"

"With all my heart and soul," he groaned.

"And yet you want our engagement to be broken off! Why?"

"Because I am a guilty and doomed man," was his reply.

I started and felt my heart beat. Was it possible? But no—I flung the unworthy suspicion from me.

"I ought not to be in this house," continued Archie. "I ought not to have let you kiss me the night we came home. I am unworthy of you, and yet . . . My God! this misery is driving me mad."

He pushed back the hair from his forehead; there were beads of perspiration on his brow.

"If we were engaged fifty times over, our wedding would have never come off," he continued, speaking in the most reckless, exicted tone. "I can no more prevent the fate which is hanging over me, than I can get rid of that thing which has stained me. I can only say this: As Jack died so I shall die. I am doomed, and the less you have to say to me the better."

"Now, that is all nonsense," she said, in her quick way, which could, at times of intense emotion, be wonderfully matter-of-fact, and, therefore, soothing. "Whatever you have done you must tell me and you must tell Father, and you must allow us to judge as to whether it is a barrier between you and me or not. As to my love, you must have a very poor opinion of it if you think I would forsake you in an hour of trouble. Women who care for a man do not leave him when he is down. I am a woman, and, I hope, a brave one. I mean to comfort you, and to stay by you to the last, whatever has happened; yes, *whatever* has happened."

He looked at her with incredulous eyes, into which just a flicker of hope returned.

"You cannot mean it?" he cried.

"Yes, I do mean it; but I want your whole confidence, and so does Father. You are concealing something. You must tell us at once."

"Yes, speak, Archie," I said, gravely. "Vivien, my girl, come here and stand by me. Archie, this is no ordinary case. Vivien and I will deal with you with all fairness, only we must know the absolute truth."

"I meant to tell you some days ago," said Archie, fixing his eyes on my face, "but somehow I could not get the pluck. The whole thing is so horrible, and the burden on my conscience so great, that I am overcome by a ghastly fear. I cannot fight against it."

"Well, speak," I said, with impatience.

"It is the queerest thing on earth," he said slowly. "It has half stunned me. Though I consider myself pretty tough, the whole thing has knocked the pluck clean out of me."

He paused to wet his dry lips, and continued:—

"You know we were in the Mediterranean cruising about for six weeks?"

I nodded.

"We were just about to come home, when Fletcher, who was always up to a lark, suggested that we should go through the Canal, down to Jeddah, and then on to Mecca, to see the pilgrims. They would be all there, as it was the twelfth month of the Mohammedan year. I did

not mind, so we went. We left the yacht at Jeddah, and went on to
Mecca. The place was one mass of pilgrims. They were on their way to
the Kaaba, the oblong stone building within the great Mosque. You
have heard of it, of course, and also of the famous lava-like Black
Stone, to which all Moslems turn in their prayers. It was in the north-
east corner of the building. The place was in a sort of uproar, for it is a
part of the faith of every good Moslem to kiss that stone once in the
course of his life. Well, Dr. Kennedy, you would scarcely believe it,
but Fletcher, when he got into the midst of this throng, seemed to turn
quite mad. He lost his head, and insisted that we should go and see the
whole show. He intended to kiss the Black Stone, if he could. Of course,
I knew we should run into the most fearful danger, and did my best to
dissuade him, but nothing would do; go he would. He said to me:—

"'You may stay away, old boy; you are engaged to be married, and
perhaps ought to consider your life a little bit, but with me it is different.
When I want a lark, I must have it at all risks. I am going; you can
please yourself.'

"Of course, I didn't relish running the risk of being torn to pieces, but
I wasn't the fellow to see him start off alone, so at last I agreed to go
with him. We put on the *Ihram*, the woolen thing worn by the Arabs
around the waist and shoulders, got some sandals, and went bareheaded
with the crowd of pilgrims to the Mosque. We joined the procession
and managed to get right inside, and Jack got inside the Kaaba and
went up to the north-east corner of the building and kissed the Black
Stone. He told me afterwards that it is quite worn away with the kisses
of millions of human beings. I missed him in the crowd, and just as I
was looking around to see where he could have got to, I noticed one of
the Mueddins, or priests, watching me closely, and when his eyes met
mine, I can tell you I shuddered. From the moment they singled me out
he seemed never to take his gaze away, and I shall not, to my dying day,
forget the expression of cruel, fierce suspicion that was stamped on
his face, which was rendered hideous by being deeply pitted with small-
pox.

"Well, Jack turned up, and we got out all right; and Jack, poor fellow!
was in the best spirits. He said it was the biggest lark he had ever en-

joyed, and he did nothing but laugh at my fears. I told him about the priest, and said I was certain we had been discovered, but he made nothing of it.

"When we got out we were in an awful crowd, and our donkeys could scarcely move. We had just cleared the thickest of the mob, and I was hoping we were safe, when I noticed the priest, who had already observed me in the Mosque, detach himself from the crowd and move swiftly towards us. It was now nearly dark. I saw that he wanted to speak and, not knowing why I did it, reined in my donkey. He came up to my side. In his left hand he held a parchment scroll, and as I took it I saw his right hand steal down to his belt. There was the flash of steel. In an instant I should have been stabbed. I do not know what came over me; there was a ringing in my ears, and my head seemed to swim. I leaned quickly over the donkey and plunged my long hunting-knife with all my force into the man's heart. He fell without a groan. I touched Jack on the arm. We galloped madly and for our lives. The mob followed us, but we outpaced them, and at last their howls and shouts grew fainter and fainter behind us. We reached Jeddah in safety, got on board, and steamed away with all possible speed.

"'Why in the name of Heaven did you kill him, Archie?' said Jack to me then.

"'He would have killed us if we had not killed him,' was my reply, but while I spoke there was a dead-weight at my heart, and wherever I turned I seemed to see the dying eyes of the man, and to hear the thud of his body as he fell to the ground.

"'Have you got the parchment he put into your hand?' continued Jack.

"I had. He took it from me and opened it. It had some writing on it in Arabic, which we could both read and speak. Jack copied it out in English and here it is."

As he spoke Archie produced from his pocket-book a piece of parchment and an old envelope, and read as follows: "The vengeance of Mahomet rests upon the two infidels and unbelievers who have profaned the Prophet. Their days are numbered, and before the sun rise on the Festival of Eed-Al-Kurban in the month of Dsul Heggeh they will be no more."

"There," said Archie standing up, "that is what was written; and now, Dr. Kennedy, that I have had courage to tell you my story, I want to ask you a question. Do you think it is within the bounds of probability, or even possibility, that poor Fletcher's sudden death could have had any connection with this affair?"

"Absolutely out of the question," was my first remark, but then I paused to think the situation over.

"You certainly did a mad thing," I said then; "not only did you profane the religious rights of these fanatics, but you, in especial, killed one of their priests. Under such circumstances there is little doubt that they would do much to compass their revenge, but that they would follow you both to England seems on the face of it ridiculous. No, no, Archie; it is an unpleasant business, and I am sorry you did not tell me before, but that Jack's death has anything to do with that paper is the wildest fiction."

"I do not believe you," he answered. "I am firmly convinced that the Mueddin whom I killed will be revenged. Jack is already dead and the words of the prophecy will come true, with regard to me. I shall not live after sunrise on the festival of Eed-Al-Kurban, whenever that is."

While he was speaking Vivien had remained absolutely quiet. She went up to him now, and put her hand on his shoulder.

"Why do you touch me?" he said, starting away from her. "I have that man's blood on my hands."

"You did it in self-defense," she answered.

"But we must not think of that at all now. Father"—she turned to me—"I agree with Archie: I believe that his life is in grave danger. We must save him; that is our present business. Nothing else can be thought of until his life is safe."

"I have one thing more to say," continued Archie. "Last night I saw one of the Mueddins in London. I knew him; I could not mistake him; he resembled the priest I had killed. He was standing under a lamp-post, opposite St. George's Hospital. He fixed his eyes on my face. I believe he is the man who compassed poor Jack's death, and mine is only a matter of time."

"Come, come, this is nonsense," I answered. "Fletcher was not murdered."

"What did he die of?" asked Archie, gloomily. "You say yourself that he was thoroughly healthy; he was in the prime of youth. Do healthy men in the prime of youth die suddenly without any discoverable cause? I ask you a straight question."

"The death was a strange one," I could not help replying.

"Very strange," echoed Vivien, "strange enough," she added, "to account for Archie's fears. The Moslems have threatened the deaths of both Archie and Jack. Jack is dead. Archie is the most guilty man of the two, for he killed their priest. They will certainly not leave a stone unturned to kill him."

"Yes, my days are numbered," said Forbes; "there is no getting over the fact. Vivien, our engagement must come to an end, and in any case I feel now that I have no right to marry you."

Vivien's brows contracted in a nervous frown.

"We will not talk of our marriage at present," she said, with some impatience; "but why should we not consult Dr. Khan?"

"Dr. Khan!" I cried. "Do you mean the Persian?"

"Yes; why should not we all three go to him at once? He knows much more about these Arabs and their queer ways and their sorceries than anyone else in London."

"Upon my word, it is a capital idea," I said. "Khan does know strange things, and is up to all the lore of the East. He is in some ways one of the cleverest follows I know. He does not practice, but he has gone in for chemical research and forensic medicine as a hobby. There is no one in London whose opinion would be of more value in a difficult case like the present, and, being a Mohammedan by religion, he can help us with the side issues of this most extraordinary affair. Archie, you have to pull yourself together, my boy, if for no other reason, for Vivien's sake. Come, we will go down to Professor Khan's chambers in Gray's Inn at once, and tell him the whole story."

"And Dr. Khan is a special friend of mine," said Vivien, brightly. "Oh, now that we are doing something to help you, Archie, I can live."

I crossed the room to order the carriage. As I did so I heard Archie say to her, in a low tone:—

"And you love me still?"

"I love you still," was her reply.

He drew himself up; the color returned to his ashen cheeks and the light to his eyes.

In half an hour we were all driving to Hussein Khan's chambers, in Gray's Inn. When we reached them I rang the outer bell. It seemed ages before anyone came. At last the door was opened by an old housekeeper, in his shirt sleeves. He recognized me, and nodded when I spoke to him.

"Is Dr. Khan in?" I asked.

"Yes, sir; you know your way," was the answer.

We hurried up the uncarpeted stairs to the second floor, and pressed the electric bell. There was the sound of the latch being drawn back inside; I pushed the panel, and we all three entered; the door closed automatically behind us, and stretched on the sofa at the far end of a long room, in a loose dressing-gown and slippers, lay the Persian. He was smoking a long opium pipe. The moment his eyes rested upon Vivien he put down the pipe and stood up. He looked us all over with heavy, lusterless eyes, and nodded slowly. He was evidently only half awake.

"I am sorry to disturb you, Professor," I said, apologetically. "You know my daughter, of course?"

Vivien came forward and offered her hand. Khan bent over it, and then raised it respectfully to his lips.

"I have not forgotten Miss Vivien," he said.

"I have come here to-day because I am in great trouble, and because I want your advice," she said at once. "It has to do with this gentleman. May I introduce him? Mr. Forbes—Dr. Khan."

Dr. Khan slowly turned his heavy eyes in Archie's direction. He looked him all over from head to foot, and then, rather to my astonishment, I observed a lightning look of intelligence and remarkable interest fill his eyes.

"Has the trouble anything to do with Mr. Forbes?" he said, glancing at Vivien.

"It has."

"Then I believe I may help you. Sit down, sir, pray; and tell me at once what is the matter."

Archie told his strange tale. While he spoke I closely watched the effect on my friend; but, once the narrative had begun, the expression on the Persian's face never altered. After that first glance of interest, it had settled down into a stolid, Oriental indifference.

"What do you think of it all?" I said, as Archie ceased to speak.

"Let me examine the parchment, please," he replied, with deliberate composure.

Archie gave it to him. He took it and read it over and over again, muttering the words to himself.

"You could find no cause for your friend's death?"

"None."

"You are quite certain, Mr. Forbes, that the man you saw yesterday outside St. George's Hospital was one of the Mueddins whom you had already noticed in the Mosque?"

"Quite."

"Well, my dear friend, I am sorry to say it looks a very queer business."

"And do you really believe that Jack's death was the work of the Mueddin?" I cried, aghast at his words.

"No; I only say that it is quite possible. I recall a similar case; the same thing may happen again. The Arabians, upon whose early researches the whole science of Europe was founded, possess, of course, secrets unknown to our Western scientists of the present day. I have seen some strange things done by them. The act of sacrilege you both committed was one of the gravest offenses possible, but it is just within the realm of possibility that such a crime might have been looked over; but as you, my friend, killed one of the priests as well, the Mohammedans whom you so deeply insulted would not leave a stone unturned to compass your end. The marvel is that you escaped immediate death. But now let us quite clearly sum up the position as it stands."

As he spoke the Persian stood up. He remained quiet for a moment thinking deeply, then he crossed the room and took down a volume in Arabic from a shelf. With pencil and paper he began working some calculations, referring now and then to an almanac, and once to a map of Asia.

We all three watched him in intense silence. After a moment or two he looked up.

"Assuming for the sake of argument that the Mueddin whom you saw last night has undertaken this work of revenge," he continued, "the position is this. Owing to the Arabs' year being a lunar one, the festival of Eed-Al-Kurban does not occur at the same date each year. I see, however, that it will commence according to our calendar to-morrow, the 8th of June, at daybreak, or Subh. At daybreak or Subh the first call to prayer is given by the Mueddin from the Mosque. Now, Mecca is exactly 40 degrees longitude east of Greenwich, and, therefore, day will break with them two hours and forty minutes earlier than with us—that is, at seven minutes past one o'clock to-morrow morning. Of course, the Mueddin, whom you believe to have followed you, would know all this. And as, according to the words of the parchment, you are both to be dead *before* sunrise on the festival of Eed-Al-Kurban, so also, *failing* the fulfillment of this vow, you are perfectly safe when that hour has passed."

"Then you believe that Archie is in grave danger until after one o'clock to-morrow morning?" exclaimed Vivien.

"That is my belief," answered Dr. Khan, bowing to her.

"But all this is most unsatisfactory," I cried, getting up. "Surely, Dr. Khan, even granted that it is as you say, we can easily protect Forbes. He has but to stay quietly at home until the hour of danger is past. These Arabs are not magicians: they cannot hurt a man in his own house, for instance?"

"How was it your friend died?" said the Persian, looking full into Archie's face.

"That I cannot say," was the reply.

Dr. Khan shrugged his shoulders.

"You declare that the Arabs are not magicians," he said, turning to me, "but that is just the point. They *are!* I can tell you things which I have seen with my own eyes which happened in Arabia that you would find hard to believe."

"Very likely," I answered, "but they require the Oriental stage and surroundings for the exhibition of the so-called phenomena. They cannot use magic within the four-mile radius of Charing Cross, under the vigilant eye of the Metropolitan police."

Dr. Khan did not immediately answer. He remained motionless in deep thought.

"What do you intend to do to-night?" he said then, turning to Archie.

"I have made no plans," was the low, indifferent reply. "I am so certain of my impending end," he continued, "that nothing seems to make any difference."

"You must come home with us, Archie," cried Vivien. "Dr. Khan declares that after one o'clock you are safe. Until one o'clock you must be with us; and suppose, Dr. Khan," she added, "you come too? Suppose we spend this momentous evening together? What do you say, Father?"

Before I could answer the Persian said, slowly:—

"I was going to ask you to invite me. Yes, I will come, with pleasure."

"One more question," said Vivien; "you do firmly believe that Archie will be safe *after* one o'clock to-morrow morning?"

"Yes; the words on the parchment point distinctly to his death on or before the commencement of the festival. The Mohammedans keep their vows to the letter, or not at all."

As he spoke Dr. Khan got up slowly, went into his bedroom, and reappeared ready dressed for the evening. It was already nearly seven o'clock. We got into my carriage and returned to Harley Street. I sent a servant for Archie's evening dress to the hotel, and at eight o'clock we found ourselves seated round the dinner-table. It was a strange and silent meal, and I do not think we any of us had much appetite.

I am naturally not a superstitious man, but matters were sufficiently queer and out-of-the-way to excite a certain foreboding which I could neither account for nor dismiss. The Persian looked utterly calm and indifferent, as betokened his race. But I noticed that from time to time he fixed his deep-set, brilliant eyes on Forbes's haggard face, as if he would read him through.

The night happened to be the hottest of that year. There was not a breath of air, and the heat inside the house was stifling.

When dinner was over, Vivien suggested that we should go into my smoking-room. The house was a corner one, and the windows of the smoking-room were on the ground floor, and looked into a side street.

She seated herself by Archie's side. He took little or no notice of her. Khan continued to give him anxious glances from time to time. Vivien was restless, often rising from her seat.

"Sit down, Miss Vivien," said Dr. Khan, suddenly. "I know exactly what you feel, but the time will soon pass. Let me tell you something interesting."

She shook her head. It was almost beyond her power to listen. The gloomy face of her lover, the slightly bent figure which had been so athletic and upright, the change in the whole man, absorbed her entire attention.

"Save him—give him back to me if you can," was the unspoken wish in her eyes, as they fixed themselves for a moment on Dr. Khan's face.

He gave her a strange smile, and then turning addressed me. He was the most brilliant talker I ever met, and on this occasion he roused all the power of his great intellect to make his conversation interesting. He related some of his own experiences in the East, and made many marvelous revelations with regard to modern science.

Eleven and twelve chimed from a neighboring church clock. Soon after midnight the Persian, who had been silent for several moments, said, suddenly, "During this last hour of suspense, I should like to put out the electric light."

As he spoke he crossed the room, and was about to switch off the current when our attention was suddenly attracted to Vivien. She had sunk back in her seat with a deep sigh. The intense heat of the room had been too much for her.

"Air! Air!" I cried.

Archie laid his hand on the heavy sash of one of the windows and raised it. There seemed to be a hush everywhere—I had never known so still a night. But just at that instant I saw—or fancied I saw—the tassel of the blind move, as though the air had quivered.

The next instant Khan uttered a sharp cry.

"He is there—he has done it—I thought so!"

The words died on his lips, for Archie Forbes reeled, clutched wildly at the lintel of the window, and then with a heavy thud lay like a log on the floor.

I had always looked upon the Persian as a man of exceptional promptitude and great strength of character, but never for a moment had I realized his lightning grasp of an emergency.

"Artificial respiration—don't lose a moment. Take his chest, man; we shall save him!" he cried. As he spoke he leaped through the open window, vaulted the railings, and was in the street.

The shock acted upon Vivien like a charm. With her assistance I tore open Forbes's collar and shirt, and began applying artificial respiration with all my might. In less than a minute the Persian came back. He carried a small box in his hand.

"The solution of the mystery," he said. "I will explain presently. Now to save him. I believe we shall do it."

He fell on his knees and helped me with the artificial respiration with all his might. For five long minutes there was not the slightest result. Then there came a feeble gasp. It was followed by another. We redoubled our efforts and waited for a moment. Forbes began to breathe again; we drew back and dashed the sweat from our streaming faces.

"He will do now," whispered Khan; "leave him quiet."

"What is it? For God's sake, what is it?" I said, as soon as I could get my voice to speak.

"I will tell you. This has been the most dastardly and awful thing. I have been trying to get at the solution the whole evening, and just grasped it as Mr. Forbes stood up to open that window. I was too late. He got what they meant for him, but he will do. Yes, his pulse is stronger."

I laid my hand on the victim's wrist: the beats came more regularly each moment, though he was still only half-conscious.

"But what can it be?" I cried; "what have you discovered?"

Khan's eyes were blazing with excitement.

"What has happened?" I continued. "A bullet through the brain could not have been more instantaneous; but, silent and unseen, before our very eyes the blow fell and left no trace. This is magic with a vengeance."

"I will explain it," said Khan. "I have been hammering out the solution all the evening, and, fool that I was, never suspected the real thing until just too late. Look here—here is something that your modern scientific criminal has never dreamed of."

"But what the deuce is it?" I said, examining a small box in much bewilderment which Khan now placed in my hands. Three of the sides and the top and bottom were made of wood, but across one end was stretched some material which looked like indiarubber. At the opposite end to this was a small circular opening, which could be closed by a hinged flap.

"Explain what this means, for God's sake," I cried. As I spoke I bent my nose towards the box, and instantly was seized by a catching sensation at the back of the throat.

"Ah, you had better not come too close to it," cried Khan. "This box contained the most deadly gas known to modern chemists: the vapor of concentrated anhydrous hydrogen cyanide."

I started back. Well did I know the action of this most infernally potent and deadly gas. Still, the mystery of how the gas reached Forbes was unexplained.

"How was it done?" I cried, staring at Khan in absolute bewilderment.

"Simply in this way," he answered. As he spoke he lit a cigarette, and at the same time laid his hand on the box. "The poison was projected as a vortex ring in the marvellous and mysterious rotational motion which vortex rings assume. This motion can be imparted to gas, but even scientists of the present day cannot explain it, although the study has given rise to Thompson's fascinating theory on the constitution of matter. All we know is this," continued Khan, "that, projected by the operator, a ring of that gas would move through the air as a solid body, and would burst as true as a shot from a rifle, and slay as quickly, only it would be perfectly silent and invisible. When made with smoke these rings are visible, of course, and we can watch their motion—so." He shot a ring of cigarette smoke from his mouth, and I watched it as it sailed across the room and burst at last into curling wreaths.

"With this apparatus," he continued, pointing to the box, "an enormous velocity could be given to a vortex ring. Even in broad daylight its approach could not be seen, and, breaking on the mouth and nostrils of a man, it would instantly kill him unless artificial respiration were immediately resorted to. Yes," he added, "the modern detective has a lot to learn."

"But the man who did it?" I cried.

"Gone! We shall never see or hear of him again. He must have seen me when I leapt from the window, and dropped the box in his hasty flight. Of course he followed us here, and crept up to the open window. This was the Mueddin's chance—he projected the vortex ring straight into Archie's face. Thank Heaven, the instant remedies employed have saved him. One second's delay, and he must have died."

Forbes had now staggered to a sitting posture, and Vivien had fallen on her knees by his side.

"Leave us alone, father," she said to me; "yes, leave us alone for a little."

And the Persian and I slowly left the room.

My girl is now married to Archie Forbes. She loves him, as only such women can love. He has recovered his manhood and his pluck, but there is a shadow on his face which I think will stay there while he lives.

# Footsteps in the Supernatural: Sheridan Lefanu, Ambrose Bierce, and Amelia Edwards (The Golden Age of the Ghost Story)

# MADAM CROWL'S GHOST

## BY SHERIDAN LEFANU

THE VICTORIAN period was particularly appreciative of the ghost story, but the ghost has always been one of the most enduring figures in supernatural fiction. The ghost was at home in ancient Greece, the Middle Ages; he or she appeared ethereally and pitifully in gothic romance; more aggressively in stories of today.

One of the greatest of all writers in the ghostly vein was an Irishman, Joseph Sheridan LeFanu.

LeFanu was a brilliant scholar. He inundated himself in the occult, in theosophical and religious studies, and in the history of magic. His ghost stories—he wrote about thirty of them in a period of ten years—also were some of the first to have a psychological background. LeFanu was always aware of the dark parts of the mind that make the supernatural story so haunting. He was also influenced by the growth of mystical societies in Ireland, which would culminate in the affection for the supernatural that was represented by such great writers as William Butler Yeats.

Not only did he write short stories, but he wrote fourteen novels, most of them all forgotten. His supernatural tales, however, are still widely appreciated by the aficionados of the ghost story. Henry James said that there should always be a LeFanu story for the bed table, "The ideal reading in a country house for the hours after midnight."  &

TWENTY YEARS have passed since you last saw Mrs. Jolliffe's tall slim figure. She is now past seventy, and can't have many mile-stones more to count on the journey that will bring her to her long home. The hair has grown white as snow, that is parted under her cap, over her shrewd, but kindly face. But her figure is still straight, and her step light and active.

She has taken of late years to the care of adult invalids, having surrendered to younger hands the little people who inhabit cradles, and crawl on all-fours. Those who remember that good-natured face among the earliest that emerge from the darkness of non-entity, and who owe to their first lessons in the accomplishment of walking, and a delighted appreciation of their first babblings and earliest teeth, have "spired up" into tall lads and lasses, now. Some of them shrew streaks of white by this time, in brown locks, "the bonny gouden" hair, that she was so proud to brush and shew to admiring mothers, who are seen no more on the green of Golden Friars, and whose names are traced now on the flat gray stones in the church-yard.

So the time is ripening some, and searing others; and the saddening and tender sunset hour has come; and it is evening with the kind old north-country dame, who nursed pretty Laura Mildmay, who now stepping into the room, smiles so gladly, and throws her arms around the old woman's neck, and kisses her twice.

"Now, this is so lucky!" said Mrs. Jenner, "you have just come in time to hear a story."

"Really! That's delightful."

"Na, na, od wite it! no story, ouer true for that, I sid it a wi my aan eyen. But the barn here, would not like, at these hours, just goin' to her bed, to hear tell of freets and boggarts."

"Ghosts? The very thing of all others I should most likely to hear of."

"Well, dear," said Mrs. Jenner, "if you are not afraid, sit ye down here, with us."

"She was just going to tell me all about her first engagement to attend a dying old woman," says Mrs. Jenner, "and of the ghost she saw there. Now, Mrs. Jolliffe, make your tea first, and then begin."

The good woman obeyed, and having prepared a cup of that companionable nectar, she sipped a little, drew her brows slightly together to collect her thoughts, and then looked up with a wondrous solemn face to begin.

Good Mrs. Jenner, and the pretty girl, each gazed with eyes of solemn expectation in the face of the old woman, who seemed to gather awe from the recollections she was summoning.

The old room was a good scene for such a narrative, with the oak-wainscoting, quaint, and clumsy furniture, the heavy beams that crossed its ceiling, and the tall four-post bed, with dark curtains, within which you might imagine what shadows you please.

Mrs. Jolliffe cleared her voice, rolled her eyes slowly around, and began her tale in these words:

"I'm an ald woman now, and I was but thirteen, my last birthday, the night I came to Applewale House. My aunt was the housekeeper there, and a sort o' one-horse carriage was down at Lexhoe waitin' to take me and my box up to Applewale.

"I was a bit frightened by the time I got to Lexhoe, and when I saw the carriage and horse, I wished myself back again with my mother at Hazelden. I was crying when I got into the 'shay'—that's what we used to call it—and old John Mulbery that drove it, and was a good-natured fellow, bought me a handful of apples at the Golden Lion to cheer me up a bit; and he told me that there was a currant-cake, and tea, and pork chops, waiting for me, all hot, in my aunt's room at the great house. It was a fine moonlight night, and I eat the apples, lookin' out o' the shay winda.

"It's a shame for gentlemen to frighten a poor foolish child like I was. I sometimes think it might be tricks. There was two on 'em on the tap o' the coach beside me. And they began to question me after nightfall, when the moon rose, where I was going to. Well, I told them it was to wait on Dame Arabella Crowl, of Applewale House, near by Lexhoe.

" 'Ho, then,' says one of them, 'you'll not be long there!'

"And I looked at him as much as to say 'Why not?' for I had spoken out when I told them where I was goin', as if 'twas something clever I hed to say.

"'Because,' says he, 'and don't you for your life tell no one, only watch her and see—she's possessed by the devil, and more an half a ghost. Have you got a Bible?'

"'Yes, sir,' says I. For my mother put my little Bible in my box, and I knew it was there: and by the same token, though the print's too small for my ald eyes, I have it in my press to this hour.

"As I looked up at him saying 'Yes, sir,' I thought I saw him winkin' at his friend; but I could not be sure.

"'Well,' says he, 'be sure you put it under your bolster every night, it will keep the ald girl's claws aff ye.'

"And I got such a fright when he said that, you wouldn't fancy! And I'd a liked to ask him a lot about the ald lady, but I was too shy, and he and his friend began talkin' together about their own consarns, and dowly enough I got down, as I told ye, at Lexhoe. My heart sank as I drove into the dark avenue. The trees stand very thick and big, as ald as the ald house almost, and four people, with their arms out and fingertips touchin', barely girds round some of them.

"Well my neck was stretched out o' the winda, looking for the first view o' the great house; and all at once we pulled up in front of it.

"A great white-and-black house it is, wi' great black beams across and right up it, and gables lookin' out, as white as a sheet, to the moon, and the shadows o' the trees, two or three up and down in front, you could count the leaves on them, and all the little diamond-shaped winda-panes, glimmering on the great hall winda, and great shutters, in the old fashion, hinged on the wall outside, boulted across all the rest o' the windas in front, for there was but three or four servants, and the old lady in the house, and most o' t'rooms was locked up.

"My heart was in my mouth when I sid the journey was over, and this the great house afoore me, and I sa near my aunt that I never sid till noo, and Dame Crowl, that I was come to wait upon, and was afeard on already.

"My aunt kissed me in the hall, and brought me to her room. She was tall and thin, wi' a pale face and black eyes, and long thin hands wi' black mittins on. She was pasty fifty, and her word was short; but her word was law. I hev no complaints to make of her; but she was a hard woman, and I think she would hev bin kinder to me if I had bin her sister's child in place of her brother's. But all that's o' no consequence noo.

"The squire—his name was Mr. Chevenix Crowl, he was Dame Crowl's grandson—came down there, by way of seeing that the old lady was well treated, about twice or thrice in the year. I sid him but twice all the time I was at Applewale House.

"I can't say but she was well taken care of, notwithstanding; but that was because my aunt and Meg Wyvern, that was her maid, had a conscience, and did their duty by her.

"Mrs. Wyvern—Meg Wyvern my aunt called her to herself, and Mrs. Wyvern to me—was a fat, jolly lass of fifty, a good height and a good breadth, always good-humoured and walked slow. She had fine wages, but she was a bit stingy, and kept all her fine clothes under lock and key, and wore, mostly, a twilled chocolate cotton, wi' red, and yellow, and green sprigs and balls on it, and it lasted wonderful.

"She never gave me nout, not the vally o' a brass thimble, all the time I was there; but she was good-humored, and always laughin', and she talked no end o' proas over her tea; and, seeing me sa sackless and dowly, she roused me up wi' her laughin' and stories; and I think I liked her better than my aunt—children is so taken wi' a bit o' fun or a story— though my aunt was very good to me, but a hard woman about some things, and silent always.

"My aunt took me into her bedchamber, that I might rest myself a bit while she was settin' the tea in her room. But first, she patted me on the shouther, and said I was a tall lass o' my years, and has spired up well, and asked me if I could do plain work and stitchin'; and she looked in my face, and said I was like my father, her brother, that was dead and gone, and she hoped I was a better Christian, and wad na du a' that lids (would not do anything of that sort).

"It was a hard sayin' the first time I set foot in her room, I thought.

"When I went into the next room, the housekeeper's room—very comfortable, yak (oak) all round—there was a fine fire blazin' away, wi' coal, and peat, and wood, all in a low together, and tea on the table, and hot cake, and smokin' meat; and there was Mrs. Wyvern, fat, jolly, and talkin' away, more in an hour than my aunt would in a year.

"While I was still at my tea my aunt went upstairs to see Madam Crowl.

"'She's agone up to see that old Judith Squailes is awake,' says Mrs. Wyvern. 'Judith sits with Madam Crowl when me and Mrs. Shutters'—that was my aunt's name—'is away. She's a troublesome old lady. Ye'll hev to be sharp wi' her, or she'll be into the fire, or out o' t' winda. She goes on wires, she does, old though she be.'

"'How old, ma'am?' says I.

"'Ninety-three her last birthday, and that's eight months gone,' says she; and she laughed. 'And don't be askin' questions about her before your aunt—mind, I tell ye; just take her as you find her, and that's all.'

"'And what's to be my business about her, please, ma'am?' says I.

"'About the old lady? Well,' says she, 'your aunt, Mrs. Shutters, will tell you that; but I suppose you'll hev to sit in the room with your work, and see she's at no mischief, and let her amuse herself with her things on the table, and get her food or drink as she calls for it, and keep her out o' mischief, and ring the bell hard if she's troublesome.'

"'Is she deaf, ma'am?'

"'No, nor blind,' says she; 'as sharp as a needle, but she's gone quite aupy, and can't remember nout rightly; and Jack the Giant Killer, or Goody Twoshoes will please her as well as the king's court, or the affairs of the nation.'

"'And what did the little girl go away for, ma'am, that went on Friday last? My aunt wrote to my mother she was to go.'

"'Yes; she's gone.'

"'What for?' says I again.

"'She didn't answer Mrs. Shutters, I do suppose,' says she. 'I don't know. Don't be talkin'; your aunt can't abide a talkin' child.'

"'And please, ma'am, is the old lady well in health?' says I.

"'It ain't no harm to ask that,' says she. 'She's torflin a bit lately, but better this week past, and I dare say she'll last out her hundred years yet. Hish! Here's your aunt coming down the passage.'

In comes my aunt, and begins talkin' to Mrs. Wyvern, and I, beginnin' to feel more comfortable and at home like, was walkin' about the room lookin' at this thing and at that. There was pretty old china things on the cupboard, and pictures again the wall; and there was a door open in the wainscot, and I sees a queer old leathern jacket, wi' straps and buckles to it, and sleeves as long as the bed-post hangin' up inside.

"What's that you're at, child?' says my aunt, sharp enough, turning about when I thought she least minded. 'What's that in your hand?'

"'This, ma'am?' says I, turning about with the leathern jacket. 'I don't know what it is, ma'am.'

"Pale as she was, the red came up in her cheeks, and her eyes flashed wi' anger, and I think only she had half a dozen steps to take, between her and me, she'd a gev me a sizzup. But she did gie me a shake by the shouther, and she plucked the thing out o' my hand, and says she, 'While ever you stay here, don't ye meddle wi' nout that don't belong to ye,' and she hung it up on the pin that was there, and shut the door wi' a bang and locked it fast.

"Mrs. Wyvern was liftin' up her hands and laughin' all this time, quietly, in her chair, rolling herself a bit in it, as she used when she was kinkin'.

"The tears was in my eyes, and she winked at my aunt, and says she, dryin' her own eyes that was wet wi' the laughin', 'Tut, the child meant no harm—come here to me, child. It's only a pair o' crutches for lame ducks, and ask us no questions mind, and we'll tell ye no lies; and come here and sit down, and drink a mug o' beer before ye go to your bed.'

"My room, mind ye, was upstairs, next to the old lady's, and Mrs. Wyvern's bed was near hers in her room, and I was to be ready at call, if need should be.

"The lady was in one of her tantrums that night and part of the day before. She used to take fits o' the sulks. Sometimes she would not let them dress her, and at other times she would not let them take her clothes off. She was a great beauty, they said, in her day. But there was no one about Applewale that remembered her in her prime. And she was dreadful fond o' dress, and had thick silks, and stiff satins, and velvets, and laces, and all sorts, enough to set up seven shops at the least. All her dresses was old-fashioned and queer, but worth a fortune.

"Well, I went to my bed. I lay for a while awake; for a' things was new to me; and I think the tea was in my nerves, too, for I wasn't used to it, except now and then on a holiday, or the like. And I heard Mrs. Wyvern talkin', and I listened with my hand to my ear; but I could not hear Mrs. Crowl, and I don't think she said a word.

"There was great care took of her. The people at Applewale knew that when she died they would every one get the sack; and their situations was well paid and easy.

"The doctor came twice a week to see the old lady, and you may be sure they all did as he bid them. One thing was the same every time; they were never to cross or frump her, any way, but to humor and please her in everything.

"So she lay in her clothes all that night, and next day, not a word she said, and I was at my needlework all that day, in my own room, except when I went down to my dinner.

"I would a liked to see the ald lady, and even hear her speak. But she might as well a' bin in Lunnon a' the time for me.

"When I had my dinner my aunt sent me out for a walk for an hour. I was glad when I came back, the trees was so big, and the place so dark and lonesome, and 'twas a cloudy day, and I cried a deal, thinkin' of home, while I was walkin' alone there. That evening, the candles bein' alight, I was sittin' in my room, and the door was open into Madam Crowl's chamber, where my aunt was. It was, then, for the first time I heard what I suppose was the ald lady talking.

"It was a queer noise like, I couldn't well say which, a bird, or a beast, only it had a bleatin' sound in it, and was very small.

"I pricked my ears to hear all I could. But I could not make out one word she said. And my aunt answered:

"'The evil one can't hurt no one, ma'am, bout the Lord permits.'

"Then the same queer voice from the bed says something more that I couldn't make head nor tail on.

"And my aunt med answer again: 'Let them pull faces, ma'am, and say what they will; if the Lord be for us, who can be against us?'

"I kept listenin' with my ear turned to the door, holdin' my breath, but not another word or sound came in from the room. In about twenty minutes, as I was sittin' by the table, lookin' at the pictures in the old Aesop's Fables, I was aware o' something moving at the door, and lookin' up I sid my aunt's face lookin' in at the door, and her hand raised.

"'Hish!' says she, very soft, and comes over to me on tiptoe, and she says in a whisper: 'Thank God, she's asleep at last, and don't ye make no noise till I come back, for I'm goin' down to take my cup o' tea, and I'll be back i' noo—me and Mrs. Wyvern, and she'll be sleepin' in the room, and you can run down when we come up, and Judith will gie ye yaur supper in my room.'

"And with that she goes.

"I kep' looking at the picture-book, as before, listenin' every noo and then, but there was no sound, not a breath, that I could hear; an' I began whisperin' to the pictures and talkin' to myself to keep my heart up, for I was growin' feared in that big room.

"And at last up I got, and began walkin' about the room, lookin' at this and peepin' at that, to amuse my mind, ye'll understand. And at last what sud I do but peeps into Madam Crowl's bedchamber.

"A grand chamber it was, wi' a great four-poster, wi' flowered silk curtains as tall as the ceilin', and foldin' down on the floor, and drawn close all round. There was a lookin'-glass, the biggest I ever sid before, and the room was a blaze o' light. I counted twenty-two wax candles, all alight. Such was her fancy, and no one dared say her nay.

"I listened at the door, and gaped and wondered all round. When I heard there was not a breath, and did not see so much as a stir in the curtains, I took heart, and walked into the room on tiptoe, and looked round again. Then I takes a keek at myself in the big glass; and at last it came in my head, 'Why couldn't I ha' a keek at the ald lady herself in the bed?'

"Ye'd think me a fule if ye knew half how I longed to see Dame Crowl, and I thought to myself if I didn't peep now I might wait many a day before I got so gude a chance again.

"Well, my dear, I came to the side o' the bed, the curtains bein' close, and my heart a'most failed me. But I took courage, and I slips my finger in between the thick curtains, and then my hand. So I waits a bit, but all was still as death. So, softly, softly I draws the curtain, and there, sure enough, I sid before me, stretched out like the painted lady on the tomb-stean in Lexhoe Church, the famous Dame Crowl, of Applewale House. There she was, dressed out. You never sid the like in they days. Satin and silk, and scarlet and green, and gold and pint lace; by Jen! 'twas a sight! A big powdered wig, half as high as herself, was a-top o' her head, and, wow!—was ever such wrinkles?—and her old baggy throat all powdered white, and her cheeks rouged, and mouse-skin eybrows, that Mrs. Wyvern used to stick on, and there she lay proud and stark, wi' a pair o' clocked silk hose on, and heels to her shoon as tall as ninepins. Lawd! But her nose was crooked and thin, and half the whites o' her eyes was open. She used to stand, dressed as she was, gigglin' and dribblin' before the lookin'-glass, wi' a fan in her hand and a big nosegay in her bodice. Her wrinkled little hands was stretched down by her sides, and such long nails, all cut into points, I never sid in my days. Could it even a bin the fashion for grit fowk to wear their fingernails so?

"Well, I think ye'd a-bin frightened yourself if ye'd a sid such a sight. I couldn't let go the curtain, nor move an inch, nor take my eyes off her; my very heart stood still. And in an instant she opens her eyes and up she sits, and spins herself round, and down wi' her, wi' a clack on her two tall heels on the floor, facin' me, ogglin' in my face wi' her two great glassy eyes, and a wicked simper wi' her wrinkled lips, and lang fause teeth.

"Well, a corpse is a natural thing; but this was the dreadfullest sight I ever sid. She had her fingers straight out pointin' at me, and her back was crooked, round again wi' age. Says she:

"'Ye little limb! what for did ye say I killed the boy? I'll tickle ye till ye're stiff!'

"If I'd a thought an instant, I'd a turned about and run. But I couldn't take my eyes off her, and I backed from her as soon as I could; and she came clatterin' after like a thing on wires, with her fingers pointing to my throat, and she makin' all the time a sound with her tongue like zizz-zizz-zizz.

"I kept backin' and backin' as quick as I could, and her fingers was only a few inches away from my throat, and I felt I'd lose my wits if she touched me.

"I went back this way, right into the corner, and I gev a yellock, ye'd think saul and body was partin', and that minute my aunt, from the door, calls out wi' a blare, and the ald lady turns round on her, and I turns about, and ran through my room, and down the stairs, as hard as my legs could carry me.

"I cried hearty, I can tell you, when I got down to the housekeeper's room. Mrs. Wyvern laughed a deal when I told her what happened. But she changed her key when she heard the ald lady's words.

" 'Say them again,' says she.

"So I told her.

" 'Ye little limb! What for did ye say I killed the boy? I'll tickle ye till ye're stiff.'

" 'And did ye say she killed a boy?' says she.

" 'Not I, ma'am, says I.

Judith was always up with me, after that, when the two elder women was away from her. I would a jumped out at winda, rather than stay alone in the same room wi' her.

"It was about a week after, as well as I can remember, Mrs. Wyvern, one day when me and her was alone, told me a thing about Madam Crowl that I did not know before.

"She being young and a great beauty, full seventy year before, had married Squire Crowl, of Applewale. But he was a widower, and had a son about nine years old.

"There never was tale or tidings of this boy after one mornin'. No one could say where he went to. He was allowed too much liberty, and used to be off in the morning, one day, to the keeper's cottage and breakfast wi' him, and away to the warren, and not home, mayhap, till evening; and another time down to the lake, and bathe there, and spend the day fishin' there, or paddlin' about in the boat. Well, no one could say what was gone wi' him; only this, that his hat was found by the lake, under a haathorn that grows thar to this day, and 'twas thought he was drowned bathin'. And the squire's son, by his second marriage, with this Madam Crowl that lived sa dreadful lang came in far the estates. It was his son, the ald lady's grandson, Squire Chevenix Crowl, that owned the estates at the time I came to Applewale.

"There was a deal o' talk lang before my aunt's time about it; and 'twas said the step-mother knew more than she was like to let out. And

she managed her husband, the ald squire, wi' her white-heft and flat-
teries. And as the boy was never seen more, in course of time the thing
died out of fowks' minds.

"I'm goin' to tell ye noo about what I sid wi' my own een.

"I was not there six months, and it was winter time, when the ald
lady took her last sickness.

"The doctor was afeard she might a took a fit o' madness, as she did
fifteen years befoore, and was buckled up, many a time, in a strait-
waistcoat, which was the very leathern jerkin I sid in the closet, off
my aunt's room.

"Well, she didn't. She pined, and windered, and went off, torflin',
torflin', quiet enough, till a day or two before her flittin', and then she
took to rabblin', and sometimes skirlin' in the bed, ye'd think a robber
had a knife to her throat, and she used to work out o' the bed, and not
being strong enough, then, to walk or stand, she'd fall on the flure, wi'
her ald wizened hands stretched before her face, and skirlin' still for
mercy.

"Ye may guess I didn't go into the room, and I used to be shiverin'
in my bed wi' fear, at her skirlin' and scrafflin' on the flure, and blarin'
out words that id make your skin turn blue.

"My aunt, and Mrs. Wyvern, and Judith Squailes, and a woman
from Lexhoe, was always about her. At last she took fits, and they wore
her out.

"'T' sir was there, and prayed for her; but she was past praying with.
I suppose it was right, but none could think there was much good in
it, and sa at lang last she made her flittin', and a' was over, and old
Dame Crowl was shrouded and coffined, and Squire Chevenix was wrote
for. But he was away in France, and the delay was sa lang, that t' sir and
doctor both agreed it would not du to keep her langer out o' her place,
and no one cared but just them two, and my aunt and the rest o' us, from
Applewale, to go to the buryin'. So the old lady of Applewale was laid
in the vault under Lexhoe Church; and we lived up at the great house
till such time as the squire should come to tell his will about us, and
pay off such as he chose to discharge.

"I was put into another room, two doors away from what was Dame

Crowl's chamber, after her death, and this thing happened the night before Squire Chevenix came to Applewale.

"The room I was in now was a large square chamber, covered wi' yak pannels, but unfurnished except for my bed, which had no curtains to it, and a chair and a table, or so, that looked nothing at all in such a big room. And the big looking-glass, that the old lady used to keek into and admire herself from head to heel, now that there was na mair o' that wark, was put out of the way, and stood against the wall in my room, for there was shiftin' o' many things in her chamber ye may suppose, when she came to be coffined.

"The news had come that day that the squire was to be down next morning at Applewale; and not sorry was I, for I thought I was sure to be sent home again to my mother. And right glad was I, and I was thinkin' of a' at hame, and my sister Janet, and the kitten and the pymag, and Trimmer the tike, and all the rest, and I got sa fidgetty, I couldn't sleep, and the clock struck twelve, and me wide awake, and the room as dark as pick. My back was turned to the door, and my eyes toward the wall opposite.

"Well, it could na be a full quarter past twelve, when I sees a lightin' on the wall befoore me, as if something took fire behind, and the shadas o' the bed, and the chair, and my gown, that was hangin' from the wall, was dancin' up and down on the ceilin' beams and the yak pannels; and I turns my head ower my shouther quick, thinkin' something must a gone a' fire.

"And what sud I see, by Jen! but the likeness o' the ald beldame, bedizened out in her satins and velvets, on her dead body, simperin', wi' her eyes as wide as saucers, and her face like the fiend himself. 'Twas a red light that rose about her in a fuffin low, as if her dress round her feet was blazin'. She was drivin' on right for me, wi' her ald shriveled hands crooked as if she was goin' to claw me. I could not stir, but she passed me straight by, wi' a blast o' cald air, and I sid her, at the wall, in the alcove as my aunt used to call it, which was a recess where the state bed used to stand in ald times wi' a door open wide, and her hands gropin' in at somethin' was there. I never sid that door befoore. And she turned round to me, like a thing on a pivot, flyrin', and all at once the room was dark, and I standin' at the far side o' the bed; I don't know how I got there, and I found my tongue at last, and if I did na blare a yellock, rennin' down the gallery and almost pulled Mrs. Wyvern's door off t' hooks, and frighted her half out o' wits.

"Ye may guess I did na sleep that night; and wi' the first light, down wi' me to my aunt, as fast as my two legs cud carry me.

"Well my aunt did na frump or flite me, as I thought she would, but she held me by the hand, and looked hard in my face all the time. And she telt me not to be feared; and says she:

"'Hed the appearance a key in its hand?'

"'Yes', says I, bringin' it to mind. 'a key in a queer brass handle.'

"'Stop a bit,' says she, lettin' go ma hand, and openin' the cupboard door. 'Was it like this?' says she, takin' one out in her fingers, and showing it to me, with a dark look in my face.

"'That was it,' says I, quick enough.

"'Are ye sure?' she says, turnin' it round.

"'Sart,' says I, and I felt like I was gain' to faint when I sid it.

"'Well, that will do, child,' says she, saftly thinkin', and she locked it up again.

"'The squire himself will be here today, before twelve o'clock, and ye must tell him all about it,' says she, thinkin', 'and I suppose I'll be leavin' soon, and so the best thing for the present is, that ye should go home this afternoon, and I'll look out another place for you when I can.'

"Fain was I, ye may guess, at that word.

"My aunt packed up my things for me, and the three pounds that was due to me, to bring home, and Squire Crowl himself came down to Applewale that day, a handsome man, about thirty years ald. It was the second time I sid him. But this was the first time he spoke to me.

"My aunt talked wi' him in the housekeeper's room, and I don't know what they said. I was a bit feared on the squire, he bein' a great gentleman down in Lexhoe, and I darn't go near till I was called. And says he, smilin':

"'What's a' this ye a sen, child? it mun be a dream, for ye know there's na sic a thing as a bo or a freet in a' the world. But whatever it was, ma little maid, sit ye down and tell all about it from first to last.'

"Well, so soon as I made an end, he thought a bit, and says he to my aunt:

"'I mind the place well. In old Sir Olivur's time lame Wyndel told me there was a door in that recess, to the left, where the lassie dreamed she saw my grandmother open it. He was past eighty when he told me that, and I but a boy. It's twenty year sen. The plate and jewels used to be kept there, long ago, before the iron closet was made in the arras chamber, and he told me the key had a brass handle, and this ye say was found in the bottom o' the kist where she kept her old fans. Now, would not it be a queer thing if we found some spoons or diamonds forgot there? Ye mun come up wi' us, lassie, and point to the very spot.'

"Loth was I, and my heart in my mouth, and fast I held by my aunt's hand as I stept into that awesome room, and showed them both how she came and passed me by, and the spot where she stood, and where the door seemed to open.

"There was an ald empty press against the wall then, and shoving it aside, sure enough there was the tracing of a door in the wainscot, and a keyhole stopped with wood, and planed across as smooth as the rest, and the joining of the door all stopped wi' putty the color o' yak, and, but for the hinges that showed a bit when the press was shoved aside, ye would not consayt there was a door there at all.

"'Ha!' says he, wi' a queer smile, 'this looks like it.'

"It took some minutes wi' a small chisel and hammer to pick the bit o' wood out o' the keyhole. The key fitted, sure enough, and, wi' a strang twist and a lang skreak, the boult went back and he pulled the door open.

"There was another door inside, stranger than the first, but the lacks was gone, and it opened easy. Inside was a narrow floor and walls and vault o' brick; we could not see what was in it, for 'twas dark as pick.

"When my aunt had lighted the candle, the squire held it up and stept in.

"My aunt stood on tiptoe tryin' to look over his shouther, and I did na see nout.

"'Ha! ha!' says the squire, steppin' backward. 'What's that? Gi' ma the poker—quick!' says he to my aunt. And as she went to the hearth I peeps beside his arm, and I sid squat down in the far corner a monkey or a flayin' on the chest, or else the maist shriveled up, wizzened ald wife that ever was sen on yearth.

"'By Jen!' says my aunt, as puttin' the poker in his hand, she keeked by his shouther, and sid the ill favored thing, 'hae a care, sir, what ye're doin'. Back wi' ye, and shut to the door!'

"But in place o' that he steps in saftly, wi' the poker pointed like a swoord, and he gies it a poke, and down it a' tumbles together, head and a', in a heap o' bayans and dust, little meyar an' a hatful.

"'Twas the bayans o' a child; a' the rest went to dust at a touch. They said nout for a while, but he turns round the skull, as it lay on the floor.

"Young as I was, I consayted I knew well enough what they was thinkin' on.

"'A dead cat!' says he, pushin' back and blowin' out the can'le, and shuttin' to the door. 'We'll come back, you and me, Mrs. Shutters, and look on the shelves by-and-bye. I've other matters first to speak to ye about; and this little girl's goin' hame, ye say. She has her wages, and I mun mak' her a present,' says he, pattin' my shouther wi' his hand.

"And he did gimma a goud pound and I went aff to Lexhoe about an hour after, and sa hame by the stagecoach, and fain was I to be at hame again; and I never sid Dame Crowl o' Applewale, God be thanked, either in appearance or in dream, at-efter. But when I was grown to be a woman, my aunt spent a day and night wi' me at Littleham, and she telt me there was no doubt it was the poor little boy that was missing sa lang sen, that was shut up to die thar in the dark by that wicked beldame, whar his skirls, or his prayers, or his thumpin' cud na be heard, and his hat was left by the water's edge, whoever did it, to mak' belief he was drowned. The clothes, at the first touch, a' ran into a snuff o' dust in the cell whar the bayans was found. But there was a handful o' jet buttons, and a knife with a green heft, together wi' a couple o' pennies the poor little fella had in his pocket, I suppose, when he was decoyed in thar, and sid his last o' the light. And there was, amang the squire's papers, a copy o' the notice that was prented after he was lost, when the ald squire thought he might 'a run away, or bin took by gipsies, and it said he had a green-hefted knife wi' him, and that his buttons were o' cut jet. Sa that is a' I hev to say consarnin' ald Dame Crowl, o' Applewale House."

# THE PHANTOM COACH

## BY AMELIA B. EDWARDS

A MELIA B. EDWARDS was one of these extraordinary, liberated, Victorian women whose good works were legion. She was a brilliant amateur archaeologist and founder of the Egypt Exploration Fund. She was also a superb writer of ghost stories.

It was a period in which women were trying to express themselves through writing and, often, under enormous difficulties. They rarely had rooms of their own; they scratched their stories on wrapping paper placed on old atlases on their knees. They carried dozens of plots in their heads as they went about their daily routines. Often, they had difficulty getting published. Amelia Edwards' work, however, seemed made for the market that loved a ghost story, and her handful of tales are memorable. ৡৡ

THE CIRCUMSTANCES I am about to relate to you have truth to recommend them. They happened to myself, and my recollection of them is as vivid as if they had taken place only yesterday. Twenty years, however, have gone by since that night. During those twenty years I have told the story to but one other person. I tell it now with a reluctance which I find it difficult to overcome. All I entreat, meanwhile, is that you will abstain from forcing your own conclusions upon me. I want nothing explained away. I desire no arguments. My mind on this subject is quite made up, and, having the testimony of my own senses to rely upon, I prefer to abide by it.

Well! It was just twenty years ago, and within a day or two of the end of the grouse season. I had been out all day with my gun, and had had no sport to speak of. The wind was due east; the month, December; the place, a bleak wide moor in the far north of England. And I had lost my way. It was not a pleasant place in which to lose one's way, with the first feathery flakes of a coming snowstorm just fluttering down upon the heather, and the leaden evening closing in all round. I shaded my eyes with my hand, and stared anxiously into the gathering darkness, where the purple moorland melted into a range of low hills, some ten or twelve miles distant. Not the faintest smoke-wreath, not the tiniest cultivated patch, or fence, or sheep-track, met my eyes in any direction. There was nothing for it but to walk on, and take my chance of finding what shelter I could, by the way. So I shouldered my gun again, and pushed wearily forward; for I had been on foot since an hour after daybreak, and had eaten nothing since breakfast.

Meanwhile, the snow began to come down with ominous steadiness, and the wind fell. After this, the cold became more intense, and the night came rapidly up. As for me, my prospects darkened with the darkening sky, and my heart grew heavy as I thought how my young wife was already watching for me through the window of our little inn parlor, and thought of all the suffering in store for her throughout this weary night. We had been married four months, and, having spent our autumn in the Highlands, were now lodging in a remote little village situated just on the verge of the great English moorlands. We were very much in love, and, of course, very happy. This morning, when we parted, she had implored me to return before dusk, and I had promised her that I would. What would I not have given to have kept my word!

Even now, weary as I was, I felt that with a supper, an hour's rest, and a guide, I might still get back to her before midnight, if only guide and shelter could be found.

And all this time, the snow fell and the night thickened. I stopped and shouted every now and then, but my shouts seemed only to make the silence deeper. Then a vague sense of uneasiness came upon me, and I began to remember stories of travelers who had walked on and on in the falling snow until, wearied out, they were fain to lie down and sleep their lives away. Would it be possible, I asked myself, to keep on thus through all the long dark night? Would there not come a time when my limbs must fail and my resolution give way? When I, too, must sleep the sleep of death. Death! I shuddered. How hard to die just now, when life lay all so bright before me! How hard for my darling, whose whole loving heart—but that thought was not to be borne! To banish it, I shouted again, louder and longer, and then listened eagerly. Was my shout answered, or did I only fancy that I heard a far off cry? I halloed again, and again the echo followed. Then a wavering speck of light came suddenly out of the dark, shifting, disappearing, growing momentarily nearer and brighter. Running toward it at full speed, I found myself to my great joy, face to face with an old man and a lantern.

"Thank God!" was the exclamation that burst involuntarily from my lips.

Blinking and frowning, he lifted his lantern and peered into my face.

"What for?" growled he, sulkily.

"Well—for you. I began to fear I should be lost in the snow."

"Eh, then, folks do get cast away hereabouts fra' time to time, an' what's to hinder you from bein' cast away likewise, if the Lord's so minded?"

"If the Lord is so minded that you and I shall be lost together, friend, we must submit," I replied; "but I don't mean to be lost without you. How far am I now from Dwolding?"

"A gude twenty mile, more or less."

"And the nearest village?"

"The nearest village is Wyke, an' that's twelve mile t'other side."

"Where do you live, then?"

"Out yonder," said he, with a vague jerk of the lantern.

"You're going home, I presume?"

"Maybe I am."

"Then I'm going with you."

The old man shook his head, and rubbed his nose reflectively with the handle of the lantern.

"It ain't o' no use," growled he. "He 'ont let you in—not he."

"We'll see about that," I replied briskly. "Who is He?"

"The master."

"Who is the master?"

"That's nowt to you," was the unceremonious reply.

"Well, well; you lead the way, and I'll engage that the master shall give me shelter and a supper tonight."

"Eh, you can try him!" muttered my reluctant guide; and, still shaking his head, he hobbled, gnome-like, away through the falling snow. A large mass loomed up presently out of the darkness, and a huge dog rushed out, barking furiously.

"Is this the house?" I asked.

"Ay, it's the house. Down, Bey!" And he fumbled in his pocket for the key.

I drew up close behind him, prepared to lose no chance of entrance, and saw in the little circle of light shed by the lantern that the door was heavily studded with iron nails, like the door of a prison. In another minute he had turned the key and I had pushed past him into the house.

Once inside, I looked round with curiosity, and found myself in a great raftered hall, which served, apparently, a variety of uses. One end was piled to the roof with corn, like a barn. The other was stored with flour sacks, agricultural implements, casks, and all kinds of miscellaneous lumber; while from the beams overhead hung rows of hams, flitches, and bunches of dried herbs for winter use. In the center of the floor stood some huge object gauntly dressed in a dingy wrapping-cloth, and reaching half-way to the rafters. Lifting a corner of this cloth, I saw to my surprise, a telescope of very considerable size, mounted on a rude movable platform, with four small wheels. The tube was made of painted wood, bound round with bands of metal rudely fashioned; the speculum, so far as I could estimate its size in the dim light, measured at least fifteen inches in diameter. While I was yet examining the instrument, and asking myself whether it was not the work of some self-taught optician, a bell rang sharply.

"That's for you," said my guide, with a malicious grin, "Yonder's his room."

He pointed to a low black door at the opposite side of the hall. I crossed over, rapped somewhat loudly, and went in, without waiting for an invitation. A huge, white-haired old man rose from a table covered with books and papers, and confronted me sternly.

"Who are you?" said he. "How came you here? What do you want?"

"James Murray, barrister-at-law. On foot across the moor. Meat, drink and sleep."

He bent his bushy brows into a portentous frown.

"Mine is not a house of entertainment," he said, haughtily. "Jacob, how dared you admit this stranger?"

"I didn't admit him," grumbled the old man. "He followed me over the muir, and shouldered his way in before me. I'm no match for six foot two."

"And pray, sir, by what right have you forced an entrance into my house?"

"The same by which I should have clung to your boat, if I were drowning. The right of self-preservation."

"Self-preservation?"

"There's an inch of snow on the ground already," I replied, briefly; "and it would be deep enough to cover my body before daybreak."

He strode to the window, pulled aside a heavy curtain, and looked out.

"It is true," he said. "You can stay, if you choose, till morning. Jacob, serve the supper."

With this he waved me to a seat, resumed his own, and became at once absorbed in the studies from which I had disturbed him.

I placed my gun in a corner, drew a chair to the hearth, and examined my quarters at leisure. Smaller and less incongruous in its arrangements than the hall, this room contained, nevertheless, much to awaken my curiosity. The floor was carpetless. The whitewashed walls were in parts scrawled over with strange diagrams, and in others covered with shelves crowded with philosophical instruments, the uses of many of which were unknown to me. On one side of the fireplace, stood a bookcase filled with dingy folios; on the other, a small organ, fantastically decorated with painted carvings of medieval saints and devils. Through the half-opened door of a cupboard at the further end of the room, I saw a long array of geological specimens, surgical preparations, crucibles, retorts, and jars of chemicals; while on the mantelshelf beside me, amid a number of small objects, stood a model of the solar system, a small galvanic battery, and a microscope. Every chair had its burden. Every corner was heaped high with books. The very floor was littered over with maps, casts, papers, tracings, and learned lumber of all conceivable kinds.

I stared about me with an amazement increased by every fresh object upon which my eyes chanced to rest. So strange a room I had never seen; yet seemed it stranger still, to find such a room in a lone farmhouse amid those wild and solitary moors! Over and over again, I looked from my host to his surroundings, and from his surroundings back to my host, asking myself who and what he could be? His head was singularly fine; but it was more the head of a poet than of a philosopher. Broad in the temples, prominent over the eyes, and clothed with a rough profusion of perfectly white hair, it had all the ideality and much of the ruggedness that characterizes the head of Louis von Beethoven. There were the same deep lines about the mouth, and the same stern furrows in the brow. There was the same concentration of expression. While I was yet observing him, the door opened, and Jacob brought in the supper. His master then closed his book, rose, and with more courtesy of manner than he had yet shown, invited me to the table.

A dish of ham and eggs, a loaf of brown bread, and a bottle of admirable sherry, were placed before me.

"I have but the homeliest farmhouse fare to offer you, sir," said my entertainer. "Your appetite, I trust, will make up for the deficiencies of our larder."

I had already fallen upon the viands, and now protested, with the enthusiasm of a starving sportsman, that I had never eaten anything so delicious.

He bowed stiffly, and sat down to his own supper, which consisted, primitively, of a jug of milk and a basin of porridge. We ate in silence, and, when we had done, Jacob removed the tray. I then drew my chair back to the fireside. My host, somewhat to my surprise, did the same, and turning abruptly toward me, said:

"Sir, I have lived in strict retirement for three-and-twenty years. During that time, I have not seen as many strange faces, and I have not read a single newspaper. You are the first stranger who has crossed my threshold for more than four years. Will you favor me with a few words of information respecting that outer world from which I have parted company so long?"

"Pray interrogate me," I replied. "I am heartily at your service."

He bent his head in acknowledgment; leaned forward, with his elbows resting on his knees and his chin supported in the palms of his hands; stared fixedly into the fire; and proceeded to question me.

His inquiries related chiefly to scientific matters, with the later progress of which, as applied to the practical purposes of life, he was almost wholly unacquainted. No student of science myself, I replied as well as my slight information permitted; but the task was far from easy, and I was much relieved when, passing from interrogation to discussion, he began pouring forth his own conclusions upon the facts which I had been attempting to place before him. He talked, and I listened spellbound. He talked till I believe he almost forgot my presence, and only thought aloud. I had never heard anything like it then; I have never heard anything like it since. Familiar with all systems of all philosophies, subtle in analysis, bold in generalization, he poured forth his thought in an uninterrupted stream, and, still leaning forward in the same moody attitude with his eyes fixed upon the fire, wandered from topic to topic, from speculation to speculation like an inspired dreamer. From practical science to mental philosophy; from electricity in the wire to electricity in the nerve; from Watts to Mesmer, from Mesmer to Reichenbach, from Reichenbach to Swedenborg, Spinoza, Condillac, Descartes, Berkeley, Aristotle, Plato, and the Magi and mystics of the East, were transitions which, however bewildering in their variety and scope, seemed easy and harmonious upon his lips as sequences in music. By-and-by—I forget now by what link of conjecture or illustration—he passed on to that field which lies beyond the boundary line of even conjectural philosophy, and reaches no man knows whither. He spoke of the soul and its aspirations; of the spirit and its powers; of second sight; of prophecy; of those phenomena which, under the names of ghosts, specters, and supernatural appearances, have been denied by the sceptics and attested by the credulous of all ages.

"The world," he said, "grows hourly more and more skeptical of all that lies beyond its own narrow radius; and our men of science foster the fatal tendency. They condemn as fable all that resists experiment. They reject as false all that cannot be brought to the test of the laboratory or the dissecting room. Against what superstition have they waged so long and obstinate a war, as against the belief in apparitions? And yet what superstition has maintained its hold upon the minds of men so long and so firmly? Show me any fact in physics, history, in archaeology, which is supported by testimony so wide and so various. Attested by all races of men, in all ages, and in all climates, by the soberest sages of antiquity, by the rudest savage of today, by the Christian, the Pagan, the Pantheist, the Materialist, this phenomenon is treated as a nursery tale by the philosophers of our century. Circumstantial evidence weighs with them as a feather in the balance. The comparison of causes with effects, however valuable in physical science, is put aside as worthless and unreliable. The evidence of competent witnesses, however conclusive in a court of justice, counts for nothing. He who pauses before he pronounces, is condemned as a trifler. He who believes, is a dreamer or a fool."

He spoke with bitterness, and, having said thus, relapsed for some minutes into silence. Presently he raised his head from his hands, and added, with an altered voice and manner:

"I, sir, paused, investigated, believed, and was not ashamed to state my convictions to the world. I, too, was branded as a visionary, held up to ridicule by my contemporaries, and hooted from that field of science in which I had labored with honor during all the best years of my life. These things happened just three-and-twenty years ago. Since then, I have lived as you see me living now, and the world has forgotten me, as I have forgotten the world. You have my history."

"It is a very sad one," I murmured, scarcely knowing what to answer.

"It is a very common one," he replied. "I have only suffered for the truth, as many a better and wiser man has suffered before me."

He rose, as if desirous of ending the conversation, and went over to the window.

"It has ceased snowing," he observed, as he dropped the curtain, and came back to the fireside.

"Ceased!" I exclaimed, starting eagerly to my feet. "Oh, if it were only possible—but no! it is hopeless. Even if I could find my way across the moor, I could not walk twenty miles tonight."

"Walk twenty miles tonight!" repeated my host. "What are you thinking of?"

"Of my wife," I replied, impatiently. "Of my young wife, who does not know that I have lost my way, and who is at this moment breaking her heart with suspense and terror."

"Where is she?"

"At Dwolding, twenty miles away."

"At Dwolding," he echoed, thoughtfully. "Yes, the distance, it is true, is twenty miles; but—are you so very anxious to save the next six or eight hours?"

"So very, very anxious, that I would give ten guineas at this moment for a guide and a horse."

"Your wish can be gratified at a less costly rate," said he, smiling. "The night mail from the north, which changes horses at Dwolding, passes within five miles of this spot, and will be due at a certain cross-road in about an hour and a quarter. If Jacob were to go with you across the moor, and put you into the old coach-road, you could find your way, I suppose, to where it joins the new one?"

"Easily—gladly."

He smiled again, rang the bell, gave the old servant his directions, and, taking a bottle of whiskey and a wineglass from the cupboard in which he kept his chemicals, said:

"The snow lies deep, and it will be difficult walking tonight on the moor. A glass of usquebaugh before you start?"

I would have declined the spirit, but he pressed it on me, and I drank it. It went down my throat like liquid flame, and almost took my breath away.

"It is strong," he said; "but it will keep out the cold. And now you have no moments to spare. Good night!"

I thanked him for his hospitality, and would have shaken hands, but that he had turned away before I could finish my sentence. In another minute I had traversed the hall, Jacob had locked the outer door behind me, and we were out on the wide white moor.

Although the wind had fallen, it was still bitterly cold. Not a star glimmered in the vault overhead. Not a sound, save the rapid crunching of the snow beneath our feet, disturbed the heavy stillness of the night. Jacob, not too well pleased with his mission, shambled on before in sullen silence, his lantern in his hand, and his shadow at his feet. I followed, with my gun over my shoulder, as little inclined for conversation as himself. My thoughts were full of my late host. His voice yet rang in my ears. His eloquence yet held my imagination captive. I remember to this day, with surprise, how my over excited brain retained whole sentences and parts of sentences, troops of brilliant images, and fragments of splendid reasoning, in the very words in which he had uttered them. Musing thus over what I had heard, and striving to recall a lost link here and there, I strode on at the heels of my guide, absorbed and unobservant. Presently—at the end, as it seemed to me, of only a few minutes—he came to a sudden halt, and said:

"Yon's your road. Keep the stone fence to your right hand, and you can't fail of the way."

"This, then, is the old coach-road?"

"Ay, 'tis the old coach-road."

"And how far do I go, before I reach the cross-roads?"

"Nigh upon three mile."

I pulled out my purse, and he became more communicative.

"The road's a fair road enough," said he, "for foot passengers; but 'twas over steep and narrow for the northern traffic. You'll mind where the parapet's broken away, close again the sign-post. It's never been mended since the accident."

"What accident?"

"Eh, the night mail pitched right over into the valley below—a gude fifty feet an' more—just at the worst bit o' road in the whole country."

"Horrible! Were many lives lost?"

"All. Four were found dead, and t'other two died next morning."

"How long is it since this happened?"

"Just nine year."

"Near the sign-post, you say? I will bear it in mind. Good night."

"Gude night, sir, and thankee." Jacob pocketed his half-crown, made a faint pretense of touching his hat, and trudged back by the way he had come.

I watched the light of his lantern till it quite disappeared, and then turned to pursue my way alone. This was no longer matter of the slightest difficulty, for, despite the dead darkness overhead, the line of stone fence showed distinctly enough against the pale gleam of the snow. How silent it seemed now, with only my footsteps to listen to; how silent and how solitary! A strange disagreeable sense of loneliness stole over me. I walked faster. I hummed a fragment of a tune. I cast up enormous sums in my head, and accumulated them at compound interest. I did my best, in short, to forget the startling speculations to which I had but just been listening, and, to some extent, I succeeded.

Meanwhile, the night air seemed to become colder and colder, and though I walked fast I found it impossible to keep myself warm. My feet were like ice. I lost sensation in my hands, and grasped my gun mechanically. I even breathed with difficulty, as though, instead of traversing a quiet north-country highway, I were scaling the uppermost heights of some gigantic Alp. This last symptom became presently so distressing, that I was forced to stop for a few minutes, and lean against the stone fence. As I did so, I chanced to look back up the road, and there, to my infinite relief, I saw a distant point of light, like the gleam of an approaching lantern. I at first concluded that Jacob had retraced his steps and followed me; but even as the conjecture presented itself, a second light flashed into sight—a light evidently parallel with the first, and approaching at the same rate of motion. It needed no second thought to show me that these must be the carriage-lamps of some private vehicle, though it seemed strange that any private vehicle should take a road professedly disused and dangerous.

There could be no doubt, however, of the fact, for the lamps grew larger and brighter every moment, and I even fancied I could already see the dark outline of the carriage between them. It was coming up very fast, and quite noiselessly, the snow being nearly a foot deep under the wheels.

And now the body of the vehicle became distinctly visible behind the lamps. It looked strangely lofty. A sudden suspicion flashed upon me. Was it possible that I had passed the cross-roads in the dark without observing the sign-post, and could this be the very coach which I had come to meet?

No need to ask myself that question a second time, for here it came around the bend of the road, guard and driver, one outside passenger, and four steaming greys, all wrapped in a soft haze of light, through which the lamps blazed out, like a pair of fiery meteors.

I jumped forward, waved my hat, and shouted. The mail came down at full speed, and passed me. For a moment I feared that I had not been seen or heard, but it was only for a moment. The coachman pulled up; the guard, muffled to the eyes in capes and comforters, and apparently sound asleep in the rumble, neither answered my hail nor made the slightest effort to dismount; the outside passenger did not even turn his head. I opened the door for myself, and looked in. There were but three travelers inside, so I stepped in, shut the door, slipped into the vacant corner, and congratulated myself on my good fortune.

The atmosphere of the coach seemed, if possible, colder than that of the outside air, and was pervaded by a singularly damp and disagreeable smell. I looked around at my fellow-passengers. They were all three men, and all silent. They did not seem to be asleep, but each leaned back in his corner of the vehicle, as if absorbed in his own reflections. I attempted to open a conversation.

"How intensely cold it is tonight," I said, addressing my opposite neighbor.

He lifted his head, looked at me, but made no reply.

"The winter," I added, "seems to have begun in earnest."

Although the corner in which he sat was so dim that I could distinguish none of his features very clearly, I saw that his eyes were still turned full upon me. And yet he answered never a word.

At any other time I should have felt, and perhaps expressed, some annoyance, but at the moment I felt too ill to do either. The icy coldness of the night air had struck a chill to my very marrow, and the strange smell inside the coach was affecting me with an intolerable nausea. I shivered from head to foot, and, turning to my left-hand neighbor, asked if he had any objection to an open window?

He neither spoke nor stirred.

I repeated the question more loudly, but with the same result. Then I lost patience, and let the sash down. As I did so the leather strap broke in my hand, and I observed that the glass was covered with a thick coat of mildew, the accumulation, apparently, of years. My attention being thus drawn to the condition of the coach, I examined it more narrowly, and saw by the uncertain light of the outer lamps that it was in the last stage of dilapidation. Every part of it was not only out of repair, but in a condition of decay. The sashes splintered at a touch. The leather fittings were crusted over with mold, and literally rotting from the woodwork. The floor was almost breaking away beneath my feet. The whole machine, in short, was foul with damp, and had evidently been dragged from some outhouse in which it had been moldering away for years, to do another day or two of duty on the road.

I turned to the third passenger, whom I had not yet addressed, and hazarded one more remark.

"This coach," I said, "is in a deplorable condition. The regular mail, I suppose, is under repair?"

He moved his head slowly, and looked me in the face, without speaking a word. I shall never forget that look while I live. I turned cold at heart under it. I turn cold at heart even now when I recall it. His eyes glowed with a fiery unnatural luster. His face was livid as the face of a corpse. His bloodless lips were drawn back as if in the agony of death, and showed the gleaming teeth between.

The words that I was about to utter died upon my lips, a strange horror—a dreadful horror—came upon me. My sight had by this time become used to the gloom of the coach, and I could see with tolerable distinctness. I turned to my opposite neighbor. He, too, was looking at me, with the same startling pallor in his face, and the same stony glitter in his eyes. I passed my hand across my brow. I turned to the passenger on the seat beside my own, and saw—oh heaven! how shall I describe what I saw? I saw that he was no living man—that none of them were living men, like myself! A pale phosphorescent light—the light of putrefaction—played upon their awful faces; upon their hair, dank with the dews of the grave; upon their clothes, earth-stained and dropping to pieces; upon their hands, which were as the hands of corpses long buried. Only their eyes, their terrible eyes, were living; and those eyes were all turned menacingly upon me!

A shriek of terror, a wild unintelligible cry for help and mercy, burst from my lips as I flung myself against the door, and strove in vain to open it.

In that single instant, brief and vivid as a landscape beheld in the flash of summer lightning, I saw the moon shining down through a rift of stormy cloud—the ghastly sign-post rearing its warning finger by the wayside—the broken parapet—the plunging horses—the black gulf below. Then, the coach reeled like a ship at sea. Then, came a mighty crash—a sense of crushing pain—and then, darkness.

It seemed as if years had gone by when I awoke one morning from a deep sleep, and found my wife watching by my bedside. I will pass over the scene that ensued, and give you, in half a dozen words, the tale she told me with tears of thanksgiving. I had fallen over a precipice, close against the junction of the old coach-road and the new, and had only been saved from certain death by lighting upon a deep snowdrift that had accumulated at the foot of the rock beneath. In this snowdrift I was discovered at daybreak, by a couple of shepherds, who carried me to the nearest shelter, and brought a surgeon to my aid. The surgeon found me in a state of raving delirium with a broken arm and a compound fracture of the skull. The letters in my pocketbook showed my name and address; my wife was summoned to nurse me; and, thanks to youth and a fine constitution, I came out of danger at last. The place of my fall, I need scarcely say, was precisely that at which a frightful accident had happened to the north mail nine years before.

I never told my wife the fearful events which I have just related to you. I told the surgeon who attended me; but he treated the whole adventure as a mere dream born of the fever in my brain. We discussed the question over and over again, until we found that we could discuss it with temper no longer, and then we dropped it. Others may form what conclusions they please—I *know* that twenty years ago I was the fourth inside passenger in that Phanton Coach.

# THE STRANGER

## BY AMBROSE BIERCE

THE THREE-DECKER gothic novels of the late eighteenth and early nineteenth centuries contained ghosts with single-track brains. The atmosphere was filled with clanking armor, magic helmets, haunted castles and corridors, great groans, magic potions. The gothic ghosts, like the primitive ghosts of earlier literature, were very elemental. Love and hate were their two themes. The gothic ghosts were always haunting some villain or villainess in order to foil them in some wicked deed or eternally pursue them for an ancient crime. Occasionally they were good ghosts, comforting the hero or heroine, chaperoning them and even advising them.

Starting with Ambrose Bierce, ghosts became far more subtle. Dorothy Scarborough, a historian of the ghost story, has said: "The modern ghost is not satisfied with such sit-by-the-fire jobs. They like to keep in the van of activity and do what mortals do. They run the whole scale of human motions and emotions and one needs as much handy psychology to interpret their hauntings as to read George Meredith. They are actuated by subtle motivations of jealousy, ardent love, tempered friendship, curiosity, mischief, vindictiveness, revenge, hate, gratitude, and all other conceivable impulses." ৯৯

A MAN stepped out of the darkness into the little illuminated circle about our failing camp-fire and seated himself upon a rock.

"You are not the first to explore this region," he said gravely.

Nobody controverted his statement; he was himself proof of its truth, for he was not of our party and must have been somewhere near when we camped. Moreover, he must have companions not far away; it was not a place where one would be living or traveling alone. For more than a week we had seen, besides ourselves and our animals, only such living things as rattlesnakes and horned toads. In an Arizona desert one does not long coexist with only such creatures as these; one must have pack animals, supplies, arms—"an outfit." And all these imply comrades. It was, perhaps, a doubt as to what manner of men this unceremonious stranger's comrades might be, together with something in his words interpretable as a challenge, that caused every man of our half-dozen "gentlemen adventurers" to rise to a sitting posture and lay his hand upon a weapon—an act signifying, in that time and place, a policy of expectation. The stranger gave the matter no attention, and began again to speak in the same deliberate, uninflected monotone in which he had delivered his first sentence:

"Thirty years ago Ramon Gallegos, William Shaw, George W. Kent and Berry Davis, all of Tucson, crossed the Santa Catalina Mountains and traveled due west, as nearly as the configuration of the country permitted. We were prospecting and it was our intention, if we found nothing, to push through to the Gila river at some point near Big Bend, where we understood there was a settlement. We had a good outfit but no guide—just Ramon Gallegos, William Shaw, George W. Kent and Berry Davis."

The man repeated the names slowly and distinctly, as if to fix them in the memories of his audience, every member of which was now attentively observing him, but with a slackened apprehension regarding his possible companions somewhere in the darkness whch seemed to enclose us like a black wall, for in the manner of this volunteer historian was no suggestion of an unfriendly purpose. His act was rather that of a harmless lunatic than an enemy. We were not so new to the country as not to know that the solitary life of many a plainsman had a tendency to develop eccentricities of conduct and character not always easily distinguishable from mental aberration. A man is like a tree: in a forest of his fellows he will grow as straight as his generic and individual nature permits; alone, in the open, he yields to the deforming stresses and tortions that environ him. Some such thoughts were in my mind as I watched the man from the shadow of my hat, pulled low to shut out the firelight. A witless fellow, no doubt, but what could he be doing there in the heart of a desert?

Nobody having broken the silence, the visitor went on to say: "This country was not then what it is now. There was not a ranch between the Gila and the Gulf. There was a little game here and there in the mountains, and near the infrequent water-holes grass enough to keep our animals from starvation. If we should be so fortunate as to encounter no Indians we might get through. But within a week the purpose of the expedition had altered from discovery of wealth to preservation of life. We had gone too far to go back, for what was ahead could be no worse than what was behind; so we pushed on, riding by night to avoid Indians and the intolerable heat, and concealing ourselves by day as best we could. Sometimes, having exhausted our supply of wild meat and emptied our casks, we were days without food and drink; then a water-hole or a shallow pool in the bottom of an arroyo so restored our strength and sanity that we were able to shoot some of the wild animals that sought it also. Sometimes it was a bear, sometimes an antelope, a coyote, a cougar—that was as God pleased; all were food.

"One morning as we skirted a mountain range, seeking a practicable pass, we were attacked by a band of Apaches who had followed our trail up a gulch—it is not far from here. Knowing that they outnumbered us ten to one, they took none of their usual cowardly precautions, but dashed upon us at a gallop, firing and yelling. Fighting was out of the question. We urged our feeble animals up the gulch as far as there was footing for a hoof, then threw ourselves out of our saddles and took to the chaparral on one of the slopes, abandoning our entire outfit to the enemy. But we retained our rifles, every man—Ramon Gallegos, William Shaw, George W. Kent and Berry Davis."

"Same old crowd," said the humorist of the party. A gesture of disapproval from our leader silenced him, and the stranger proceeded with his tale:

"The savages dismounted also, and some of them ran up the gulch beyond the point at which we had left it, cutting off further retreat in that direction and forcing us on up the side. Unfortunately the chaparral extended only a short distance up the slope, and as we came into the open ground above we took the fire of a dozen rifles; but Apaches shoot badly when in a hurry, and God so willed it that none of us fell. Twenty yards up the slope, beyond the edge of the brush, were vertical cliffs, in which, directly in front of us, was a narrow opening. Into that we ran, finding ourselves in a cavern about as large as an ordinary room. Here for a time we were safe. A single man with a repeating rifle could defend the entrance against all the Apaches in the land. But against hunger and thirst we had no defense. Courage we still had, but hope was a memory.

"Not one of those Indians did we afterwards see, but by the smoke and glare of their fires in the gulch we knew that by day and by night they watched with ready rifles in the edge of the bush—knew that if we made a sortie not a man of us would live to take three steps into the open. For three days, watching in turn, we held out, before our suffering became insupportable. Then—it was the morning of the fourth day—Ramon Gallegos said:

"'Señores, I know not well of the good God and what please him. I have lived without religion, and I am not acquaint with that of you. Pardon, señores, if I shock you, but for me the time is come to beat the game of the Apache.'

"He knelt upon the rock floor of the cave and pressed his pistol against his temple. 'Madre de Dios,' he said, 'comes now the soul of Ramon Gallegos.'

"And so he left us—William Shaw, George W. Kent and Berry Davis.

"I was the leader. It was for me to speak.

"'He was a brave man,' I said. 'He knew when to die, and how. It is foolish to go mad from thirst and fall by Apache bullets, or be skinned alive—it is in bad taste. Let us join Ramon Gallegos.'

"'That is right,' said William Shaw.

"'That is right,' said George W. Kent.

"I straightened the limbs of Ramon Gallegos and put a handkerchief over his face. Then William Shaw said: 'I should like to look like that a little while.'

"And George W. Kent said that he felt that way too.

"'It shall be so,' I said. 'The red devils will wait a week. William Shaw and George W. Kent, draw and kneel.'

"They did so and I stood before them.

"'Almighty God, our Father,' said I.

"'Almighty God, our Father,' said William Shaw.

"'Almighty God, our Father,' said George W. Kent.

"'Forgive us our sins,' said I.

"'Forgive us our sins,' said they.

"'And receive our souls.'

"'And receive our souls.'

"'Amen!'

"'Amen!'

"I laid them beside Ramon Gallegos and covered their faces."

There was a quick commotion on the opposite side of the camp fire. One of our party had sprung to his feet, pistol in hand.

"And you!" he shouted, "you dared to escape?—you dare to be alive? You cowardly hound, I'll send you to join them if I hang for it!"

But with the leap of a panther the captain was upon him, grasping his wrist. "Hold it in, Sam Yountsey, hold it in!"

We were now all upon our feet—except the stranger, who sat motionless and apparently inattentive. Someone seized Yountsey's other arm.

"Captain," I said, "there is something wrong here. This fellow is either a lunatic or merely a liar—just a plain, everyday liar that Yountsey has no call to kill. If this man was of that party it had five members, one of whom—probably himself—he has not named."

"Yes," said the captain, releasing the insurgent, who sat down, "there is something—unusual. Years ago four dead bodies of white men, scalped and shamefully mutilated, were found about the mouth of that cave. They are buried there; I have seen the graves—we shall all see them tomorrow."

The stranger rose, standing tall in the light of the expiring fire, which in our breathless attention to his story we had neglected to keep going.

"There were four," he said. "Ramon Gallegos, William Shaw, George W. Kent and Berry Davis."

With this reiterated roll call of the dead he walked into the darkness and we saw him no more.

At that moment one of our party, who had been on guard, strode in among us, rifle in hand and somewhat excited.

"Captain," he said, "for the last half-hour three men have been standing out there on the *mesa*." He pointed in the direction taken by the stranger. "I could see them distinctly, for the moon is up, but as they had no guns and I had them covered with mine, I thought it was their move. They have made none, but, damn it! They got on my nerves."

"Go back to your post, and stay till you see them again," said the captain. "The rest of you lie down again, or I'll kick you all into the fire."

The sentinel obediently withdrew, swearing, and did not return. As we were arranging our blankets, the fiery Yountsey said: "I beg your pardon, Captain, but who the devil do you take them to be?"

"Ramon Gallegos, William Shaw and George W. Kent."

"But how about Berry Davis? I ought to have shot him."

"Quite needless; you couldn't have made him any deader. Go to sleep."

# ENTERTAINERS IN THE PSYCHOLOGICAL SUSPENSE STORY: ROBERT LOUIS STEVENSON, MARY WILKINS FREEMAN, AND GRAHAM GREENE

## (THE PSYCHOLOGY OF EVIL)

# THE BODY-SNATCHER

## BY R. L. STEVENSON

*Let the sound of Stevenson go through your mind empty and you will realize that he never took himself other than as an amusement.*

This comment was made about Robert Louis Stevenson by Robert Frost in a letter maintaining that a writer's stye and his material always indicates to the reader how seriously an author approaches his own writing. Robert Louis Stevenson wrote with an enormous felicity of style, a superb sense of ease, and a masterful grasp of his material. But it would be incorrect to think that Stevenson was not a thoroughly serious writer trying to cope with his own time with many of the psychological concepts that would be common knowledge in our own time.

Stevenson's great novel "Dr. Jekyll and Mr. Hyde" is one of the greatest psychological suspense stories of all time. The best-known of all dual personality stories, it deals with the psychology of evil in a story that explores the physical form of evil in one man's nature by depicting it as having a separate existence of its own.

*The Body-snatcher* has the same compelling quality as an adventure into the macabre. Although Stevenson was a very serious writer, Robert Frost was right in this instance that he was "an amusement." His ideas of good and evil always permeated his work, but he was always determined to be, above all, just what he was, a great storyteller. ৡ৶

EVERY NIGHT in the year, four of us sat in the small parlor of the George at Debenham—the undertaker, and the landlord, and Fettes, and myself. Sometimes there would be more; but blow high, blow low, come rain or snow or frost, we four would be each planted in his own particular armchair. Fettes was an old drunken Scotchman, a man of education obviously, and a man of some property, since he lived in idleness. He had come to Debenham years ago, while still young, and by a mere continuance of living had grown to be an adopted townsman. His blue camlet cloak was a local antiquity, like the church spire. His place in the parlor at the George, his absence from church, his old, crapulous, disreputable vices, were all things of course in Debenham. He had some vague Radical opinions and some fleeting infidelities, which he would now and again set forth and emphasize with tottering slaps upon the table. He drank rum—five glasses regularly every evening; and for the greater portion of his nightly visit to the George sat, with his glass in his right hand, in a state of melancholy alcoholic saturation. We called him the Doctor, for he was supposed to have some special knowledge of medicine, and had been known, upon a pinch, to set a fracture or reduce a dislocation; but beyond these slight particulars, we had no knowledge of his character and antecedents.

One dark winter night—it had struck nine sometime before the landlord joined us—there was a sick man in the George, a great neighboring proprietor suddenly struck down with apoplexy on his way to Parliament; and the great man's still greater London doctor had been telegraphed to his bedside. It was the first time that such a thing had happened in Debenham, for the railway was but newly open, and we were proportionately moved by the occurrence.

"He's come," said the landlord, after he had filled and lighted his pipe.

"He?" said I. "Who?—not the doctor?"

"Himself," replied our host.

"What is his name?"

"Dr. Macfarlane," said the landlord.

Fettes was far through his third tumbler, stupidly fuddled, now nodding over, now staring mazily around him; but at the last word he seemed to awaken, and repeated the name "Macfarlane" twice, quietly enough the first time, but with sudden emotion at the second.

"Yes," said the landlord, "that's his name, Doctor Wolfe Macfarlane."

Fettes became instantly sober; his eyes awoke, his voice became clear, loud, and steady, his language forcible and earnest. We were all startled by the transformation, as if a man had risen from the dead.

"I beg your pardon," he said, "I am afraid I have not been paying much attention to your talk. Who is this Wolfe Macfarlane?" And then, when he had heard the landlord out, "It cannot be, it cannot be," he added; "and yet I would like well to see him face to face."

"Do you know him, Doctor?" asked the undertaker, with a gasp.

"God forbid!" was the reply. "And yet the name is a strange one; it were too much to fancy two. Tell me, landlord, is he old?"

"Well," said the host, "he's not a young man, to be sure, and his hair is white; but he looks younger than you."

"He is older, though; years older. But," with a slap upon the table, "it's the rum you see in my face—rum and sin. This man, perhaps, may have an easy conscience and a good digestion. Conscience! Hear me speak. You would think I was some good, old, decent Christian, would you not? But no, not I; I never canted. Voltaire might have canted if he'd stood in my shoes; but the brains"—with a rattling fillip on his bald head—"the brains were clear and active, and I saw and made no deductions."

"If you know this doctor," I ventured to remark, after a somewhat awful pause, "I should gather that you do not share the landlord's good opinion."

Fettes paid no regard to me.

"Yes," he said, with sudden decision, "I must see him face to face."

There was another pause, and then a door was closed rather sharply on the first floor, and a step was heard upon the stair.

"That's the doctor," cried the landlord. "Look sharp and you can catch him."

It was but two steps from the small parlor to the door of the old George Inn; the wide oak staircase landed almost in the street; there was room for a Turkey rug and nothing more between the threshold and the last round of the descent; but this little space was every evening brilliantly lit up, not only by the light upon the stair and the great signal lamp below the sign, but by the warm radiance of the barroom window. The George thus brightly advertised itself to passers-by in the cold street. Fettes walked steadily to the spot, and we, who were hanging behind, beheld the two men meet, as one of them had phrased it, face to face. Dr. Macfarlane was alert and vigorous. His white hair set off his pale and placid, although energetic, countenance. He was richly dressed in the finest of broadcloth and the whitest of linen, with a great gold watch chain, and studs and spectacles of the same precious material. He wore a broadfolded tie, white and speckled with lilac, and he carried on his arm a comfortable driving coat of fur. There was no doubt but he became his years, breathing, as he did, of wealth and consideration; and it was a surprising contrast to see our parlor sot— bald, dirty, pimpled, and robed in his old camlet cloak—confront him at the bottom of the stairs.

"Macfarlane!" he said somewhat loudly, more like a herald than a friend.

The great doctor pulled up short on the fourth step, as though the familiarity of the address surprised and somewhat shocked his dignity.

"Toddy Macfarlane!" repeated Fettes.

The London man almost staggered. He stared for the swiftest of seconds at the man before him, glanced behind him with a sort of scare, and then in a startled whisper, "Fettes!" he said, "you!"

"Ay," said the other, "me! Did you think I was dead too? We are not so easy shut of our acquaintance."

"Hush, hush!" exclaimed the doctor. "Hush, hush! This meeting is so unexpected—I can see you are unmanned. I hardly knew you, I confess, at first; but I am overjoyed—overjoyed to have this opportunity. For the present it must be how-d'ye-do and good-bye, in one, for my fly is waiting, and I must not fail the train; but you shall—let me see—yes— you shall give me your address, and you can count on early news of me. We must do something for you, Fettes. I fear you are out at elbows; but we must see to that for auld lang syne, as once we sang at suppers."

"Money!" cried Fettes; "money from you! The money that I had from you is lying where I cast it in the rain."

Dr. Macfarlane had talked himself into some measure of superiority and confidence, but the uncommon energy of this refusal cast him back into his first confusion.

A horrible, ugly look came and went across his almost venerable countenance. "My dear fellow," he said, "be it as you please; my last thought is to offend you. I would intrude on none. I will leave you my address, however——"

"I do not wish it—I do not wish to know the roof that shelters you," interrupted the other. "I heard your name; I feared it might be you; I wished to know if, after all, there were a God; I know now that there is none. Begone!"

He still stood in the middle of the rug, between the stair and doorway; and the great London physician, in order to escape, would be forced to step to one side. It was plain that he hesitated before the thought of this humiliation. White as he was, there was a dangerous glitter in his spectacles; but while he still paused uncertain, he became aware that the driver of his fly was peering in from the street at this unusual scene and caught a glimpse at the same time of our little body from the parlor, huddled by the corner of the bar. The presence of so many witnesses decided him at once to flee. He crouched together, brushing on the wainscot, and made a dart like a serpent, striking for the door. But his tribulation was not yet entirely at an end, for even as he was passing, Fettes clutched him by the arm and these words came in a whisper, and yet painfully distinct, "Have you seen it again?"

The great rich London doctor cried out aloud with a sharp, throttling cry; he dashed his questioner across the open space, and, with his hands over his head, fled out of the door like a detected thief. Before it had occurred to one of us to make a movement the fly was already rattling toward the station. The scene was over like a dream, but the dream had left proofs and traces of its passage. Next day the servant found the fine gold spectacles broken on the threshold, and that very night we were all standing breathless by the barroom window, and Fettes at our side, sober, pale and resolute in look.

"God protect us, Mr. Fettes!" said the landlord, coming first into possession of his customary senses. "What in the universe is all this? These are strange things you have been saying."

Fettes turned toward us; he looked us each in succession in the face. "See if you can hold your tongues," said he. "That man Macfarlane is not safe to cross; those that have done so already have repented it too late."

And then, without so much as finishing his third glass, far less waiting for the other two, he bade us good-bye and went forth, under the lamp of the hotel, into the black night.

We three turned to our places in the parlor, with the big red fire and four clear candles; and as we recapitulated what had passed, the first chill of our surprise soon changed into a glow of curiosity. We sat late; it was the latest session I have known in the old George. Each man, before we parted, had his theory that he was bound to prove; and none of us had any nearer business in this world than to track out the past of our condemned companion, and surprise the secret that he shared with the great London doctor. It is no great boast, but I believe I was a better hand at worming out a story than either of my fellows at the George; and perhaps there is now no other man alive who could narrate to you the following foul and unnatural events.

In his young days Fettes studied medicine in the schools of Edinburgh. He had talent of a kind, the talent that picks up swiftly what it hears and readily retails it for its own. He worked little at home; but he was civil, attentive, and intelligent in the presence of his masters. They soon picked him out as a lad who listened closely and remembered well; nay, strange as it seemed to me when I first heard it, he was in those days well favored, and pleased by his exterior. There was, at that period, a certain extramural teacher of anatomy, whom I shall here designate by the letter K. His name was subsequently too well known. The man who bore it skulked through the streets of Edinburgh in disguise, while the mob that applauded at the execution of Burke called loudly for the blood of his employer. But Mr. K—— was then at the top of his vogue; he enjoyed a popularity due partly to his own talent and address, partly to the incapacity of his rival, the university professor. The students, at least, swore by his name, and Fettes believed himself, and was believed by others, to have laid the foundations of success when he had acquired the favor of this meteorically famous man. Mr. K—— was a *bon vivant* as well as an accomplished teacher; he liked a sly illusion no less than a careful preparation. In both capacities Fettes enjoyed and deserved his notice, and by the second year of his attendance he held the half-regular position of second demonstrator or sub-assistant in his class.

In this capacity, the charge of the theater and lecture room devolved in particular upon his shoulders. He had to answer for the cleanliness of the premises and the conduct of the other students, and it was a part of his duty to supply, receive, and divide the various subjects. It was with a view to this last—at that time very delicate—affair that he was lodged by Mr. K—— in the same wynd, and at last in the same building, with the dissecting rooms. Here, after a night of turbulent pleasures, his hand still tottering, his sight still misty and confused, he would be called out of bed in the black hours before the winter dawn by the unclean and desperate interlopers who supplied the table. He would open the door to these men, since infamous throughout the land. He would help them with their tragic burden, pay them their sordid price, and remain alone, when they were gone, with the unfriendly relics of humanity. From such a scene he would return to snatch another hour or two of slumber, to repair the abuses of the night, and refresh himself for the labors of the day.

Few lads could have been more insensible to the impressions of a life thus passed among the ensigns of mortality. His mind was closed against all general considerations. He was incapable of interest in the fate and fortunes of another, the slave of his own desires and low ambitions. Cold, light, and selfish in the last resort, he had that modicum of prudence, miscalled morality, which keeps a man from inconvenient drunkenness or punishable theft. He coveted, besides, a measure of consideration from his masters and his fellow pupils and he had no desire to fail conspicuously in the external parts of life. Thus he made it his pleasure to gain some distinction in his studies, and day after day rendered unimpeachable eye service to his employer, Mr. K——. For his day of work he indemnified himself by nights of roaring, blackguardly enjoyment; and when that balance had been struck, the organ that he called his conscience declared itself content.

The supply of subjects was a continual trouble to him as well as to his master. In that large and busy class, the raw material of the anatomists kept perpetually running out; and the business thus rendered necessary was not only unpleasant in itself, but threatened dangerous consequences to all who were concerned. It was the policy of Mr. K—— to ask no questions in his dealings with the trade. "They bring the body, and we pay the price," he used to say, dwelling on the alliteration— "*Quid pro quo.*" And, again, and somewhat profanely, "Ask no questions," he would tell his assistants, "for conscience sake." There was no understanding that the subjects were provided by the crime of murder. Had that idea been broached to him in words, he would have recoiled in horror; but the lightness of his speech upon so grave a matter was, in itself, an offense against good manners, and a temptation to the men with whom he dealt. Fettes, for instance, had often remarked to himself upon the singular freshness of the bodies. He had been struck again and again by the hangdog, abominable looks of the ruffians who came to him before the dawn; and putting things together clearly in his private thoughts, he perhaps attributed a meaning too immoral and too categorical to the unguarded counsels of his master. He understood his duty, in short, to have three branches: to take what was brought, to pay the price, and to avert the eye from any evidence of crime.

One November morning this policy of silence was put sharply to the test. He had been awake all night with a racking toothache—pacing his room like a caged beast or throwing himself in fury on his bed—and had fallen at last into that profound, uneasy slumber that so often follows on a night of pain, when he was awakened by the third or fourth angry repetition of the concerted signal. There was a thin, bright moonshine; it was bitter cold, windy, and frosty; the town had not yet awakened, but an indefinable stir already preluded the noise and business of the day. The ghouls had come later than usual, and they seemed more than usually eager to be gone. Fettes, sick with sleep, lighted them upstairs. He heard their grumbling Irish voices through a dream; and as they stripped the sack from their sad merchandise he leaned dozing, with his shoulder propped against the wall; he had to shake himself to find the men their money. As he did so his eyes lighted on the dead face. He started; he took two steps nearer, with the candle raised.

"God Almighty!" he cried. "That is Jane Galbraith!"

The men answered nothing, but they shuffled nearer the door.

"I know her, I tell you," he continued. "She was alive and hearty yesterday. It's impossible she can be dead; it's impossible you should have got this body fairly."

"Sure, sir, you're mistaken entirely," said one of the men.

But the other looked Fettes darkly in the eyes, and demanded the money on the spot.

It was impossible to misconceive the threat or to exaggerate the danger. The lad's heart failed him. He stammered some excuses, counted out the sum, and saw his hateful visitors depart. No sooner were they gone than he hastened to confirm his doubts. By a dozen unquestionable marks he identified the girl he had jested with the day before. He saw, with horror, marks upon her body that might well betoken violence. A panic seized him, and he took refuge in his room. There he reflected at length over the discovery that he had made; considered soberly the bearing of Mr. K——'s instructions and the danger to himself of interference in so serious a business, and at last, in sore perplexity, determined to wait for the advice of his immediate superior, the class assistant.

This was a young doctor, Wolfe Macfarlane, a high favorite among all the reckless students, clever, dissipated, and unscrupulous to the last degree. He had traveled and studied abroad. His manners were agreeable and a little forward. He was an authority on the stage, skillful on the ice or the links with skate or golf club; he dressed with nice audacity, and, to put the finishing touch upon his glory, he kept a gig and a strong trotting horse. With Fettes he was on terms of intimacy; indeed, their relative positions called for some community of life; and when subjects were scarce the pair would drive far into the country in Macfarlane's gig, visit and desecrate some lonely graveyard, and return before dawn with their booty to the door of the dissecting room.

On that particular morning Macfarlane arrived somewhat earlier than his wont. Fettes heard him, and met him on the stairs, told him his story, and showed him the cause of his alarm. Macfarlane examined the marks on her body.

"Yes," he said with a nod, "it looks fishy."

"Well, what should I do?" asked Fettes.

"Do?" repeated the other. "Do you want to do anything? Least said soonest mended, I should say."

"Someone else might recognize her," objected Fettes. "She was as well known as the Castle Rock."

"We'll hope not," said Macfarlane, "and if anybody does—well, you didn't, don't you see, and there's an end. The fact is, this has been going on too long. Stir up the mud, and you'll get K—— into the most unholy trouble; you'll be in a shocking box yourself. So will I, if you come to that. I should like to know how any one of us would look, or what the devil we should have to say for ourselves, in any Christian witness box. For me, you know there's one thing certain—that, practically speaking, all our subjects have been murdered."

"Macfarlane!" cried Fettes.

"Come now!" sneered the other. "As if you hadn't suspected it yourself!"

"Suspecting is one thing——"

"And proof another. Yes, I know; and I'm as sorry as you are this should have come here," tapping the body with his cane. "The next best thing for me is not to recognize it; and," he added coolly, "I don't. You may, if you please. I don't dictate, but I think a man of the world would do as I do; and I may add, I fancy that is what K—— would look for at our hands. The question is, Why did he choose us two for his assistants? And I answer, because he didn't want old wives."

This was the tone of all others to affect the mind of a lad like Fettes. He agreed to imitate Macfarlane. The body of the unfortunate girl was duly dissected, and no one remarked or appeared to recognize her.

One afternoon, when his day's work was over, Fettes dropped into a popular tavern and found Macfarlane sitting with a stranger. This was a small man, very pale and dark, with coal-black eyes. The cut of his features gave a promise of intellect and refinement which was but feebly realized in his manners, for he proved, upon a nearer acquaintance, coarse, vulgar, and stupid. He exercised, however, a very remarkable control over Macfarlane; issued orders like the Great Bashaw; became inflamed at the least discussion or delay, and commented rudely on the servility with which he was obeyed. This most offensive person took a fancy to Fettes on the spot, plied him with drinks, and honored him with unusual confidences on his past career. If a tenth part of what he confessed were true, he was a very loathsome rogue; and the lad's vanity was tickled by the attention of so experienced a man.

"I'm a pretty bad fellow myself," the stranger remarked, "but Macfarlane is the boy—Toddy Macfarlane I call him. Toddy, order your friend another glass." Or it might be, "Toddy, you jump up and shut the door." "Toddy hates me," he said again. "Oh, yes, Toddy, you do!"

"Don't you call me that confounded name," growled Macfarlane.

"Hear him! Did you ever see the lads play knife? He would like to do that all over my body," remarked the stranger.

"We medicals have a better way than that," said Fettes. "When we dislike a dead friend of ours, we dissect him."

Macfarlane looked up sharply, as though this jest were scarcely to his mind.

The afternoon passed. Gray, for that was the stranger's name, invited Fettes to join them at dinner, ordered a feast so sumptuous that the tavern was thrown in commotion, and when all was done commanded Macfarlane to settle the bill. It was late before they separated; the man Gray was incapably drunk. Macfarlane, sobered by his fury, chewed the cud of the money he had been forced to squander and the slights he had been obliged to swallow. Fettes, with various liquors singing in his head, returned home with devious footsteps and a mind entirely in abeyance. Next day Macfarlane was absent from the class, and Fettes smiled to himself as he imagined him still squiring the intolerable Gray from tavern to tavern. As soon as the hour of liberty had struck he posted from place to place in quest of his last night's companions. He could find them, however, nowhere; so returned early to his rooms, went early to bed, and slept the sleep of the just.

At four in the morning he was awakened by the well-known signal.

Descending to the door, he was filled with astonishment to find Macfarlane with his gig, and in the gig one of those long and ghastly packages with which he was so well acquainted.

"What?" he cried. "Have you been out alone? How did you manage?"

But Macfarlane silenced him roughly, bidding him turn to business. When they had got the body upstairs and laid it on the table, Macfarlane made at first as if he were going away. Then he paused and seemed to hesitate; and then, "You had better look at the face," said he, in tones of some constraint. "You had better," he repeated, as Fettes only stared at him in wonder.

"But where, and how, and when did you come by it?" cried the other.

"Look at the face," was the only answer.

Fettes was staggered; strange doubts assailed him. He looked from the young doctor to the body, and then back again. At last, with a start, he did as he was bidden. He had almost expected the sight that met his eyes, and yet the shock was cruel. To see, fixed in the rigidity of death and naked on that coarse layer of sackcloth, the man whom he had left well clad and full of meat and sin upon the threshold of a tavern, awoke, even in the thoughtless Fettes, some of the terrors of the conscience. It was a *cras tibi* which re-echoed in his soul, that two whom he had known should have come to lie upon these icy tables. Yet these were only secondary thoughts. His first concern regarded Wolfe. Unprepared for a challenge so momentous, he knew not how to look his comrade in the face. He durst not meet his eye, and he had neither words nor voice at his command.

It was Macfarlane himself who made the first advance. He came up quietly behind and laid his hand gently but firmly on the other's shoulder.

"Richardson," said he, "may have the head."

Now Richardson was a student who had long been anxious for that portion of the human subject to dissect. There was no answer, and the murderer resumed: "Talking of business, you must pay me; your accounts, you see, must tally."

Fettes found a voice, the ghost of his own: "Pay you!" he cried. "Pay you for that?"

"Why, yes, of course you must. By all means and on every possible account, you must," returned the other. "I dare not give it for nothing, you dare not take it for nothing; it would compromise us both. This is another case like Jane Galbraith's. The more things are wrong the more we must act as if all were right. Where does old K—— keep his money?"

"There," answered Fettes hoarsely, pointing to a cupboard in the corner.

"Give me the key, then," said the other calmly, holding out his hand.

There was an instant's hesitation, and the die was cast. Macfarlane could not suppress a nervous twitch, the infinitesimal mark of an immense relief, as he felt the key between his fingers. He opened the cupboard, brought out pen and ink and a paper book that stood in one compartment, and separated from the funds in a drawer a sum suitable to the occasion.

"Now, look here," he said, "there is the payment made—first proof of your good faith: first step to your security. You have now to clinch it by a second. Enter the payment in your book, and then you for your part may defy the devil."

The next few seconds were for Fettes an agony of thought; but in balancing his terrors it was the most immediate that triumphed. Any future difficulty seemed almost welcome if he could avoid a present quarrel with Macfarlane. He set down the candle which he had been carrying all this time, and with a steady hand entered the date, the nature, and the amount of the transaction.

"And now," said Macfarlane, "it's only fair that you should pocket the lucre. I've had my share already. By the bye, when a man of the world falls into a bit of luck, has a few shillings extra in his pocket—I'm ashamed to speak of it, but there's a rule of conduct in the case. No treating, no purchase of expensive class books, no squaring of old debts; borrow, don't lend."

"Macfarlane," began Fettes, still somewhat hoarsely, "I have put my neck in a halter to oblige you."

"To oblige me?" cried Wolfe. "Oh, come! You did, as near as I can see the matter, what you downright had to do in self-defense. Suppose I got into trouble, where would you be? This second little matter flows clearly from the first. Mr. Gray is the continuation of Miss Galbraith.

You can't begin and then stop. If you begin, you must keep on beginning; that's the truth. No rest for the wicked."

A horrible sense of blackness and the treachery of fate seized hold upon the soul of the unhappy student.

"My God!" he cried, "but what have I done? and when did I begin? To be made a class assistant—in the name of reason, where's the harm in that? Service wanted the position; Service might have got it. Would *he* have been where *I* am now?"

"My dear fellow," said Macfarlane, "what a boy you are! What harm *has* come to you? What harm *can* come to you if you hold your tongue? Why, man, do you know what this life is? There are two squads of us—the lions and the lambs. If you're a lamb, you'll come to lie upon these tables like Gray or Jane Galbraith; if you're a lion, you'll live and drive a horse like me, like K——, like all the world with any wit or courage. You're staggered at the first. But look at K——! My dear fellow, you're clever, you have pluck. I like you, and K—— likes you. You were born to lead the hunt; and I tell you, on my honor and my experience of life, three days from now you'll laugh at all these scarecrows like a high-school boy at a farce."

And with that Macfarlane took his departure and drove off up the wynd in his gig to get under cover before daylight. Fettes was thus left alone with his regrets. He saw the miserable peril in which he stood involved. He saw, with inexpressible dismay, that there was no limit to his weakness, and that, from concession to concession, he had fallen from the arbiter of Macfarlane's destiny to his paid and helpless accomplice. He would have given the world to have been a little braver at the time, but it did not occur to him that he might still be brave. The secret of Jane Galbraith and the cursed entry in the daybook closed his mouth.

Hours passed; the class began to arrive; the members of the unhappy Gray were dealt out to one and to another, and received without remark. Richardson was made happy with the head; and before the hour of freedom rang Fettes trembled with exultation to perceive how far they had already gone toward safety.

For two days he continued to watch, with increasing joy, the dreadful process of disguise.

On the third day Macfarlane made his appearance. He had been ill, he said; but he made up for lost time by the energy with which he directed the students. To Richardson in particular he extended the most valuable assistance and advice, and that student, encouraged by the praise of the demonstrator, burned high with ambitious hopes, and saw the medal already in his grasp.

Before the week was out Macfarlane's prophecy had been fulfilled. Fettes had outlived his terrors and had forgotten his baseness. He began to plume himself upon his courage, and had so arranged the story in his mind that he could look back on these events with an unhealthy pride. Of his accomplice he saw but little. They met, of course, in the business of the class; they received their orders together from Mr. K——. At times they had a word or two in private, and Macfarlane was from first to last particularly kind and jovial. But it was plain that he avoided any reference to their common secret; and even when Fettes whispered to him that he had cast in his lot with the lions and foresworn the lambs, he only signed to him smilingly to hold his peace.

At length an occasion arose which threw the pair once more into a closer union. Mr. K—— was again short of subjects; pupils were eager, and it was a part of this teacher's pretensions to be always well supplied. At the same time there came the news of a burial in the rustic graveyard of Glencorse. Time has little changed the place in question. It stood then, as now, upon a crossroad, out of call of human habitations, and buried fathom deep in the foliage of six cedar trees. The cries of the sheep upon the neighboring hills, the streamlets upon either hand, one loudly singing among pebbles, the other dripping furtively from pond to pond, the stir of the wind in mountainous old flowering chestnuts, and once in seven days the voice of the bell and the old tunes of the precentor, were the only sounds that disturbed the silence around the rural church. The Resurrection Man—to use a byname of the period —was not to be deterred by any of the sanctities of customary piety. It was part of his trade to despise and desecrate the scrolls and trumpets of old tombs, the paths worn by the feet of worshipers and mourners, and the offerings and the inscriptions of bereaved affection. To rustic neighborhoods, where love is more than commonly tenacious, and where some bonds of blood or fellowship unite the entire society of a parish, the body-snatcher, far from being repelled by natural respect, was attracted by the ease and safety of the task. To bodies that had been laid in earth, in joyful expectation of a far different awakening, there came that hasty, lamp-lit, terror-haunted resurrection of the spade and mattock. The coffin was forced, the cerements torn, and the melancholy relics, clad in sackcloth, after being rattled for hours on moonless byways, were at length exposed to uttermost indignities before a class of gaping boys.

Somewhat as two vultures may swoop upon a dying lamb, Fettes and Macfarlane were to be let loose upon a grave in that green and quiet resting place. The wife of a farmer, a woman who had lived for sixty years, and been known for nothing but good butter and a godly conversation, was to be rooted from her grave at midnight and carried, dead and naked, to that far-away city that she had always honored with her Sunday's best; the place beside her family was to be empty till the crack of doom; her innocent and almost venerable members to be exposed to that last curiosity of the anatomist.

Late one afternoon the pair set forth, well wrapped in cloaks and furnished with a formidable bottle. It rained without remission—a cold, dense, lashing rain. Now and again there blew a puff of wind, but these sheets of falling water kept it down. Bottle and all, it was a sad and silent drive as far as Penicuik, where they were to spend the evening. They stopped once, to hide their implements in a thick bush not far from the churchyard, and once again at the Fisher's Tryst, to have a toast before the kitchen fire and vary their nips of whisky with a glass of ale. When they reached their journey's end the gig was housed, the horse was fed and comforted, and the two young doctors in a private room sat down to the best dinner and the best wine the house afforded. The lights, the fire, the beating rain upon the window, the cold, incongruous work that lay before them, added zest to their enjoyment of the meal. With every glass their cordiality increased. Soon Macfarlane handed a little pile of gold to his companion.

"A compliment," he said. "Between friends these little d——d accommodations ought to fly like pipe lights."

Fettes pocketed the money, and applauded the sentiment to the echo. "You are a philosopher," he cried. "I was an ass till I knew you.

You and K—— between you, by the Lord Harry! But you'll make a man of me."

"Of course we shall," applauded Macfarlane. "A man? I tell you, it required a man to back me up the other morning. There are some big, brawling, forty-year-old cowards who would have turned sick at the look of the d——d thing; but not you—kept your head. I watched you."

"Well, and why not?" Fettes thus vaunted himself. "It was no affair of mine. There was nothing to gain on the one side but disturbance, and on the other I could count on your gratitude, don't you see?" And he slapped his pocket till the gold pieces rang.

Macfarlane somehow felt a certain touch of alarm at these unpleasant words. He may have regretted that he had taught his young companion so successfully, but he had no time to interfere, for the other noisily continued in this boastful strain:

"The great thing is not to be afraid. Now, between you and me, I don't want to hang—that's practical; but for all cant, Macfarlane, I was born with a contempt. Hell, God, Devil, right, wrong, sin, crime, and all the old gallery of curiosities—they may frighten boys, but men of the world, like you and me, depise them. Here's to the memory of Gray!"

It was by this time growing somewhat late. The gig, according to order, was brought round to the door with both lamps brightly shining, and the young men had to pay their bill and take the road. They announced that they were bound for Peebles, and drove in that direction till they were clear of the last houses of the town; then, extinguishing the lamps, returned upon their course, and followed a byroad toward Glencorse. There was no sound but that of their own passage, and the incessant, strident pouring of the rain. It was pitch dark; here and there a white gate or a white stone in the wall guided them for a short space across the night; but for the most part it was at a foot pace, and almost groping, that they picked their way through that resonant blackness to their solemn and isolated destination. In the sunken woods that traverse the neighborhood of the burying ground the last glimmer failed them, and it became necessary to kindle a match and re-illumine one of the lanterns of the gig. Thus, under the dripping trees, and environed by huge and moving shadows, they reached the scene of their unhallowed labors.

They were both experienced in such affairs, and powerful with the spade; and they had scarce been twenty minutes at their task before they were rewarded by a dull rattle on the coffin lid. At the same moment Macfarlane, having hurt his hand upon a stone, flung it carelessly above his head. The grave, in which they now stood almost to the shoulders, was close to the edge of the plateau of the graveyard; and the gig lamp had been propped, the better to illuminate their labors, against a tree, and on the immediate verge of the steep bank descending to the stream. Chance had taken a sure aim with the stone. Then came a clang of broken glass; night fell upon them; sounds alternately dull and ringing announced the bounding of the lantern down the bank, and its occasional collision with the trees. A stone or two, which it had dislodged in its descent, rattled behind it into the profundities of the glen; and then silence, like night, resumed its sway; and they might bend their hearing to its utmost pitch, but naught was to be heard except the rain, now marching to the wind, now steadily falling over miles of open country.

They were so nearly at an end of their abhorred task that they judged it wisest to complete it in the dark. The coffin was exhumed and broken open; the body inserted in the dripping sack and carried between them to the gig; one mounted to keep it in its place, and the other, taking the horse by the mouth, groped along by wall and bush until they reached the wider road by the Fisher's Tryst. Here was a faint, diffused radiancy, which they hailed like daylight; by that they pushed the horse to a good pace and began to rattle along merrily in the direction of the town.

They had both been wetted to the skin during their operations, and now, as the gig jumped among the deep ruts, the thing that stood propped between them fell now upon one and now upon the other. At every repetition of the horrid contact each instinctively repelled it with the greater haste; and the process, natural although it was, began to tell upon the nerves of the companions. Macfarlane made some ill-favored jest about the farmer's wife, but it came hollowly from his lips, and was allowed to drop in silence. Still their unnatural burden bumped from side to side; and now the head would be laid, as if in confidence, upon their shoulders, and now the drenching sackcloth would flap icily about their faces. A creeping chill began to possess the soul of Fettes. He peered at the bundle, and it seemed somehow larger than at first. All over the countryside, and from every degree of distance, the farm dogs accompanied their passage with tragic ululations; and it grew and grew upon his mind that some unnatural miracle had been accomplished, that some nameless change had befallen the dead body, and that it was in fear of their unholy burden that the dogs were howling.

"For God's sake," said he, making a great effort to arrive at speech, "for God's sake, let's have a light!"

Seemingly Macfarlane was affected in the same direction; for, though he made no reply, he stopped the horse, passed the reins to his companion, got down, and proceeded to kindle the remaining lamp. They had by that time got no farther than the crossroad down to Auchenclinny. The rain still poured as though the deluge were returning, and it was no easy matter to make a light in such a world of wet and darkness. When at last the flickering blue flame had been transferred to the wick and began to expand and clarify, and shed a wide circle of misty brightness round the gig, it became possible for the two young men to see each other and the thing they had along with them. The rain had molded the rough sacking to the outlines of the body underneath; the head was distinct from the trunk, the shoulders plainly modeled; something at once spectral and human riveted their eyes upon the ghastly comrade of their drive.

For some time Macfarlane stood motionless, holding up the lamp. A nameless dread was swathed, like a wet sheet, about the body, and tightened the white skin upon the face of Fettes; a fear that was meaningless, a horror of what could not be, kept mounting to his brain. Another beat of the watch, and he had spoken. But his comrade forestalled him.

"That is not a woman," said Macfarlane, in a hushed voice.

"It was a woman when we put her in," whispered Fettes.

"Hold that lamp," said the other. "I must see her face."

And as Fettes took the lamp his companion untied the fastenings of the sack and drew down the cover from the head. The light fell very clear upon the dark, well-molded features and smooth-shaven cheeks of a too familiar countenance, often beheld in dreams of both of these young men. A wild yell rang up into the night; each leaped from his own side into the roadway; the lamp fell, broke, and was extinguished; and the horse, terrified by this unusual commotion, bounded and went off toward Edinburgh at a gallop, bearing along with it, sole occupant of the gig, the body of the dead and long-dissected Gray.

# LUELLA MILLER

## BY MARY WILKINS FREEMAN

THE PSYCHOLOGY of evil was well understood by the great New
England writer Nathaniel Hawthorne. Evil was to him, as H. P. Lovecraft has said, a lurking and conquering adversary. The New England he
knew, with its history of witch trials, haunted houses, ancient graves, and
tired specters, was familiar to many other writers as well.

Mary Wilkins Freeman wrote a series of suspense horror tales all set
against a background of staid New England communities, stiff unused parlors,
long rambling hallways, and ghosts that shook even rose bushes.

Mrs. Freeman's work illustrates the progression that ghost and horror stories
had made by the late nineteenth and early twentieth century. All her effects
were subtle. The horror was kept in the background, always hovering, but
never sitting down to be greeted in the front parlor. She used sight, sound,
odors, feelings; these were the new elements that would replace the creaking
phantom ghost of the early nineteenth century. Her horrors are generally
nameless. Sometimes they are but haunting shadows, but in this great story,
Luella Miller is very much a real woman. ⚮

CLOSE TO the village street stood the one-story house in which Luella
Miller, who had an evil name in the village, had dwelt. She had been
dead for years, yet there were those in the village who, in spite of the
clearer light which comes on a vantage-point from a long-past danger,
half believed in the tale which they had heard from their childhood. In

their hearts, although they scarcely would have owned it, was a survival of the wild horror and frenzied fear of their ancestors who had dwelt in the same age with Luella Miller. Young people even would stare with a shudder at the old house as they passed, and children never played around it as was their wont around an untenanted building. Not a window in the old Miller house was broken: the panes reflected the morning sunlight in patches of emerald and blue, and the latch of the sagging front door was never lifted, although no bolt secured it. Since Luella Miller had been carried out of it, the house had had no tenant except one friendless old soul who had no choice between that and the far-off shelter of the open sky. This old woman, who had survived her kindred and friends, lived in the house one week, then one morning no smoke came out of the chimney, and a body of neighbors, a score strong, entered and found her dead in her bed. There were dark whispers as to the cause of her death, and there were those who testified to an expression of fear so exalted that it showed forth the state of the departing soul upon the dead face. The old woman had been hale and hearty when she entered the house, and in seven days she was dead; it seemed that she had fallen a victim to some uncanny power. The minister talked in the pulpit with covert severity against the sin of superstition; still the belief prevailed. Not a soul in the village but would have chosen the almshouse rather than that dwelling. No vagrant, if he heard the tale, would seek shelter beneath that old roof, unhallowed by nearly half a century of superstitious fear.

There was only one person in the village who had actually known Luella Miller. That person was a woman well over eighty, but a marvel of vitality and unextinct youth. Straight as an arrow, with the spring of one recently let loose from the bow of life, she moved about the streets, and she always went to church, rain or shine. She had never married, and had lived alone for years in a house across the road from Luella Miller's.

This woman had none of the garrulousness of age, but never in all her life had she ever held her tongue for any will save her own, and she never spared the truth when she essayed to present it. She it was who bore testimony to the life, evil, though possibly wittingly or designedly so, of Luella Miller, and to her personal appearance. When this old woman spoke—and she had the gift of description, although her thoughts were clothed in the rude vernacular of her native village—one could seem to see Luella Miller as she had really looked. According to this woman, Lydia Anderson by name, Luella Miller had been a beauty of a type rather unusual in New England. She had been a slight, pliant sort of creature, as ready with a strong yielding to fate and as unbreakable as a willow. She had glimmering lengths of straight, fair hair, which she wore softly looped round a long, lovely face. She had blue eyes full of soft pleading, little slender, clinging hands, and a wonderful grace of motion and attitude.

"Luella Miller used to sit in a way nobody else could if they sat up and studied a week of Sundays," said Lydia Anderson, "and it was a sight to see her walk. If one of them willows over there on the edge of the brook could start up and get its roots free of the ground, and move off, it would go just the way Luella Miller used to. She had a green shot silk she used to wear, too, and a hat with green ribbon streamers, and a lace veil blowing across her face and out sideways, and a green ribbon flyin' from her waist. That was what she come out bride in when she married Erastus Miller. Her name before she was married was Hill. There was always a sight of "l's" in her name, married or single. Erastus Miller was good lookin', too, better lookin' than Luella. Sometimes I used to think that Luella wa'n't so handsome after all. Erastus just about worshiped her. I used to know him pretty well. He lived next door to me, and we went to school together. Folks used to say he was waitin' on me, but he wa'n't. I never thought he was except once or twice when he said things that some girls might have suspected meant somethin'. That was before Luella came here to teach the district school. It was funny how she came to get it, for folks said she hadn't any education, and that one of the big girls, Lottie Henderson, used to do all the teachin' for her, while she sat back and did embroidery work on a cambric pocket-handkerchief. Lottie Henderson was a real smart girl, a splendid scholar, and she just set her eyes by Luella, as all the girls did. Lottie would have made a real smart woman, but she died when Luella had been here about a year—just faded away and died: nobody knew what ailed her. She dragged herself to that schoolhouse and helped Luella teach till the very last minute. The committee all knew how Luella didn't do much of the work herself, but they winked at it. It wa'n't long after Lottie died that Erastus married her. I always thought he hurried it up because she wa'n't fit to teach. One of the big boys used to help her after Lottie died, but he hadn't much government, and the school didn't do very well, and Luella might have had to give it up, for the committee couldn't have shut their eyes to things much longer. The boy that helped her was a real honest, innocent sort of fellow, and he was a good scholar, too. Folks said he overstudied, and that was the reason he was took crazy the year after Luella married, but I don't know. And I don't know what made Erastus Miller go into consumption of the blood the year after he was married: consumption wa'n't in his family. He just grew weaker and weaker, and went almost bent double when he tried to wait on Luella, and he spoke feeble, like an old man. He worked terrible hard till the last trying to save up a little to leave Luella. I've seen him out in the worst storms on a wood-sled—he used to cut and sell wood—and he was hunched up on top lookin' more dead than alive. Once I couldn't stand it: I went over and helped him pitch some wood on the cart—I was always strong in my arms. I wouldn't stop for all he told me to, and I guess he was glad enough for the help. That was only a week before he died. He fell on the kitchen floor while he was gettin' breakfast and let Luella lay abed. He did all the sweepin' and the washin' and the ironin' and most of the cookin'. He couldn't bear to have Luella lift her finger, and she let him do for her. She lived like a queen for all the work she did. She didn't even do her sewin'. She said it made her shoulder ache to sew, and poor Erastus's sister Lily used to do all her sewin'. She wa'n't able to, either; she was never strong in her back, but she did it beautifully. She had to, to suit Luella, she was so dreadful particular, I never saw anythin' like the fagottin' and hemstitchin' that Lily Miller did for Luella. She made all Luella's weddin' outfit, and that green silk dress, after Maria Babbit cut it. Maria she cut it for nothin', and she did a lot more cuttin' and fittin' for nothin' for Luella, too. Lily Miller went to live with Luella after Erastus died. She gave up her home, though she was real attached to it and wa'n't a mite afraid to stay alone. She rented it and she went to live with Luella right away after the funeral."

Then this old woman, Lydia Anderson, who remembered Luella Miller, would go on to relate the story of Lily Miller. It seemed that on the removal of Lily Miller to the house of her dead brother, to live with his widow, the village people first began to talk. This Lily Miller had been hardly past her first youth, and a most robust and blooming woman, rosy-cheeked, with curls of strong, black hair overshadowing round, candid temples and bright dark eyes. It was not six months after she had taken up her residence with her sister-in-law that her rosy color faded and her pretty curves became wan hollows. White shadows began to show in the black rings of her hair, and the light died out of her eyes, her features sharpened, and there were pathetic lines at her mouth, which yet wore always an expression of utter sweetness and even happiness. She was devoted to her sister; there was no doubt that she loved her with her whole heart, and was perfectly content in her service. It was her sole anxiety lest she should die and leave her alone.

"The way Lily Miller used to talk about Luella was enough to make you mad and enough to make you cry," said Lydia Anderson. "I've been in there sometimes toward the last when she was too feeble to cook and carried her some blanc-mange or custard—somethin' I thought she might relish, and she'd thank me, and when I asked her how she was, say she felt better than she did yesterday, and asked me if I didn't think she looked better, dreadful pitiful, and say poor Luella had an awful time takin' care of her and doin' the work—she wa'n't strong enough to do anythin'—when all the time Luella wa'n't liftin' her finger and poor Lily didn't get any care except what the neighbors gave her, and Luella eat up everythin' that was carried in for Lily. I had it real straight that she did. Luella used to just sit and cry and do nothin'. She did act real fond of Lily, and she pined away considerable, too. There was those that thought she'd go into a decline herself. But after Lily died, her Aunt Abby Mixter came, and then Luella picked up and grew as fat and rosy as ever. But poor Aunt Abby begun to droop just the way Lily had, and I guess somebody wrote to her married daughter, Mrs. Sam Abbot, who lived in Barre, for she wrote her mother that she must leave right away and come and make her a visit, but Aunt Abby wouldn't go. I can see her now. She was a real good-lookin' woman, tall and large, with a big, square face and a high forehead that looked of itself kind of benevolent and good. She just tended out on Luella as if she had been a baby, and when her married daughter sent for her she wouldn't stir one inch. She'd always thought a lot of her daughter, too, but she said Luella needed her and her married daughter didn't. Her daughter kept writin' and writin', but it didn't do any good. Finally she came, and when she saw how bad her mother looked, she broke down and cried and all but went on her knees to have her come away. She spoke her mind out to Luella, too. She told her that she'd killed her husband and everybody that had anythin' to do with her, and she'd thank her to leave her mother alone. Luella went into hysterics, and Aunt Abby was so frightened that she called me after her daughter went. Mrs. Sam Abbot she went away fairly cryin' out loud in the buggy, the neighbors heard her, and well she might, for she never saw her mother again alive. I went in that night when Aunt Abby called for me, standin' in the door with her little green-checked shawl over her head. I can see her now. 'Do come over here, Miss Anderson,' she sung out, kind of gasping for breath. I didn't stop for anythin'. I put over as fast as I could, and when I got there, there was Luella laughin' and cryin' all together, and Aunt Abby trying to hush her, and all the time she herself was white as a sheet and shakin' so she could hardly stand. 'For the land sakes, Mrs. Mixter,' says I, 'you look worse than she does. You ain't fit to be up out of your bed.'

" 'Oh, there ain't anythin' the matter with me,' says she. Then she went on talkin' to Luella. 'There, there, don't, don't, poor little lamb,' says she. 'Aunt Abby is here. She ain't goin' away and leave you. Don't, poor little lamb.'

" 'Do leave her with me, Mrs. Mixter, and you get back to bed,' says I, for Aunt Abby had been layin' down considerable lately, though somehow she contrived to do the work.

" 'I'm well enough,' says she. 'Don't you think she had better have the doctor, Miss Anderson?'

" 'The doctor,' says I, 'I think *you* had better have the doctor. I think you need him much worse than some folks I could mention.' And I looked right straight at Luella Miller laughin' and cryin' and goin' on as if she was the center of all creation. All the time she was actin' so—seemed as if she was too sick to sense anythin'—she was keepin' a sharp lookout as to how we took it out of the corner of one eye. I see her. You could never cheat me about Luella Miller. Finally I got real mad and I run home and I got a bottle of valerian I had, and I poured some boilin' hot water on a handful of catnip, and I mixed up that catnip tea with most half a wineglass of valerian, and I went with it over to Luella's. I marched right up to Luella, a-holdin' out of that cup, all smokin'. 'Now,' says I, 'Luella Miller, *you swaller this!*'

" 'What is—what is it, oh, what is it?' she sort of screeches out. Then she goes off a-laughin' enough to kill.

" 'Poor lamb, poor little lamb,' says Aunt Abby, standin' over her, all kind of tottery, and tryin' to bathe her head with camphor.

" '*You swaller this right down,*' says I. And I didn't waste any ceremony. I just took hold of Luella Miller's chin and I tipped her head back, and I caught her mouth open with laughin', and I clapped that cup to her lips, and I fairly hollered at her: 'Swaller, swaller, swaller!' and she gulped it right down. She had to, and I guess it did her good. Anyhow, she stopped cryin' and laughin' and let me put her to bed, and she went to sleep like a baby inside of half an hour. That was more than poor Aunt Abby did. She lay awake all that night and I stayed with her, though she tried not to have me; said she wa'n't sick enough for watchers. But I stayed, and I made some good cornmeal gruel and I fed her a teaspoon every little while all night long. It seemed to me as if she was jest dyin' from bein' all wore out. In the mornin' as soon as it was light I run over to the Bisbees and sent Johnny Bisbee for the doctor. I told him to tell the doctor to hurry, and he come pretty quick. Poor Aunt Abby didn't seem to know much of anythin' when he got there. You couldn't hardly tell she breathed, she was so used up. When the doctor had gone, Luella came into the room lookin' like a baby in her ruffled nightgown. I can see her now. Her eyes were as blue and her face all pink and white like a blossom, and she looked at Aunt Abby in the bed sort of innocent and surprised. 'Why,' says she, 'Aunt Abby ain't got up yet?'

" 'No, she ain't,' says I, pretty short.

" 'I thought I didn't smell the coffee,' says Luella.

" 'Coffee,' says I. 'I guess if you have coffee this mornin' you'll make it yourself.'

"'I never made the coffee in all my life,' says she, dreadful astonished. 'Erastus always made the coffee as long as he lived, and then Lily she made it, and then Aunt Abby made it. I don't believe I *can* make the coffee, Miss Anderson.'

"'You can make it or go without, jest as you please,' says I.

"'Aint Aunt Abby goin' to get up?' says she.

"'I guess she won't get up,' says I, 'sick as she is.' I was gettin' madder and madder. There was somethin' about that little pink-and-white thing standin' there and talkin' about coffee, when she had killed so many better folks than she was, and had jest killed another, that made me feel 'most as if I wished somebody would up and kill her before she had a chance to do any more harm.

"'Is Aunt Abby sick?' says Luella, as if she was sort of aggrieved and injured.

"'Yes,' says I, 'she's sick, and she's goin' to die, and then you'll be left alone, and you'll have to do for yourself and wait on yourself, or do without things.' I don't know but I was sort of hard, but it was the truth, and if I was any harder than Luella Miller had been I'll give up. I ain't never been sorry that I said it. Well, Luella, she up and had hysterics again at that, and I jest let her have 'em. All I did was to bundle her into the room on the other side of the entry where Aunt Abby couldn't hear her, if she wa'n't past it—I don't know but she was —and set her down hard in a chair and told her not to come back into the other room, and she minded. She had her hysterics in there till she got tired. When she found out that nobody was comin' to coddle her and do for her she stopped. At least I suppose she did. I had all I could do with poor Aunt Abby tryin' to keep the breath of life in her. The doctor had told me that she was dreadful low, and give me some very strong medicine to give to her in drops real often, and told me real particular about the nourishment. Well, I did as he told me real faithful till she wa'n't able to swaller any longer. Then I had her daughter sent for. I had begun to realize that she wouldn't last any time at all. I hadn't realized it before, though I spoke to Luella the way I did. The doctor he came, and Mrs. Sam Abbot, but when she got there it was too late; her mother was dead. Aunt Abby's daughter just give one look at her mother layin' there, then she turned sort of sharp and sudden and looked at me.

" 'Where is she?' says she, and I knew she meant Luella.

" 'She's out in the kitchen,' says I. 'She's too nervous to see folks die. She's afraid it will make her sick.'

"The Doctor he speaks up then. He was a young man. Old Doctor Park had died the year before, and this was a young fellow just out of college. 'Mrs. Miller is not strong,' says he, kind of severe, 'and she is quite right in not agitating herself.'

" 'You are another, young man; she's got her pretty claw on you,' thinks I, but I didn't say anythin' to him. I just said over to Mrs. Sam Abbot that Luella was in the kitchen, and Mrs. Sam Abbot she went out there, and I went, too, and I never heard anythin' like the way she talked to Luella Miller. I felt pretty hard to Luella myself, but this was more than I ever would have dared to say. Luella she was too scared to go into hysterics. She jest flopped. She seemed to jest shrink away to nothin' in that kitchen chair, with Mrs. Sam Abbot standin' over her and talkin' and tellin' her the truth. I guess the truth was most too much for her and no mistake, because Luella presently actually did faint away, and there wa'n't any sham about it, the way I always suspected there was about them hysterics. She fainted dead away and we had to lay her flat on the floor, and the Doctor he came runnin' out and he said somethin' about a weak heart dreadful fierce to Mrs. Sam Abbot, but she wa'n't a mite scared. She faced him jest as white as even Luella was layin' there lookin' like death and the Doctor feelin' of her pulse.

" 'Weak heart,' says she, 'weak heart; weak fiddlesticks! There ain't nothin' weak about that woman. She's got strength enough to hang onto other folks till she kills 'em. Weak? It was my poor mother that was weak: this woman killed her as sure as if she had taken a knife to her.'

"But the Doctor he didn't pay much attention. He was bendin' over Luella layin' there with her yellow hair all streamin' and her pretty pink-and-white face all pale, and her blue eyes like stars gone out, and he was holdin' onto her hand and smoothin' her forehead, and tellin' me to get the brandy in Aunt Abby's room, and I was sure as I wanted to be that Luella had got somebody else to hang onto, now Aunt Abby was gone, and I thought of poor Erastus Miller, and I sort of pitied the poor young Doctor, led away by a pretty face, and I made up my mind I'd see what I could do.

"I waited till Aunt Abby had been dead and buried about a month, and the Doctor was goin' to see Luella steady and folks were beginnin' to talk; then one evenin', when I knew the Doctor had been called out of town and wouldn't be round, I went over to Luella's. I found her all dressed up in a blue muslin with white polka dots on it, and her hair curled jest as pretty, and there wa'n't a young girl in the place could compare with her. There was somethin' about Luella Miller seemed to draw the heart right out of you, but she didn't draw it out of *me*. She was settin' rocking in the chair by her sittin'-room window, and Maria Brown had gone home. Maria Brown had been in to help her, or rather to do the work, for Luella wa'n't helped when she didn't do anythin'. Maria Brown was real capable and she didn't have any ties; she wa'n't married, and lived alone, so she'd offered. I couldn't see why she should do the work any more than Luella; she wa'n't any too strong; but she seemed to think she could and Luella seemed to think so, too, so she went over and did all the work—washed, and ironed, and baked, while Luella sat and rocked. Maria didn't live long afterward. She began to fade away just the same fashion the others had. Well, she was warned, but she acted real mad when folks said anythin': said Luella was a poor, abused woman, too delicate to help herself, and they'd ought to be ashamed, and if she died helpin' them that couldn't help themselves she would—and she did.

"'I s'pose Maria has gone home,' says I to Luella, when I had gone in and sat down opposite her.

"'Yes, Maria went half an hour ago, after she had got supper and washed the dishes,' says Luella, in her pretty way.

"'I suppose she has got a lot of work to do in her own house tonight,' says I, kind of bitter, but that was all thrown away on Luella Miller. It seemed to her right that other folks that wa'n't any better able than she was herself should wait on her, and she couldn't get it through her head that anybody should think it *wa'n't* right.

" 'Yes,' says Luella, real sweet and pretty, 'yes, she said she had to do her washin' tonight. She has let it go for a fortnight along of comin' over here.'

" 'Why don't she stay home and do her washin' instead of comin' over here and doin' *your* work, when you are just as well able, and enough sight more so, than she is to do it?' says I.

"Then Luella she looked at me like a baby who has a rattle shook at it. She sort of laughed as innocent as you please. 'Oh, I can't do the work myself, Miss Anderson,' says she. 'I never did. Maria *has* to do it.'

"Then I spoke out: 'Has to do it!' says I. 'Has to do it!' She don't have to do it, either. Maria Brown has her own home and enough to live on. She ain't beholden to you to come over here and slave for you and kill herself.'

"Luella she jest set and stared at me for all the world like a doll-baby that was so abused that it was comin' to life.

" 'Yes,' says I, 'she's killin' herself. She's goin' to die just the way Erastus did, and Lily, and your Aunt Abby. You're killin' her jest as you did them. I don't know what there is about you, but you seem to bring a curse,' says I. 'You kill everybody that is fool enough to care anythin' about you and do for you.'

"She stared at me and she was pretty pale.

" 'And Maria ain't the only one you're goin' to kill,' says I. 'You're goin' to kill Doctor Malcom before you're done with him.'

"Then a red color came flamin' all over her face. 'I ain't goin' to kill him, either,' says she, and she begun to cry.

"Yes, you *be!*' says I. Then I spoke as I had never spoke before. You see, I felt it on account of Erastus. I told her that she hadn't any business to think of another man after she'd been married to one that had died for her: that she was a dreadful woman; and she was, that's true enough, but sometimes I have wondered lately if she knew it—if she wa'n't like a baby with scissors in its hand cuttin' everybody without knowin' what it was doin'.

"Luella she kept gettin' paler and paler, and she never took her eyes off my face. There was somethin' awful about the way she looked at me and never spoke one word. After awhile I quit talkin' and I went home. I watched that night, but her lamp went out before nine o'clock, and when Doctor Malcom came drivin' past and sort of slowed up he see there wa'n't any light and he drove along. I saw her sort of shy out of meetin' the next Sunday, too, so he shouldn't go home with her, and I begun to think mebbe she did have some conscience after all. It was only a week after that that Maria Brown died—sort of sudden at the last, though everybody had seen it was comin'. Well, then there was a good deal of feelin' and pretty dark whispers. Folks said the days of witchcraft had come again, and they were pretty shy of Luella. She acted sort of offish to the Doctor and he didn't go there, and there wa'n't anybody to do anythin' for her. I don't know how she *did* get along. I wouldn't go in there and offer to help her—not because I was afraid of dyin' like the rest, but I thought she was just as well able to do her own work as I was to do it for her, and I thought it was about time that she did it and stopped killin' other folks. But it wa'n't very long before folks began to say that Luella herself was goin' into a decline jest the way her husband, and Lily, and Aunt Abby and the others had, and I saw myself that she looked pretty bad. I used to see her goin' past from the store with a bundle as if she could hardly crawl, but I remembered how Erastus used to wait and 'tend when he couldn't hardly put one foot before the other, and I didn't go out to help her.

"But at last one afternoon I saw the Doctor come drivin' up like mad with his medicine chest, and Mrs. Babbit came in after supper and said that Luella was real sick.

" 'I'd offer to go in and nurse her,' says she, 'but I've got my children to consider, and mebbe it ain't true what they say, but it's queer how many folks that have done for her have died.'

"I didn't say anythin', but I considered how she had been Erastus's wife and how he had set his eyes by her, and I made up my mind to go in the next mornin', unless she was better, and see what I could do; but the next mornin' I see her at the window, and pretty soon she came steppin' out as spry as you please, and a little while afterward Mrs. Babbit came in and told me that the Doctor had got a girl from out of town, a Sarah Jones, to come there, and she said she was pretty sure that the Doctor was goin' to marry Luella.

"I saw him kiss her in the door that night myself, and I knew it was true. The woman came that afternoon, and the way she flew around was a caution. I don't believe Luella had swept since Maria died. She swept and dusted, and washed and ironed; wet clothes and dusters and carpets were flyin' over there all day, and every time Luella set her foot out when the Doctor wa'n't there there was that Sarah Jones helpin' of her up and down the steps, as if she hadn't learned to walk.

"Well, everybody knew that Luella and the Doctor were goin' to be married, but it wa'n't long before they began to talk about his lookin' so poorly, jest as they had about the others; and they talked about Sarah Jones, too.

"Well, the Doctor did die, and he wanted to be married first, so as to leave what little he had to Luella, but he died before the minister could get there, and Sarah Jones died a week afterward.

"Well, that wound up everything for Luella Miller. Not another soul in the whole town would lift a finger for her. There got to be a sort of panic. Then she began to droop in good earnest. She used to have to go to the store herself, for Mrs. Babbit was afraid to let Tommy go for her, and I've seen her goin' past and stoppin' every two or three steps to rest. Well, I stood it as long as I could, but one day I see her comin' with her arms full and stoppin' to lean against the Babbit fence, and I run out and took her bundles and carried them to her house. Then I went home and never spoke one word to her though she called after me dreadful kind of pitiful. Well, that night I was taken sick with a chill, and I was sick as I wanted to be for two weeks. Mrs. Babbit had seen me run out to help Luella and she came in and told me I was goin' to die on account of it. I didn't know whether I was or not, but I considered I had done right by Erastus's wife.

"That last two weeks Luella she had a dreadful hard time, I guess. She was pretty sick, and as near as I could make out nobody dared go near her. I don't know as she was really needin' anythin' very much, for there was enough to eat in her house and it was warm weather, and she made out to cook a little flour gruel every day, I know, but I guess she had a hard time, she that had been so petted and done for all her life.

"When I got so I could go out, I went over there one morning. Mrs. Babbit had just come in to say she hadn't seen any smoke and she didn't know but it was somebody's duty to go in, but she couldn't help thinkin' of her children, and I got right up, though I hadn't been out of the house for two weeks, and I went in there, and Luella she was layin' on the bed, and she was dyin'.

"She lasted all that day and into the night. But I sat there after the new doctor had gone away. Nobody else dared to go there. It was about midnight that I left her for a minute to run home and get some medicine I had been takin', for I begun to feel rather bad.

"It was a full moon that night, and just as I started out of my door to cross the street back to Luella's, I stopped short, for I saw something."

Lydia Anderson at this juncture always said with a certain defiance that she did not expect to be believed, and then proceeded in a hushed voice:

"I saw what I saw, and I know I saw it, and I will swear on my death bed that I saw it. I saw Luella Miller and Erastus Miller, and Lily, and Aunt Abby, and Maria, and the Doctor, and Sarah, all goin' out of her door, and all but Luella shone white in the moonlight, and they were all helpin' her along till she seemed to fairly fly in the midst of them. Then it all disappeared. I stood a minute with my heart poundin', then I went over there. I thought of goin' for Mrs. Babbit, but I thought she'd be afraid. So I went alone, though I knew what had happened. Luella was layin' real peaceful, dead on her bed."

This was the story that the old woman, Lydia Anderson, told, but the sequel was told by the people who survived her, and this is the tale which had become folklore in the village.

Lydia Anderson died when she was eighty-seven. She had continued wonderfully hale and hearty for one of her years until about two weeks before her death.

One bright moonlight evening she was sitting beside a window in her parlor when she made a sudden exclamation, and was out of the house and across the street before the neighbor who was taking care of her could stop her. She followed as fast as possible and found Lydia Anderson stretched on the ground before the door of Luella Miller's deserted house, and she was quite dead.

The next night there was a red gleam of fire athwart the moonlight and the old house of Luella Miller was burned to the ground. Nothing is now left of it except a few old cellar stones and a lilac bush, and in summer a helpless trail of morning glories among the weeds, which might be considered emblematic of Luella herself.

# A REVOLVER IN THE CORNER CUPBOARD

## BY GRAHAM GREENE

GRAHAM GREENE, a distant relative of Robert Louis Stevenson, has referred to many of his own novels as "entertainments." Just as Stevenson was an amusement, Greene is an entertainer, but that does not mean that he is not one of the major novelists today, or the one who has not handled the deepest and most painful material of human suffering.

Graham Greene was one of the first writers of our time to realize that the concept of the hero in writing had disappeared. All his heroes are anti-heroes; they are men and women threatened by the anxieties of our times, subject to such pain and suffering, often of their own making, that they take on a new dimension of heroic stature. Greene is very much influenced by the Greek idea of tragedy as well as by the old Christian concept of the fall of man. Every Greene hero goes through some crisis of personal degradation. The remarkable "A Revolver in the Corner Cupboard" has the excoriating suspense of an anti-hero who plays the most dangerous game—in which a young man is his own most desperate enemy. ৯৯

I CAN REMEMBER very clearly the afternoon I found the revolver in the brown deal corner cupboard in the bedroom which I shared with my elder brother. It was the early autumn of 1922. I was seventeen and terribly bored and in love with my sister's governess—one of those miserable, hopeless, romantic loves of adolescence that set in many minds the idea that love and despair are inextricable and that successful love hardly deserves the name. At that age one may fall irrevocably in love with failure, and success of any kind loses half its savour before it is experienced. Such a love is surrendered once and for all to the singer at the pavement's edge, the bankrupt, the old school friend who wants to touch you for a dollar. Perhaps in many so conditioned it is the love for God that mainly survives, because in his eyes they can imagine themselves remaining always drab, seedy, unsuccessful, and therefore worthy of notice.

The revolver was a small genteel object with six chambers like a tiny egg stand, and there was a cardboard box of bullets. It has only recently occurred to me that they may have been blanks; I always assumed them to be live ammunition, and I never mentioned the discovery to my brother because I had realized the moment I saw the revolver the use I intended to make of it. (I don't to this day know why he possessed it; certainly he had no license, and he was only three years older than myself. A large family is as departmental as a Ministry.)

My brother was away—probably climbing in the Lake District—and until he returned the revolver was to all intents mine. I knew what to do with it because I had been reading a book (the name Ossendowski comes to mind as the possible author) describing how the White Russian officers, condemned to inaction in South Russia at the tail-end of the counter-revolutionary war, used to invent hazards with which to escape boredom. One man would slip a charge into a revolver and turn the chambers at random, and his companion would put the revolver to his head and pull the trigger. The chance, of course, was six to one in favor of life.

How easily one forgets emotions. If I were dealing now with an imaginary character, I would feel it necessary for verisimilitude to make him hesitate, put the revolver back into the cupboard, return to it again after an interval, reluctantly and fearfully, when the burden of boredom became too great. But in fact I think there was no hesitation at all, for the next I can remember is crossing Berkhamsted Common, gashed here and there between the gorse bushes with the stray trenches of the first Great War, toward the Ashridge beeches. Perhaps before I had made the discovery, boredom had already reached an intolerable depth.

I think the boredom was far deeper than the love. It had always been a feature of childhood: it would set in on the second day of the school holidays. The first day was all happiness, and, after the horrible confinement and publicity of school, seemed to consist of light, space, and silence. But a prison conditions its inhabitants. I never wanted to return to it (and finally expressed my rebellion by the simple act of running away), but yet I was so conditioned that freedom bored me unutterably.

The psychoanalysis that followed my act of rebellion had fixed the boredom as hypo fixes the image on the negative. I emerged from those delightful months in London spent at my analyst's house—perhaps the happiest months of my life—correctly orientated, able to take a proper extrovert interest in my fellows (the jargon rises to the lips), but wrung dry. For years, it seems to me, I could take no aesthetic interest in any visual thing at all: staring at a sight that others assured me was beautiful, I would feel nothing. I was fixed in my boredom. (Writing this I come on a remark of Rilke: 'Psychoanalysis is too fundamental a help for me, it helps you once and for all, it clears you up, and to find myself finally cleared up one day might be even more helpless than this chaos.')

Now with the revolver in my pocket I was beginning to emerge. I had stumbled on the perfect cure. I was going to escape in one way or another, and because escape was inseparably connected with the Common in my mind, it was there that I went.

The wilderness of gorse, old trenches, abandoned butts was the unchanging backcloth of most of the adventures of childhood. It was to the Common I had decamped for my act of rebellion some years before, with the intention, expressed in a letter left after breakfast on the heavy black sideboard, that there I would stay, day and night, until either I had starved or my parents had given in; when I pictured war it was always in terms of this Common, and myself leading a guerilla campaign in the ragged waste, for no one, I was persuaded, knew its paths so intimately (how humiliating that in my own domestic campaign I was ambushed by my elder sister after a few hours).

Beyond the Common lay a wide grass ride known for some reason as Cold Harbour to which I would occasionally with some fear take a horse, and beyond this again stretched Ashridge Park, the smooth olive skin of beech trees and the thick last year's quagmire of leaves, dark like old pennies. Deliberately I chose my ground, I believe without any real fear —perhaps because I was uncertain myself whether I was playacting; perhaps because so many acts which my elders would have regarded as neurotic, but which I still consider to have been under the circumstances highly reasonable, lay in the background of this more dangerous venture.

There had been, for example, perhaps five or six years before, the disappointing morning in the dark room by the linen cupboard on the eve of term when I had patiently drunk a quantity of hypo under the impression that it was poisonous: on another occasion the blue glass bottle of hay fever lotion which as it contained a small quantity of cocaine had probably been good for my mood: the bunch of deadly nightshade that I had eaten with only a slight narcotic effect: the twenty aspirins I had taken before swimming in the empty out-of-term school baths (I can still remember the curious sensation of swimming through wool): these acts may have removed all sense of strangeness as I slipped a bullet into a chamber and, holding the revolver behind my back, spun the chambers round.

Had I romantic thoughts about the governess? Undoubtedly I must have had, but I think that at the most they simply eased the medicine down. Boredom, aridity, those were the main emotions. Unhappy love has, I suppose, sometimes driven boys to suicide, but this was not suicide, whatever a coroner's jury might have said of it: it was a gamble with six chances to one against an inquest. The romantic flavor—the autumn scene, the small heavy compact shape lying in the fingers— that perhaps was a tribute to adolescent love, but the discovery that it was possible to enjoy again the visible world by risking its total loss was one I was bound to make sooner or later.

I put the muzzle of the revolver in my right ear and pulled the trigger. There was a minute click, and looking down at the chamber I could see that the charge had moved into place. I was out by one. I remember an extraordinary sense of jubilation. It was as if a light had been turned on. My heart was knocking in its cage, and I felt that life contained an infinite number of possibilities. It was like a young man's first successful experience of sex—as if in that Ashridge glade one had passed a test of manhood. I went home and put the revolver back in the corner cupboard.

The odd thing about this experience was that it was repeated several times. At fairly long intervals I found myself craving for the drug. I took the revolver with me when I went up to Oxford and I would walk out from Headington towards Elsfield down what is now a wide arterial road, smooth and shiny like the walls of a public lavatory. Then it was a sodden unfrequented country lane. The revolver would be whipped behind my back, the chambers twisted, the muzzle quickly and surreptitiously inserted beneath the black and ugly winter tree, the trigger pulled.

Slowly the effect of the drug wore off—I lost the sense of jubilation, I began to gain from the experience only the crude kick of excitement. It was like the difference between love and lust. And as the quality of the experience deteriorated so my sense of responsibility grew and worried me. I wrote a very bad piece of free verse (free because it was easier in that way to express my meaning without literary equivocation) describing how, in order to give a fictitious sense of danger, I would 'press the trigger of a revolver I already know to be empty'. This piece of verse I would leave permanently on my desk, so that if I lost my gamble, there would be incontrovertible evidence of an accident, and my parents, I thought, would be less troubled than by an apparent suicide—or than by the rather bizarre truth.

But it was back at Berkhamsted that I paid a permanent farewell to the drug. As I took my fifth dose it occurred to me that I wasn't even excited: I was beginning to pull the trigger about as casually as I might take an aspirin tablet. I decided to give the revolver—which was six chambered—a sixth and last chance. Twirling the chambers round, I put the muzzle to my ear for the last time and heard the familiar empty click as the chambers revolved. I was through with the drug, and walking back over the Common, down the new road by the ruined castle, past the private entrance to the gritty old railway station—reserved for the use of Lord Brownlow—my mind was already busy on other plans. One campaign was over, but the war against boredom had got to go on.

I put the revolver back in the corner cupboard, and going downstairs I lied gently and convincingly to my parents that a friend had invited me to join him in Paris.

# Horror Explorers Out of Time and Space: Fitz-James O'Brien, H. P. Lovecraft & August Derleth (The Science Fiction Horror Story)

# THE WONDERSMITH

## BY FITZ-JAMES O'BRIEN

*Science fiction,* one of the most popular forms of writing today, has been known by that term less than fifty years. Of course, Mary Shelley's great *Frankenstein* was an early precursor of the genre and many nineteenth-century writers tried their hand at it.

One of the greatest was Fitz-James O'Brien, who was born in Ireland in 1828. During his young manhood he published extensively in Ireland, Scotland, and England. Always extravagant, he ran through a small fortune as a man, and sailed for the United States to try to make a new life for himself.

In the Bohemia of New York he soon became a colorful, even outrageous character. Living in the same Greenwich Village as had Edgar Allan Poe, O'Brien inundated himself in the mystery and horror tales of that master. His first famous short story, "The Diamond Lens," was very much influenced by Poe and Nathaniel Hawthorne.

In the *Atlantic Monthly* for October 1859, he wrote a science fiction horror story called "The Wondersmith" which is one of the most remarkably individualistic stories in American literature. It is a story of great historical importance because it is one of the earliest robot stories ever written. Gilbert Seldes has said "Nothing in the story of Frankenstein's monster, nothing in the crushing fury of Capek's robots gives the same sense of horror as the description of the bloodthirsty stabbing of galvanized manikins of this story." ঙ৯

### 1. GOLOSH STREET AND ITS PEOPLE

A SMALL lane, the name of which I have forgotten, or do not choose to remember, slants suddenly off from Chatham Street (before that headlong thoroughfare rushes into the Park), and retreats suddenly down toward the East River, as if it were disgusted with the smell of old clothes, and had determined to wash itself clean. This excellent intention it has, however, evidently contributed toward the making of that imaginary pavement mentioned in the old adage; for it is still emphatically a dirty street. It has never been able to shake off the taint of filth which it inherits from the ancestral thoroughfare. It is slushy and greasy.

I like a dirty slum; not because I am naturally unclean but because I generally find a certain sediment of philosophy precipitated in its gutters. A clean street is terribly prosaic. There is no food for thought in carefully swept pavements, barren kennels, and vulgarly spotless houses. But when I go down a street which has been left so long to itself that it has acquired a distinct outward character, I find plenty to think about. The scraps of sodden letters lying in the ash-barrel have their meaning: desperate appeals, perhaps, from Tom, the baker's assistant, to Amelia, the daughter of the dry-goods retailer, who is always selling at a sacrifice in consequence of the late fire. That may be Tom himself who is now passing me in a white apron, and I look up at the windows of the house (which does not, however, give any signs of a recent conflagration) and almost hope to see Amelia wave a white pocket-handkerchief.

The bit of orange-peel lying on the sidewalk inspires thought. Who will fall over it? who but the industrious mother of six children, the youngest of which is only nine months old, all of whom are dependent on her exertions for support? I see her slip and tumble. I see the pale face convulsed with agony, and the vain struggle to get up; the pitying crowd closing her off from all air; the anxious young doctor who happened to be passing by; the manipulation of the broken limb, the shake of the head, the moan of the victim, the litter borne on men's shoulders, the gates of the New York hospital unclosing, the subscription taken up on the spot.

There is some food for speculation in that three-year-old, tattered child, masked with dirt, who is throwing a brick at another three-year-old, tattered child, masked with dirt. It is not difficult to perceive that he is destined to lurk, as it were, through life. His bad, flat face—or, at least, what can be seen of it—does not look as if it were made for the light of day. The mire in which he wallows now is but a type of the moral mire in which he will wallow hereafter. The feeble little hand lifted at this instant to smite his companion, half in earnest, half in jest, will be raised against his fellow-beings for evermore.

Golosh Street—as I will call this nameless lane before alluded to—is an interesting locality. All the oddities of trade seemed to have found their way thither and made an eccentric mercantile settlement. There is a bird-shop at one corner wainscoted with little cages containing linnets, wax-wings, canaries, black-birds, Mino-birds, with a hundred other varieties, known only to naturalists. Immediately opposite is an establishment where they sell nothing but ornaments made out of the tinted leaves of autumn, varnished and gummed into various forms. Further down is a secondhand book-stall which looks like a sentry-box mangled out flat, and which is remarkable for not containing a complete set of any work. There is a small chink between two ordinary-sized houses, in which a little Frenchman makes and sells artificial eyes, specimens of which, ranged on a black velvet cushion, stare at you unwinkingly through the window as you pass, until you shudder and hurry on, thinking how awful the world would be if everyone went about without eyelids. There are junk-shops in Golosh Street that seem to have got hold of all the old nails in the ark and all the old brass of Corinth. Madame Filomel, the fortune-teller, lives at No. 12 Golosh Street, second story front, pull the bell on the left-hand side. Next door to Madame is the shop of Herr Hippe, commonly called the Wondersmith.

Herr Hippe's shop is the largest in Golosh Street, and to all appearance is furnished with the smallest stock. Beyond a few packing-cases, a turner's lathe, and a shelf laden with dissected maps of Europe, the interior of the shop is entirely unfurnished. The window, which is lofty and wide, but much begrimed with dirt, contains the only pleasant object in the place. This is a beautiful little miniature theater—that is to say, the orchestra and stage. It is fitted with charmingly painted scenery and all the appliances for scenic changes. There are tiny traps, and delicately constructed "lifts," and real foot-lights fed with burning fluid, and in the orchestra sits a diminutive conductor before his desk, surrounded by musical manikins, all provided with the smallest of violoncellos, flutes, oboes, drums, and such like.

There are characters also on the stage. A Templar in a white cloak is dragging a fainting female form to the parapet of a ruined bridge, while behind a great black rock on the left one can see a man concealed, who, kneeling, levels an arquebuse at the knight's heart. But the orchestra is silent; the conductor never beats the time, the musicians never play a note; the Templar never drags his victim an inch nearer to the bridge; the masked avenger takes an eternal aim with his weapon. This repose appears unnatural; for so admirably are the figures executed that they seem replete with life. One is almost led to believe, in looking on them, that they are resting beneath some spell which hinders their motion. One expects every moment to hear the loud explosion of the arquebuse —to see the blue smoke curling, the Templar falling—to hear the orchestra playing the requiem of the guilty.

Few people knew what Herr Hippe's business or trade really was. That he worked at something was evident; else why the shop? Some people inclined to the belief that he was an inventor, or mechanician. His workshop was in the rear of the store, and into that sanctuary no one but himself had admission. He arrived in Golosh Street eight or ten years ago, and one fine morning the neighbors, taking down their shutters, observed that No. 13 had got a tenant. A tall, thin, sallow-faced man stood on a ladder outside the shop entrance, nailing up a large board, on which "Herr Hippe, Wondersmith," was painted in black letters on a yellow ground. The little theater stood in the window, where it stood ever after, and Herr Hippe was established.

But what was a Wondersmith? people asked each other. No one could reply. Madame Filomel was consulted; but she looked grave, and said that it was none of her business. Mr. Pippel, the bird-fancier, who was a German, and ought to know best, thought it was the English for some singular Teutonic profession; but his replies were so vague that Golosh Street was as unsatisfied as ever. Solon, the little humpback, who kept the odd-volume book-stall at the lowest corner, could throw no light upon it. And at length people had to come to the conclusion that Herr Hippe was either a coiner or a magician, and opinions were divided.

## 2.   A BOTTLEFUL OF SOULS

IT WAS a dull December evening. There was little trade doing in Golosh Street, and the shutters were up at most of the shops. Hippe's store had been closed at least an hour, and the Mino-birds and Bohemian wax-wings at Mr. Pippel's had their heads tucked under their wings in their first sleep.

Herr Hippe sat in his parlor, which was lit by a pleasant wood-fire. There were no candles in the room, and the flickering blaze played fantastic tricks on the pale gray walls. It seemed the festival of shadows. Processions of shapes, obscure and indistinct, passed across the leaden-hued panels and vanished in the dusk corners. Every fresh blaze flung up by the wayward logs created new images. Now it was a funeral throng, with the bowed figures of mourners, the shrouded coffin, the plumes that waved like extinguished torches; now a knightly cavalcade with flags and lances, and weird horses, that rushed silently along until they met the angle of the room, when they pranced through the wall and vanished.

On a table close to where Herr Hippe sat was placed a large square box of some dark wood, while over it was spread a casing of steel, so elaborately wrought in an open arabesque pattern that it seemed like a shining blue lace which was lightly stretched over its surface.

Herr Hippe lay luxuriously in his armchair, looking meditatively into the fire. He was tall and thin, and his skin was of a dull saffron hue. Long, straight hair, sharply cut, regular features, a long, thin mustache, that curled like a dark asp around his mouth, the expression of which was so bitter and cruel that it seemed to distill the venom of the ideal serpent, and a bony, muscular form, were the prominent characteristics of the Wondersmith.

The profound silence that reigned in the chamber was broken by a peculiar scratching at the panel of the door, like that which at the French court was formerly substituted for the ordinary knock, when it was necessary to demand admission to the royal apartments. Herr Hippe started, raised his head, which vibrated on his long neck like the head of a cobra when about to strike, and after a moment's silence uttered a strange guttural sound. The door unclosed, and a squat, broad shouldered woman, with large, wild, oriental eyes, entered softly.

"Ah! Filomel, you are come!" said the Wondersmith, sinking back in his chair. "Where are the rest of them?"

"They will be here presently," answered Madame Filomel, seating herself in an armchair much too narrow for a person of her proportions, and over the sides of which she bulged like a pudding.

"Have you brought the souls?" asked the Wondersmith.

"They are here," said the fortune-teller, drawing a large pot-bellied black bottle from under her cloak. "Ah! I have had such trouble with them!"

"Are they of the right brand—wild, tearing, dark, devilish fellows? We want no essence of milk and honey, you know. None but souls bitter as hemlock or scorching as lightning will suit our purpose."

"You will see, you will see, Grand Duke of Egypt! They are ethereal demons, every one of them. They are the pick of a thousand births. Do you think that I, old midwife that I am, don't know the squall of the demon child from that of the angel child, the very moment they are delivered? Ask a musician how he knows, even in the dark, a note struck by Thalberg from one struck by Liszt!"

"I long to test them," cried Wondersmith, rubbing his hands joyfully. "I long to see how little devils will behave when I give them their shapes. Ah! it will be a proud day for us when we let them loose upon the cursed Christian children! Through the length and breadth of the land they will go; wherever our wandering people set foot, and wherever they are, the children of the Christians shall die. Then we, the despised Bohemians, the gypsies, as they call us, will be once more lords of the earth, as we were in the days when the accursed things called cities did not exist, and men lived in the free woods and hunted the game of the forest. Toys indeed! Ay, ay, we will give the little dears toys! toys that all day will sleep calmly in their boxes, seemingly stiff and wooden and without life—but at night, when the souls enter them, will arise and surround the cots of the sleeping children, and pierce their hearts with

their keen, envenomed blades! Toys indeed! Oh, yes, I will sell them
toys!"

And the Wondersmith laughed horribly, while the snaky mustache
on his upper lip writhed as if it had truly a serpent's power and could
sting.

"Have you got your first batch, Herr Hippe?" asked Madame Filomel.
"Are they all ready?"

"Oh ay! they are ready," answered the Wondersmith with gusto,
opening, as he spoke, the box covered with the blue steel lacework;
"they are here."

The box contained a quantity of exquisitely carved wooden manikins
of both sexes, painted with great dexterity so as to present a miniature
resemblance to nature. They were, in fact, nothing more than admirable specimens of those toys which children delight in placing in various
positions on the table—in regiments, or sitting at meals, or grouped
under the stiff green trees which always accompany them in the boxes
in which they are sold at the toy shops.

The peculiarity, however, about the manikins of Herr Hippe was
not alone the artistic truth with which the limbs and the features were
gifted; but on the countenance of each little puppet the carver's art had
wrought an expression of wickedness that was appalling. Every tiny
face had its special stamp of ferocity. The lips were thin and brimful
of malice; the small black bead-like eyes glittered with the fire of a universal hate. There was not one of the manikins, male or female, that
did not hold in his or her hand some miniature weapon. The little men,
scowling like demons, clasped in their wooden fingers swords delicate
as a housewife's needle. The women, whose countenances expressed
treachery and cruelty, clutched infinitesimal daggers, with which they
seemed about to take some terrible vengeance.

"Good!" said Madame Filomel, taking one of the manikins out of
the box and examining it attentively; "you work well, Duke Balthazar!
These little ones are of the right stamp; they look as if they had mischief in them. Ah! here come our brothers."

At this moment the same scratching that preceded the entrance of
Madame Filomel was heard at the door, and Herr Hippe replied with a

hoarse, guttural cry. The next moment two men entered. The first was a small man with very brilliant eyes. He was wrapt in a long shabby cloak, and wore a strange nondescript species of cap on his head, such a cap as one sees only in the low billiard rooms in Paris. His companion was tall, long-limbed, and slender; and his dress, although of the ordinary cut, either from the disposition of colors or from the careless, graceful attitudes of the wearer, assumed a certain air of picturesqueness. Both the men possessed the same marked oriental type of countenance which distinguished the Wondersmith and Madame Filomel. True gypsies they seemed, who would not have been out of place telling fortunes, or stealing chickens in the green lanes of England, or wandering with their wild music and their sleight-of-hand tricks through Bohemian villages.

"Welcome, brothers!" said the Wondersmith; "you are in time. Sister Filomel has brought the souls, and we are about to test them. Monsieur Kerplonne, take off your cloak. Brother Oaksmith, take a chair. I promise you some amusement this evening; so make yourselves comfortable. Here is something to aid you."

And while the Frenchman Kerplonne and his tall companion, Oaksmith, were obeying Hippe's invitation, he reached over to a little closet let into the wall, and took thence a squat bottle and some glasses, which he placed on the table.

"Drink, brothers!" he said: "it is not Christian blood, but good stout wine of Oporto. It goes right to the heart, and warms one like the sunshine of the south."

"It is good," said Kerplonne, smacking his lips with enthusiasm.

"Why don't you keep brandy? Hang wine!" cried Oaksmith, after having swallowed two bumpers in rapid successsion.

"Bah! Brandy has been the ruin of our race. It has made us sots and thieves. It shall never cross my threshold," cried the Wondersmith, with a somber indignation.

"A little of it is not bad, though, Duke," said the fortune-teller. "It consoles us for our misfortunes; it gives us the crowns we once wore; it restores to us the power we once wielded; it carries us back, as if by magic, to that land of the sun from which fate has driven us; it darkens the memory of all the evils that we have for centuries suffered."

"It is a devil; may it be cursed!" cried Herr Hippe, passionately. "It is a demon that stole from me my son, the finest youth in all Courland. Yes! my son, the son of the Waywode Balthazar, Grand Duke of Lower Egypt, died raving in a gutter, with an empty brandy-bottle in his hands. Were it not that the plant is a sacred one to our race, I would curse the grape and the vine that bore it."

This outburst was delivered with such energy that the three gypsies kept silence. Oaksmith helped himself to another glass of port, and the fortune-teller rocked to and fro in her chair, too much overawed by the Wondersmith's vehemence of manner to reply. The little Frenchman, Kerplonne, took no part in the discussion, but seemed lost in admiration of the manikins, which he took from the box in which they lay, handling them with the greatest care.

After the silence had lasted for about a minute, Herr Hippe broke it with the sudden question, "How does your eye get on, Kerplonne?"

"Excellently, Duke. It is finished. I have it here." And the little Frenchman put his hand into his breeches pocket and pulled out a large artificial human eye. Its great size was the only thing in this eye that would lead anyone to suspect its artificiality. It was at least twice the size of life; but there was a fearful speculative light in its iris, which seemed to expand and contract like the eye of a living being, that rendered it a horrible staring paradox. It looked like the naked eye of the Cyclops, torn from his forehead, and still burning with wrath and the desire for vengeance.

The little Frenchman laughed pleasantly as he held the eye in his hand, and gazed down on that huge, dark pupil, that stared back at him, it seemed, with an air of defiance and mistrust.

"It is a devil of an eye," said the little man, wiping the enameled surface with an old silk pocket-handkerchief; "it reads like a demon. My niece—the unhappy one—has a wretch of a lover, and I have a long time feared that she would run away with him. I could not read her correspondence, for she kept her writing desk closely locked. But I asked her yesterday to keep this eye in some very safe place for me. She put it, as I knew she would, into her desk, and by its aid I read every one of her letters. She was to run away next Monday, the ungratefull! but she will find herself disappointed."

And the little man laughed heartily at the success of his stratagem, and polished and fondled the great eye until that optic seemed to grow sore with rubbing.

"And you have been at work too, I see, Herr Hippe. Your manikins are excellent. But where are the souls?"

"In that bottle," answered the Wondersmith, pointing to the pot-bellied black bottle that Madame Filomel had brought with her. "Yes, Monsieur Kerplonne," he continued, "my manikins are well made. I invoked the aid of Abigor, the demon of soldiery, and he inspired me. The little fellows will be famous assassins when they are animated. We will try them tonight."

"Good!" cried Kerplonne, rubbing his hands joyously. "It is close upon New Year's day. We will fabricate millions of the little murderers by New Year's eve, and sell them in large quantities; and when the households are all asleep, and the Christian children are waiting for Santa Claus to come, the small ones will troop from their boxes, and the Christian children will die. It is famous! Health to Abigor!"

"Let us try them at once," said Oaksmith. "Is your daughter, Zonéla, in bed, Herr Hippe? Are we secure from intrusion?"

"No one is stirring about the house," replied the Wondersmith, gloomily.

Filomel leaned over to Oaksmith, and said in an undertone, "Why do you mention his daughter? You know he does not like to have her spoken about."

"I will take care that we are not disturbed," said Kerplonne, rising. "I will put my eye outside the door, to watch."

He went to the door and placed his great eye upon the floor with tender care. As he did so, a dark form, unseen by him or his second vision, glided along the passage noiselessly, and was lost in the darkness.

"Now for it!" exclaimed Madame Filomel, taking up her fat black bottle. "Herr Hippe, prepare your manikins!"

The Wondersmith took the little dolls out, one by one, and set them upon the table. Such an array of villainous countenances was never seen. An army of Italian bravoes, seen through the wrong end of a telescope, or a band of prisoners at the galleys in Lilliput, will give some faint idea of the appearance they presented. While Madame Filomel uncorked the black bottle, Herr Hippe covered the dolls with a species of linen tent, which he took also from the box. This done, the fortune-teller held the mouth of the bottle to the door of the tent, gathering the loose cloth closely around the glass neck. Immediately tiny noises were heard inside the tent. Madame Filomel removed the bottle, and the Wondersmith lifted the covering in which he had enveloped his little people.

A wonderful transformation had taken place. Wooden and inflexible no longer, the crowd of manikins were now in full motion. The bead-like eyes turned, glittering, on all sides; the thin, wicked lips quivered with bad passions; the tiny hands sheathed and unsheathed the little swords and daggers. Episodes, common to life, were taking place in every direction. Here two martial manikins paid court to a pretty, sly-faced female, who smiled on each alternately, but gave her hand to be kissed to a third manikin, an ugly little scoundrel, who crouched behind her. There a pair of friendly dolls walked arm in arm, apparently on the best terms, while, all the time, one was watching his opportunity to stab the other in the back.

"I think they'll do," said the Wondersmith, chuckling as he watched these various incidents. "Treacherous, cruel, bloodthirsty. All goes marvelously well. But stay! I will put the grand test to them."

So saying, he drew a gold dollar from his pocket, and let it fall on the table, in the very midst of the throng of manikins. It had hardly touched the table when there was a pause on all sides. Every head was turned toward the dollar. Then about twenty of the little creatures rushed toward the glittering coin. One, fleeter than the rest, leaped upon it and drew his sword. The entire crowd of little people had now gathered around this new center of attraction. Men and women struggled and shoved to get nearer to the piece of gold. Hardly had the first Lilliputian mounted upon the treasure, when a hundred blades flashed back a defiant answer to his, and a dozen men, sword in hand, leaped upon the yellow platform and drove him off at the sword's point. Then commenced a general battle. The miniature faces were convulsed with rage and avarice. Each furious doll tried to plunge dagger or sword into his or her neighbor, and the women seemed possessed by a thousand devils.

"They will break themselves into atoms," cried Filomel, as she watched with eagerness this savage *mêlée*. "You had better gather them up, Herr Hippe. I will exhaust my bottle and suck all the souls back from them."

"Oh, they are perfect devils! they are magnificent little demons!" cried the Frenchman, with enthusiasm. "Hippe, you are a wonderful man. Brother Oaksmith, you have no such man as Hippe among your English gypsies."

"Not exactly," answered Oaksmith, rather sullenly, "not exactly. But we have men there who can make a twelve-year-old horse look like a four-year-old—and who can take you and Herr Hippe up with one hand, and throw you over their shoulders."

"The good God forbid!" said the little Frenchman. "I do not love such play. It is incommodious."

While Oaksmith and Kerplonne were talking, the Wondersmith had placed the linen tent over the struggling dolls, and Madame Filomel, who had been performing some mysterious manipulations with her black bottle, put the mouth once more to the door of the tent. In an instant the confused murmur within ceased. Madame Filomel corked the bottle quickly. The Wondersmith withdrew the tent, and, lo! the furious dolls were once more wooden-jointed and inflexible; and the old sinister look was again frozen on their faces.

"They must have blood, though," said Herr Hippe, as he gathered them up and put them into their box. "Mr. Pippel, the bird-fancier, is asleep. I have a key that opens his door. We will let them loose among the birds; it will be rare fun."

"Magnificent!" cried Kerplonne. "Let us go on the instant. But first let me gather up my eye."

The Frenchman pocketed his eye, after having given it a polish with the silk handkerchief; Herr Hippe extinguished the lamp; Oaksmith took a last bumper of port; and the four gypsies departed for Mr. Pippel's, carrying the box of manikins with them.

## 3. SOLON

THE SHADOW that glided along the dark corridor, at the moment that Monsieur Kerplonne deposited his sentinel eye outside the door of

the Wondersmith's apartment, sped swiftly through the passage and
ascended the stairs to the attic. Here the shadow stopped at the entrance to one of chambers and knocked at the door. There was no reply.

"Zonéla, are you asleep?" said the shadow, softly.

"Oh, Solon, is it you?" replied a sweet low voice from within. "I
thought it was Herr Hippe. Come in."

The shadow opened the door and entered. There were neither candles
nor lamp in the room; but through the projecting window, which was
open, there came the faint gleams of the starlight, by which one could
distinguish a female figure seated on a low stool in the middle of the
floor.

"Has he left you without light again, Zonéla?" asked the shadow,
closing the door of the apartment. "I have brought my little lantern
with me, though."

"Thank you, Solon," answered she called Zonéla? "you are a good
fellow. He never gives me any light of an evening, but bids me go to
bed. I like to sit sometimes and look at the moon and the stars—the
stars more than all; for they seem all the time to look right back into
my face, very sadly, as if they would say, 'We see you, and pity you, and
would help you, if we could.' But it is so mournful to be always looking
at such myraids of melancholy eyes! and I long so to read those nice
books that you lend me, Solon!"

By this time the shadow had lit the lantern and was a shadow no
longer. A large head, covered with a profusion of long blond hair, which
was cut after that fashion known as *aux enfants d'Edouard*; a beautiful
pale face, lit with wide, blue, dreamy eyes; long arms and slender hands,
attenuated legs, and—an enormous hump;—such was Solon, the shadow.
As soon as the humpback had lit the lamp, Zonéla arose from the low
stool on which she had been seated, and took Solon's hand affectionately
in hers.

Zonéla was surely not of gypsy blood. That rich auburn hair, that
looked almost black in the lamplight, that pale, transparent skin, tinged
with an under-glow of warm rich blood, the hazel eyes, large and soft as
those of a fawn, were never begotten of a Zingaro. Zonéla was seemingly
about sixteen; her figure, although somewhat thin and angular, was
full of the unconscious grace of youth. She was dressed in an old cotton

print, which had been once of an exceedingly boisterous pattern, but was now a mere suggestion of former splendor; while around her head was twisted, in fantastic fashion, a silk handkerchief of green ground spotted with bright crimson. This strange head-dress gave her an elfish appearance.

"I have been out all day with the organ, and I am so tired, Solon!—not sleepy, but weary, I mean. Poor Furbelow was sleepy, though, and he's gone to bed."

"I'm weary, too, Zonéla; not weary as you are, though, for I sit in my little book-stall all day long, and do not drag round an organ and a monkey and play old tunes for pennies—but weary of myself, of life, of the load that I carry on my shoulders"; and, as he said this, the poor humpback glanced sideways, as if to call attention to his deformed person.

"Well, but you ought not to be melancholy amidst your books, Solon. Gracious! If I could only sit in the sun and read as you do, how happy I should be! But it's very tiresome to trudge around all day with that nasty organ, and look up at the houses, and know that you are annoying the people inside; and then the boys play such bad tricks on poor Furbelow, throwing him hot pennies to pick up, and burning his poor little hands; and oh! sometimes, Solon, the men in the street make me so afraid—they speak to me and look at me so oddly!—I'd a great deal rather sit in your book-stall and read."

"I have nothing but odd volumes in my stall," answered the hump-back. "Perhaps that's right, though; for, after all, I'm nothing but an odd volume myself."

"Come, don't be melancholy, Solon. Sit down and tell me a story. I'll bring Furbelow to listen."

So saying, she went to a dusky corner of the cheerless attic room, and returned with a little Brazilian monkey in her arms—a poor, mild, drowsy thing, that looked as if it had cried itself to sleep. She sat down on her little stool, with Furbelow in her lap, and nodded her head to Solon, as much as to say, "Go on; we are attentive."

"You want a story, do you?" said the humpback, with a mournful smile. "Well, I'll tell you one. Only what will your father say, if he catches me here?"

"Herr Hippe is not my father," cried Zonéla, indignantly. "He's a gypsy, and I know I'm stolen; and I'd run away from him, if I only knew where to run to. If I were his child, do you think that he would treat me as he does? make me trudge around the city all day long, with a barrel-organ and a monkey—though I love poor, dear little Furbelow —and keep me up in a garret, and give me ever so little to eat? I know I'm not his child, for he hates me."

"Listen to my story, Zonéla, and we'll talk of that afterward. Let me sit at your feet"; and, having coiled himself up at the little maiden's feet, he commenced:

"There once lived in a great city, just like this city of New York, a poor little hunchback. He kept a second-hand book-stall, where he made barely enough money to keep body and soul together. He was very sad at times, because he knew scarce anyone, and those that he did know did not love him. He had passed a sickly, secluded youth. The children of his neighborhood would not play with him, for he was not made like them; and the people in the streets stared at him with pity, or scoffed at him when he went by. Ah! Zonéla, how his poor heart was wrung with bitterness when he beheld the procession of shapely men and fine women that every day passed him by in the thoroughfares of the great city! How he repined and cursed his fate as the torrent of fleet-footed firemen dashed past him to the toll of the bells, magnificent in their overflowing vitality and strength! But there was one consolation left him—one drop of honey in the jar of gall, so sweet that it ameliorated all the bitterness of life. God had given him a deformed body, but his mind was straight and healthy. So the poor hunchback shut himself into the world of books, and was, if not happy, at least contented. He kept company with courteous paladins, and romantic heroes, and beautiful women; and this society was of such excellent breeding that it never so much as once noticed his poor crooked back or his lame walk.

"The love of books grew upon him with his years. He was remarked for his studious habits; and when, one day, the obscure people that he called father and mother—parents only in name—died, a compassionate book vender gave him enough stock in trade to set up a little stall of his own. Here, in his book-stall, he sat in the sun all day, waiting for the customers that seldom came, and reading the fine deeds of the people of the ancient time, or the beautiful thoughts of the poets that had warmed millions of hearts before that hour, and still glowed for him with undiminished fire.

"One day, when he was reading some book, that, small as it was, was big enough to shut the whole world out from him, he heard some music in the street. Looking up from his book, he saw a little girl, with large eyes, playing an organ, while a monkey begged for alms from a crowd of idlers who had nothing in their pockets but their hands. The girl was playing, but she was also weeping. The merry notes of the polka were ground out to a silent accompaniment of tears. She looked very sad, this organ-girl, and her monkey seemed to have caught the infection, for his large brown eyes were moist, as if he also wept.

"The poor hunchback was struck with pity, and called the little girl over to give her a penny—not, dear Zonéla, because he wished to bestow alms, but because he wanted to speak with her. She came, and they talked together. She came the next day—for it turned out that they were neighbors—and the next, and, in short, every day. They became friends. They were both lonely and afflicted, with this difference, that she was beautiful, and he—was a hunchback."

"Why, Solon," cried Zonéla, "that's the very way you and I met!"

"It was then," continued Solon, with a faint smile, "that life seemed to have its music. A great harmony seemed to the poor cripple to fill the world. The carts that took the flour-barrels from the wharves to the storehouses seemed to emit joyous melodies from their wheels. The hum of the great business streets sounded like grand symphonies of triumph. As one who has been traveling through a barren country without much heed feels with singular force the sterility of the lands he has passed through when he reaches the fertile plains that lie at the end of his journey, so the humpback, after his vision had been freshened with this blooming flower, remembered for the first time the misery of the life that he had led. But he did not allow himself to dwell upon the past. The present was so delightful that it occupied all his thoughts. Zonéla, he was in love with the organ girl."

"Oh, that's so nice!" said Zonéla, innocently—pinching poor Furbelow, as she spoke, in order to dispel a very evident snooze that was creeping over him. "It's going to be a love story."

"Ah! but, Zonéla, he did not know whether she loved him in return. You forget that he was deformed."

"But," answered the girl gravely, "he was good."

A light like the flash of an aurora illuminated Solon's face for an instant. He put out his hand suddenly, as if to take Zonéla's and press it to his heart; but an unaccountable timidity seemed to arrest the impulse, and he only stroked Furbelow's head—upon which that individual opened one large brown eye to the extent of the eighth of an inch, and, seeing that it was only Solon, instantly closed it again, and resumed his dream of a city where there were no organs and all the copper coin of the realm was iced.

"He hoped and feared," continued Solon, in a low, mournful voice; "but at times he was very miserable, because he did not think it possible that so much happiness was reserved for him as the love of this beautiful, innocent girl. At night, when he was in bed, and all the world was dreaming, he lay awake looking up at the old books against the walls, thinking how he could bring about the charming of her heart.

"One night, when he was thinking of this, with his eyes fixed upon the moldy backs of the odd volumes that lay on their shelves, and looked back at him wistfully, as if they would say, 'We also are like you, and wait to be completed,' it seemed as if he heard a rustle of leaves. Then one by one, the books came down from their places to the floor, as if shifted by invisible hands, opened their worm-eaten covers, and from between the pages of each the hunchback saw issue forth a curious throng of little people that danced here and there through the apartment. Each one of these little creatures was shaped so as to bear resemblance to some one of the letters of the alphabet. One tall, long legged fellow seemed like the letter A; a burly fellow, with a big head and a paunch, was the model of B; another leering little chap might have passed for a Q; and so on through the whole. These fairies—for fairies they were—climbed upon the hunchback's bed, and clustered thick as bees upon his pillow.

"'Come!' they cried to him, 'we will lead you into fairyland.'

"So saying, they seized his hand, and he suddenly found himself in a beautiful country, where the light did not come from sun or moon or stars, but floated round and over and in everything like the atmosphere. On all sides he heard mysterious melodies sung by strangely musical voices. None of the features of the landscape was definite; yet when he looked on the vague harmonies of color that melted one into another before his sight he was filled with a sense of inexplicable beauty. On every side of him fluttered radiant bodies, which darted to and fro through the illumined space. They were not birds, yet they flew like birds; and as each one crossed the path of his vision he felt a strange delight flash through his brain, and straightway an interior voice seemed to sing beneath the vaulted dome of his temples a verse containing some beautiful thought. The little fairies were all this time dancing and fluttering around him, perching on his head, on his shoulders, or balancing themselves on his fingertips.

" 'Where am I?' he asked, at last, of his friends, the fairies.

" 'Ah, Solon!' he heard them whisper, in tones that sounded like the distant tinkling of silver bells, 'this land is nameless; but those whom we lead hither, who tread its soil, and breathe its air, and gaze on its floating sparks of light, are poets for evermore.'

"Having said this, they vanished, and with them the beautiful indefinite land, and the flashing lights, and illumined air; and the hunchback found himself again in bed, with the moonlight quivering on the floor, and the dusty books on their shelves, grim and moldy as ever."

"You have betrayed yourself. You called yourself Solon," cried Zonéla. "Was it a dream?"

"I do not know," answered Solon; "but since that night I have been a poet."

"A poet?" screamed the little organ girl—"a real poet, who makes verses which everyone reads and everyone talks of?"

"The people call me a poet," answered Solon, with a sad smile. "They do not know me by the name of Solon, for I write under an assumed title; but they praise me, and repeat my songs. But Zonéla, I can't sing this load off my back, can I?"

"Oh, bother the hump!" said Zonéla, jumping up suddenly. "You're

a poet, and that's enough, isn't it? I'm so glad you're a poet, Solon!
You must repeat all your best things to me, won't you?"

Solon nodded assent.

"You don't ask me," he said, "who was the little girl that the hunchback loved."

Zonéla's face flushed crimson. She turned suddenly away, and ran
into a dark corner of the room. In a moment she returned with an old
hand-organ in her arms.

"Play, Solon, play!" she cried. "I am so glad that I want to dance.
Furbelow, come and dance in honor of Solon the Poet."

It was her confession. Solon's eyes flamed, as if his brain had suddenly ignited. He said nothing; but a triumphant smile broke over his
countenance. Zonéla, the twilight of whose cheeks was still rosy with
the setting blush, caught the lazy Furbelow by his little paws; Solon
turned the crank of the organ, which wheezed out as merry a polka as
its asthma would allow, and the girl and the monkey commenced their
fantastic dance. They had taken but a few steps when the door suddenly opened, and the tall figure of the Wondersmith appeared on the
threshold. His face was convulsed with rage, and the black snake that
quivered on his upper lip seemed to rear itself as if about to spring upon
the hunchback.

## 4. THE MANIKINS AND THE MINOS

THE FOUR gypsies left Herr Hippe's house cautiously, and directed
their steps toward Mr. Pippel's bird shop. Golosh Street was asleep.
Nothing was stirring in that tenebrous slum, save a dog that savagely
gnawed a bone which lay on a dust-heap, tantalizing him with the
flavor of food without its substance. As the gypsies moved stealthily
along in the darkness they had a sinister and murderous air that would
not have failed to attract the attention of the policeman of the quarter,
if that worthy had not at the moment been comfortably ensconced in
the neighboring "Rainbow" bar-room, listening to the improvisations of
that talented vocalist, Mr. Harrison, who was making impromptu verses
on every possible subject, to the accompaniment of a cithern which was
played by a sad little Italian in a large cloak, to whom the host of the

"Rainbow" gave so many toddies and a dollar for his nightly performance.

Mr. Pippel's shop was but a short distance from the Wondersmith's house. A few moments, therefore, brought the gypsy party to the door, when, by the aid of a key which Herr Hippe produced, they silently slipped into the entry. Here the Wondersmith took a dark-lantern from under his cloak, removed the cap that shrouded the light, and led the way into the shop, which was separated from the entry only by a glass door, that yielded, like the outer one, to a key which Hippe took from his pocket. The four gypsies now entered the shop and closed the door behind them.

It was a little world of birds. On every side, whether in large or small cages, one beheld balls of various-colored feathers standing on one leg and breathing peacefully. Lovebirds, nestling shoulder to shoulder, with their heads tucked under their wings and all their feathers puffed out, so that they looked like globes of malachite; English bullfinches, with ashen-colored backs, in which their black heads were buried, and corselets of a rosy down; Java sparrows, fat and sleek and cleanly; troupials, so glossy and splendid in plumage that they looked as if they were dressed in the celebrated armor of the Black Prince, which was jet, richly damascened with gold; a cock of the rock, gleaming, a ball of tawny fire, like a setting sun; the campanero of Brazil, white as snow, with his dilatable tolling-tube hanging from his head, placid and silent;—these, with a humbler crowd of linnets, canaries, robins, mocking-birds, and phoebes, slumbered calmly in their little cages, that were hung so thickly on the wall as not to leave an inch of it visible.

"Splendid little morsels, all of them!" exclaimed Monsieur Kerplonne. "Ah, we are going to have a rare beating!"

"So Pippel does not sleep in his shop," said the English gypsy, Oaksmith.

"No. The fellow lives somewhere up one of the avenues," answered Madame Filomel. "He came, the other evening, to consult me about his fortune. I did not tell him," she added with a laugh, "that he was going to have so distinguished a sporting party on his premises."

"Come," said the Wondersmith, producing the box of manikins, "get ready with souls, Madame Filomel. I am impatient to see my little men letting out lives for the first time." Just at the moment that the Wondersmith uttered this sentence, the four gypsies were startled by a hoarse voice issuing from a corner of the room, and propounding in the most guttural tones the intemperate query of "What'll you take?" This sottish invitation had scarce been given, when a second extremely thick voice replied from an opposite corner, in accents so rough that they seemed to issue from a throat torn and furrowed by the liquid lava of many bar-rooms, "Brandy and water."

"Holla! who's here?" muttered Herr Hippe, flashing the light of his lantern around the shop.

Oaksmith turned up his coat-cuffs, as if to be ready for a fight; Madame Filomel glided, or rather rolled, toward the door; while Kerplonne put his hand into his pocket, as if to assure himself that his supernumerary optic was all right.

"What'll you take?" croaked the voice in the corner, once more.

"Brandy and water," rapidly replied the second voice in the other corner. And then, as if by a concerted movement, a series of bibular invitations and acceptances were rolled backwards and forwards with a volubility of utterance that threw Patter versus Clatter into the shade.

"What the devil can it be?" muttered the Wondersmith, flashing his lantern here and there. "Ah! it is those Minos."

So saying, he stopped under one of the wicker cages that hung high up on the wall, and raised the lantern above his head, so as to throw the light upon that particular cage. The hospitable individual who had been extending all these hoarse invitations to partake of intoxicating beverages was an inhabitant of the cage. It was a large Mino-bird, who now stood perched on his cross-bar, with his yellowish-orange bill sloped slightly over his shoulder, and his white eye cocked knowingly upon the Wondersmith. The respondent voice in the other corner came from another Mino-bird, who sat in the dusk in a similar cage, also attentively watching the Wondersmith. These Mino-birds have a singular aptitude for acquiring phrases.

"What'll you take?" repeated the Mino, cocking his other eye upon Herr Hippe.

"*Mon Dieu!* what a bird!" exclaimed the little Frenchman. "He is, in truth, polite."

"I don't know what I'll take," said Hippe, as if replying to the Mino-bird; "but I know what you'll get, old fellow! Filomel, open the cage doors, and give me the bottle."

Filomel opened, one after another, the doors of the numberless little cages, thereby arousing from slumber their feathered occupants, who opened their beaks, and stretched their claws, and stared with great surprise at the lantern and the midnight visitors.

By this time the Wondersmith had performed the mysterious ma-nipulations with the bottle, and the manikins were once more in full motion, swarming out of their box, sword and dagger in hand, with their little black eyes glittering fiercely, and their white teeth shining. The little creatures seemed to scent their prey. The gypsies stood in the cen-ter of the shop, watching the proceedings eagerly, while the Lilliputians made in a body toward the wall and commenced climbing from cage to cage. Then was heard a tremendous fluttering of wings, and faint, de-spairing "quirks" echoed on all sides. In almost every cage there was a fierce manikin thrusting his sword or dagger vigorously into the body of some unhappy bird. It recalled the antique legend of the battles of the Pygmies and the Cranes. The poor love-birds lay with their emerald feathers dabbled in their heart's blood, shoulder to shoulder in death as in life. Canaries gasped at the bottom of their cages, while the water in their little glass fountains ran red. The bullfinches wore an unnatural crimson on their breasts. The mocking-bird lay on his back, kicking spasmodically, in the last agonies, with a tiny sword-thrust cleaving his melodious throat in twain, so that from the instrument which used to gush with wondrous music only scarlet drops of blood now trickled.

The manikins were ruthless. Their faces were ten times wickeder than ever, as they roamed from cage to cage, slaughtering with a fury that seemed entirely unappeasable. Presently the feathery rustlings became fewer and fainter, and the little pipings of despair died away; and in every cage lay a poor murdered minstrel, with the song that abode within him forever quenched—in every cage but two, and those two were high up on the wall; and in each glared a pair of wild, white eyes; and an orange beak, tough as steel, pointed threateningly down. With the needles which they grasped as swords all wet and warm with blood, and their bead-like eyes flashing in the light of the lantern, the Lilliputian assassins swarmed up the cages in two separate bodies, until they reached the wickets of the habitations in which the Minos abode.

Mino saw them coming—had listened attentively to the many death struggles of his comrades, and had, in fact, smelt a rat. Accordingly he was ready for the manikins. There he stood at the barbican of his castle, with formidable beak couched like a lance. The manikins made a gallant charge. "What'll you take?" was rattled out by the Mino, in a deep bass, as with one plunge of his sharp bill he scattered the ranks of the enemy, and sent three of them flying to the floor, where they lay with broken limbs. But the manikins were brave automata, and again they closed and charged the gallant Mino. Again the wicked white eyes of the bird gleamed, and again the orange bill dealt destruction.

Everything seemed to be going on swimmingly for Mino, when he found himself attacked in the rear by two treacherous manikins, who had stolen upon him from behind, through the lattice-work of the cage. Quick as lightning the Mino turned to repel this assault, but all too late; two slender, quivering threads of steel crossed in his poor body, and he staggered into a corner of the cage. His white eyes closed, then opened; a shiver passed over his body, beginning at his shoulder-tips and dying off in the extreme tips of the wings; he gasped as if for air, and then, with a convulsive shudder, which ruffled all his feathers, croaked out feebly his little speech. "What'll you take?" Instantly from the opposite corner came the old response still feebler than the question—a mere gurgle, as it were, of "Brandy and water." Then all was silent. The Mino-birds were dead.

"They spill blood like Christians," said the Wondersmith, gazing fondly on the manikins. "They will be famous assassins.

## 5. TIED UP

HERR HIPPE stood in the doorway, scowling. His eyes seemed to scorch the poor hunchback, whose form, physically inferior, crouched before that baneful, blazing glance, while its head, mentally brave, reared itself as if to redeem the cowardice of the frame to which it belonged. So the attitude of the serpent: the body pliant, yielding, supple;

but the crest thrown aloft, erect, and threatening. As for Zonéla, she was
frozen in the attitude of motion—a dancing nymph in colored marble;
agility stunned; elasticity petrified.

Furbelow, astonished at this sudden change, and catching, with all
the mysterious rapidity of instinct peculiar to the lower animals, at
the enigmatical character of the situation, turned his pleading, melancholy eyes from one to another of the motionless three, as if begging
that his humble intellect (pardon me, naturalists, for the use of this
word "intellect" in the matter of a monkey) should be enlightened as
speedily as possible. Not receiving the desired information, he, after the
manner of trained animals, returned to his muttons; in other words, he
conceived that this unusual entrance, and consequent dramatic tab-
leau, meant "shop." He therefore dropped Zonéla's hand, and pattered
on his velvety feet over toward the grim figure of the Wondersmith,
holding out his poor little paw for the customary copper. He had but
one idea drilled into him—soulless creature that he was—and that was
alms. But I have seen creatures that professed to have souls, and that
would have been indignant if you had denied them immortality, who
took to the soliciting of alms as naturally as if beggary had been the original sin, and was regularly born with them, and never baptized out of
them. I will give these Bandits of the Order of Charity this credit, however, that they knew the best highways and the richest founts of benevo-
lence—unlike to Furbelow, who, unreasoning and undiscriminating,
begged from the first person that was near. Furbelow, owing to this intel-
lectual inferiority to the before-mentioned Alsatians, frequently got more
kicks than coppers, and the present supplication which he indulged in
toward the Wondersmith was a terrible confirmation of the rule. The reply to the extended pleading paw was what might be called a double-
barreled kick—a kick to be represented by the power of two when the
foot touched the object, multiplied by four when the entire leg formed
an angle of forty-five degrees with the spinal column. The long, nervous leg of the Wondersmith caught the little creature in the center of
the body, doubled up his brown, hairy form, till he looked like a fur
driving-glove, and sent him whizzing across the room into a far corner,
where he dropped senseless and flaccid.

This vengeance which Herr Hippe executed upon Furbelow seemed to have operated as a sort of escape-valve, and he found voice. He hissed out the question, "Who are you?" to the hunchback; and in listening to that essence of sibilation it really seemed as if it proceeded from the serpent that curled upon his upper lip.

"Who are you? Deformed dog, who are you? What do you here?"

"My name is Solon," answered the fearless head of the hunchback, while the frail, cowardly body shivered and trembled inch by inch into a corner.

"So you come to visit my daughter in the night-time, when I am away?" continued the Wondersmith, with a sneering tone that dropped from his snake wreathed mouth like poison. "You are a brave and gallant lover, are you not? Where did you win that Order of the Curse of God that decorates your shoulders? The women turn their heads and look after you in the street, when you pass, do they not? lost in admiration of that symmetrical figure, those graceful limbs, that neck pliant as the stem that moors the lotus! Elegant, conquering, Christian cripple, what do you here in my daughter's room?"

Can you imagine Jove, limitless in power and wrath, hurling from his vast grasp mountain after mountain upon the struggling Enceladus— and picture the Titan sinking, sinking deeper and deeper into the earth, crushed and dying, with nothing visible through the superincumbent masses of Pelion and Ossa but a gigantic head and two flaming eyes, that, despite the death which is creeping through each vein, still flash back defiance to the divine enemy? Well, Solon and Herr Hippe presented such a picture, seen through the wrong end of a telescope—reduced in proportion, but alike in action. Solon's feeble body seemed to sink into utter annihilation beneath the horrible taunts that his enemy hurled at him, while the large, brave brow and unconquered eyes still sent forth a magnetic resistance.

Suddenly the poor hunchback felt his arm grasped. A thrill seemed to run through his entire body. A warm atmosphere, invigorating and full of delicious odor, surrounded him. It appeared as if invisible bandages were twisted all about his limbs, giving him a strange strength. His sinking legs straightened. His powerless arms were braced. Astonished, he glanced around for an instant, and beheld Zonéla, with a world of love burning in her large lambent eyes, wreathing her round white arms about his humped shoulders. Then the poet knew the great sustaining power of love. Solon reared himself boldly.

"Sneer at my poor form," he cried in strong, vibrating tones, flinging out one long arm and one thin finger at the Wondersmith, as if he would have impaled him like a beetle. "Humiliate me if you can. I care not. You are a wretch, and I am honest and pure. This girl is not your daughter. You are like one of those demons in the fairy-tales that held beauty and purity locked in infernal spells. I do not fear you, Herr Hippe. There are stories abroad about you in the neighborhood, and when you pass people say that they feel evil and blight covering over their threshold. You persecute this girl. You are her tyrant. You hate her. I am a cripple. Providence has cast this lump upon my shoulders. But that is nothing. The camel, that is the salvation of the children of the desert, has been given his hump in order that he might bear his human burden better. This girl, who is homeless as the Arab, is my appointed load in life, and please God, I will carry her on this back, hunched though it may be. I have come to see her because I love her— because she loves me. You have no claim on her; so I will take her from you."

Quick as lightning the Wondersmith had stridden a few paces, and grasped the poor cripple, who was yet quivering with the departing thunder of his passion. He seized him in his bony, muscular grasp, as he would have seized a puppet, and held him at arm's length, gasping and powerless; while Zonéla, pale, breathless, entreating, sank half kneeling on the floor.

"Your skeleton will be interesting to science when you are dead, Mr. Solon," hissed the Wondersmith. "But before I have the pleasure of reducing you to an anatomy, which I will assuredly do, I wish to compliment you on your power of penetration, or sources of information; for I know not if you have derived your knowledge from your own mental research or the efforts of others. You are perfectly correct in your statement that this charming young person, who day after day parades the streets with a barrel-organ and a monkey—the last unhappily indisposed at present—listening to the degrading jokes of ribald boys and depraved men—you are quite correct, sir, in stating that she is not my daughter. On the contrary, she is the daughter of an Hungarian noble-man who had the misfortune to incur my displeasure.

"I had a son, crooked spawn of a Christian!—a son, not like you, can-kered, gnarled stump of life that you are—but a youth tall and fair and noble in aspect, as became a child of one whose lineage makes Pharaoh modern—a youth whose foot in the dance was as swift and beautiful to look at as the golden sandals of the sun when he dances upon the sea in summer. This youth was virtuous and good; and being of a good race, and dwelling in a country where his rank, gypsy as he was, was recog-nized, he mixed with the proudest of the land.

"One day he fell in with this accursed Hungarian, a fierce drinker of that devil's blood called brandy. My child until that hour had avoided this bane of our race. Generous wine he drank, because the soul of the sun, our ancestor, palpitated in its purple waves. But brandy, which is fallen and accursed wine, as devils are fallen and accursed angels, had never crossed his lips, until in an evil hour he was seduced by this Chris-tian hog, and from that day forth his life was one firey debauch, which set only in the black waves of death. I vowed vengeance on the de-stroyer of my child, and I kept my word. I have destroyed *his* child—not compassed her death, but blighted her life, steeped her in misery and poverty, and now, thanks to the thousand devils, I have discovered a new torture for her heart. She thought to solace her life with a love-episode! Sweet little epicure that she was! She shall have her little crooked lover, shan't she? Oh, yes! she shall have him, cold and stark and livid, with that great, black, heavy hunch, which no back, however broad, can bear, Death, sitting between his shoulders!"

There was something so awful and demoniac in this entire speech and the manner in which it was delivered, that it petrified Zonéla into a mere inanimate figure, whose eyes seemed unalterably fixed on the fierce, cruel face of the Wondersmith. As for Solon, he was paralyzed in the grasp of his foe. He heard, but could not reply. His large eyes, di-lated with horror to far beyond their ordinary size, expressed unutter-able agony.

The last sentence had hardly been hissed out by the gypsy when he took from his pocket a long, thin coil of whip-cord, which he entangled in a complicated mesh around the cripple's body. It was not the ordinary binding of a prisoner. The slender lash passed and repassed in a thousand intricate folds over the powerless limbs of the poor hunchback. When the operation was completed, he looked as if he had been sewed from head to foot in some singularly ingenious species of network.

"Now, my pretty lop-sided little lover," laughed Herr Hippe, flinging Solon over his shoulder as a fisherman might fling a netful of fish, "we will proceed to put you into your little cage until your little coffin is quite ready. Meanwhile we will lock up your darling beggar-girl to mourn over your untimely end."

So saying, he stepped from the room with his captive, and securely locked the door behind him.

When he had disappeared, the frozen Zonéla thawed, and with a shriek of anguish flung herself on the inanimate body of Furbelow.

## 6. THE POISONING OF THE SWORDS

IT WAS New Year's eve, and 11 o'clock at night. All over this great land, and in every great city in the land, curly heads were lying on white pillows, dreaming of the coming of the generous Santa Claus. Innumerable stockings hung by countless bedsides. Visions of beautiful toys, passing in splendid pageantry through myriads of dimly lit dormitories, made millions of little hearts palpitate in sleep. Ah! what heavenly toys those were that the children of this soil beheld, that mystic night, in their dreams! Painted cars with orchestral wheels, making music more delicious than the roll of planets. Agile men, of cylindrical figure, who sprang unexpectedly out of meek-looking boxes, with a supernatural fierceness in their crimson cheeks and fur-whiskers. Herds of marvelous sheep, with fleeces as impossible as the one that Jason sailed after; animals entirely indifferent to grass and water and "rot" and "ticks." Horses spotted with an astounding regularity, and furnished with the most ingenious methods of locomotion. Slender foreigners, attired in painfully short tunics, whose existence passed in continually turning heels over head down a steep flight of steps, at the bottom of which they lay in an exhausted condition with dislocated limbs, until they were restored to their former elevation, when they went at it again as if

nothing had happened. Stately swans, that seemed to have a touch of
the ostrich in them; for they swam continually after a piece of iron
which was held before them, as if consumed with a ferruginous hunger.
Whole farmyards of roosters, whose tails curled the wrong way—a
slight defect, that was, however, amply atoned for by the size and
brilliancy of their scarlet combs, which, it would appear, Providence
had intended for pen-wipers. Pears, that, when applied to youthful lips,
gave forth sweet and inspiring sounds. Regiments of soldiers, that performed neat but limited evolutions on cross-jointed contractile battle-
fields. All these things, idealized, transfigured, and illuminated by the
powers and atmosphere and colored lamps of dreamland, did the millions of dear sleeping children behold, the night of the New Year's eve
of which I speak.

It was on this night, when Time was preparing to shed his skin, and
come out young and golden and glossy as ever—when, in the vast chambers of the universe, silent and infallible preparations were making for
the wonderful birth of the coming year—when mystic dews were se-
creted for his baptism, and mystic instruments were tuned in space
to welcome him—it was at this solemn hour that the Wondersmith
and his three companions sat in close conclave in the little parlor before
mentioned.

There was a fire roaring in the grate. On a table, nearly in the center
of the room, stood a huge decanter of port wine, that glowed in the
blaze which lit the chamber like a flask of crimson fire. On every side,
piled in heaps, inanimate, but scowling with the same old wondrous
scowl, lay myriads of the manikins, all clutching in their wooden hands
their tiny weapons. The Wondersmith held in one hand a small silver
bowl filled with a green, glutinous substance, which he was delicately
applying, with the aid of a camel's-hair brush, to the tips of tiny swords
and daggers. A horrible smile wandered over his sallow face—a smile
as unwholesome in appearance as the sickly light that plays above reek-
ing graveyards.

"Let us drink great drafts, brothers," he cried, leaving off his strange
anointment for a while, to lift a great glass, filled with sparkling liquor,
to his lips. "Let us drink to our approaching triumph. Let us drink to
the great poison, Macousha. Subtle seed of Death—swift hurricane that

sweeps away Life—fast hammer that crushes brain and heart and artery with its resistless weight—I drink to it."

"It is a noble decoction, Duke Balthazar," said the old fortune-teller and mid-wife, Madame Filomel, nodding in her chair as she swallowed her wine in great gulps. "Where did you obtain it?"

"It is made," said the Wondersmith, swallowing another great draft of wine ere he replied, "in the wild woods of Guiana, in silence and in mystery. But one tribe of Indians, the Macoushi Indians, know the secret. It is simmered over fires built of strange woods, and the maker of it dies in the making. The place, for a mile around the spot where it is fabricated, is shunned as accursed. Devils hover over the pot in which it stews; and the birds of the air, scenting the smallest breath of its vapors from far away, drop to earth with paralyzed wings, cold and dead."

"It kills, then, fast?" asked Kerplonne, the artificial-eye maker—his own eyes gleaming, under the influence of the wine, with a sinister luster, as if they had been fresh from the factory, and were yet untarnished by use.

"Kills?" echoed the Wondersmith, derisively; "it is swifter than thunder-bolts, stronger than lightning. But you shall see it proved before we let forth our army on the city accursed. You shall see a wretch die, as if smitten by a falling fragment of the sun."

"What? Do you mean Solon?" asked Oaksmith and the fortune-teller together.

"Ah, you mean the young man who makes the commerce with books?" echoed Kerplonne. "It is well. His agonies will instruct us."

"Yes! Solon," answered Hippe, with a savage accent. "I hate him, and he shall die this horrid death. Ah! how the little fellows will leap upon him, when I bring him in, bound and helpless, and give their beautiful wicked souls to them! How they will pierce him in ten thousand spots with their poisoned weapons, until his skin turns blue and violet and crimson, and his form swells with the venom—until his hump is lost in shapeless flesh! He hears what I say, every word of it. He is in the closet next door, and is listening. How comfortable he feels! How the sweat of terror rolls on his brow! How he tries to loosen his bonds, and curses all earth and heaven when he finds that he cannot! Ho! Ho! Handsome lover of Zonéla, will she kiss you when you are livid and swollen? Brothers, let us drink again—drink always. Here, Oaksmith, take these brushes—and you, Filomel—and finish the anointing of these swords. This wine is grand. This poison is grand. It is fine to have good wine to drink, and good poison to kill with; is it not?"— and, with flushed face and rolling eyes, the Wondersmith continued to drink and use his brush alternately.

The others hastened to follow his example. It was a horrible scene: those four wicked faces; those myriads of tiny faces, just as wicked; the certain unearthly air that pervaded the apartment; the red, unwholesome glare cast by the fire; the wild and reckless way in which the weird company drank the red-illumined wine.

The anointing of the swords went on rapidly, and the wine went as rapidly down the throats of the four poisoners. Their faces grew more and more inflamed each instant; their eyes shone like rolling fireballs; their hair was moist and disheveled. The old fortune-teller rocked to and fro in her chair, like those legless plaster figures that sway upon convex loaded bottoms. All four began to mutter incoherent sentences, and babble unintelligible wickedness. Still the anointing of the swords went on.

"I see the faces of millions of young corpses," babbled Herr Hippe, gazing, with swimming eyes, into the silver bowl that contained the Macousha poison, "all young, all Christians—and the little fellows dancing, dancing, and stabbing, stabbing. Filomel, Filomel, I say!"

"Well, Grand Duke," snored the old woman, giving a violent lurch.

"Where's the bottle of souls?"

"In my right-hand pocket, Herr Hippe"; and she felt, so as to assure herself that it was there. She half drew out the black bottle, before described in this narrative, and let it slide again into her pocket—let it slide again, but it did not completely regain its former place. Caught by some accident, it hung half out, swaying over the edge of the pocket, as the fat midwife rolled backwards and forwards in her drunken efforts at equilibrium.

"All right," said Herr Hippe, "perfectly right! Let's drink."

He reached out his hand for his glass, and, with a dull sigh, dropped on the table, in the instantaneous slumber of intoxication. Oaksmith soon fell back in his chair, breathing, heavily. Kerplonne followed. And the heavy, stertorous breathing of Filomel told that she slumbered also; but still her chair retained its rocking motion, and still the bottle of souls balanced itself on the edge of her pocket.

### 7. LET LOOSE

SURE ENOUGH, Solon heard every word of the fiendish talk of the Wondersmith. For how many days he had been shut up, bound in the terrible net, in that dark closet, he did not know; but now he felt that his last hour was come. His little strength was completely worn out in efforts to disentangle himself. Once a day a door opened, and Herr Hippe placed a crust of bread and a cup of water within his reach. On this meager fare he had subsisted. It was a hard life; but, bad as it was, it was better than the horrible death that menaced him. His brain reeled with terror at the prospect of it. Then, where was Zonéla? Why did she not come to his rescue? But she was, perhaps, dead. The darkness, too, appalled him. A faint light, when the moon was bright, came at night through a chink far up in the wall; and the only other hole in the chamber was an aperture through which, at some former time, a stove-pipe had been passed. Even if he were free, there would have been small hope of escape; but, laced as it were in a network of steel, what was to be done? He groaned and writhed upon the floor, and tore at the boards with his hands, which were free from the wrists down. All else was as solidly laced up as an Indian papoose. Nothing but pride kept him from shrieking aloud, when, on the night of New Year's eve, he heard the fiendish Hippe recite the program of his murder.

While he was thus wailing and gnashing his teeth in darkness and torture, he heard a faint noise above his head. Then something seemed to leap from the ceiling and alight softly on the floor. He shuddered with terror. Was it some new torture of the Wondersmith's invention? The next moment, he felt some small animal crawling over his body, and a soft, silky paw was pushed timidly across his face. His heart leaped with joy.

"It is Furbelow!" he cried. "Zonéla has sent him. He came through the stove-pipe hole."

It was Furbelow, indeed, restored to life by Zonéla's care, and who had come down a narrow tube, that no human being could have threaded, to console the poor captive. The monkey nestled closely into the hunchback's bosom, and, as he did so, Solon felt something cold and hard hanging from his neck. He touched it. It was sharp. By the dim light that struggled through the apperture high up in the wall, he discovered a knife, suspended by a bit of cord. Ah! how the blood came rushing through the veins that crossed over and through his heart, when life and liberty came to him in this bit of rusty steel! With his manacled hands he loosened the heaven-sent weapon; a few cuts were rapidly made in the cunning network of cord that enveloped his limbs, and in a few seconds he was free!—cramped and faint with hunger, but free!—free to move, to use the limbs that God had given him for his preservation—free to fight—to die fighting, perhaps—but still to die free. He ran to the door. The bolt was a weak one, for the Wondersmith had calculated more surely on his prison of cords than any jail of stone—and more; and with a few efforts the door opened. He went cautiously out into the darkness, with Furbelow perched on his shoulder, pressing his cold muzzle against his cheek. He had made but a few steps when a trembling hand was put into his, and in another moment Zonéla's palpitating heart was pressed against his own. One long kiss, an embrace, a few whispered words, and the hunchback and the girl stole softly toward the door of the chamber in which the four gypsies slept. All seemed still; nothing but the hard breathing of the sleepers and the monotonous rocking of Madame Filomel's chair broke the silence. Solon stooped down and put his eye to the keyhole, through which a red bar of light streamed into the entry. As he did so, his foot crushed some brittle substance that lay just outside the door; at the same moment a howl of agony was heard to issue from the room within. Solon started; nor did he know that at that instant he had crushed into dust Monsieur Kerplonne's supernumerary eye, and the owner, though wrapt in a drunken sleep, felt the pang quiver through his brain.

While Solon peeped through the keyhole, all in the room was motionless. He had not gazed, however, for many seconds, when the chair of the fortune-teller gave a sudden lurch, and the black bottle, already hanging half out of her wide pocket, slipped entirely from its resting-place, and, falling heavily to the ground, shivered into fragments.

Then took place an astonishing spectacle. The myriads of armed dolls, that lay in piles about the room, became suddenly imbued with motion. They stood straight, their tiny limbs moved, their black eyes flashed with wicked purposes, their thread-like swords gleamed as they waved them to and fro. The villainous souls imprisoned in the bottle began to work within them. Like the Lilliputians, when they found the giant Gulliver asleep, they scaled in swarms the burly sides of the four sleeping gypsies. At every step they took, they drove their thin swords and quivering daggers into the flesh of the drunken authors of their be-ing. To stab and kill was their mission, and they stabbed and killed with incredible fury. They clustered on the Wondersmith's sallow cheeks and sinewy throat, piercing every portion with their diminutive poisoned blades. Filomel's fat carcass was alive with them. They blackened the spare body of Monsieur Kerplonne. They covered Oaksmith's huge form like a cluster of insects.

Overcome completely with the fumes of wine, these tiny wounds did not for a few moments awaken the sleeping victims. But the swift and deadly poison Macousha, with which the weapons had been so fiend-ishly anointed, began to work. Herr Hippe, stung into sudden life, leaped to his feet, with a dwarf army clinging to his clothes and his hands—always stabbing, stabbing, stabbing. For an instant, a look of stupid bewilderment clouded his face; then the horrible truth burst upon him. He gave a shriek like that which a horse utters when he finds himself fettered and surrounded by fire—a shriek that curdled the air for miles and miles.

"Oaksmith! Kerplonne! Filomel! Awake! awake! We are lost! The souls have got loose! We are dead! poisoned! O accursed ones! O demons, ye are slaying me! Ah! fiends of hell!"

Aroused by these frightful howls, the three gypsies sprang also to their feet, to find themselves stung to death by the manikins. They raved, they shrieked, they swore. They staggered around the chamber. Blinded in the eyes by the ever stabbing weapons—with the poison already burning in their veins like red-hot lead—their forms swelling and discoloring visibly every moment—their howls and attitudes and furious gestures made the scene look like a chamber in hell.

Maddened beyond endurance, the Wondersmith, half blinded and choking with the venom that had congested all the blood-vessels of his body, seized dozens of the manikins and dashed them into the fire, trampling them down with his feet.

"Ye shall die too, if I die," he cried, with a roar like that of a tiger. "Ye shall burn, if I burn. I gave ye life—I give ye death. Down!—down!—burn! flame! Fiends that ye are, to slay us! Help me, brothers! Before we die, let us have our revenge!"

On this, the other gypsies, themselves maddened by approaching death, began hurling manikins, by handfuls, into the fire. The little creatures, being wooden of body, quickly caught the flames, and an awful struggle for life took place in miniature in the grate. Some of them escaped from between the bars and ran about the room, blazing, writhing in agony, and igniting the curtains and other draperies that hung around. Others fought and stabbed one another in the very core of the fire, like combating salamanders. Meantime, the motions of the gypsies grew more languid and slow, and their curses were uttered in choked guttural tones. The faces of all four were spotted with red and green and violet, like so many egg-plants. Their bodies were swollen to a frightful size, and at last they dropped on the floor, like over-ripe fruit shaken from the boughs by the winds of autumn.

The chamber was now a sheet of fire. The flames roared around and around, as if seeking for escape, licking every projecting cornice and sill with greedy tongues, as the serpent licks his prey before he swallows it. A hot, putrid breath came through the keyhole, and smote Solon and Zonéla like a wind of death. They clasped each other's hands with a moan of terror, and fled from the house.

The next morning, when the young year was just unclosing its eyes, and the happy children all over the great city were peeping from their beds into the myriads of stockings hanging near by, the blue skies of heaven shone through a black network of stone and charred rafters. These were all that remained of the habitation of Herr Hippe, the Wondersmith.

# THE DARK BROTHERHOOD

## BY H. P. LOVECRAFT
## & AUGUST DERLETH

THE SHADOW of Edgar Allan Poe is often seen in the pages of this book. Because his tales are so familiar, we have not represented him here, but it seems only fitting that he should be especially treated in this brilliant story by H. P. Lovecraft and August Derleth.

H. P. Lovecraft, the extraordinary recluse of Providence, Rhode Island, has been called the most important supernatural storyteller since Poe. He was also tremendously adept at the science fiction story and often combined both in a weird phantasmagoria of horror. His ability to handle such stories came from his own recognition of the creative power of fear.

"The oldest and strongest emotion of mankind," he said, "is fear, and the oldest and strongest kind of fear is fear of the unknown. These facts few psychologists will dispute, and their admitted truth must establish for all time the genuineness and dignity of the weirdly horrible tales as a literary form. Against it are discharged all the shafts of a materialistic sophistication which clings to frequently felt emotions and external events, and of a naively inspired idealism which deprecates the aesthetic motive and calls for a didactic literature to 'uplift' the reader toward a suitable degree of smirking optimism. But in spite of all this opposition the weird tale has survived, developed, and attained remarkable heights of perfection; founded as it is on a profound and elementary principle whose appeal, if not always universal, must necessarily be poignant and permanent to minds of the requisite sensitiveness."

August Derleth, a superb science fiction writer in his own right, was the founder of the great science fiction publishing house called Arkham House.  ࿋

IT IS PROBABLE that the facts in regard to the mysterious destruction by fire of an abandoned house on a knoll along the shore of the Seekonk in a little habited district between the Washington and Red Bridges, will never be entirely known. The police have been beset by the usual number of cranks, purporting to offer information about the matter, none more insistent than Arthur Phillips, the descendant of an old East Side family, long resident on Angell Street, a somewhat confused but earnest young man who prepared an account of certain events he alleges led to the fire. Though police have interviewed all persons concerned and mentioned in Mr. Phillips' account, no corroboration—save for a statement from a librarian at the Athenaeum, attesting only to the fact that Mr. Phillips did once meet Miss Rose Dexter there—could be found to support Mr. Phillips' allegations. The manuscript follows.

I

THE NOCTURNAL streets of any city along the Eastern Seaboard afford the nightwalker many a glimpse of the strange and terrible, the macabre and *outré*, for darkness draws from the crevices and crannies, the attic rooms and cellar hideways of the city those human beings who, for obscure reasons lost in the past, choose to keep the day secure in their gray niches—the misshapen, the lonely, the sick, the very old, the haunted, and those lost souls who are forever seeking their identities under cover of the night, which is beneficent for them as the cold light of day can never be. These are the hurt by life, the maimed, men and women who have never recovered from the traumas of childhood or who have willingly sought after experiences not meant for man to know, and every place where the human society has been concentrated for any considerable length of time abounds with them, though they are seen only in the dark hours, emerging like nocturnal moths to move about in their narrow environs for a few brief hours before they must escape daylight once more.

Having been a solitary child, and much left to my own devices because of the persistent ill-health which was my lot, I developed early a propensity for roaming abroad by night, at first only in the Angell Street neighborhood where I lived during much of my childhood, and then, little by little, in a widened circle in my native Providence. By day, my health permitting, I haunted the Seekonk River from the city into the open country, or, when my energy was at its height, played with a few carefully chosen companions at a "clubhouse" we had painstakingly constructed in wooded areas not far out of the city. I was also much given to reading, and spent long hours in my grandfather's extensive library, reading without discrimination and thus assimilating a vast amount of knowledge, from the Greek philosophies to the history of the English monarchy, from the secrets of ancient alchemists to the experiments of Niels Bohr, from the lore of Egyptian papyri to the regional studies of Thomas Hardy, since my grandfather was possessed of very catholic tastes in books and, spurning specialization, bought and kept only what in his mind was good, by which he meant that which involved him.

But the nocturnal city invariably drew me from all else; walking abroad was my preference above all other pursuits, and I went out and about at night all through the later years of my childhood and throughout my adolescent years, in the course of which I tended—because sporadic illness kept me from regular attendance at school—to grow ever more self-sufficient and solitary. I could not now say what it was I sought with such determination in the nighted city, what it was in the ill-lit streets that drew me, why I sought old Benefit Street and the shadowed environs of Poe Street, almost unknown in the vastness of Providence, what it was I hoped to see in the furtively glimpsed faces of other night-wanderers slipping and slinking along the dark lanes and byways of the city, unless perhaps it was to escape from the harsher realities of daylight coupled with an insatiable curiosity about the secrets of city life which only the night could disclose.

When at last my graduation from high school was an accomplished fact, it might have been assumed that I would turn to other pursuits; but it was not so, for my health was too precarious to warrant matriculation at Brown University, where I would like to have gone to continue my studies, and this deprivation served only to enhance my solitary occupations—I doubled my reading hours and increased the time I spent abroad by night, by the simple expedient of sleeping during the daylight hours. And yet I contrived to lead an otherwise normal existence; I did not abandon my widowed mother or my aunts, with whom we lived, though the companions of my youth had grown away from me, and I managed to discover Rose Dexter, a dark-eyed descendant of the first English families to come into old Providence, one singularly favored in the proportions of her figure and in the beauty of her features, whom I persuaded to share my nocturnal pursuits.

With her I continued to explore nocturnal Providence, and with new zest, eager to show Rose all I had already discovered in my wanderings about the city. We met originally at the old Athenaeum, and we continued to meet there of evenings, and from its portals ventured forth into the night. What began lightheartedly for her soon grew into dedicated habit; she proved as eager as I to inquire into hidden byways and long disused lanes, and she was soon as much at home in the night-held city as I. She was little inclined to irrelevant chatter, and thus proved admirably complementary to my person.

We had been exploring Providence in this fashion for several months when, one night on Benefit Street, a gentleman wearing a knee-length cape over wrinkled and ill-kept clothing accosted us. He had been standing on the walk not far ahead of us when first we turned into the street, and I had observed him when we went past him; he had struck me as oddly disquieting, for I thought his moustached, dark-eyed face with the unruly hair of his hatless head strangely familiar; and, at our passing, he had set out in pursuit until, at last, catching up to us, he touched me on the shoulder and spoke.

"Sir," he said, "could you tell me how to reach the cemetery where once Poe walked?"

I gave him directions, and then, spurred by a sudden impulse, suggested that we accompany him to the goal he sought; almost before I understood fully what had happened, we three were walking along together. I saw almost at once with what a calculating air the fellow scrutinized my companion, and yet any resentment I might have felt was dispelled by the ready recognition that the stranger's interest was inoffensive, for it was rather more coolly critical than passionately involved. I took the opportunity, also, to examine him as carefully as I could in the occasional patches of streetlight through which we passed, and was increasingly disturbed at the gnawing certainty that I knew him or had known him.

He was dressed almost uniformly in somber black, save for his white shirt and the flowing Windsor tie he affected. His clothing was unpressed, as if it had been worn for a long time without having been attended to, but it was not unclean, as far as I could see. His brow was high, almost dome-like; under it his dark eyes looked out hauntingly, and his face narrowed to his small, blunt chin. His hair, too, was longer than most men of my generation wore it, and yet he seemed to be of that same generation, not more than five years past my own age. His clothing, however, was definitely not of my generation; indeed, it seemed, for all that it had the appearance of being new, to have been cut to a pattern of several generations before my own.

"Are you a stranger to Providence?" I asked him presently.

"I am visiting," he said shortly.

"You are interested in Poe?"

He nodded.

"How much do you know of him?" I asked then.

"Little," he replied. "Perhaps you could tell me more?"

I needed no second invitation, but immediately gave him a biographical sketch of the father of the detective story and a master of the macabre tale whose work I had long admired, elaborating only on his romance with Mrs. Sarah Helen Whitman, since it involved Providence and the visit with Mrs. Whitman to the cemetery whither we were bound. I saw that he listened with almost rapt attention, and seemed to be setting down in memory everything I said, but I could not decide from his expressionless face whether what I told him gave him pleasure or displeasure, and I could not determine what the source of his interest was.

For her part, Rose was conscious of his interest in her, but she was not embarrassed by it, perhaps sensing that his interest was other than amorous. It was not until he asked her name that I realized we had not had his. He gave it now as "Mr. Allan," at which Rose smiled almost imperceptibly; I caught it fleeting as we passed under a streetlamp.

Having learned our names, our companion seemed interested in nothing more, and it was in silence that we reached the cemetery at last. I had thought Mr. Allan would enter it, but such was not his intention; he had evidently meant only to discover its location, so that he could return to it by day, which was manifestly a sensible conclusion, for—though I knew it well and had walked there on occasion by night—it offered little for a stranger to view in the dark hours.

We bade him good-night at the gate and went on.

"I've seen that fellow somewhere before," I said to Rose once we had passed beyond his hearing. "But I can't think where it was. Perhaps in the library."

"It must have been in the library," answered Rose with a throaty chuckle that was typical of her. "In a portrait on the wall."

"Oh, come!" I cried.

"Surely you recognized the resemblance, Arthur!" she cried. "Even to his name. He looks like Edgar Allan Poe."

And, of course, he did. As soon as Rose had mentioned it, I recognized the strong resemblance, even to his clothing, and at once set Mr. Allan down as a harmless idolater of Poe's, so obsessed with the man that he must fashion himself in his likeness, even to his outdated clothing—another of the curious specimens of humanity thronging the night streets of the city.

"Well, that one is the oddest fellow we've met in all the while we've walked out," I said.

Her hand tightened on my arm. "Arthur, didn't you *feel* something —something *wrong* about him?"

"Oh, I suppose there is something 'wrong' in that sense about all of us who are haunters of the dark," I said. "Perhaps, in a way, we prefer to make our own reality."

But even as I answered her, I was aware of her meaning, and there was no need of the explanation she tried so earnestly to make in the spate of words that followed—there was something wrong in the sense that there was about Mr. Allan a profound note of error. It lay, now that I faced and accepted it, in a number of trivial things, but particularly in the lack of expressiveness in his features; his speech, limited though it had been, was without modulation, almost mechanical; he had not smiled, nor had he been given to any variation in facial expression whatsoever; he had spoken with a precision that suggested an icy detachment and aloofness foreign to most men. Even the manifest interest he showed in Rose was far more clinical than anything else. At the same time that my curiosity was quickened, a note of apprehension began to make itself manifest, as a result of which I turned our conversation into other channels and presently walked Rose to her home.

## II

I suppose it was inevitable that I should meet Mr. Allan again, and but two nights later, this time not far from my own door. Perhaps it was absurd to think so, but I could not escape the impression that he was waiting for me, that he was as anxious to encounter me again as I was to meet him.

I greeted him jovially, as a fellow haunter of the night, and took quick notice of the fact that, though his voice simulated my own joviality, there was not a flicker of emotion on his face; it remained completely placid—"wooden," in the words of the romantic writers, not the hint of a smile touched his lips, not a glint shone in his dark eyes. And now that I had had it called to my attention, I saw that the resemblance to Poe was remarkable, so much so, that had Mr. Allan put forth any reasonable claim to being a descendant of Poe's, I could have been persuaded to belief.

It was, I thought, a curious coincidence, but hardly more, and Mr. Allan on this occasion made no mention of Poe or anything relating to him in Providence. He seemed, it was soon evident, more intent on listening to me; he was as singularly uncommunicative as he had been at our first meeting, and in an odd way his manner was precisely the same—as if we had not actually met before. But perhaps it was that he simply sought some common ground, for, once I mentioned that

I contributed a weekly column on astronomy to the Providence *Journal*, he began to take part in our conversation; what had been for several blocks virtually a monologue on my part, became a dialogue.

It was immediately apparent to me that Mr. Allan was not a novice in astronomical matters. Anxious as he seemed to be for my views, he entertained some distinctly different views of his own, some of them highly debatable. He lost no time in setting forth his opinion that not only was interplanetary travel possible, but that countless stars—not alone some of the planets in our own solar system—were inhabited.

"By human beings?" I asked incredulously.

"Need it be?" he replied. "Life is unique—not man. Even here on this planet life takes many forms."

I asked him then whether he had read the works of Charles Fort.

He had not. He knew nothing of him, and, at his request, I outlined some of Fort's theories, together with the facts Fort had adduced in support of those theories. I saw that from time to time, as we walked along, my companion's head moved in a curt nod, though his unemotional face betrayed no expression; it was as if he agreed. And on one occasion, he broke into words.

"Yes, it is so. What he says is so."

I had at the moment been speaking of the sighting of unidentified flying objects near Japan during the latter half of the nineteenth century.

"How can you say so?" I cried.

He launched at once into a lengthy statement, the gist of which was that every advanced scientist in the domain of astronomy was convinced that earth was not unique in having life, and that it followed therefore that, just as it could be concluded that some heavenly bodies had lower life forms than our own, so others might well support higher forms, and, accepting that premise, it was perfectly logical that such higher forms had mastered interplanetary travel and might, after decades of observation, be thoroughly familiar with earth and its inhabitants as well as with its sister planets.

"To what purpose?" I asked. "To make war on us? To invade us?"

"A more highly developed form of life would hardly need to use such primitive methods," he pointed out. "They watch us precisely as we watch the moon and listen for radio signals from the planets—we here are still in the earliest stages of interplanetary communication and, be-yond that, space travel, whereas other races on remote stars have long since achieved both."

"How can you speak with such authority?" I asked then.

"Because I am convinced of it. Surely you must have come face to face with similar conclusions."

I admitted that I had.

"And you remain open-minded?"

I admitted this as well.

"Open-minded enough to examine certain proof it it were offered to you?"

"Certainly," I replied, though my skepticism could hardly have gone unnoticed.

"That is good," he said. "Because if you will permit my brothers and me to call on you at your home on Angell Street, we may be able to convince you that there is life in space—not in the shape of men, but life, and life possessing a far greater intelligence than that of your most intelligent men."

I was amused at the breadth of his claim and belief, but I did not betray it by any sign. His confidence made me to reflect again upon the infinite variety of characters to be found among the nightwalkers of Providence; clearly Mr. Allan was a man who was obsessed by his ex-traordinary beliefs, and, like most of such men, eager to proselytize, to make converts.

"Whenever you like," I said by way of invitation. "Except that I would prefer it to be late rather than early, to give my mother time to get to bed. Anything in the way of an experiment might disturb her."

"Shall we say next Monday night?"

"Agreed."

My companion thereafter said no more on this subject. Indeed, he said scarcely anything on any subject, and it was left for me to do the talking. I was evidently not very entertaining, for in less than three blocks we came to an alley and there Mr. Allan abruptly bade me good night, after which he turned into the alley and was soon swallowed in its darkness.

Could his house abut upon it? I wondered. If not, he must inevitably come out the other end. Impulsively I hurried around one end of that block and stationed myself deep in the shadows of the parallel street, where I could remain well hidden from the alley entrance and yet keep it in view.

Mr. Allan came leisurely out of the alley before I had quite recovered my breath. I expected him to pursue his way through the alley, but he did not; he turned down the street, and, accelerating his pace a little, he proceeded on his way. Impelled by curiosity now, I followed, keeping myself as well hidden as possible. But Mr. Allan never once looked around; he set his face straight ahead of him and never, as far as I could determine, even glanced to left or right; he was clearly bound for a destination that could only be his home, for the hour was past midnight.

I had little difficulty following my erstwhile companion, for I knew these streets well, I had known them since my childhood. Mr. Allan was bound in the direction of the Seekonk, and he held to his course without deviation until he reached a somewhat rundown section of Providence, where he made his way up a little knoll to a long-deserted house at its crest. He let himself into it and I saw him no more. I waited a while longer, expecting a light to go up in the house, but none did, and I could only conclude that he had gone directly to bed.

Fortunately, I had kept myself in the shadows, for Mr. Allan had evidently not gone to bed. Apparently he had gone through the house and around the block, for suddenly I saw him approach the house from the direction we had come, and once more he walked on, past my place of concealment, and made his way into the house, again without turning on a light.

This time, certainly, he had remained there. I waited for five minutes or a trifle more; then turned and made my way back toward my own home on Angell Street, satisfied that I had done no more in following Mr. Allan than he had evidently done on the night of our initial meeting in following me, for I had long since concluded that our meeting tonight had not been by chance, but by design.

Many blocks from the Allan house, however, I was startled to see approaching me from the direction of Benefit Street, my erstwhile companion! Even as I wondered how he had managed to leave the house again and make his way well around me in order to enable him to come toward me, trying in vain to map the route he could have taken to accomplish this, he came up and passed me by without so much as a flicker of recognition.

Yet it was he, undeniably—the same Poesque appearance distinguished him from any other nightwalker. Stilling his name on my tongue, I turned and looked after him. He never turned his head, but walked steadily on, clearly bound for the scene I had not long since quitted. I watch him out of sight, still trying—in vain—to map the route he might have taken among the lanes and byways and streets so familiar to me in order to meet me so once more, face to face.

We had met on Angell Street, walked on to Benefit and north, then turned riverward once more. Only by dint of hard running could he have cut around me and come back. And what purpose would he have had to follow such a course? It left me utterly baffled, particularly since he had given me not the slightest sign of recognition, his entire mien suggesting that we were perfect strangers!

But if I was mystified at the occurrences of the night, I was even more puzzled at my meeting with Rose at the Athenaeum the following night. She had clearly been waiting for me, and hastened to my side as soon as she caught sight of me.

"Have you see Mr. Allan?" she asked.

"Only last night," I answered, and would have gone on to recount the circumstances had she not spoken again.

"So did I! He walked me out from the library and home."

I stifled my response and heard her out. Mr. Allan had been waiting for her to come out of the library. He had greeted her and asked whether he might walk with her, after having ascertained that I was not with her. They had walked for an hour with but little conversation, and this only of the most superficial—relative to the antiquities of the city, the architecture of certain houses, and similar matters, just such as one interested in the older aspects of Providence would find of interest—and then he had walked her home. She had, in short, been with Mr. Allan in one part of the city at the same time that I had been with him in another; and clearly neither of us had the slightest doubt of the identity of our companions.

"I saw him after midnight," I said, which was part of the truth but not all the truth.

This extraordinary coincidence must have some logical explanation, though I was not disposed to discuss it with Rose, lest I unduly alarm her. Mr. Allan had spoken of his "brothers"; it was therefore entirely likely that Mr. Allan was one of a pair of identical twins. But what explanation could there be for what was an obvious and designed deception? One of our companions was *not*, could not have been the same Mr. Allan with whom we had previously walked. But which? I was satisfied that my companion was identical with Mr. Allan met but two nights before.

In as casual a manner as I could assume in the circumstances, I asked such questions of Rose as were designed to satisfy me in regard to the identity of her companion, in the anticipation that somewhere in our dialogue she would reveal some doubt of the identity of hers. She betrayed no such doubt; she was innocently convinced that her companion was the same man who had walked with us two nights ago, for he had obviously made references to the earlier nocturnal walk, and Rose was completely convinced that he was the same man. She had no reason for doubt, however, for I held my tongue; there was some perplexing mystery here, for the brothers had some obscure reason for interesting themselves in us—certainly other than that they shared our interest in the nightwalkers of the city and the hidden aspects of urban life that appeared only with the dusk and vanished once more into their seclusion with the dawn.

My companion, however, had made an assignation with me, whereas Rose said nothing to indicate that her companion had planned a further meeting with her. And why had he waited to meet her in the first place? But this line of inquiry was lost before the insistant cognizance that neither of the meetings I had had after leaving my companion at his residence last night could have been Rose's companion, for Rose lived rather too far from the place of my final meeting last night to have permitted her companion to meet me at the point we met. A disquieting sense of uneasiness began to rise in me. Perhaps there were three Allans—all identical—triplets? Or four? But no, surely the second Mr. Allan encountered on the previous night had been identical with the first, even if the third encounter could not have been the same man.

No matter how much thought I applied to it, the riddle remained insoluble. I was, therefore, in a challenging frame of mind for my Monday night appointment with Mr. Allan, now but two days away.

### III

EVEN SO, I was ill-prepared for the visit of Mr. Allan and his brothers on the following Monday night. They came at a quarter past ten o'clock; my mother had just gone upstairs to bed. I had expected, at most, three of them; there were seven—and they were as alike as peas in a pod, so much so that I could not pick from among them the Mr. Allan with whom I had twice walked the nocturnal streets of Providence, though I assumed it was he who was the spokesman for the group.

They filed into the living room, and Mr. Allan immediately set about arranging chairs in a semicircle with the help of his brothers, murmuring something about the "nature of the experiment," though, to tell the truth, I was still much too amazed and disquieted at the appearance of seven identical men, all of whom bore so strong a resemblance to Edgar Allan Poe as to startle the beholder, to assimilate what was being said. Moreover, I saw now by the light of my Welsbach gas lamp, that all seven of them were of a pallid, waxen complexion, not of such a nature as to give me any doubt of their being flesh and bone like myself, but rather such as to suggest that one and all were afflicted with some kind of disease—anemia, perhaps, or some kindred illness which would leave their faces colorless; and their eyes, which were very dark, seemed to stare fixedly and yet without seeing, though they suffered no lack of perception and seemed to perceive by means of some extra sense not visible to me. The sensation that rose in me was not predominantly one of fear, but one of overwhelming curiosity tinged with a spreading sense of something utterly alien not only to my experience but to my existence.

Thus far, little had passed between us, but now that the semicircle had been completed, and my visitors had seated themselves, their spokesman beckoned me forward and indicated a chair placed within the arc of the semicircle facing the seated men.

"Will you sit here, Mr. Phillips?" he asked.

I did as he asked, and found myself the object of all eyes, but not essentially so much their object as their focal point, for the seven men seemed to be looking not so much at me as through me.

"Our intention, Mr. Phillips," explained their spokesman—whom I took to be the gentleman I had encountered on Benefit Street—"is to produce for you certain impressions of extraterrestrial life. All that is necessary for you to do is to relax and to be receptive."

"I am ready," I said.

I had expected that they would ask for the light to be lowered, which seems to be integral to all such seance-like sessions, but they did not do so. They waited upon silence, save for the ticking of the hall clock and the distant hum of the city, and then they began what I can only describe as singing—a low, not unpleasant, almost lulling humming, increasing in volume, and broken with sounds I assumed were words though I could not make out any of them. The song they sang and the way they sang it was indescribably foreign; the key was minor, and the tonal intervals did not resemble any terrestrial musical system with which I was familiar, though it seemed to me more Oriental than Occidental.

I had little time to consider the music, however, for I was rapidly overcome with a feeling of profound malaise, the faces of the seven men grew dim and coalesced to merge into one swimming face, and an intolerable consciousness of unrolled eons of time swept over me. I concluded that some form of hypnosis was responsible for my condition, but I did not have any qualms about it; it did not matter, for the experience I was undergoing was utterly novel and not unpleasant, though there was inherent in it a discordant note, as of some lurking evil looming far behind the relaxing sensations that crowded upon me and swept me before them. Gradually, the lamp, the walls, and the men before me faded and vanished and, though I was still aware of being in my quarters on Angell Street, I was also cognizant that somehow I had been transported to new surroundings, and an element of alarm at the strangeness of these surroundings, together with one of repulsion and alienation began to make themselves manifest. It was as if I feared losing consciousness in an alien place without the means of returning to earth—for it was an extraterrestrial scene that I witnessed, one of great and magnificent grandeur in its proportions, and yet one completely incomprehensible to me.

Vast vistas of space whirled before me in an alien dimension, and central in them was an aggregation of gigantic cubes, scattered along a gulf of violet and agitated radiation—and other figures moving among them—enormous, iridescent, rugose cones, rising from a base almost ten feet wide to a height of over ten feet, and composed of ridgy, scaly, semi-elastic matter, and sporting from their apexes four flexible, cylindrical members, each at least a foot thick, and of a similar substance, though more fleshlike, as that of the cones, which were presumably bodies for the crowning members, which, as I watched, had an ability to contract or expand, sometimes to lengthen to a distance equal to the height of the cone to which they adhered. Two of these members were terminated with enormous claws, while a third wore a crest of four red, trumpetlike appendages, and the fourth ended in a great yellow globe two feet in diameter, in the center of which were three enormous eyes, darkly opalescent, which, because of their position in the elastic member, could be turned in any direction whatsoever. It was such a scene as exercised the greatest fascination upon me and yet at the same time spread in me a repellance inspired by its total alienation and the aura of fearful disclosures which alone could give it meaning and a lurking terror. Moreover, as I saw the moving figures, which seemed to be *tending* the great cubes, with greater clarity and more distinctness, I saw that their strange heads were crowned by four slender gray stalks carrying flowerlike appendages, as well as, from its nether side, eight sinuous, elastic tentacles, moss green in color, which seemed to be constantly agitated by serpentine motion, expanding and contracting, lengthening and shortening and whipping around as if with life independent of that which animated, more sluggishly, the cones themselves. The whole scene was bathed in a wan, red glow, as from some dying sun which, failing its planet, now took second place to the violet radiation from the gulf.

The scene had an indescribable effect on me; it was as if I had been permitted a look into another world, one incredibly vaster than our own, distinguished from our own by antipodally different values and life forms, and remote from ours in time and space, and as I gazed at this far world, I became aware—as were this intelligence being funneled into me by some psychic means—that I looked upon a dying race which must escape its planet or perish. Spontaneously then, I seemed to recognize the burgeoning of a menacing evil, and with an urgent, violent effort, I threw off the bondage of the chant that held me in its spell, gave vent to the uprushing of fear I felt in a cry of protest, and rose to my feet, while the chair on which I sat fell backward with a crash.

Instantly the scene before my mind's eye vanished and the room returned to focus. Across from me sat my visitors, the seven gentlemen in the likeness of Poe, impassive and silent, for the sounds they had made, the humming and the odd word-like tonal noises, had ceased.

I calmed down, my pulse began to slow.

"What you saw, Mr. Phillips, was a scene on another star, remote from here," said Mr. Allan. "Far out in space—indeed, in another universe. Did it convince you?"

"I've seen enough," I cried.

I could not tell whether my visitors were amused or scornful; they remained without expression, including their spokesman, who only inclined his head slightly and said, "We will take our leave then, with your permission."

And silently, one by one, they all filed out into Angell Street.

I was most disagreeably shaken. I had no proof of having seen anything on another world, but I could testify that I had experienced an extraordinary hallucination, undoubtedly through hypnotic influence.

But what had been its reason for being? I pondered that as I set about to put the living room to rights, but I could not adduce any profound reason for the demonstration I had witnessed. I was unable to deny that my visitors had shown themselves to be possessed of extraordinary faculties—but to what end? And I had to admit to myself that I was as much shaken by the appearance of no less than seven identical men as I was by the hallucinatory experience I had just passed through. Quintuplets were possible, yes—but had anyone ever heard of septuplets? Nor were multiple births of identical children usual. Yet here were seven men, all of very much the same age, identical in appearance, for whose existence there was not a scintilla of explanation.

Nor was there any graspable meaning in the scene that I had witnessed during the demonstration. Somehow I had understood that the great cubes were sentient beings for whom the violet radiation was life-giving; I had realized that the cone-creatures served them in some fashion or other, but nothing had been disclosed to show how. The whole vision was meaningless; it was just such a scene as might have been created by a highly organized imagination and telepathically conveyed to a willing subject, such as myself. That it proved the existence of extraterrestrial life was ridiculous; it proved no more than that I had been the victim of an induced hallucination.

But, once more, I came full circle. As hallucination, it was completely without reason for being.

Yet I could not escape an insistent disquiet that troubled me long that night before I was able to sleep.

IV

STRANGELY ENOUGH, my uneasiness mounted during the course of the following morning. Accustomed as I was to the human curiosities, to the often incredible characters and unusual sights to be encountered on the nocturnal walks I took about Providence, the circumstances surrounding the Poesque Mr. Allan and his brothers were so *outré* that I could not get them out of mind.

Acting on impulse, I took time off from my work that afternoon and made my way to the house on the knoll along the Seekonk, determined to confront my nocturnal companion. But the house, when I came to it, wore an air of singular desertion; badly worn curtains were drawn down to the sills of the windows, in some places blinds were up; and the whole milieu was the epitome of abandonment.

Nevertheless, I knocked at the door and waited.

There was no answer. I knocked again.

No sound fell to ear from inside the house.

Powerfully impelled by curiosity now, I tried the door. It opened to my touch. I hesitated still, and looked all around me. No one was in sight, at least two of the houses in the neighborhood were unoccupied, and if I was under surveillance it was not apparent to me.

I opened the door and stepped into the house, standing for a few moments with my back to the door to accustom my eyes to the twilight that filled the rooms. Then I moved cautiously through the small vestibule into the adjacent room, a parlor sparely occupied by horsehair furniture at least two decades old. There was no sign here of occupation by any human being, though there was evidence that someone had not long since walked here, making a path through dust visible on the uncarpeted flooring. I crossed the room and entered a small dining room, and crossed this, too, to find myself in a kitchen, which, like the other rooms, bore little sign of having been used, for there was no food of any kind in evidence, and the table appeared not to have been used for years. Yet here, too, were footprints in substantial numbers, testifying to the habitation of the house. And the staircase revealed steady use, as well.

But it was the far side of the house that afforded the most disturbing disclosures. This side of the building consisted of but one large room, though it was instantly evident that it had been three rooms at one time, but the connecting walls had been removed without the finished repair of the junctions at the outer wall. I saw this in a fleeting glance, for what was in the center of the room caught and held my fascinated attention. The room was bathed in violet light, a soft glowing that emanated from what appeared to be a long, glass-encased slab, which, with a second, unlit similar slab, stood surrounded by machinery the like of which I had never seen before save in dreams.

I moved cautiously into the room, alert for anyone who might prevent my intrusion. No one and nothing moved. I drew closer to the violet-lit glass case and saw that something lay within, though I did not at first encompass this because I saw what it laid upon—nothing less than a lifesized reproduction of a likeness of Edgar Allan Poe, which, like everything else, was illuminated by the same pulsing violet light, the source of which I could not determine, save that it was enclosed by the glass-like substance which made up the case. But when at last I looked upon that which lay upon the likeness of Poe, I almost cried out in fearful surprise, for it was, in miniature, a precise reproduction of one of the rugose cones I had seen only last night in the hallucination induced in my home on Angell Street! And the sinuous movement of the tentacles on its head—or what I took to be its head—was indisputable evidence that it was alive!

I backed hastily away with only enough of a glance at the other case to assure myself that it was bare and unoccupied, though connected by many metal tubes to the illumined case parallel to it; then I fled, as noiselessly as possible, for I was convinced that the nocturnal brotherhood slept upstairs and in my confusion at this inexplicable revelation that placed my hallucination of the previous night into another perspective, I wished to meet no one. I escaped from the house undetected, though I thought I caught a glimpse of a Poesque face at one of the upper windows. I ran down the road and back along the streets that bridged the distance from the Seekonk to the Providence River, and ran so for many blocks before I slowed to a walk, for I was beginning to attract attention in my wild flight.

As I walked along, I strove to bring order to my chaotic thoughts. I could not adduce an explanation for what I had seen, but I knew intuitively that I had stumbled upon some menacing evil too dark and forbidding and perhaps too vast as well for my comprehension. I hunted for meaning and found none; mine had never been a scientifically oriented mind, apart from chemistry and astronomy, so that I was not equipped to understand the use of the great machines I had seen in that house ringing that violet-lit slab where that rugose body lay in warm, life-giving radiation—indeed, I was not even able to assimilate the machinery itself, for there was only a remote resemblance to anything I had ever before seen, and that the dynamos in a powerhouse. They had all been connected in some way to the two slabs, and the glass cases—if the substance were glass—the one occupied, the other dark and empty, for all the tubing that tied them each to each.

But I had seen enough to be convinced that the dark-clad brotherhood who walked the streets of Providence by night in the guise of Edgar Allan Poe had a purpose other than mine in doing so; theirs was no simple curiosity about the nocturnal characters, about fellow walkers of the night. Perhaps darkness was their natural element, even as daylight was that of the majority of their fellowmen; but that their motivation was sinister, I could not now doubt. Yet at the same time I was at a loss as to what course next to follow.

I turned my steps at last toward the library, in the vague hope of grasping at something that might lead me to some clue by means of which I could approach an understanding of what I had seen.

But there was nothing. Search as I might, I found no key, no hint, though I read widely through every conceivable reference—even to those on Poe in Providence on the shelves, and I left the library late in the day as baffled as I had entered.

Perhaps it was inevitable that I would see Mr. Allan again that night. I had no way of knowing whether my visit to his home had been observed, despite the observer I thought I had glimpsed in an upper window in my flight, and I encountered him therefore in some trepidation. But this was evidently ill-founded, for when I greeted him on Benefit Street there was nothing in his manner or in his words to suggest any change in his attitude, such as I might have expected had he been aware of my intrusion. Yet I knew full well his capacity for being without expression—humor, disgust, even anger or irritation were alien to his features, which never changed from that introspective mask which was essentially that of Poe.

"I trust you have recovered from our experiment, Mr. Phillips," he said after exchanging the customary amenities.

"Fully," I answered, though it was not the truth. I added something about a sudden spell of dizziness to explain my bringing the experiment to its precipitate end.

"It is but one of the worlds outside you saw, Mr. Phillips," Mr. Allan went on. "There are many. As many as a hundred thousand. Life is not the unique property of Earth. Nor is life in the shape of human beings. Life takes many forms on other planets and far stars, forms that would seem bizarre to humans, as human life is bizarre to other life forms."

For once, Mr. Allan was singularly communicative, and I had little to say. Clearly, whether or not I laid what I had seen to hallucination—even in the face of my discovery in my companion's house—he himself believed implicitly in what he said. He spoke of many worlds, as if he were familiar with them. On occasion he spoke almost with reverence

of certain forms of life, particularly those with the astonishing adapta-
bility of assuming the life forms of other planets in their ceaseless
quest for the conditions necessary to their existence.

"The star I looked upon," I broke in, "was dying."

"Yes," he said simply.

"You have seen it?"

"I have seen it, Mr. Phillips."

I listened to him with relief. Since it was manifestly impossible to
permit any man sight of the intimate life of outer space, what I had
experienced was nothing more than the communicated hallucination
of Mr. Allan and his brothers. Telepathic communication certainly,
aided by a form of hypnosis I had not previously experienced. Yet I
could not rid myself of the disquieting sense of evil that surrounded my
nocturnal companion, nor of the uneasy feeling that the explanation
which I had so eagerly accepted was unhappily glib.

As soon as I decently could, thereafter, I made excuses to Mr. Allan
and took my leave of him. I hastened directly to the Athenaeum in the
hope of finding Rose Dexter there, but if she had been there, she had already gone. I went then to a public telephone in the building and
telephoned her home.

Rose answered, and I confess to an instantaneous feeling of gratifica-
tion.

"Have you seen Mr. Allan tonight?" I asked.

"Yes," she replied. "But only for a few moments. I was on my way to
the library."

"So did I."

"He asked me to his home some evening to watch an experiment,"
she went on.

"Don't go," I said at once.

There was a long moment of silence at the other end of the wire.
Then, "Why not?" Unfortunately, I failed to acknowledge the edge of
truculence in her voice.

"It would be better not to go," I said, with all the firmness I could
muster.

"Don't you think, Mr. Phillips, I am the best judge of that?"

I hastened to assure her that I had no wish to dictate her actions, but meant only to suggest that it might be dangerous to go.

"Why?"

"I can't tell you over the telephone," I answered, fully aware of how lame it sounded, and knowing even as I said it that perhaps I could not put into words at all the horrible suspicions which had begun to take shape in my mind, for they were so fantastic, so *outré*, that no one could be expected to believe in them.

"I'll think it over," she said crisply.

"I'll try to explain when I see you," I promised.

She bade me good-night and rang off with an intransigence that boded ill, and left me profoundly disturbed.

## V

I COME now to the final, apocalyptic events concerning Mr. Allan and the mystery surrounding the house on the forgotten knoll. I hesitate to set them down even now, for I recognize that the charge against me will only be broadened to include grave questions about my sanity. Yet I have no other course. Indeed, the entire future of humanity, the whole course of what we call civilization may be affected by what I do or do not write of this matter. For the culminating events followed rapidly and naturally upon my conversation with Rose Dexter, that unsatisfactory exchange over the telephone.

After a restless, uneasy day at work, I concluded that I must make a tenable explanation to Rose. On the following evening, therefore, I went early to the library, where I was accustomed to meeting her, and took a place where I could watch the main entrance. There I waited for well over an hour before it occurred to me that she might not come to the library that night.

Once more I sought the telephone, intending to ask whether I might come over and explain my request of the previous night.

But it was her sister-in-law, not Rose, who answered my ring.

Rose had gone out. "A gentleman called for her."

"Did you know him?" I asked.

"No, Mr. Phillips."

"Did you hear his name?"

She had not heard it. She had, in fact, caught only a glimpse of him as Rose hurried out to meet him, but, in answer to my insistent probing, she admitted that Rose's caller had had a moustache.

Mr. Allan! I had no further need to inquire.

For a few moments after I had hung up, I did not know what to do. Perhaps Rose and Mr. Allan were only walking the length of Benefit Street. But perhaps they had gone to that mysterious house. The very thought of it filled me with such apprehension that I lost my head.

I rushed from the library and hurried home. It was ten o'clock when I reached the house on Angell Street. Fortunately, my mother had retired; so I was able to procure my father's pistol without disturbing her. So armed, I hastened once more into night-held Providence and ran, block upon block, toward the shore of the Seekonk and the knoll upon which stood Mr. Allan's strange house, unaware in my incautious haste of the spectacle I made for other nightwalkers and uncaring, for perhaps Rose's life was at stake—and beyond that, vaguely defined, loomed a far greater and hideous evil.

When I reached the house into which Mr. Allan had disappeared I was taken aback by its solitude and unlit windows. Since I was winded, I hesitated to advance upon it, and waited for a minute or so to catch my breath and quiet my pulse. Then, keeping to the shadows, I moved silently up to the house, looking for any sliver of light.

I crept from the front of the house around to the back. Not the slightest ray of light could be seen. But a low humming sound vibrated just inside the range of my hearing, like the hum of a power line responding to the weather. I crossed to the far side of the house—and there I saw the hint of light—not yellow light, as from a lamp inside, but a pale lavender radiance that seemed to glow faintly, ever so faintly, from the wall itself.

I drew back, recalling only too sharply what I had seen in that house.

But my role now could not be a passive one. I had to know whether Rose was in that darkened house—perhaps in that very room with the unknown machinery and the glass case with the monster in the violet radiance.

I slipped back to the front of the house and mounted the steps to the front door.

Once again, the door was not locked. It yielded to the pressure of my hands. Pausing only long enough to take my loaded weapon in hand, I pushed open the door and entered the vestibule. I stood for a moment to accustom my eyes to that darkness; standing there, I was even more aware of the humming sound I had heard—and of more—the same kind of chant which had put me into that hypnotic state in the course of which I had witnessed that disturbing vision purporting to be that of life in another world.

I apprehended its meaning instantly, I thought. Rose must be with Mr. Allan and his brothers, undergoing a similar experience.

Would that it had been no more!

For when I pushed my way into that large room on the far side of the house, I saw that which will be forever indelibly imprinted on my mind. Lit by the radiance from the glass case, the room disclosed Mr. Allan and his identical brothers all prone upon the floor around the twin cases, making their chanting song. Beyond them, against the far wall, lay the discarded life-size likeness of Poe I had seen beneath that weird creature in the glass case bathed in violet radiance. But it was not Mr. Allan and his brothers that so profoundly shocked and repelled me—it was what I saw in the glass cases!

For in the one that lit the room with its violently pulsating and agitated violet radiation lay Rose Dexter, fully clothed, and certainly under hypnosis—and on top of her lay, greatly elongated and with its tentacles flailing madly, the rugose cone-like figure I had last seen shrunken on the likeness of Poe. And in the connected case adjacent to it—I can hardly bear to set it down even now—lay, identical in every detail, *a perfect duplicate of Rose!*

What happened next is confused in my memory. I know that I lost control, that I fired blindly at the glass cases, intending to shatter them. Certainly I struck one or both of them, for with the impact the radiance vanished, the room was plunged into utter darkness, cries of fear and alarm rose from Mr. Allan and his brothers, and, amid a succession of explosive sounds from the machinery, I rushed forward and picked up Rose Dexter.

Somehow I gained the street with Rose.

Looking back, I saw that flames were appearing at the windows of that accursed house, and then, without warning, the north wall of the house collapsed, and something—an object I could not identify—burst from the now burning house and vanished aloft. I fled, still carrying Rose.

Regaining her senses, Rose was hysterical, but I succeeded in calming her, and at last she fell silent and would say nothing. And in silence I took her safely home, knowing how frightening her experience must have been, and resolved to say nothing until she had fully recovered.

In the week that followed, I came to see clearly what was taking place in that house on the knoll. But the charge of arson—lodged against me in lieu of a far more serious one because of the pistol I abandoned in the burning house—has blinded the police to anything but the most mundane matters. I have tried to tell them, insisting that they see Rose Dexter when she is well enough to talk—and willing to do so. I cannot make them understand what I now understand only too well. Yet the facts are there, inescapably.

They say the charred flesh found in that house is not human, most of it. But could they have expected anything else? Seven men in the likeness of Edgar Allan Poe! Surely they must understand that whatever it was in that house came from another world, a dying world, and sought to invade and ultimately take over Earth by reproducing themselves in the shape of men! Surely they must know that it must have been only by coincidence that the model they first chose was a likeness of Poe, chosen because they had no knowledge that Poe did not represent the average among men? Surely they must know, as I came to know, that the rugose, tentacled cone in the violet radiance was the source of their material selves, that the machinery and the tubing—which they say was too much damaged by the fire to identify, as if they could have identified its functions even undamaged!—manufactured from the material simulating flesh supplied by the cone in the violet light creatures in the shape of men from the likeness of Poe!

"Mr. Allan" himself afforded me the key, though I did not know it at the time, when I asked him why mankind was the object of interplanetary scrutiny—"To make war on us? To invade us?"—and he replied: "*A more highly developed form of life would hardly need to use such primitive methods.*" Could anything more plainly set forth the explanation for the strange occupation of the house along the Seekonk? Of course, it is evident now that what "Mr. Allan" and his identical brothers afforded me in my own house was a glimpse of life on the planet of the cubes and rugose cones, which was their own.

And surely, finally, most damning of all—it must be evident to any unbiased observer why they wanted Rose. They meant to reproduce their kind in the guise of men and women, so that they could mingle with us, undetected, unsuspected, and slowly, over decades—perhaps centuries, while their world died, take over and prepare our Earth for those who would come after.

God alone knows how many of them may be here, among us, even now!

Later. I have been unable to see Rose until now, tonight, and I am hesitant to call for her. For something unutterably terrible has happened to me. I have fallen prey to horrible doubts. While it did not occur to me during that frightful experience in the shambles following my shots in that violet-lit room, I have now begun to wonder, and my concern has grown hour by hour until I find it now almost unbearable. How can I be sure that, in those frenzied minutes, I rescued the *real* Rose Dexter? If I did, surely she will reassure me tonight. If I did not— God knows what I may unwittingly have loosed upon Providence and the world!

From *The Providence Journal*—July 17
LOCAL GIRL SLAYS ATTACKER

Rose Dexter, the daughter of Mr. and Mrs. Elisha Dexter of 127 Benevolent Street, last night fought off and killed a young man she charged with attacking her. Miss Dexter was apprehended in an hysterical condition as she fled down Benefit Street in the vicinity of the Cathedral of St. John, near the cemetery attached to which the attack took place.

Her attacker was identified as an acquaintance, Arthur Phillips . . .

# DETECTIVES OF THE GOLDEN AGE: GOLDEN AGE: ELLERY QUEEN, DOROTHY L. SAYERS

## (THE PICTURE OF THE TRADITIONAL DETECTIVE STORY)

# ABRAHAM LINCOLN'S CLUE

## BY ELLERY QUEEN

E LLERY QUEEN—the *nom de plume* of two cousins, Frederic Dannay and Manfred B. Lee—is one of the most accomplished practitioners of the contemporary detective story. But he is more than that. He is the proud possessor of the most complete library of detective short stories in the world. He is the foremost authority on the subject.

Ellery Queen has pointed out that the first violent crime of literature was a very short, short story. It was a murder complete with victim, criminal and motive; it was of course Chapter Four of Genesis, "Cain rose up against Abel his brother, and slew him."

Most contemporary readers of detective stories think of them primarily as novels, but the first true form has always been the short story, starting with Edgar Allan Poe's "Murders in the Rue Morgue." "Actually," says Ellery Queen, "the detective novel is a short story, inflated by characterization and description, and romantic nonsense too often for purposes of padding, and adds only one innovation to the short story form; the by-plot or red herring, which when badly used serves only to irritate, when it is meant to confuse."

Ellery Queen writes without any such padding and the result is always a masterly short story. ࿇

FOURSCORE AND eighteen years ago, Abraham Lincoln brought forth (in this account) a new notion, conceived in secrecy and dedicated to the proposition that even an Honest Abe may borrow a leaf from Edgar A. Poe.

It is altogether fitting and proper that Mr. Lincoln's venture into the detective story should come to its final resting place in the files of a man named Queen. For all his life Ellery has consecrated Father Abraham as the noblest projection of the American dream; and, insofar as it has been within his poor power to add or detract, he has given full measure of devotion, testing whether that notion, or any notion so conceived and so dedicated, deserves to endure.

Ellery's service in running the Lincoln clue to earth is one the world has little noted nor, perhaps, will long remember. That he shall not have served in vain, this account:

THE CASE began on the outskirts of an upstate-New York city with the dreadful name of Eulalia, behind the flaking shutters of a fat and curlicued house with architectural dandruff, recalling for all the world some blowsy ex-Bloomer Girl from the Gay Nineties of its origin.

The owner, a formerly wealthy man named DiCampo, possessed a grandeur not shared by his property, although it was no less fallen into ruin. His falcon's face, more Florentine than Victorian, was—like the house—ravaged by time and the inclemencies of fortune; but haughtily so, and indeed DiCampo wore his scurfy purple velvet house jacket like the prince he was entitled to call himself, but did not. He was proud, and stubborn, and useless; and he had a lovely daughter named Bianca, who taught at a Eulalia grade school, and through marvels of economy, supported them both.

How Lorenzo San Marco Borghese-Ruffo DiCampo came to this decayed estate is no concern of ours. The presence there this day of a man named Harbidger and a man named Tungston, however, is to the point: they had come, Harbidger from Chicago, Tungston from Philadelphia, to buy something each wanted very much, and DiCampo had summoned them in order to sell it. The two visitors were collectors, Harbidger's passion being Lincoln, Tungston's Poe.

The Lincoln collector, an elderly man who looked like a migrant fruit picker, had plucked his fruits well: Harbidger was worth about $40,000,000, every dollar of which was at the beck of his mania for Lincolniana. Tungston, who was almost as rich, had the aging body of a poet and the eyes of a starving panther, armament that had served him well in the wars of Poeana.

"I must say, Mr. DiCampo," remarked Harbidger, "that your letter surprised me." He paused to savor the wine his host had poured from an ancient and honorable bottle (DiCampo had filled it with California claret before their arrival). "May I ask what has finally induced you to offer the book and document for sale?"

"To quote Lincoln in another context, Mr. Harbidger," said Di-Campo with a shrug of his wasted shoulders, "'the dogmas of the quiet past are inadequate to the stormy present.' In short, a hungry man sells his blood."

"Only if it's of the right type," said old Tungston, unmoved. "You've made that book and document less accessible to collectors and historians, DiCampo, than the gold in Fort Knox. Have you got them here? I'd like to examine them."

"No other hand will ever touch them except by right of ownership," Lorenzo DiCampo replied bitterly. He had taken a miser's glee in his lucky finds, vowing never to part with them; now forced by his need to sell them, he was like a suspicion-caked old prospector who, stumbling at last on pay dirt, draws cryptic maps to keep the world from stealing the secret of its location. "As I informed you gentlemen, I represent the book as bearing the signatures of Poe and Lincoln, and the document as being in Lincoln's hand; I am offering them with the customary proviso that they are returnable if they should prove to be not as represented; and if this does not satisfy you," and the old prince actually rose, "let us terminate our business here and now."

"Sit down, sit down, Mr. DiCampo," Harbidger said.

"No one is questioning your integrity," snapped old Tungston. "It's just that I'm not used to buying sight unseen. If there's a money-back guarantee, we'll do it your way."

Lorenzo DiCampo reseated himself stiffly. "Very well, gentlemen. Then I take it you are both prepared to buy?"

"Oh, yes!" said Harbidger. "What is your price?"

"Oh, no," said DiCampo. "What is your bid?"

The Lincoln collector cleared his throat, which was full of slaver. "If the book and document are as represented, Mr. DiCampo, you might hope to get from a dealer or realize at auction—oh—$50,000. I offer you $55,000."

"$56,000," said Tungston.

"$57,000," said Harbidger.

"$58,000," said Tungston.

"$59,000," said Harbidger.

Tungston showed his fangs. "$60,000," he said.

Harbidger fell silent, and DiCampo waited. He did not expect miracles. To these men, five times $60,000 was of less moment than the undistinguished wine they were smacking their lips over; but they were veterans of many a hard auction-room campaign, and a collector's victory tastes very nearly as sweet for the price as for the prize.

So the impoverished prince was not surprised when the Lincoln collector suddenly said, "Would you be good enough to allow Mr. Tungston and me to talk privately for a moment?"

DiCampo rose and strolled out of the room, to gaze somberly through a cracked window at the jungle growth that had once been his Italian formal gardens.

It was the Poe collector who summoned him back. "Harbidger has convinced me that for the two of us to try to outbid each other would simply run the price up out of all reason. We're going to make you a sporting proposition."

"I've proposed to Mr. Tungston, and he has agreed," nodded Harbidger, "that our bid for the book and document be $65,000. Each of us is prepared to pay that sum, and not a penny more."

"So that is how the screws are turned," said DiCampo, smiling. "But I do not understand. If each of you makes the identical bid, which of you gets the book and document?"

"Ah," grinned the Poe man, "that's where the sporting proposition comes in."

"You see, Mr. DiCampo," said the Lincoln man, "we are going to leave that decision to you."

Even the old prince, who had seen more than his share of the astonishing, was astonished. He looked at the two rich men really for the first

time. "I must confess," he murmured, "that your compact is an amusement. Permit me?" He sank into thought while the two collectors sat
expectantly. When the old man looked up he was smiling like a fox.
"The very thing, gentlemen! From the typewritten copies of the document I sent you, you both know that Lincoln himself left a clue to a
theoretical hiding place for the book which he never explained. Some
time ago I arrived at a possible solution to the President's little mystery. I propose to hide the book and document in accordance with it."

"You mean whichever of us figures out your interpretation of the
Lincoln clue and finds the book and document where you will hide
them, Mr. DiCampo, gets both for the agreed price?"

"That is it exactly."

The Lincoln collector looked dubious. "I don't know . . ."

"Oh, come, Harbidger," said Tungston, eyes glittering. "A deal is a
deal. We accept, DiCampo! Now what?"

"You gentlemen will of course have to give me a little time. Shall
we say three days?"

Ellery let himself into the Queen apartment, tossed his suitcase
aside, and set about opening windows. He had been out of town for a
week on a case, and Inspector Queen was in Atlantic City attending a
police convention.

Breathable air having been restored, Ellery sat down to the week's
accumulation of mail. One envelope made him pause. It had come by
air-mail special delivery, it was postmarked four days earlier, and in the
lower left corner, in red, flamed the word URGENT. The printed return
address on the flap said: *L.S.M.B.-R. DiCampo, Post Office Box 69,
Southern District, Eulalia, N.Y.* The initials of the name had been
crossed out and "Bianca" written above them.

The enclosure, in a large agitated female hand on inexpensive notepaper, said:

Dear Mr. Queen,
    The most important detective book in the world has disap-
peared. Will you please find it for me?
    Phone me on arrival at the Eulalia RR station or airport
I will pick you up.

                                                    BIANCA DiCAMPO

A yellow envelope then caught his eye. It was a telegram, dated the previous day:

WHY HAVE I NOT HEARD FROM YOU STOP AM IN DESPERATE
NEED YOUR SERVICES

                                           BIANCA DICAMPO

He had no sooner finished reading the telegram than the telephone on his desk trilled. It was a long-distance call.

"Mr. Queen?" throbbed a contralto voice. "Thank heaven I've finally got through to you! I've been calling all day—"

"I've been away," said Ellery, "and you would be Miss Bianca Di-Campo of Eulalia. In two words, Miss DiCampo: Why me?"

"In two words, Mr. Queen: Abraham Lincoln."

Ellery was startled. "You plead a persuasive case," he chuckled. "It's true, I'm an incurable Lincoln addict. How did you find out? Well, never mind. Your letter refers to a book, Miss DiCampo. Which book?"

The husky voice told him, and certain other provocative things as well. "So will you come, Mr. Queen?"

"Tonight if I could! Suppose I drive up first thing in the morning. I ought to make Eulalia by noon. Harbidger and Tungston are still around, I take it?"

"Oh, yes. They're staying at a motel downtown."

"Would you ask them to be there?"

The moment he hung up Ellery leaped to his bookshelves. He snatched out his volume of *Murder for Pleasure*, the historical work on detective stories by his good friend Howard Haycraft, and found what he was looking for on page 26: "And . . . young William Dean Howells thought it significant praise to assert of a nominee for President of the United States: 'The bent of his mind is mathematical and metaphysical, and he is therefore pleased with the absolute and logical method of Poe's tales and sketches, in which the problem of mystery is given, and wrought out into everyday facts by processes of cunning analysis. It is said that he suffers no year to pass without a perusal of this author.' Abraham Lincoln subsequently confirmed this statement, which appeared in his little-known 'campaign biography' by Howells in 1860 . . . The instance is chiefly notable, of course, for its revelation of a little-suspected affinity between two great Americans . . ."

Very early the next morning Ellery gathered some papers from his files, stuffed them into his briefcase, scribbled a note for his father, and ran for his car, Eulalia-bound.

He was enchanted by the DiCampo house, which looked like something out of Poe by Charles Addams; and, for other reasons, by Bianca, who turned out to be a genetic product supreme of northern Italy, with titian hair and Mediterranean blue eyes and a figure that needed only some solid steaks to qualify her for Miss Universe competition. Also, she was in deep mourning; so her conquest of the Queen heart was immediate and complete.

"He died of a cerebral hemorrhage, Mr. Queen," Bianca said, dabbing her absurd little nose. "In the middle of the second night after his session with Mr. Harbidger and Mr. Tungston."

So Lorenzo San Marco Borghese-Ruffo DiCampo was unexpectedly dead, bequeathing the lovely Bianca near-destitution and a mystery.

"The only things of value father really left me are that book and the Lincoln document. The $65,000 they now represent would pay off father's debts and give me a fresh start. But I can't find them, Mr. Queen, and neither can Mr. Harbidger and Mr. Tungston—who'll be here soon, by the way. Father hid the two things, as he told them he would; but where? We've ransacked the place."

"Tell me more about the book, Miss DiCampo."

"As I said over the phone, it's called *The Gift: 1845*. The Christmas annual that contained the earliest appearance of Edgar Allan Poe's *The Purloined Letter*."

"Published in Philadelphia by Carey & Hart? Bound in red?" At Bianca's nod Ellery said, "You understand that an ordinary copy of *The Gift: 1845* isn't worth more than about $50. What makes your father's copy unique is that double autograph you mentioned."

"That's what he said, Mr. Queen. I wish I had the book here to show you—that beautifully handwritten *Edgar Allan Poe* on the flyleaf, and under Poe's signature the signature *Abraham Lincoln*."

"Poe's own copy, once owned, signed, and read by Lincoln," Ellery said slowly. "Yes, that would be a collector's item for the ages. By the way, Miss DiCampo, what's the story behind the other piece—the Lincoln document?"

Bianca told him what her father had told her.

One morning in the spring of 1865, Abraham Lincoln opened the rosewood door of his bedroom in the southwest corner of the second floor of the White House and stepped out into the red-carpeted hall at the unusually late hour—for him—of 7:00 A.M.; he was more accustomed to beginning his work day at six.

But (as Lorenzo DiCampo had reconstructed events) Mr. Lincoln that morning had lingered in his bedchamber. He had awakened at his usual hour but, instead of leaving immediately on dressing for his office, he had pulled one of the cane chairs over to the round table, with its gas-fed reading lamp, and sat down to reread Poe's *The Purloined Letter* in his copy of the 1845 annual; it was a dreary morning, and the natural light was poor. The President was alone; the folding doors to Mrs. Lincoln's bedroom remained closed.

Impressed as always with Poe's tale, Mr. Lincoln on this occasion was struck by a whimsical thought; and, apparently finding no paper handy, he took an envelope from his pocket, discarded its enclosure, slit the two short edges so that the envelope opened out into a single sheet, and began to write on the blank side.

"Describe it to me, please."

"It's a long envelope, one that must have contained a bulky letter. It is addressed to the White House, but there is no return address, and father was never able to identify the sender from the handwriting. We do know that the letter came through the regular mails because there are two Lincoln stamps on it, lightly but unmistakably canceled."

"May I see your father's transcript of what Lincoln wrote out that morning on the inside of the envelope?"

Bianca handed him a typewritten copy and, in spite of himself, Ellery felt goose flesh rise as he read:

*Apr. 14, 1865*

Mr. Poe's The Purloined Letter is a work of singular originality. Its simplicity is a master-stroke of cunning, which never fails to arouse my wonder.

Reading the tale over this morning has given me a "notion." Suppose I wished to hide a book, this very book, perhaps? Where best to do so? Well, as Mr. Poe in his tale hid a letter *among letters*, might not a book be hidden *among books?* Why, if this very copy of the tale were to be deposited in a library and on purpose not recorded—would not the Library of Congress make a prime depository!—well might it repose there, undiscovered, for a generation.

On the other hand, let us regard Mr. Poe's "notion" turnabout: Suppose the book were to be placed, not amongst other books, but *where no book would reasonably be expected?* (I may follow the example of Mr. Poe, and, myself, compose a tale of "ratiocination"!)

The "notion" beguiles me, it is nearly seven o'clock. Later to-day, if the vultures and my appointments leave me a few moments of leisure, I may write further of my imagined hiding-place.

In self-reminder: The hiding-place of the book is in 30d, which

Ellery looked up. "The document ends there?"

"Father said that Mr. Lincoln must have glanced again at his watch, and shamefacedly jumped up to go to his office, leaving the sentence unfinished. Evidently he never found the time to get back to it."

Ellery brooded. Evidently indeed. From the moment when Abraham Lincoln stepped out of his bedroom that Good Friday morning, fingering his thick gold watch on its vest chain, to bid the still-unrelieved night guard his customary courteous "Good morning" and make for his office at the other end of the hall, his day was spoken for. The usual patient push through the clutching crowd of favor-seekers, many of whom had bedded down all night on the hall carpet; sanctuary in his sprawling office, where he read official correspondence; by 8:00 A.M. having breakfast with his family—Mrs. Lincoln chattering away about plans for the evening, 12-year-old Tad of the cleft palate lisping a complaint that "nobody asked me to go," and young Robert Lincoln, just returned from duty, bubbling with stories about his hero Ulysses Grant and the last days of the war; then back to the presidential office to look over the morning newspapers (which Lincoln had once remarked he "never" read, but these were happy days, with good news everywhere), sign two documents, and signal the soldier at the door to admit the morning's first caller, Speaker of the House Schuyler Colfax (who was angling for a Cabinet post and had to be tactfully handled); and so on throughout the day—the historic Cabinet meeting at 11:00 A.M., attended by General Grant himself, that stretched well into the afternoon; a hurried lunch at almost half-past two with Mrs. Lincoln (had this 45-pounds-underweight man eaten his usual midday meal of a biscuit, a glass of milk, and an apple?); more visitors to see in his office (including the unscheduled Mrs. Nancy Bushrod, escaped slave and wife of an escaped slave and mother of three small children, weeping that Tom, a soldier in the Army of the Potomac, was no longer getting his pay: "You are entitled to your husband's pay. Come this time tomorrow," and the tall President escorted her to the door, bowing her out "like I was a natural-born lady"); the late afternoon drive in the barouche to the Navy Yard and back with Mrs. Lincoln; more work, more visitors, into the evening . . . until finally, at five minutes past 8:00 P.M., Abraham Lincoln stepped into the White House formal coach after his wife, waved, and sank back to be driven off to see a play he did not much want to see, *Our American Cousin*, at Ford's Theatre . . .

Ellery mused over that black day in silence. And, like a relative hanging on the specialist's yet undelivered diagnosis, Bianca DiCampo sat watching him with anxiety.

Harbidger and Tungston arrived in a taxi to greet Ellery with the fervor of castaways grasping at a smudge of smoke on the horizon.

"As I understand it, gentlemen," Ellery said when he had calmed them down, "neither of you has been able to solve Mr. DiCampo's interpretation of the Lincoln clue. If I succeed in finding the book and paper where DiCampo hid them, which of you gets them?"

"We intend to split the $65,000 payment to Miss DiCampo," said Harbidger, "and take joint ownership of the two pieces."

"An arrangement," growled old Tungston, "I'm against on principle, in practice, and by plain horse sense."

"So am I," sighed the Lincoln collector, "but what else can we do?"

"Well," and the Poe man regarded Bianca DiCampo with the icy intimacy of the cat that long ago marked the bird as its prey, "Miss DiCampo, who now owns the two pieces, is quite free to renegotiate a sale on her own terms."

"Miss DiCampo," said Miss DiCampo, giving Tungston stare for stare, "considers herself bound by her father's wishes. His terms stand."

"In all likelihood, then," said the other millionaire, "one of us will retain the book, the other the document, and we'll exchange them every year, or some such thing." Harbidger sounded unhappy.

"Only practical arrangement under the circumstances," grunted Tungston, and *he* sounded unhappy. "But all this is academic, Queen, unless and until the book and document are found."

Ellery nodded. "The problem, then, is to fathom DiCampo's interpretation of that 30*d* in the document. 30*d* . . . I notice, Miss DiCampo—or, may I? Bianca?—that your father's typewritten copy of the Lincoln holograph text runs the 3 and 0 and *d* together—no spacing in between. It that the way it occurs in the longhand?"

"Yes."

"Hmm. Still . . . 30*d* . . . Could *d* stand for *days* . . . or the British *pence* . . . or *died*, as used in obituaries? Does any of these make sense to you, Bianca?"

"No."

"Did your father have any special interest in, say, pharmacology? chemistry? physics? algebra? electricity? Small *d* is an abbreviation used in all those." But Bianca shook her splendid head. "Banking? Small *d* for *dollars, dividends*?"

"Hardly," the girl said with a sad smile.

"How about theatricals? Was your father ever involved in a play production? Small *d* stands for *door* in playscript stage directions."

"Mr. Queen, I've gone through every darned abbreviation my dictionary lists, and I haven't found one that has a point of contact with any interest of my father's."

Ellery scowled. "At that—I assume the typewritten copy is accurate—the manuscript shows no period after the *d*, making an abbreviation unlikely. 30*d* . . . let's concentrate on the number. Does the number 30 have any significance for you?"

"Yes, indeed," said Bianca, making all three men sit up. But then they sank back. "In a few years it will represent my age, and that has enormous significance. But only for me, I'm afraid."

"You'll be drawing wolf whistles at twice thirty," quoth Ellery warmly. "However! Could the number have cross-referred to anything in your father's life or habits?"

"None that I can think of, Mr. Queen. And," Bianca said, having grown roses in her cheeks, "thank you."

"I think," said old Tungston testily, "we had better stick to the subject."

"Just the same, Bianca, let me run over some 'thirty' associations as they come to mind. Stop me if one of them hits a nerve. The Thirty Tyrants—was your father interested in classical Athens? Thirty Years' War—in Seventeenth Century European history? Thirty all—did he play or follow tennis? Or . . . did he ever live at an address that included the number 30?"

Ellery went on and on, but to each suggestion Bianca DiCampo could only shake her head.

"The lack of spacing, come to think of it, doesn't necessarily mean that Mr. DiCampo chose to view the clue that way," said Ellery thoughtfully. "He might have interpreted it arbitrarily as 3-space-o-d."

"Three od?" echoed old Tungston. "What the devil could that mean?"

"Od? Od is the hypothetical force or power claimed by Baron von Reichenbach—in 1850, wasn't it?—to pervade the whole of nature. Manifests itself in magnets, crystals, and such, which according to the excited Baron explained animal magnetism and mesmerism. Was your father by any chance interested in hypnosis, Bianca? Or the occult?"

"Not in the slightest."

"Mr. Queen," exclaimed Harbidger, "are you serious about all this —this semantic sludge?"

"Why, I don't know," said Ellery. "I never know till I stumble over something. Od . . . the word was used with prefixes, too—*biod*, the force of animal life; *elod*, the force of electricity; and so forth. *Three* od . . . or *triod*, the triune force—it's all right, Mr. Harbidger, it's not ignorance on your part, I just coined the word. But it does rather suggest the Trinity, doesn't it? Bianca, did your father tie up to the Church in a personal, scholarly, or any other way? No? That's too bad, really, because Od—capitalized—has been a minced form of the word God since the Sixteenth Century. Or . . . you wouldn't happen to have three Bibles on the premises, would you? Because—"

Ellery stopped with the smashing abruptness of an ordinary force meeting an absolutely immovable object. The girl and the two collectors gawped. Bianca had idly picked up the typewritten copy of the Lincoln document. She was not reading it, she was simply holding it on her knees; but Ellery, sitting opposite her, had shot forward in a crouch, rather like a pointer, and he was regarding the paper in her lap with a glare of pure discovery.

"That's it!" he cried.

"What's it, Mr. Queen?" the girl asked, bewildered.

"Please—the transcript!" He plucked the paper from her. "Of course. Hear this: 'On the other hand, let us regard Mr. Poe's "notion" turnabout.' *Turn-about.* Look at the 30d 'turn-about'—as I just saw it!"

He turned the Lincoln message upside down for their inspection. In that position the 30d became:

30d

"*Poe!*" exploded Tungston.

"Yes, crude but recognizable," Ellery said swiftly. "So now we read the Lincoln clue as: 'The hiding-place of the book is in *Poe*'!"

There was a silence.

"In Poe," said Harbidger blankly.

"In Poe?" muttered Tungston. "There are only a couple of trade editions of Poe in DiCampo's library, Harbidger, and we went through those. We looked in every book here."

"He might have meant among the Poe books in the *public* library. Miss DiCampo—"

"Wait." Bianca sped away. But when she came back she was drooping. "It isn't. We have two public libraries in Eulalia, and I know the head librarian in both. I just called them. Father didn't visit either library."

Ellery gnawed a fingernail. "Is there a bust of Poe in the house, Bianca? Or any other Poe-associated object, aside from books?"

"I'm afraid not."

"Queer," he mumbled. "Yet I'm positive your father interpreted 'the hiding-place of the book' as being 'in Poe.' So he'd have hidden it 'in Poe' . . ."

Ellery's mumbling dribbled away into a tormented sort of silence: his eyebrows worked up and down, Groucho Marx fashion; he pinched the tip of his nose until it was scarlet; he yanked at his unoffending ears; he munched on his lip . . . until, all at once, his face cleared; and he sprang to his feet. "Bianca, may I use your phone?"

The girl could only nod, and Ellery dashed. They heard him telephoning in the entrance hall, although they could not make out the words. He was back in two minutes.

"One thing more," he said briskly, "and we're out of the woods. I suppose your father had a key ring or a key case, Bianca? May I have it, please?"

She fetched a key case. To the two millionaires it seemed the sorriest of objects, a scuffed and dirty tan leatherette case. But Ellery received it from the girl as if it were an artifact of historic importance from a newly discovered IV Dynasty tomb. He unsnapped it with concentrated love; he fingered its contents like a scientist. Finally he decided on a certain key.

"Wait here!" Thus Mr. Queen; and exit, running.

"I can't decide," old Tungston said after a while, "whether that fellow is a genius or an escaped lunatic."

Neither Harbidger nor Bianca replied. Apparently they could not decide, either.

They waited through twenty elongated minutes; at the twenty-first they heard his car, champing. All three were in the front doorway as Ellery strode up the walk.

He was carrying a book with a red cover, and smiling. It was a compassionate smile, but none of them noticed.

"You—" said Bianca. "—found—" said Tungston. "—the book!" shouted Harbidger. "Is the Lincoln holograph in it?"

"It is," said Ellery. "Shall we all go into the house, where we may mourn in decent privacy?"

"Because," Ellery said to Bianca and the two quivering collectors as they sat across a refectory table from him, "I have foul news. Mr. Tungston, I believe you have never actually seen Mr. DiCampo's book. Will you now look at the Poe signature on the flyleaf?"

The panther claws leaped. There, toward the top of the flyleaf, in faded inkscript, was the signature *Edgar Allan Poe*.

The claws curled, and old Tungston looked up sharply. "DiCampo never mentioned that it's a full autograph—he kept referring to it as 'the Poe signature.' Edgar *Allan* Poe . . . Why, I don't know of a single instance after his West Point days when Poe wrote out his middle name in an autograph! And the earliest he could have signed this 1845 edition is obviously when it was published, which was around the fall of 1844. In 1844 he'd surely have abbreviated the 'Allan,' signing Edgar A. Poe,' the way he signed everything! This is a forgery."

"My God," murmured Bianca, clearly intending no impiety; she was as pale as Poe's Lenore. "Is that true, Mr. Queen?"

"I'm afraid it is," Ellery said sadly. "I was suspicious the moment you told me the Poe signature on the flyleaf contained the Allan.' And if the Poe signature is a forgery, the book itself can hardly be considered Poe's own copy."

Harbidger was moaning. "And the Lincoln signature underneath the Poe, Mr. Queen! DiCampo never told me it reads *Abraham* Lincoln— the full Christian name. Except on official documents, Lincoln practically always signed his name 'A. Lincoln.' Don't tell me this Lincoln autograph is a forgery, too?"

Ellery forbore to look at poor Bianca. "I was struck by the 'Abraham' as well, Mr. Harbidger, when Miss DiCampo mentioned it to me, and I came equipped to test it. I have here"—and Ellery tapped the pile of documents he had taken from his briefcase—"facsimiles of Lincoln signatures from the most frequently reproduced of the historic documents he signed. Now I'm going to make a precise tracing of the Lincoln signature on the flyleaf of the book"—he proceeded to do so—

"and I shall superimpose the tracing on the various signatures of the authentic Lincoln documents. So."

He worked rapidly. On his third superimposition Ellery looked up. "Yes. See here. The tracing of the purported Lincoln signature from the flyleaf fits in minutest detail over the authentic Lincoln signature on this facsimile of the Emancipation Proclamation. It's a fact of life that's tripped many a forger that *nobody ever writes his name exactly the same way twice*. There are always variations. If two signatures are identical, then, one must be a tracing of the other. So the 'Abraham Lincoln' signed on this flyleaf can be dismissed without further consideration as a forgery also. It's a tracing of the Emancipation Proclamation signature.

"Not only was this book not Poe's own copy; it was never signed—and therefore probably never owned—by Lincoln. However your father came into possession of the book, Bianca, he was swindled."

It was the measure of Bianca DiCampo's quality that she said quietly, "Poor, poor father," nothing more.

Harbidger was poring over the worn old envelope on whose inside appeared the dearly beloved handscript of the Martyr President. "At least," he muttered, "we have *this*."

"Do we?" asked Ellery gently. "Turn it over, Mr. Harbidger."

Harbidger looked up, scowling. "No! You're not going to deprive me of this, too!"

"Turn it over," Ellery repeated in the same gentle way. The Lincoln collector obeyed reluctantly. "What do you see?"

"An authentic envelope of the period! With two authentic Lincoln stamps!"

"Exactly. And the United States has never issued postage stamps depicting living Americans; you have to be dead to qualify. The earliest U.S. stamp showing a portrait of Lincoln went on sale April 15, 1866—a year to the day after his death. Then a living Lincoln could scarcely have used this envelope, with these stamps on it, as writing paper. The document is spurious, too. I am so very sorry, Bianca."

Incredibly, Lorenzo DiCampo's daughter managed a smile with her "*Non importa, signor.*" He could have wept for her. As for the two collectors, Harbidger was in shock; but old Tungston managed to croak, "Where the devil did DiCampo hide the book, Queen? And how did you know?"

"Oh, that," said Ellery, wishing the two old men would go away so that he might comfort this admirable creature. "I was convinced that DiCampo interpreted what we now know was the forger's, not Lincoln's, clue, as 30d read upside down; or, crudely, *Poe*. But 'the hiding-place of the book is in Poe' led nowhere.

"So I reconsidered, P, o, e. If those three letters of the alphabet didn't mean Poe, what could they mean? Then I remembered something about the letter you wrote me, Bianca. You'd used one of your father's envelopes, on the flap of which appeared his address: *Post Office Box 69, Southern District, Eulalia, N.Y.* If there was a Southern District in Eulalia, it seemed reasonable to conclude that there were post offices for other points of the compass, too. As, for instance, an Eastern District. Post Office Eastern, P.O. East. P.O.E."

"Poe!" cried Bianca.

"To answer your question, Mr. Tungston: I phoned the main post office, confirmed the existence of a Post Office East, got directions as to how to get there, looked for a postal box key in Mr. DiCampo's key case, found the right one, located the box DiCampo had rented especially for the occasion, unlocked it—and there was the book." He added, hopefully, "And that is that."

"And that *is* that," Bianca said when she returned from seeing the two collectors off. "I'm not going to cry over an empty milk bottle, Mr. Queen. I'll straighten out father's affairs somehow. Right now all I can think of is how glad I am he didn't live to see the signatures and documents declared forgeries publicly, as they would surely have been when they were expertised."

"I think you'll find there's still some milk in the bottle, Bianca."

"I beg your pardon?" said Bianca.

Ellery tapped the pseudo-Lincolnian envelope. "You know, you didn't do a very good job describing this envelope to me. All you said was that there were two canceled Lincoln stamps on it."

"Well, there are."

"I can see you misspent your childhood. No, little girls don't collect things, do they? Why, if you'll examine these 'two canceled Lincoln stamps,' you'll see that they're a great deal more than that. In the first place, they're not separate stamps. They're a vertical pair—that is, one stamp is joined to the other at the horizontal edges. Now look at this upper stamp of the pair."

The Mediterranean eyes widened. "It's upside down, isn't it?"

"Yes, it's upside down," said Ellery, "and what's more, while the pair have perforations all around, there are no perforations between them, where they're joined.

"What you have here, young lady—and what our unknown forger didn't realize when he fished around for an authentic White House cover of the period on which to perpetrate the Lincoln forgery—is what stamp collectors might call a double printing error: a pair of 1866 black 15-cent Lincolns imperforate horizontally, with one of the pair printed upside down. No such error of the Lincoln issue has ever been reported. You're the owner, Bianca, of what may well be the rarest item in U.S. philately, and the most valuable."

The world will little note, nor long remember.

But don't try to prove it by Bianca DiCampo.

# ABSOLUTELY ELSEWHERE

## BY DOROTHY L. SAYERS

DOROTHY SAYERS, one of the greatest practitioners of the detective story, has speculated on the future of the detective story by contemplating the known methods of murder.

"It is fortunate for the mystery-monger that, whereas, up to the present, there is only one known way of getting born, there are endless ways of getting killed. Here is a brief selection of handy short cuts to the grave: Poisoned tooth-stoppings; licking poisoned stamps; shaving-brushes inoculated with dread diseases; poisoned boiled eggs (a bright thought); poison-gas; a cat with poisoned claws; poisoned mattresses; knives dropped through the ceiling; stabbing with a sharp icicle; electrocution by telephone; biting by plague-rats and typhoid-carrying lice; boiling lead in the ears (much more effective than cursed verbena in a vial); air-bubbles injected into the arteries; explosion of a gigantic "Prince Rupert's drop"; frightening to death; hanging head-downwards; freezing to atoms in liquid air; hypodermic injections shot from air-guns; exposure, while insensible, to extreme cold; guns concealed in cameras; a thermometer which explodes a bomb when the temperature of the room reaches a certain height; and so forth."

Miss Sayers' list makes us wonder what future methods may still be around the corner.

Dorothy Sayers was as remarkable as her beloved character, Lord Peter Wimsey. A scholar and a poet, she translated Dante's *Divine Comedy*. She was also a dramatist and a superb historian of all fields of the macabre. ઠ⊷

LORD PETER WIMSEY sat with Chief-Inspector Parker, of the C.I.D., and Inspector Henley, of the Baldock police, in the library at "The Lilacs."

"So you see," said Parker, "that all the obvious suspects were elsewhere at the time."

"What do you mean by 'elsewhere'?" demanded Wimsey, peevishly. Parker had hauled him down to Wapley, on the Great North Road, without his breakfast, and his temper had suffered. "Do you mean that they couldn't have reached the scene of the murder without traveling at over 186,000 miles a second? Because, if you don't mean that, they weren't absolutely elsewhere. They were only relatively and apparently elsewhere."

"For heaven's sake, don't go all Eddington. Humanly speaking, they were elsewhere, and if we're going to nail one of them we shall have to do it without going into their Fitzgerald contractions and coefficients of spherical curvature. I think, Inspector, we had better have them in one by one, so that I can hear all their stories again. You can check them up if they depart from their original statements at any point. Let's take the butler first."

The Inspector put his head out into the hall and said: "Hamworthy."

The butler was a man of middle age, whose spherical curvature was certainly worthy of consideration. His large face was pale and puffy, and he looked unwell. However, he embarked on his story without hesitation.

"I have been in the late Mr. Grimbold's service for twenty years, gentlemen, and have always found him a good master. He was a strict gentleman, but very just. I know he was considered very hard in business matters, but I suppose he had to be that. He was a bachelor, but he brought up his two nephews, Mr. Harcourt and Mr. Neville, and was very good to them. In his private life I should call him a kind and considerate man. His profession? Yes, I suppose you would call him a money-lender.

"About the events of last night, sir, yes. I shut up the house at 7.30 as usual. Everything was done exactly to time, sir,—Mr. Grimbold was very regular in his habits. I locked all the windows on the ground floor, as was customary during the winter months. I am quite sure I didn't miss anything out. They all have burglar-proof bolts and I should have noticed if they had been out of order. I also locked and bolted the front door and put up the chain."

"How about the conservatory door?"

"That, sir, is a Yale lock. I tried it, and saw that it was shut. No, I didn't fasten the catch. It was always left that way, sir, in case Mr. Grimbold had business which kept him in Town late, so that he could get in without disturbing the household."

"But he had no business in Town last night?"

"No, sir, but it was always left that way. Nobody could get in without the key, and Mr. Grimbold had that on his ring."

"Is there no other key in existence?"

"I believe"—the butler coughed—"I believe, sir, though I do not know, that there is *one*, sir,—in the possession of—of a lady, sir, who is at present in Paris."

"I see. Mr. Grimbold was about sixty years old, I believe. Just so. What is the name of this lady?"

"I see. Better make a note of that, Inspector. Now, how about the upper rooms and the back door?"

"The upper-room windows were all fastened in the same way, sir, except Mr. Grimbold's bedroom and the cook's room and mine, sir; but they couldn't be reached without a ladder, and the ladder is locked up in the tool-shed."

"Mrs. Winter, sir. She lives at Wapley, but since her husband died last month, sir, I understand she has been residing abroad."

"That's all right," put in Inspector Henley. "We went into that last night. The shed was locked and, what's more, there were unbroken cobwebs between the ladder and the wall."

"I went through all the rooms at half-past seven, sir, and there was nothing out of order."

"You may take it from me," said the Inspector, again, "that there was no interference with any of the locks. Carry on, Hamworthy."

"Yes, sir. While I was seeing to the house, Mr. Grimbold came down into the library for his glass of sherry. At 7.45 the soup was served and I called Mr. Grimbold to dinner. He sat at the end of the table as usual, facing the serving-hatch."

"With his back to the library door," said Parker, making a mark on a rough plan of the room, which lay before him. "Was that door shut?"

"Oh, yes, sir. All the doors and windows were shut."

"It looks a dashed draughty room," said Wimsey. "Two doors and a serving-hatch and two french windows."

"Yes, my lord; but they are all very well-fitting, and the curtains were drawn."

His lordship moved across to the connecting door and opened it.

"Yes," he said; "good and heavy and moves in sinister silence. I like these thick carpets, but the pattern's a bit fierce." He shut the door noiselessly and returned to his seat.

"Mr. Grimbold would take about five minutes over his soup, sir. When he had done, I removed it and put on the fish. I did not have to leave the room; everything comes through the serving-hatch. The wine —that is, the Chablis—was already on the table. That course was only a small portion of turbot, and would take Mr. Grimbold about five minutes again. I removed that, and put on the roast pheasant. I was just about to serve Mr. Grimbold with the vegetables, when the tele-phone-bell rang. Mr. Grimbold said: 'You'd better see who it is. I'll help myself.' It was not the cook's business, of course, to answer the telephone."

"Are there no other servants?"

"Only the woman who comes in to clean during the day, sir. I went out to the instrument, shutting the door behind me."

"Was that this telephone or the one in the hall?"

"The one in the hall, sir. I always used that one, unless I happened to be actually in the library at the time. The call was from Mr. Neville Grimbold in Town, sir. He and Mr. Harcourt have a flat in Jermyn Street. Mr. Neville spoke, and I recognized his voice. He said: 'Is that you, Hamworthy? Wait a moment. Mr. Harcourt wants you.' He put the receiver down and then Mr. Harcourt came on. He said: 'Hamworthy, I want to run down tonight to see my uncle, if he's at home.' I said: 'Yes, sir, I'll tell him.' The young gentlemen often come down for a night or two, sir. We keep their bedrooms ready for them. Mr. Harcourt said he would be starting at once and expected to get down by about half-past nine. While he was speaking I heard the big grandfather-clock up in their flat chime the quarters and strike eight, and immediately after, our own hall-clock struck, and then I heard the Exchange say 'Three minutes.' So the call must have come through at three minutes to eight, sir."

"Then there's no doubt about the time. That's a comfort. What next, Hamworthy?"

"Mr. Harcourt asked for another call and said: 'Mr. Neville has got something to say,' and then Mr. Neville came back to the 'phone. He said he was going up to Scotland shortly, and wanted me to send up a country suit and some stockings and shirts that he had left down here. He wanted the suit sent to the cleaner's first, and there were various other instructions, so that he asked for another three minutes. That would be at 8.3, sir, yes. And about a minute after that, while he was still speaking, the front-door bell rang. I couldn't very well leave the 'phone, so the caller had to wait, and at five past eight he rang the bell again. I was just going to ask Mr. Neville to excuse me, when I saw Cook come out of the kitchen and go through the hall to the front door. Mr. Neville asked me to repeat his instructions, and then the Exchange interrupted us again, so he rang off, and when I turned around I saw Cook just closing the library door. I went to meet her, and she said: 'Here's that Mr. Payne again, wanting Mr. Grimbold. I've put him in the library, but I don't like the looks of him.' So I said: 'All right; I'll fix him,' and Cook went back to the kitchen."

"One moment," said Parker. "Who's Mr. Payne?"

"He's one of Mr. Grimbold's clients, sir. He lives about five minutes away, across the fields, and he's been here before, making trouble. I think he owes Mr. Grimbold money, sir, and wanted more time to pay."

"He's here, waiting in the hall," added Henley.

"Oh?" said Wimsey. "The unshaven party with the scowl and the ash plant, and the blood-stained coat?"

"That's him, my lord," said the butler. "Well, sir,"—he turned to Parker again, "I started to go along to the library, when it come over me sudden-like that I'd never taken in the claret—Mr. Grimbold would be getting very annoyed. So I went back to my pantry—you see where that is, sir,—and fetched it from where it was warming before the fire. I had a little hunt then for the salver, sir, till I found I had put down my evening paper on top of it, but I wasn't more than a minute, sir, before I got back into the dining-room. And then, sir"—the butler's voice faltered—"then I saw Mr. Grimbold fallen forward on the table, sir, all across his plate, like. I thought he must have been took ill, and I hurried up to him and found—I found he was dead, sir, with a dreadful wound in his back."

"No weapon anywhere?"

"Not that I could see, sir. There was a terrible lot of blood. It made me feel shockingly faint, sir, and for a minute I didn't hardly know what to do. As soon as I could think of anything, I rushed over to the serving-hatch and called Cook. She came hurrying in and let out an awful scream when she saw the master. Then I remembered Mr. Payne and opened the library door. He was standing there, and he began at once, asking how long he'd have to wait. So I said: 'Here's an awful thing! Mr. Grimbold has been murdered!' and he pushed past me into the dining-room, and the first thing he said was: 'How about those windows?' He pulled back the curtain of the one nearest the library, and there was the window standing open. 'This is the way he went,' he said, and started to rush out. I said, 'no, you don't'—thinking he meant to get away, and I hung on to him. He called me a lot of names, and then he said: 'Look here, my man, be reasonable. The fellow's getting away all this time. We must have a look for him.' So I said, 'Not without I go with you.' So I told Cook not to touch anything but to ring up the police, and Mr. Payne and I went out after I'd fetched my torch from the pantry."

"Did Payne go with you to fetch it?"

"Yes, sir. Well, him and me went out and we searched about in the garden, but we couldn't see any footprints or anything, because it's an asphalt path all around the house and down to the gate. And we couldn't see any weapon, either. So then he said: 'We'd better go back and get the car and search the roads,' but I said: 'No, he'll be away by then,' because it's only a quarter of a mile from our gate to the Great North Road, and it would take us five or ten minutes before we could start. So Mr. Payne said: 'Perhaps you're right,' and came back to the house with me. Well, then, sir, the constable came from Wapley, and after a bit, the Inspector here and Dr. Crofts from Baldock, and they made a search and asked a lot of questions, which I answered to the best of my ability, and I can't tell you no more, sir."

"Did you notice," asked Parker, "whether Mr. Payne had any stains of blood about him?"

"No, sir,—I can't say that he had. When I first saw him, he was standing in here, right under the light, and I think I should have seen it if there was anything, sir. I can't say fairer than that."

"Of course you've searched this room, Inspector, for bloodstains or a weapon or for anything such as gloves or a cloth, or anything that might have been used to protect the murderer from bloodstains?"

"Yes, Mr. Parker. We searched very carefully."

"Could anybody have come downstairs while you were in the dining room with Mr. Grimbold?"

"Well, sir, I suppose they might. But they'd have to have got into the house before half-past seven, sir, and hidden themselves somewhere. Still, there's no doubt it might have happened that way. They couldn't come down by the back stairs, of course, because they'd have had to pass the kitchen, and Cook would have heard them, the passage being flagged, sir, but the front stairs—well, I don't know hardly what to say about that."

"That's how the man got in, depend upon it," said Parker. "Don't look so distressed, Hamworthy. You can't be expected to search all the cupboards in the house every evening for concealed criminals. Now I think I had better see the two nephews. I suppose they and their uncle got on together all right?"

"Oh, yes, sir. Never had a word of any sort. It's been a great blow to them, sir. They were terribly upset when Mr. Grimbold was ill in the summer—"

"He was ill, was he?"

"Yes, sir, with his heart, last July. He took a very bad turn, sir, and we had to send for Mr. Neville. But he pulled around wonderfully, sir, —only he never seemed to be quite such a cheerful gentleman afterwards. I think it made him feel he wasn't getting younger, sir. But I'm sure nobody ever thought he'd be cut off like this."

"How is his money left?" asked Parker.

"Well, sir, that I don't know. I believe it would be divided between the two gentlemen, sir—not but what they have plenty of their own. But Mr. Harcourt would be able to tell you, sir. He's the executor."

"Very well, we'll ask him. Are the brothers on good terms?"

"Oh, yes, indeed, sir. Most devoted. Mr. Neville would do anything for Mr. Harcourt—and Mr. Harcourt for him, I'm sure. A very pleasant pair of gentlemen, sir. You couldn't have nicer."

"Thanks, Hamworthy. That will do for the moment, unless anybody else has anything to ask?"

"How much of the pheasant was eaten, Hamworthy?"

"Well, my lord, not a great deal of it—I mean, nothing like all of what Mr. Grimbold had on his plate. But he'd ate some of it. It might have taken three or four minutes or so to eat what he had done, my lord, judging by what I helped him to."

"There was nothing to suggest that he had been interrupted, for example, by somebody coming to the windows, or of his having got up to let the person in?"

"Nothing at all, my lord, that I could see."

"The chair was pushed in close to the table when I saw him," put in the Inspector, "and his napkin was on his knees and the knife and fork lying just under his hands, as though he had dropped them when the blow came. I understand that the body was not disturbed."

"No, sir. I never moved it—except, of course, to make sure that he was dead. But I never felt any doubt of that, sir, when I saw that dreadful wound in his back. I just lifted his head and let it fall forward again, same as before."

"All right, then, Hamworthy. Ask Mr. Harcourt to come in."

Mr. Harcourt Grimbold was a brisk-looking man of about thirty-five. He explained that he was a stockbroker and his brother Neville an official in the Ministry of Public Health, and that they had been brought up by their uncle from the ages of eleven and ten respectively. He was aware that his uncle had had many business enemies, but for his own part he had received nothing from him but kindness.

"I'm afraid I can't tell you much about this terrible business, as I didn't get here till 9.45 last night, when, of course, it was all over."

"That was a little later than you hoped to be here?"

"Just a little. My tail-lamp went out between Welwyn Garden City and Welwyn, and I was stopped by a bobby. I went to a garage in Welwyn, where they found that the lead had come loose. They put it right, and that delayed me for a few minutes more."

"It's about forty miles from here to London?"

"Just over. In the ordinary way, at that time of night, I should reckon an hour and a quarter from door to door. I'm not a speed merchant."

"Did you drive yourself?"

"Yes. I have a chauffeur, but I don't always bring him down here with me."

"When did you leave London?"

"About 8.20, I should think. Neville went around to the garage and fetched the car as soon as he'd finished telephoning, while I put my toothbrush and so on in my bag."

"You didn't hear about the death of your uncle before you left?"

"No. They didn't think of ringing me up, I gather, till after I had started. The police tried to get Neville later on, but he'd gone around to the club, or something. I 'phoned him myself after I got here, and he came down this morning."

"Well, now, Mr. Grimbold, can you tell us anything about your late uncle's affairs?"

"You mean his will? Who profits, and that kind of thing? Well, I do, for one, and Neville, for another. And Mrs.—— Have you heard of a Mrs. Winter?"

"Something, yes."

"Well, she does, for a third. And then, of course, old Hamworthy gets a nice little nest-egg, and the cook gets something, and there is a legacy of £500 to the clerk at my uncle's London office. But the bulk of it goes to us and to Mrs. Winter. I know what you're going to ask—how much is it? I haven't the faintest idea, but I know it must be something pretty considerable. The old man never let on to a soul how much he really was worth, and we never bothered about it. I'm turning over a good bit, and Neville's salary is a heavy burden on a long-suffering public, so we only had a mild, academic kind of interest in the question."

"Do you suppose Hamworthy knew he was down for a legacy?"

"Oh, yes—there was no secret about that. He was to get £100 and a life interest in £200 a year, provided, of course, he was still in my uncle's service when he—my uncle, I mean—died."

"And he wasn't under notice, or anything?"

"N-no. No. Not more than usual. My uncle gave everybody notice about once a month, to keep them up to the mark. But it never came to anything. He was like the Queen of Hearts in *Alice*—he never executed nobody, you know."

"I see. We'd better ask Hamworthy about that, though. Now, this Mrs. Winter. Do you know anything about her?"

"Oh, yes. She's a nice woman. Of course, she was Uncle William's mistress for donkey's years, but her husband was practically potty with drink, and you could scarcely blame her. I wired her this morning and here's her reply, just come."

He handed Parker a telegram, dispatched from Paris, which read: "Terribly shocked and grieved. Returning immediately. Love and sympathy. Lucy."

"You are on friendly terms with her, then?"

"Good Lord, yes. Why not? We were always damned sorry for her. Uncle William would have taken her away with him somewhere, only she wouldn't leave Winter. In fact, I think they had practically settled that they were to get married now that Winter has had the grace to peg out. She's only about thirty-eight, and it's time she had some sort of show in life, poor thing."

"So, in spite of the money, she hadn't really very much to gain by your uncle's death?"

"Not a thing. Unless, of course, she wanted to marry somebody younger, and was afraid of losing the cash. But I believe she was honestly fond of the old boy. Anyhow, she couldn't have done the murder, because she's in Paris."

"H'm!" said Parker. "I suppose she is. We'd better make sure, though. I'll ring through to the Yard and have her looked out for at the ports. Is this 'phone through to the Exchange?"

"Yes," said the Inspector. "It doesn't have to go through the hall 'phone; they're connected in parallel."

"All right. Well, I don't think we need trouble you further, at the moment, Mr. Grimbold. I'll put my call through, and after that we'll send for the next witness. . . . Give me Whitehall 1212, please. . . . I suppose the time of Mr. Harcourt's call from town has been checked, Inspector?"

"Yes, Mr. Parker. It was put in at 7.57 and renewed at 8 o'clock and 8.03. Quite an expensive little item. And we've also checked upon the constable who spoke to him about his lights and the garage that put them right for him. He got into Welwyn at 9.05 and left again about 9.15. The number of the car is right, too."

"Well, he's out of it in any case, but it's just as well to check all we can. . . . Hullo, is that Scotland Yard? Put me through to Chief Inspector Hardy. Chief Inspector Parker speaking."

As soon as he had finished with his call, Parker sent for Neville Grimbold. He was rather like his brother, only a little slimmer and a little more suave in speech, as befitted a Civil Servant. He had nothing to add, except to confirm his brother's story and to explain that he had gone to a cinema from 8.20 to about 10 o'clock, and then on to his club, so that he had heard nothing about the tragedy till later in the evening.

The cook was the next witness. She had a great deal to say, but nothing very convincing to tell. She had not happened to see Hamworthy go to the pantry for the claret, otherwise she confirmed his story. She scouted the idea that somebody had been concealed in one of the upper rooms, because the daily woman, Mrs. Crabbe, had been in the house till nearly dinner-time, putting camphor bags in all the wardrobes; and, anyhow, she had no doubt but what "that Payne" had stabbed Mr. Grimbold—"a nasty, murdering beast." After which, it only remained to interview the murderous Mr. Payne.

Mr. Payne was almost aggressively frank. He had been treated very harshly by Mr. Grimbold. What with exorbitant usury and accumulated interest added to the principal, he had already paid back about

five times the original loan, and now Mr. Grimbold had refused him
any more time to pay, and had announced his intention of foreclosing
on the security, namely, Mr. Payne's house and land. It was all the more
brutal because Mr. Payne had every prospect of being able to pay off
the entire debt in six months' time, owing to some sort of interest or
share in something or other which was confidently expected to turn
up trumps. In his opinion, old Grimbold had refused to renew on purpose, so as to prevent him from paying—what *he* wanted was the
property. Grimbold's death was the saving of the situation, because it
would postpone settlement till after the confidently-expected trumps
had turned up. Mr. Payne would have murdered old Grimbold with
pleasure, but he hadn't done so, and in any case he wasn't the sort of
man to stab anybody in the back, though, if the money-lender had been
a younger man, he, Payne, would have been happy to break all his
bones for him. There it was, and they could take it or leave it. If that
old fool, Hamworthy, hadn't got his way, he'd have laid hands on the
murderer all right—if Hamworthy was a fool, which he doubted. Blood?
yes, there was blood on his coat. He had got that in struggling with
Hamworthy at the window. Hamworthy's hands had been all over
blood when he made his appearance in the library. No doubt he had
got it from the corpse. He, Payne, had taken care not to change his
clothes, because, if he had done so, somebody would have tried to
make out that he was hiding something. Actually, he had not been
home, or asked to go home, since the murder. Mr. Payne added that
he objected strongly to the attitude taken up by the local police, who
had treated him with undisguised hostility. To which Inspector Henley
replied that Mr. Payne was quite mistaken.

"Mr. Payne," said Lord Peter, "will you tell me one thing? When
you heard the commotion in the dining-room, and the cook screaming,
and so on, why didn't you go in at once to find out what was the matter?"

"Why?" retorted Mr. Payne. "Because I never heard anything of
the sort, that's why. The first thing I knew about it was seeing the butler fellow standing there in the doorway, waving his bloody hands about
and gibbering."

"Ah!" said Wimsey. "I thought it was a good, solid door. Shall we

ask the lady to go in and scream for us now, with the dining-room window open?"

The Inspector departed on this errand, while the rest of the company
waited anxiously to count the screams. Nothing happened, however,
till Henley put his head in and asked, what about it?

"Nothing," said Parker.

"It's a well-built house," said Wimsey. "I suppose any sound coming
through the window would be muffled by the conservatory. Well, Mr.
Payne, if you didn't hear the screams it's not surprising that you didn't
hear the murderer. Are those all your witnesses, Charles? Because I've
got to get back to London to see a man about a dog. But I'll leave you
two suggestions with my blessing. One is, that you should look for a
car, which was parked within a quarter of a mile of this house last night,
between 7.30 and 8.15; the second is, that you should all come and sit
in the dining-room to-night, with the doors and windows shut, and
watch the french windows. I'll give Mr. Parker a ring about eight. Oh,
and you might lend me the key of the conservatory door. I've got a
theory about it."

The Chief Inspector handed over the key, and his lordship departed.

The party assembled in the dining-room was in no very companionable mood. In fact, all the conversation was supplied by the police, who
kept up a chatty exchange of fishing reminiscences, while Mr. Payne
glowered, the two Grimbolds smoked cigarette after cigarette, and the
cook and the butler balanced themselves nervously on the extreme
edges of their chairs. It was a relief when the telephone-bell rang.

Parker glanced at his watch as he got up to answer it. "Seven-fifty-
seven," he observed, and saw the butler pass his handkerchief over his
twitching lips. "Keep your eye on the windows." He went out into the
hall.

"Hullo!" he said.

"Is that Chief-Inspector Parker?" asked a voice he knew well. "This
is Lord Peter Wimsey's man speaking from his lordship's rooms in
London. Would you hold the line a moment? His lordship wishes to
speak to you."

Parker heard the receiver set down and lifted again. Then Wimsey's voice came through: "Hullo, old man? Have you found that car yet?"

"We've heard of *a* car," replied the Chief Inspector cautiously, "at a Road House on the Great North Road, about five minutes' walk from the house."

"Was the number A B J 28?"

"Yes. How did you know?"

"I thought it might be. It was hired from a London garage at five o'clock yesterday afternoon and brought back just before ten. Have you traced Mrs. Winter?"

"Yes, I think so. She landed from the Calais boat this evening. So apparently she's O.K."

"I thought she might be. Now, listen. Do you know that Harcourt Grimbold's affairs are in a bit of a mess? He nearly had a crisis last July, but somebody came to his rescue—possibly Uncle, don't you think? All rather fishy, my informant saith. And I'm told, very confidentially, that he's got badly caught over the Biggars-Witlow crash. But of course he'll have no difficulty in raising money now, on the strength of Uncle's will. But I imagine the July business gave Uncle William a jolt. I expect——"

He was interrupted by a little burst of tinkling music, followed by the eight silvery strokes of a bell.

"Hear that? Recognize it? That's the big French clock in my sitting-room. . . . What? All right, Exchange, give me another three minutes. Bunter wants to speak to you again."

The receiver rattled, and the servant's suave voice took up the tale.

"His lordship asks me to ask you, sir, to ring off at once and go straight into the dining-room."

Parker obeyed. As he entered the room, he got an instantaneous impression of six people, sitting as he had left them, in an expectant semi-circle, their eyes strained toward the french windows. Then the library door opened noiselessly and Lord Peter Wimsey walked in.

"Good God!" exclaimed Parker, involuntarily. "How did you get here?" The six heads jerked round suddenly.

"On the back of the light waves," said Wimsey, smoothing back his hair. "I have traveled eighty miles to be with you, at 186,000 miles a second."

"It was rather obvious, really," said Wimsey, when they had secured Harcourt Grimbold (who fought desperately) and his brother Neville (who collapsed and had to be revived with brandy). "It had to be those two; they were so very much elsewhere—almost absolutely elsewhere. The murder could only have been committed between 7.57 and 8.6, and there had to be a reason for that prolonged 'phone call about something that Harcourt could very well have explained when he came. And the murderer had to be in the library before 7.57, or he would have been seen in the hall—unless Grimbold had let him in by the french window, which didn't appear likely.

"Here's how it was worked. Harcourt set off from Town in a hired car about six o'clock, driving himself. He parked the car at the Road House, giving some explanation. I suppose he wasn't known there?"

"No; it's quite a new place; only opened last month."

"Ah! Then he walked the last quarter-mile on foot, arriving here at 7.45. It was dark, and he probably wore goloshes, so as not to make a noise coming up the path. He let himself into the conservatory with a duplicate key."

"How did he get that?"

"Pinched Uncle William's key off his ring last July, when the old boy was ill. It was probably the shock of hearing that his dear nephew was in trouble that caused the illness. Harcourt was here at the time —you remember it was only Neville that had to be 'sent for'—and I suppose Uncle paid up then, on conditions. But I doubt if he'd have done as much again—especially as he was thinking of getting married. And I expect, too, Harcourt thought that Uncle might easily alter his will after marriage. He might even have founded a family, and what would poor Harcourt do then, poor thing? From every point of view, it was better that Uncle should depart this life. So the duplicate key was cut and the plot thought out, and Brother Neville, who would 'do anything for Mr. Harcourt,' was roped in to help. I'm inclined to think that Harcourt must have done something rather worse than merely lose money, and Neville may have troubles of his own. But where was I?"

"Coming in at the conservatory door."

"Oh, yes—that's the way I came tonight. He'd take cover in the garden and would know when Uncle William went into the dining-room, because he'd see the library light go out. Remember, he knew the household. He came in, in the dark, locking the outer door after him, and waited by the telephone till Neville's call came through from London. When the bell stopped ringing, he lifted the receiver in the library. As soon as Neville had spoken his little piece, Harcourt chipped in. Nobody could hear him through these sound-proof doors, and Hamworthy couldn't possibly tell that his voice wasn't coming from London. In fact, it *was* coming from London, because, as the 'phones are connected in parallel, it could only come by way of the Exchange. At eight o'clock, the grandfather clock in Jermyn Street struck—further proof that the London line was open. The minute Harcourt heard that, he called on Neville to speak again, and hung up under cover of the rattle of Neville's receiver. Then Neville detained Hamworthy with a lot of rot about a suit, while Harcourt walked into the dining-room, stabbed his uncle and departed by the window. He had five good minutes in which to hurry back to his car and drive off—and Hamworthy and Payne actually gave him a few minutes more by suspecting and hampering one another."

"Why didn't he go back through the library and conservatory?"

"He hoped everybody would think that the murderer had come in by the window. In the meantime, Neville left London at 8.20 in Harcourt's car, carefully drawing the attention of a policeman and a garage man to the license number as he passed through Welwyn. At an appointed place outside Welwyn he met Harcourt, primed him with his little story about tail-lights, and changed cars with him. Neville returned to town with the hired 'bus; Harcourt came back here with his own car. But I'm afraid you'll have a little difficulty in finding the weapon and the duplicate key and Harcourt's blood-stained gloves and coat. Neville probably took them back, and they may be anywhere. There's a good, big river in London."

# ABOUT THE AUTHORS

MARY W. SHELLEY, novelist and short story writer, was born in London in 1797. She was the only daughter of William Godwin, the social reformer and free thinker, and Mary Wollstonecraft, the author of *Vindication of the Rights of Women* (1792). In 1816 she married Percy Bysshe Shelley and went to the Continent. While abroad, she and her husband saw much of Byron, and it was at his villa on Lake Geneva that she conceived the idea of her famous novel *Frankenstein*. She wrote other novels, short stories, contributed biographies of foreign artists and authors to *Lardner's Cabinet Encyclopaedia*, and edited her husband's poems after his death. She died in 1851.

BRAM STOKER was born in Dublin, Ireland, in 1847, the son of a government official. In his childhood he was an invalid—but in after years he became one of the leading athletes of Dublin University, where he had a brilliant academic career. For ten years he worked in the Irish Civil Service, and in 1878 published *The Duties of Clerks of Petty Sessions in Ireland*. In the same year he became Henry Irving's acting manager at the Lyceum, and later (1906) he wrote *Personal Reminiscences of Henry Irving*. In 1897 he published *Dracula*, which has been called the most blood-curdling horror story in English literature and which sold over a million copies. He died in 1912.

EDITH NEWBOLD JONES WHARTON, novelist, was born in New York City in 1862. She was the youngest of three children and the only daughter of George Frederic and Lucretia (Rhinelander) Jones, both descendants of old and distinguished American families. Edith Jones was educated by governesses and tutors, and during the family's long residences abroad acquired fluency in French, German, and Italian. In 1885 she married Edward Wharton, a wealthy Bostonian, and they traveled extensively. Although she had published poetry in the *Atlantic Monthly* while still in her teens, her first fiction did not appear until she was thirty years old. Her first book was the *Decoration of Houses*, written in collaboration with Ogden Codman, Jr., and published in 1897. In 1899 she brought out her first collection of short stories, *The Greater Inclination*. Of her novels, *Ethan Frome* (1911) is sometimes considered her greatest; *The Age of Innocence* (1920), a satire on society, was awarded the Pulitzer prize, as also was *Old New York* (1924) in its dramatic form with the title *The Old Maid*. Her supernatural short stories are considered some of the greatest in literature. She died in 1937.

WILLIAM WILKIE COLLINS, English novelist, was born in 1824. He was a close friend of Charles Dickens, with whom he collaborated on a number of works. He is best remembered for *The Woman in White*, a mystery novel, and *The Moonstone*, which has been called, "the first, the longest, and the best of detective novels." He died in 1889.

CHARLES DICKENS, one of the world's greatest novelists, was born in England in 1812. The son of a navy clerk, he grew up in London. During one of his father's imprisonments for debt, the twelve-year-old Charles was apprenticed in a blacking warehouse and learned firsthand the horror of child labor. At seventeen he became a court shorthand reporter and subsequently a parliamentary reporter for the London *Morning Chronicle*. His sketches of London types (signed "Boz") began appearing in periodicals in 1833, and the collected *Sketches by Boz* (1836) enjoyed a great success. *The Posthumous Papers of the Pickwick Club* (1836–37) made Dickens and his characters Sam Weller and Mr. Pickwick famous. For his eager and ever more numerous readers Dickens worked vigorously, publishing first in monthy installments and then as books, *Oliver Twist* (1838), *Nicholas Nickleby* (1839), *The Old Curiosity Shop* (1841). He often worked on more than one novel at a time. After a visit to America in 1842, he wrote *America Notes* (1842) and *Martin Chuzzlewit* (1844), both sharply criticizing America's shortcomings. His many other novels, of which *David Copperfield* was his own favorite, were written while he was lecturing, managing his amateur theatrical company, and editing successively two magazines, *Household Words* and *All the Year Round*. Then in 1870, while finishing Chapter 23 of his crime and detective novel, *The Mystery of Edwin Drood*, Dickens became unconscious and died at the age of fifty-eight, leaving behind a work which still puzzles historians and writers of detective fiction—a mystery without a solution.

SIR ARTHUR CONAN DOYLE, novelist, medical doctor, historian, and statesman, was born in Edinburgh, Scotland, in 1859, of an Irish Roman-Catholic family. Although his uncles assured him of a ready-made medical practice if he would avow his Catholicism, he declined to do so and went off on his own. He practiced medicine at Southsea from 1882 to 1890, and it was during this period that he began to write. He soon found his writing so much in demand that he gave up medicine to devote himself exclusively to his novels, short stories, histories, and pamphlets. He served as a docter in the South African War and wrote a history of the conflict, *The Great Boer War* (1900), which won world renown. A man of great and varied talents, he did much to cement Anglo-American relations. Although the stories about his fictional character Sherlock Holmes are known and admired throughout the world, he himself preferred *The Exploits of Brigadier Gerard* (1895), *Micah Clarke* (1889), *Rodney Stone* (1896), *The White Company* (1890), and *Sir Nigel* (1906). He was knighted in 1902, and died in 1930.

L. T. MEADE (Lillie Thomasina) was born in County Cork, Ireland, in 1879. She displayed literary talent at an early age and wrote her first full-length novel when she was seventeen. She left Ireland for London to find success as a writer, and incidentally also found a husband. Mrs. Meade was for a period of time editor of a Victorian literary journal called *Atlanta*. Much of her literary output was directed to children, but the dark side of life also fascinated her and she wrote *The House of Black Magic* and a number of short stories in a similar vein. Mrs. Meade sometimes worked with "Robert Eustace," the pseudonymous scientific collaborator of a number of writers. She died in 1914.

SHERIDAN LEFANU, born in Dublin in 1814, was the son of the dean of the Irish Episcopal Church and a descendant of the famous Sheridans, of Ireland. His grandmother was Alice Sheridan LeFanu, poet and play-wright, and sister of Richard Brinsley Sheridan, author of the *Rivals* and *The School for Scandal*. While a student at Trinity College, Dublin, LeFanu contributed stories to the *Dublin University Magazine*, which he ultimately edited. Though trained as a lawyer, he decided on a literary career. LeFanu became famous overnight with the publication of two ballads, *Shamus O'Brien and Phaudhrig Crohoors*. He was fascinated by the occult and un-canny and wrote a number of horror and suspense stories which were enormously popular, some of which are considered to rank with the best of Wilkie Collins. He died in 1873.

AMELIA BLANFORD EDWARDS, English novelist and Egyptologist, was born in 1831—a Victorian woman with many talents. She was the guiding light in the founding of the Egyptian Exploration Fund and published many papers on Egyptology which were printed both in England and abroad. Her scholarly interest in the mysteries of the Egyptians probably influenced her choice of the supernatural as the theme for most of her short stories. *Debenham's Vow*, *Lord Brackenbury*, and *My Brother's Wife* were some of her successful novels. She died in 1892.

AMBROSE BIERCE, American journalist and author, was born in Meigs County, Ohio, in 1842. After scanty formal education, he joined the Indiana Infantry and served throughout the Civil War. Then, after further self-education, he worked as a journalist in America and England. His writings range from humorous sketches to weird tales of the supernatural. Some of the finest short stories in English have been judged Bierce's main contribution to American literature. He went to Mexico in 1913; there all trace of him was lost.

ROBERT LOUIS STEVENSON, Scottish novelist and poet, often referred to by his initials "R.L.S.," was born in Edinburgh in 1850. The grandson of Robert Stevenson, the famous engineer and builder of lighthouses, he first studied engineering, then law. His literary career was begun as an essayist. He described his unconventional travels in Europe in *An Inland Voyage* (1878) and *Travels with a Donkey in the Cévennes* (1879). Stevenson spent a few years in the United States, then returned to Scotland, where he wrote his best-remembered tales, including *New Arabian Nights* (1882), *Treasure Island* (1882), and *Dr. Jekyll and Mr. Hyde* (1886). He was forced by ill health, with which he was afflicted from childhood, to a voluntary exile in the Pacific Islands. When he settled in Samoa the natives made him an honorary chief under the name of "Tusitala," meaning "Teller of Tales." His later works include *The Master of Ballantrae* (1889), *Weir of Hermiston* (his last book, left unfinished), and *The South Seas*. His tales of adventure and fantasy remain fresh, and his poems for children, *A Child's Garden of Verses*, are still popular. He died in Samoa in 1894.

MARY WILKINS FREEMAN, American writer, was born in Randolph, Massachusetts, in 1852, of Puritan ancestry. Her early education, chiefly from reading and observation, was supplemented by a course at Mount Holyoke Seminary, South Hadley, Massachusetts. She subsequently lived in Brattleboro, Vermont, until her marriage in 1902 to Dr. Charles M. Freeman of Metuchen, New Jersey. She contributed poems and stories to magazines and published several books for children, including *Young Lucretia and Other Stories* (1892) and *Once Upon a Time and Other Child Verses* (1887). A *Humble Romance and Other Stories* (1887) and *A New England Nun and Other Stories* (1891) gave her a prominent place among American short story writers. Her writing showed great skill in interpreting the psychological effect of the severe and frustrating life of rural New England. She died at Metuchen, New Jersey, in 1930.

GRAHAM GREENE, English novelist, was born at Berkhamstead, Hertfordshire, England, on October 2, 1904. After attending Berkhamstead School, where his father was headmaster, he went to Oxford, and from there to a staff position on the London *Times* (1926–30). While an undergraduate at Oxford, he published his only book of poetry. His first novel, *The Man Within*, was published in 1929. He has traveled widely in Europe, Mexico, the United States, Africa, and Asia, and his experiences have supplied him with backgrounds for his writings. Nearly all of his fiction has been successful, and nearly all of the books have been made into films. He is one of the few modern writers to win acceptance from both the critics and the book-buying public. In addition to his novels, plays, and essays he has written several children's stories, "The Little Train" (1947) and "The Little Horse Bus" (1952).

FITZ-JAMES O'BRIEN, journalist and author, was born in 1828 in County Limerick, Ireland, where his father was an attorney. He was well educated and early decided upon a literary career. When he was about twenty-one he settled in London and wrote poetry and articles for English and Irish magazines. He came to America in 1852 and was quickly welcomed into New York's literary and Bohemian circles. He contributed poems, short stories, and articles to a number of periodicals, but his most important literary association was that of regular contributor to *Harper's Magazine*. From time to time he contributed to the New York *Times*, for which he was once an editorial writer. He wrote several plays, which were presented successfully as late as 1885. He died in 1862 from a war wound.

H. P. LOVECRAFT was born in Providence, Rhode Island, in 1890 and was a lifelong resident of that city. Although only forty-seven when he died, he had reached the pinnacle of his creative power. He was an antiquarian by taste and a recluse by preference. His wide reading, backed by field explorations, gave him a scholar's authority on the colonization and history of New England. This knowledge provided him with the realistic detail and visual vitality that give conviction to his tales of supernatural horror. He died in 1937.

AUGUST DERLETH, American writer, was born in Sauk City, Wisconsin, in 1909, and educated at the University of Wisconsin. He was the author of more than one hundred books in many different fields—poetry, novels, biographies, juveniles, historical novels, science fiction, detective short stories and novels, and supernatural short stories and novels. In addition to his writing, August Derleth was literary editor of the Madison, Wisconsin, newspaper, *The Capital Times*, and was owner-editor of Arkham House, which published the supernatural writings of British and American authors. He died in 1971.

ELLERY QUEEN is the name of the writing team of Frederic Dannay and Manfred B. Lee. They have written over fifty books, including those first published under their earlier pseudonym of Barnaby Ross, and they have edited more than forty-five more. Ellery Queen has won five "Edgars" (the national Mystery Writers of America award), as well as numerous other awards. Ellery Queen also has written for stage, screen, television and radio. In the 1960s the authors estimated a total sale of books in all editions and translations here and abroad as between 80 million and 100 million copies since 1929, when their first book was published. Mr. Lee died in 1971.

DOROTHY LEIGH SAYERS, writer of detective stories, was born at Oxford, where her father was a headmaster. Educated at Somerville College, she was one of the first women to get an Oxford degree. Her first detective story, *Whose Body?* was published in 1923, and introduced her now famous young nobleman detective, Lord Peter Wimsey, modeled on one of the more popular dons of her day. In addition to her original work, she is known throughout the world for her three anthologies, *Omnibuses of Crime* (in England, *Great Short Stories of Detection, Mystery, and Horror*). She also wrote a number of plays. Miss Sayers died in 1957.

Seon Manley and Gogo Lewis, who have worked together on many books, are sisters and have been collecting supernatural stories throughout their lives. Mrs. Manley lives in Greenwich, Connecticut, with her management-consultant husband, Robert, their daughter, Shivuan, two dogs, and five supernatural cats.

Mrs. Lewis (Mrs. William Lewis) lives in Bellport, Long Island, where the mist comes in from the bay with all the atmosphere of a Dickens novel. Her daughters, Carol and Sara, are also devotees of the supernatural tale.